The Earth Angel Training Academy

5 Year Anniversary Edition

Michelle Gordon

theamethystangel.com

First published in Great Britain in 2011 by The Amethyst Angel
Second Edition published in Great Britain in 2012 by The Amethyst Angel
Third Edition Published in Great Britain in 2013 by The Amethyst Angel
Special Edition Published in Great Britain in 2016 by The Amethyst Angel

Copyright © 2016 by Michelle Gordon
Cover Design by NT Chard
Graphic Design by madappledesigns

ISBN: 978-1530968299

Quote used:
"Life is a daring adventure or nothing" - Helen Keller

Special Edition

Gratitude

For this special edition, I have updated these acknowledgements to include the amazing people who have been such an integral part of my journey in the last five years.

So much love and gratitude to my mum and step-dad, who put up with me while I wrote this book in 2009. In the five years since first publishing it, they have been there the whole time, supporting me when I needed it, and encouraging me to continue pursuing my dreams. Eternal gratitude to you both.

Deep gratitude to Liz Lockwood, an Angel and my friend for the last 24 years. Liz read the very first rough draft of this book, and has edited every single one of my books since. She has been my light through the many dark times, and I know that this book would not exist without her unshakeable faith in me. Love you, Angel.

Another incredible Liz in my life is my sister. She has encouraged, supported and enabled this crazy journey of mine. She has been my cover designer as well, and her business, madappledesigns, is celebrating its 10th Anniversary this year. I am so proud of her and am so thankful that she has helped me so much with my books.

Where would I be without my inspiration and Flame, Jon? I feel so much gratitude for his strength and support, and his absolute faith and belief in me. Our time together has been the best time of my life so far, and he is the reason why my books exist in their current form – he was the one who has encouraged me to keep going, to keep writing, and to keep publishing my work. So if you love these books, I'm sure you will be very grateful for him too. I love you, Jon. For eternity.

Love and light and gratitude to my awesome Faerie and Alien friends, Niki and Dan, for their belief and healing and help over the last few years, you guys are amazing, I love you!

Thank you to my soul sister, Sarah Rebecca Vine, for her encouragement, healing, support and the crazy-long conversations. Love you, Starlight.

Gratitude to my soul twin, Tiffany Hathorn, for being an inspiration to me, and for encouraging me to keep writing. Tiffany, I can't wait to read your book when it is finished!

So many thanks to Andrew Embling, who co-hosted the live Earth Angel Training Academy classes, and who has done so much healing work with me, to help me to move forward. He has been an amazing friend and I am so glad he found this story when he needed it, because he was then there for me when I needed him.

Thank you, Neil, for the stunning artwork for the cover of this special edition. I love it, and I am so grateful to you for all the hours you spent creating it.

John Masiulionis is a force of nature who has opened up a whole new world of possibility for me and my work. His passion and enthusiasm are incredible, I feel so blessed and honoured that he is working with me to bring my books to the world. Thank you, John, for believing.

I'm not a fan of just listing all the names of people who I love and who have supported me, without describing their awesomeness in detail, but unless I want this to be novel-length, I have to. So a huge thank you to all of the following friends, family and readers, I love you all.

Marc Gordon, Annette Ecuyere, Helen Gordon, Jack Shalatain, Miranda Adams, Neale Donald Walsch, Will Richardson, Jasmine, Hannah, Luc, Lucja Fratczak-Kay, Angie Raasch, Shelly LaPointe, Megan Hiscox, Jen Hiscox, Louise Brister, Hannah Imogen Jones, Philip James, Saeed Jabbari, Malinda Rose, Anne Bull, Kelly Draper, Lisa Flowers, Ruby Al-Mokhtar, Jason Mordecai, Mim, Dawn Norman, Willow Jordan, Meredith Harwood Flanagan, Hayley Pritchard, Buckso Dhillon, John and Tish Harlow, Molly Silva, Richard Grey, Alex Lane, Nadina Schulte, Carole Stevens Bibisi, George Saava, Ray Ball, Louise Sophia Weir, Rhys Westbury, Rachael Barnwell, Lana Feeney, Roxanne Barker, Lisa Jones, Chip Jenkins, Tim Marrow, Joni Donoghue, Rosa Lewis, Wenna Macormac, Paul Killen, Cyndi Sabido, Llinos Thomas, Janet Spillane Gupwell, Lisa Fuqua, Robyn Peters, Shelley Brookdale, Xander, Jimmy, Valerie Abl, Alexandra Payne, Sian Williams, Helen Roberts, Rachel Robinson, Andrea Degan, Annemarie Harris, Debbie Freeman, Ana Dueñas León, Noelia Rodriguez, Jacqueline Wigglesworth, Nicky Lee, Cheryl Cave, Tadhg Jonathan Gardner, Wenda Prior, Laurie Huston, James John Malaniak and Robert Tremblay.

Message from Michelle

Dear Beautiful Earth Angel,

I am so very pleased you have picked up this book, and that you have come to these words at this time because it is the perfect time for you to find them.

Since publishing the first edition of The Earth Angel Training Academy five years ago, I have been on a magical journey of creating and discovering and remembering, and in that time, I have seen the amazing effect that this book, these characters and this story has had on others.

It has helped others to remember who they are, to awaken to their own purpose and to even see the point of their existence on this planet at this time.

It may be a story, but it is so much more than that to me and so many others. It is a portal to a dimension that we once knew and have since forgotten. It is a reminder that we are magical beings who have come to this world to make it a more loving place. It is full of memories and laughter and tears and joy.

You may find yourself and your loved ones within these pages, in their original forms as Old Souls, Faeries, Angels, Merpeople, Starpeople, Indigo, Crystal and Rainbow Children, and you will understand what it is that you are doing here on Earth.

Thank you for being a part of this journey, and for choosing to be here on Earth, to help with the Awakening. You are an incredible soul, and I am so very proud of you!

Please do reach out and share your insights, and if this book helps you, share it with others. It is because of beautiful Earth Angels like you that my journey with these characters and stories continues, and I am so very thankful for that.

With gratitude and love,

Michelle Gordon

May 2016.

This book is dedicated to all of the Earth Angels out there who are
bringing about the Awakening.
You are all beautiful and are doing a wonderful job.
May your life be blessed with love and light.

Chapter One

If it weren't for the way that everywhere shimmered and gleamed, you could almost believe it was somewhere on Earth.

Of course, the tiny Faerie with luminous pink dragonfly wings, zooming down the hallway, giggling, also gave away the fact that this was not an Earthly place.

Velvet sighed in satisfaction as she surveyed the spacious foyer; everything was in place. She smiled slightly as the Faerie's giggles turned into a squeal.

The new class was due to arrive today, and though the Academy had been running for quite some time now, Velvet was particularly looking forward to this new intake of trainees. For a start, it was the biggest class they'd ever had. The recruitment souls had done a fantastic job, and had reached more beings than ever before. They'd even travelled further, visiting galaxies that were previously unheard of.

Of course, Velvet knew that the increase of trainees attending the Academy was also something of a worry. It meant that the situation on Earth was deteriorating. And although Velvet had seen it all before, on many other planets as well as Earth, it still worried her. She had hoped that this time, it would be different. But despite the number of Earth Angels she had already trained and sent to Earth, it was happening again. Humans were not Awakening fast enough, and the Earth was literally spinning out of control.

Velvet took a deep breath. This class though, this class

was special. She just knew it. She glided silently down the hall, her feet barely touching the seemingly marble floor. Her robes whispered in the cool breeze that danced past her. She glanced at each door of the rooms either side of her. Their gold nameplates shone with the names of the many classes the Earth Angels had to take; Communication 101, Awakening 101, Patience 1000000001 and so on, along with the names of the Old Souls who taught them. Velvet came to a stop in front of Death 666 and paused for a moment, sensing that the professor was inside. She stepped towards the door, which vanished to let her through, reappearing behind her.

Devoid of any light and colour, Velvet's senses took a moment to adjust to her surroundings.

"Velvet," a warm voice said. Velvet turned to the voice and smiled.

"Hello, Corduroy, are you ready for the new class?"

Corduroy clicked his fingers and the room brightened to a dull orange glow. He glided towards Velvet. His thick brown robes barely rippled as he moved. Velvet glanced around the dark, empty room.

"I love what you've done with the place," she said, raising one eyebrow.

Corduroy grinned. "You know me; I love to make death as 'realistic' as possible."

Velvet laughed. "And what's the message here? That when you die, there's nothing? No colour, no light, just a black empty void?"

"That's the topic of my fourth class, I do believe," Corduroy said. "Each class is going to review a different idea held about death. After all, when you've never been to Earth before, you have to know what people's views are on such things."

"Out of interest, are you going to tell the trainees that this is not what death is like, or are you going to scare them into thinking that each idea of death is actually a reality?"

"Aww, Velvet, you're not going to spoil my fun, are you?"

Velvet shook her head in amusement. "You do know that the Angels won't believe any of it. After all, they deal with death every day; they know that no one ends up in a black void, or a fiery pit of hell for that matter."

"The Fiery Pits of Hell is the second lesson, I do believe." He clicked his fingers again. Bright orange flames leapt up around them, crackling and filling the room with a reddish-orange hue.

Velvet looked around, her eyes glowing in the flame-light. "All you need now is a guy in a black cloak with horns and a pitchfork."

Corduroy shook his head. "I prefer the scythe myself, far more terrifying." His smile would have been unnerving if Velvet hadn't known him so well.

"Just try not to be too harsh, okay? I haven't forgotten the screaming Faerie incident, you know."

"That was a one-off and you know it. How was I supposed to know that she was so sensitive? Besides, they need to be prepared." His smile vanished. "Earth isn't all flowers and love, you know."

"No, but we don't want to kill their joy before they get there. They'll need all the love and hope they've got to even try to make it on Earth."

Corduroy clicked his fingers and the flames vanished, the room glowed dully again.

"No screaming Faeries." He held up three fingers. "Scout's honour."

Velvet narrowed her eyes. "You've been a Scout on Earth?"

"Of course! In England, the year 3013 of the eleventh world. I was a Boy Scout for at least, oh, two weeks." He grinned.

Velvet shook her head, smiling. "I have to continue with my checks. The new class will be arriving soon and if I don't get everything done before they arrive, I never will."

Corduroy laughed. "No Leprechaun this time?"

Velvet groaned. "Oh, Goddess, will the class of the Leprechaun ever be forgotten?"

Corduroy chuckled. "I'll never forget the look on your face when they were called - I've never seen you so deliriously happy!"

"I have thanked the Goddess and the God every single moment since that beautiful day," Velvet said solemnly. She looked at Corduroy and they both cracked up.

"Hush, woman. Do this when the new trainees arrive and they'll think you're a foolish pixie or a crazy alien rather than a wise Old Soul with aeons of experience."

Velvet rolled her eyes. "Do you ever feel like we got a raw deal having to be so serious and wise all the time?"

Corduroy smiled. "Aww, come on, that's what we do best."

Velvet sighed. "I dream of going to the Elemental Realm sometimes."

"To do what? Whisper to a blade of grass all day long?" Corduroy reached out and put his hand on Velvet's shoulder. "What you do here, no other soul could do. This is your calling, your purpose, and you know it."

"No, what you mean is, what I do here, no other soul would *want* to do," Velvet retorted.

"Well, true, you certainly couldn't pay me enough to run this place."

"Hmm, speaking of running the place," Velvet tapped an imaginary watch on her wrist, "I have rounds to make."

Corduroy clicked his fingers and the flames leapt up again, crackling merrily as they licked the edges of their robes.

"Fine, leave me in the Fiery Pits of Hell, see if I care."

Velvet laughed. "Okay." She turned to leave. "Oh, and Corduroy?" she called over her shoulder as she left through the vanishing door. "Put some sunscreen on, Honey, I wouldn't want you to burn."

She laughed to herself as she glided down the hallway, the laughter of her dear friend fading behind her. She took a deep breath. The fun was over; it was time to get serious again.

*   *   *

"Velvet!" a voice called in her mind. Velvet followed her intuition and found herself at the end of the hallway, standing in front of a doorway bearing the sign: "Free Will 101". She passed through the door and found herself standing in a large room that resembled a theatre, with a couple dozen seats facing a huge screen. She went over to the soul standing in front of the screen, coming to a stop beside the pale woman with huge feathered wings and brocaded golden robes. She was the only Angel professor at the Academy, and a very close friend of Velvet's; they had known each other for many ages.

"You called, Athena?" Velvet asked. When there was no response, she turned to the screen to see what Athena was staring at so intently, a slight look of horror on her face.

The scene in front of them was a place on Earth. It looked like a typical street in a suburban area. Aside from a few cars driving down the road, Velvet couldn't see anything moving.

"I can't get him to listen, Velvet," Athena whispered. "I've tried everything. You know that when the others can't get through they ask me to try, but even I have failed."

"Get who to listen?" Velvet asked gently, scanning the ordinary scene, looking for any sign of a human.

"Mikey. He's about to leave the house, and exit just there, through that red gate," she said, pointing to the right-hand side of the screen. "And when he does, a green car is going to hit him." She shook her head in frustration. "I tried getting through to him, tried telling him to stay inside, but he wasn't listening, so I tried to get through to the driver of the car, to get him to slow down, but he's not listening either!"

Velvet turned to Athena. "You know you cannot go against the law of free will. They haven't asked for your help."

"But in life or death situations, when it's not their time, we do what we can to prevent it."

"And you have done what you can. You can do no more."

Athena gasped. Velvet looked back at the screen. Just then, a boy walked out of the red gate. He heard someone call behind him, and he looked back, but continued walking hurriedly towards the street. Velvet could see the green car approaching. The driver was trying to find a decent radio station and wasn't paying attention. At the current speed, Velvet knew that if the car hit the child head on – Mikey wouldn't survive it.

Athena clutched Velvet's arm. "I have to try one last time," she whispered. She cupped her hands around her mouth and screamed, "STOP!"

The child looked up, as though he had heard. His gaze seemed to be directed at Velvet and Athena. But he didn't stop. In the next moment, there was a sickening thud, a scream and the squeal of tires. Velvet couldn't tear her gaze away from the terrible scene in front of her. Athena crumpled onto her seat, wailing. "No! Why? Why didn't he listen? Why?"

On Earth, the driver jumped out of the car, and ran over to the child, shouting for someone to call an ambulance. As she stared at the lifeless form on the ground, Velvet saw the energy around it. It swirled around the body, then other energies joined it, and they all swirled upwards. She knew that in a matter of moments, the soul would be on the Other Side, being asked the Ultimate Question.

Something about the whole thing bothered her though; for some reason she felt like she recognised the energy; recognised the look in the eyes of the child. She bent down to Athena, and gave her a sideways hug, putting her arms awkwardly around her wings. "Shhh, it's okay. They've already come for him. He's safe now. Shhh." She waited patiently while Athena's sobs subsided and then turned into sniffles.

"Athena, who was the soul? Why did I recognise him?"

Athena took a couple of deep breaths and sniffed. She wiped her face with the sleeve of her robes. "It was Dictamnus,

Velvet. The fire Faerie."

Velvet looked back at the screen, her face sad. Now that she knew, she could see it clearly in the boy's features. She sighed. "He always was a stubborn one." She shook her head. "How many Earth Angels have left Earth this week?"

Athena bit her lip. "He's the twenty-third."

"In one week?" Velvet dropped her head into her hands. "At this rate there'll be more at the Academy in training than on Earth. I don't know how to stop it."

Athena rubbed Velvet's back and murmured soothingly. "It'll be okay, Velvet. You always come through. Things will work out. They always do."

Velvet shook her head and looked up at Athena. "I'm not so sure this time. I've been to speak with the Seers."

Athena's eyes widened. "And?"

"It doesn't look good," Velvet said quietly. "I think this new class is our last chance."

"Last chance? You mean…" Athena looked up at the screen, now a mass of flashing red and blue lights from the emergency vehicles.

"Everyone…everything…gone?"

Velvet looked up at the screen and nodded. "Yes."

"How long?"

"They're not sure. But considering their visions, I would estimate that we have about a hundred Earthly years left. At most."

"A hundred," Athena breathed. "Goddess help us."

"I'm hoping she will."

*   *   *

Feeling heavier and wearier than she had before answering Athena's call, Velvet continued on her rounds of the Academy, checking in with various professors and making sure that the dormitory rooms were in satisfactory order. Finally, she came to her own office. She went inside and sank into the deep, luxurious, purple velvet chair. She leaned back and closed her eyes, knowing that she didn't have long before the welcoming ceremony. She emptied her mind of the morning's events and relaxed her whole body. Though she knew that it wasn't possible to get aches and pains and illnesses here on the Other Side, sometimes her mind, still trapped in the human way of thinking, would create such things. Meditation helped her mind to release all those thoughts, and she would return to her natural, peaceful state of being.

A few moments later, feeling refreshed, Velvet took in a deep, cleansing breath and opened her eyes. She looked around her small office, from where she had run the Academy for the last fifty Earthly years. It was sparsely decorated. Because anything you could possibly desire could be manifested instantly here, Velvet felt no need to keep an excess of stuff. A quiet space, a comfortable chair and the massive bank of memories in her own mind was all she needed. She sifted through those memories now, looking for one in particular. A sunny laugh and a streak of flame signalled she had found the right memory. She smiled sadly. Dictamnus was such a happy soul. Always zooming about, leaving a trail of wispy smoke behind him. Velvet had known from the outset that he wasn't going to be suited to life on Earth. He was too much of a daredevil. But she had assumed that he would have ended up crossing over while doing something dangerous - not while doing something as innocuous as crossing a street. She wondered if he had settled on the Other Side yet, and whether he would choose to return to the Elemental Realm or stay on the Other Side as a guide.

The sound of wind chimes interrupted Velvet's memory and musings and she looked up at the wall next to her.

"Yes?" she asked.

A face appeared on the wall, it was her secretary, Beryl.

"I'm sorry to disturb you, Velvet, but I have an urgent call from Elder Damask. He wishes to speak with you. He won't specify what about though."

"That's fine, Beryl, put him through." Beryl nodded then faded into the gleaming wall. A second later, in her place, the deeply-lined face of a white-haired man appeared.

"Velvet," he said gently. "How are you? Ready for the new class?"

"Yes, Gold, we are ready. In fact I will be going to the welcoming ceremony in just a few minutes. How can I help you today?" Velvet knew that he had something pressing on his mind. Whenever Gold was a little nervous, he would get a twitch in his right eye.

"Well, I know you are aware of the crossing over of the young fire Faerie on Earth today, known as Mikey on Earth, Dictamnus at your Academy."

Velvet nodded. "Yes, I was with Athena when the crossing took place."

Gold cleared his throat. "Ahem, yes well, his soul arrived promptly on the Other Side, and when asked the Ultimate Question, he had quite an unusual answer."

"Which was?"

"That he did not want to remain on Earth, nor did he want to stay here as a guide or return to the Elemental Realm."

Velvet frowned. "Where did he want to go then?"

"He said that he wished to return to the Academy." Gold coughed; the nervous twitch got worse. "To be your apprentice, to be precise."

Velvet's eyes widened and her mouth fell open in shock. "Are you serious?"

"I'm afraid so, my dear Velvet." Gold rubbed his right eye. "I know you were never keen on taking him on as a trainee in the first place, but it seems that even though he heard the call ten years ago, he never fully integrated with the humans, never really fit in on Earth. He feels that the reason that he felt the need to be a trainee of yours was not to become an Earth Angel, but to study with you personally."

Velvet opened her mouth, then closed it. She was unable to form any thoughts in particular. Gold waited uncomfortably, his eye taking on a life of its own.

Finally she spoke. "It has never been done before. In fifty years I have never had an apprentice, nor have I needed one. Why does he think that I will need one now? And a Faerie apprentice, at that. It might be different if he were an Old Soul. Does he think I'm leaving? And even if I were, does he think that I would leave a crazy, irresponsible fire Faerie to run the place?"

"I am unsure as to his intentions. After much questioning, the only information he would give was that he felt the need to return to the Academy, to be your apprentice."

"And what do you think of this? Do you think he knows something we don't? Do you think he has some knowledge of a shift or some change that will somehow mean my absence? If anyone would know, surely it would be you?"

"I know of no such things. Maybe the call he has heard is an internal one, whose meaning will become clear with time. But the only way to find out would be to accept his request, and have him become your apprentice."

Velvet was lost in thought for a moment. "I guess you are right. But I don't want to make anyone else think that I will be leaving. That would create the wrong atmosphere for the new class, and this class is too important to have their thoughts scattered on things that we do not yet know the importance of. He will be my assistant. We will tell everyone that with the larger size of the class, I will be needing some extra help, and he has been selected because he has recently left Earth and understands the current situation there."

Gold nodded. "That all sounds very reasonable; I doubt there will be any suspicion that there is more to the story than that."

Velvet glanced at the door. "I'm afraid I have to go now, the welcoming ceremony will be starting in just a few moments. Will he be staying with you for a while or will you be sending him immediately?"

Gold closed his eyes. A second later, he opened them. "He

shall be arriving in a moment."

Velvet took a deep breath, and there was a knock at her door. She nodded at Gold. He smiled, then his face faded into the wall.

"Come in," Velvet called out. The door vanished and Dictamnus flew into the centre of the room. He hovered silently in front of her desk: his orange eyes sparkling and his tiny hands fluttering nervously at his waistcoat buttons.

Velvet looked him in the eye. "Dictamnus. I understand you wish to become my apprentice. May I ask why?"

Looking slightly scared, Dictamnus replied softly. "I'm afraid not, Ma'am. It is not something I can explain."

Velvet nodded. "As I'm sure you can understand, I do not wish to cause rumours to stir amongst the new class, therefore you will not be called my apprentice - you will be my assistant. You will be given a human appearance, a new name and you will conduct yourself in a manner that is similar to an Old Soul. There will be no foolish games, mischief or anything Faerie-like. You will comply with my requests, or you will be sent back to the Elemental Realm. Are we understood?"

Dictamnus nodded vigorously. Velvet was surprised he had agreed so quickly, but kept her expression impassive.

"Very well. Any requests?"

Dictamnus shook his head.

Velvet clicked her fingers and the Faerie's wings vanished, his legs grew longer and touched the marble floor. His bright red hair was tamed and shortened, a pair of glasses appeared on the bridge of his nose and yellow linen robes draped over his wiry shoulders.

He glanced down at his attire and smiled.

"You may go by your first or last name, which would you prefer?"

"Linen would be fine."

Velvet nodded. "Linen it is. Right then, if you could gather what you need," she waved at a small desk that had appeared to the right of her own desk. "Then follow me. We have a welcoming ceremony to attend."

Linen nodded quickly, grabbing a notebook and pen from the desk before falling behind Velvet as she swept through the vanishing door.

Chapter Two

A hundred different voices chattered in hushed tones. Some so high-pitched they barely registered, others a lower pitch that created a hum in the background.

A young Faerie with green dragonfly wings, wearing a green dress, hovered; quietly taking in all the many different beings that surrounded her. She had never felt so overwhelmed in all her life. She could see many other pairs of butterfly and dragonfly wings, fluttering rapidly, but she did not know any of the other Faeries. She also saw many feathered wings, which although were slightly intimidating, reminded her of her bird friends from home, and so gave her some comfort. She could also see beings with human forms, but with fishtails instead of legs. Watching them move was a strange experience. It was as though they were swimming, but there was no water. There were some others who looked like ordinary humans, but she couldn't see if they had any interesting features, and the little green Faerie didn't like to stare too much in case she was seen as being rude. Just then she felt a nudge at her back and she spun around, coming face to face with a feather-winged being.

"Oops! I'm so sorry little one! I didn't mean to bump into you, it's so crowded in here, I was just trying to get comfortable. I do apologise."

The Faerie looked at the being, in awe of her melodic voice and beautiful round features. The Faerie shook her head.

"It's okay," she said quietly. "You didn't hurt me." Before the being could turn away, she blurted out, "what are you?"

"I'm an Angel." She wiggled her wings. "You mean these things didn't give me away?"

The Faerie shook her head. "I've never met an Angel before. It's nice to meet you, Angel."

"My name is Amethyst. What's yours, little Faerie?"

"Um, well, we didn't have individual names in the Elemental Realm."

"So how did you know when someone was talking to you?"

"If they looked at me, I guess. But I didn't talk to many other Faeries. My friends were mostly birds and insects. I lived on my own and my job didn't require interacting with the other Faeries much."

"What was your job?"

The Faerie stared down at her feet and mumbled. "I helped grass to grow."

Amethyst reached out and lifted the Faerie's head. "Well that's a very important job, you should be proud of it."

The Faerie bit her lip. "I know. I was proud of it, but when the humans destroyed my patch of grass, I searched for another, but I couldn't find one. I had been without a job for a long time when I met the recruitment souls for the Earth Angel Training Academy. I told them that I didn't know how to do anything other than grow grass, but they said that if I came here and trained at the Academy, I could go to Earth as a human and try to stop the other humans from destroying all of the grass." She looked up at Amethyst. "But honestly, I have no skills other than growing grass; I don't know if I would be any good as a human."

Amethyst patted her on the arm. "I'm sure you will pick it all up very quickly. You have a wonderful motivation for doing so. After all, just think of how many other grass growing Faeries who might be able to keep their jobs because of you being brave enough to go to Earth as a human and change things."

The Faerie brightened up. "That's true," she said, her small smile growing into a grin. Her little wings fluttered faster. "I've never thought that I could help other Faeries before." She looked shyly at Amethyst. "Would you help me?"

"Of course, dear. That's what Angels are particularly good at, you know."

The Faerie smiled brightly. The situation didn't seem quite so overwhelming anymore.

A sudden hush brought the Faerie and Amethyst's attention to the small stage at the front of the cavernous room. Aside from the fluttering of wings, there was complete silence as a woman with long white hair and flowing purple velvet robes glided onto the stage. A tall wiry man with bright red hair and yellow robes followed just two steps behind her. She reached the centre front of the stage and stopped. She clicked her fingers and suddenly a giant image of her appeared on the white wall behind her. Up close, her wrinkled face broke into a smile. She threw out her arms.

"Welcome all! Welcome, Earth Angel Trainees!" Her ancient voice filled the room. "I am so pleased to see so many beautiful beings here. I hope your journeys were safe and smooth, and that you have already begun to befriend beings from the other realms."

Amethyst and the Faerie smiled at each other.

"My name is Purple Velvet. At the Academy, I am known by my last name. I am an Old Soul, and I have been running the Earth Angel Training Academy for the last fifty Earthly years. In that time I have seen many, many beings graduate and live very successful lives on Earth as Earth Angels." She looked around the room at the different beings, their faces watching her attentively.

"I am so pleased to welcome the biggest class that the Academy has ever seen. In fact, there are still some who have not yet arrived; they will be here in the next few days. The realms that are here though, are the Faeries," a high-pitched cheer rose from those with butterfly and dragonfly wings. "The Angels," a beautiful angelic note rose from those with feathered wings. "The Merpeople," a dolphin-like sound could be heard amongst the ones with fishtails. "And of course, the Old Souls," a low-pitched cheer scattered across the room.

"The ones who have yet to join us are the Starpeople. They are coming from several different distant galaxies, and we are pleased that such a high number will be joining us for this class." She turned to the man with red hair and ushered him forward. "This is my assistant, Linen. If there is a matter that needs my attention and I am unavailable, please inform him and he will pass it on." He gave an awkward little bow and quickly took a few steps back.

"Now then, I am sure that you are all very eager to settle into your rooms and become acclimatised. Aside from a few things, the Academy is very much like the buildings you will find on Earth. It is our intention to make sure you get used to the way things work there as quickly as possible. You will be sharing rooms, usually two or three beings to a room, and you will be mixed up to ensure that you become friends with beings from other realms. Please open your left palms and hold them up for a moment." A hundred hands went up in the air. Velvet clicked her fingers and a number appeared on each palm in purple glittery ink. A collective gasp of surprise went around the room.

"That is your room number. Please make your way to your rooms and fear not, as soon as you have memorised the number, it will disappear." She clicked her fingers again and the side and back walls of the room disappeared, so that everyone could leave quickly without having to file out through the small doors.

The green Faerie and Amethyst stayed where they were for a moment, their eyes on Velvet as she left the stage.

They turned to one another and started speaking at the same time. Laughing, Amethyst gestured for the Faerie to go first.

"What room number do you have?" she asked, squinting at the glittery digits on her own tiny palm.

"Four hundred and nine," the Angel replied, holding out her larger yet still delicate hand.

The Faerie squealed in delight and flew around Amethyst in a happy circle. "Me, too!"

Amethyst smiled. "They don't miss a thing, do they? They must have known we had become friends already. Well, roomie, shall we?" She gestured to the back of the room where the other beings were all exiting, chattering excitedly with one another and trying to find their way to their new accommodation.

The Faerie nodded happily and side by side they flew out of the room.

* * *

"I think that went well, don't you, Linen?" Velvet asked as they walked down the hallway back to the office.

"Yes, Ma'am. I think it went very well indeed. They seem to be a good group. I bet you're glad there aren't any Leprechaun though, eh?"

Velvet glanced at him, his eyes were sparkling in mischief and a tiny smirk played on his lips.

Velvet sighed and rolled her eyes. Linen chuckled.

"You know, Linen, you may call me Velvet just like everyone else, 'Ma'am' makes me feel old."

"I'm sorry, Ma- I mean, Velvet. I won't do that again."

"Thank you."

They reached the door to the office and entered. Velvet went to her chair and sunk into it happily, closing her eyes and relaxing. She heard Linen settle into his own chair and shift about until he was comfortable. She started to count to ten. She only got to three when he cleared his throat. She groaned inwardly.

"Yes, Linen?" she asked, not bothering to open her eyes.

She was beginning to regret saying yes to having him here already; would she ever get any peace and quiet again?

"What happens now? Once the new trainees have settled in?"

Velvet opened her eyes and frowned at Linen. "Don't you remember? It wasn't that long ago that you were here."

"I know it wasn't long ago, but well, Faeries have notoriously bad memories."

Velvet considered this. "Oh. I guess I didn't realise that. Once everyone is settled and has met their room-mates and has acclimatised, they will be gathered into the main hall again to be put into groups. These groups are named after the seven continents on Earth. Each group is assigned to a professor and they will go to their classrooms to get to know one another. Then, later, the class schedules will be given out, and tomorrow they will begin classes."

"What about their appearances? When do they change?"

"We usually wait to see how quickly the class progresses, but it's usually within the first few months." Velvet waited patiently for the next question that she knew was coming.

"When are the Starpeople arriving?"

Velvet clicked her fingers and a screen appeared in front of her. She looked at the symbols on it and analysed them quickly. "I would say in the next day or two. If there are no delays."

Linen nodded. He seemed to be taking note of everything she said. He was taking his role as assistant very seriously at least. After a few moments of silence, it was Velvet who disturbed the peace. "Linen?"

He looked up. "Yes?"

"What is it like on Earth right now? Did you really want to leave, or were you just unable to resist answering whatever call it was you heard?"

Linen thought for a moment. "Earth is... different to how I imagined it. Though I saw something of it while in the Elemental Realm, I really had no idea what it would be like to be trapped in such a dense body. I had underestimated how difficult it would be. But I guess if I hadn't felt such a strong pull to come back, I would have stayed a little while longer."

Velvet was silent for a moment. An image of Athena's sobbing face entered her mind. "Did you hear the Angels? Just before you crossed over?"

Linen smiled sadly. "The beautiful voice telling me to stay inside, to not leave the garden? The one that shouted 'Stop!'?"

Velvet nodded.

"Yes, I heard her. It was then that I knew how to leave. I knew that if I did exactly what the voice didn't want me to do, it would be a way to cross back over."

Velvet thought about this. She promised herself to never let Athena know that in trying to save him, she had actually helped the little boy to die. *What a lesson in free will that was,* Velvet thought wryly. No matter what they did or said on the Other Side, humans still had the complete free will to decide their own actions, and therefore their own consequences. Maybe the Angels, as well-meaning as they were, didn't always know what was best, ultimately.

"So what was pulling you back so strongly?"

Linen looked at Velvet, who was fiddling with something on her desk and wouldn't look him in the eye. "I'm sorry Velvet, I can't answer that now. But I promise you; this isn't some kind of take-over or demotion. I am just responding to the call I heard. Also, well," he looked down at his desk, embarrassed, "I had a vague memory of loving being here at the Academy, and I kind of jumped at the chance of coming back." He glanced over his shoulder. "Though I admit it doesn't seem to be quite as much fun without a pair of wings." He smiled at Velvet, attempting to dissolve the awkwardness.

Velvet nodded. Though she would have liked more information, she trusted Linen. His playful, mischievous nature seemed to be reined in and he appeared to be genuine. Velvet was a good judge of character, and she knew he would reveal more at the right time.

A silence fell between them as Linen rifled through his notepad. Velvet leant back in her chair once more and closed her eyes.

Sensing another question, Velvet headed him off. "Let me meditate for just a few minutes, then you can ask me anything you want all afternoon."

Eyes still closed, she could sense the smile on his face.

Chapter Three

"Wow! It's so beautiful!"

Amethyst and the little green Faerie gazed around their room in awe. The spacious room was bright and airy. There were three huge beds in a semi-circle, draped in beautiful linens. There was a notice board on the wall that had a large sign on it.

"Welcome new trainees! I hope your room is everything that you desire. To change the décor, simply touch the item and state your desire. To manifest anything, just speak your request out loud, three times. If there are any problems, questions or concerns, write them down on this board and they will be dealt with. We will be reconvening in the main hall later on today. See you there! Velvet."

The Faerie's eyes widened. "We just touch things, and they change? I've gotta try this!" She flew over to the nearest bed and touched the sheets. "Green!" Instantly, the sheets turned the colour of spring grass. The Faerie squealed in delight, and started zooming around the room, touching things and yelling out colours and patterns, until the room looked like the inside of a kaleidoscope.

Amethyst looked around, amusement showing on her face. "Hmm," she said. "I may just change a few things around my bed, if that's okay with you?"

The Faerie was bouncing up and down on her newly multi-coloured bed. "Okay!"

Amethyst went to the bed opposite and touched the sheets. "Amethyst," she said. Instantly the sheets turned a shimmering lilac colour. She nodded happily and touched the wall behind her. "A meadow on a breezy summer's day." The wall took on the appearance of a meadow, with a bright blue sky, lazy clouds drifting along, wild flowers in bright colours and the long grass swaying in an unfelt breeze.

"Ooh!" the Faerie said. "That's so beautiful! I'm going to try!" She flew over to her wall and touched it. "A lawn from a Faerie's point of view." Giant blades of grass appeared, a huge ladybug crawled slowly up one of them and a massive ant ambled past. The Faerie flew around in circles. "It's so life-like! It feels like I'm back home again!" She stroked the moving image of the ladybug. "I wonder how Larry is," she muttered to herself.

Sighing, she looked around at their now vibrant, colourful room. She glanced over at the third bed. "Do you think our room-mate is an alien?"

Amethyst glanced over at the empty space. "It would seem so. They are the only ones who have not yet arrived, after all."

"Wow, a being from outer space. Or even outer, outer, *outer* space! What do you think it will look like?"

"I'm not sure. In the Angelic Realm we only really dealt with human-like beings."

The Faerie looked over at Amethyst. "Human-like? Do you mean you helped beings on planets other than Earth?"

"Yes." Amethyst smiled. "Humans on Earth aren't the only beings in the Universe who need a little help every now and then." She sat on her bed and bounced lightly. "Beautiful feather mattress," she murmured to herself.

"Do Angels need to sleep? I always assumed that being pure energy, there would be no need. Fairies are a little denser - we need to rest, though not nearly as much as humans. Do you know they spend about a third of their lives sleeping?"

"Angels don't need to sleep, no. But we can, and we do like to spend some quiet time in meditation too."

"So why do you have a bed if you don't need to sleep?" the Faerie wondered.

Amethyst peered at the Faerie curiously. "Do you know what the process is like here at the Academy? Weren't you given information about the classes and the way they teach us how to be human?"

The Faerie blushed. "I think there was an information meeting in the Elemental Realm. And I do vaguely remember some leaflets. But to be honest, I didn't pay much attention. I was just so pleased to have somewhere to go and possibly be of some use again, that I didn't listen to what was said."

Amethyst shook her head. "So what *do* you know about the Academy?"

"Erm... it's been around for about fifty years, it's run by a white-haired old lady called Velvet... and we're the biggest class they've ever had!" She looked at Amethyst. "Will I get into trouble for not knowing anything?" she asked timidly.

Amethyst smiled kindly. "I shouldn't think so. They're not cruel, the Old Souls. I just think you may have a bit of a shock at what's to come in the next few weeks, that's all." She gestured around the room. "It's not all fun and magick, you know."

"Oh, I know," the Faerie said breezily. "I'm a hard worker, I'm sure I'll be just fine." She grinned. "Besides, how can I go wrong? My best friend is an Angel."

Amethyst smiled. "This course will be anything but boring, that's for sure."

"Boring? It's going to be the biggest adventure of our existence!"

Suddenly, there was a short beep from the notice board. The Faerie flew over to it, and found that the earlier welcome message had changed. She read it out to Amethyst.

"Hello, Earth Angels! I hope you are enjoying settling in and meeting your new room-mates. In the next few moments if you could please make your way to the main hall so that you can be split into groups and receive your class schedule, that would be excellent. Thank you!"

The Faerie looked down at the glittery purple numbers on her palm.

"Where do you think they'll put the class schedule? With my terrible memory, I'll spend the entire training course tattooed from head to toe in purple glitter."

She looked at Amethyst helplessly and they both broke into a fit of giggles.

*   *   *

Velvet tried, but failed, to stop herself from rolling her eyes for the tenth time in the last five minutes. Though mostly known for being extraordinarily patient, Old Souls were also known to have very short attention spans, and soon became bored with people asking seemingly ridiculous questions over and over. She took another deep breath and controlled her frustration.

"Yes, Linen. When we go back to the main hall, we will divide the class into groups, then each group will go with their assigned professors for their first session. Classes will begin in the morning."

Linen consulted his notes. "And the division of souls is based on where they will live when they are called to Earth?"

Velvet sighed. "No, Linen. The groups are named after the continents on Earth, but it doesn't mean that the Earth Angels will actually be placed on those continents."

Linen looked up at her, finally registering the note of impatience in her voice. "Oh, okay." He crossed something out on his notes. "I'm sorry if I keep asking the same thing, I just want to be sure that my notes are as accurate as possible. I don't want to miss anything out."

Velvet frowned. "Why is it so incredibly important that your notes are accurate?"

"Well, it could be another few years before another class begins, so this is the only time I can make notes about the beginning stages."

Velvet's eyes narrowed. "So you're saying that when the next new class arrives, you will be the one welcoming them, not me?"

Linen suddenly realised he may have said too much. "Um, erm, no, that's not what I meant at all. I mean, it will just be a long time before this process happens again and well, you know, as your apprent- I mean assistant, I um, just want to be thorough that's all." He looked down at the desk and pretended to reorganise things.

"Don't you know by now that it's pointless to lie to an Old Soul? Faerie or human - it doesn't matter what the being is; we can spot a lie from a mile away." She stood up from her desk and began to pace back and forth. "Please leave me for a while, I need to think."

Linen nodded, his face as red as his hair. He hastily got up from his desk, knocking over his chair as he went. He righted it and hurried out the door.

Velvet stopped pacing and closed her eyes. "What in Heaven's name is going on here?" she muttered to herself. She sighed. She could see no other way around it. She needed to visit a Seer. She consulted her mental schedule. There was just enough time. If she left now, she would be back before the Earth Angels all reached the main hall. She clicked her fingers and a note appeared on Linen's desk informing him of her whereabouts; telling him to go ahead to the main hall without her. She would meet him there. Then she clicked her fingers and disappeared.

* * *

"Velvet! I wasn't expecting to see you here today! I thought you would be rather busy with your new class."

"Some psychic you are, Magenta. Didn't you see me coming?"

Magenta chuckled. She gestured for Velvet to sit down at

the small circular table in the middle of the sandy beach. Velvet sat down and Magenta joined her. She gazed out over the ocean for a while, but conscious of her limited time, she pulled her gaze away from the mesmerising waves and turned to Magenta.

"I need to ask you a favour."

"Uh oh, sounds ominous," Magenta said playfully.

"I need you... I need you to look for my future," Velvet said slowly.

Magenta frowned. "I'm confused, is your future in question? I thought you only believed in the present moment here. The future is something that humans believe in."

Velvet sighed. "That's the thing, I have reason to believe that I may not be here soon. That I may in fact..." she struggled to say it. "Become human again."

Magenta's eyes widened. "But what about the Academy? You could never leave, who would run it?"

Velvet smiled at her friend. "I do believe that I have come to you for answers to those very questions."

"Oh! I'm sorry, of course." Magenta tapped herself on the side of the head. "Duh. Why else would you visit a Seer if not for answers?"

"One day I will visit you just for a chat."

"Yeah, yeah, whatever." Magenta waved her hand dismissively. She settled into her chair and closed her eyes. Her body relaxed and her breathing deepened. When she opened her eyes, they were focused on something just above Velvet's left shoulder.

"I can see a man with hair of flames and a mischievous soul."

Velvet sighed. "Yes, that's my new assistant, Linen."

Magenta acknowledged this and continued. "He appears to be one thing, but is in fact another."

"He's a Faerie, but to be my assistant I have told him to act like an Old Soul. I changed his appearance too. Can you see anything besides him?"

Magenta tilted her head. "He is very important. He may seem insignificant now, but that will change very soon. In fact, there will be a great many changes, ones that will completely change the course of your existence and the Academy itself."

Velvet nodded. "Okay."

Magenta stared for a few moments, then her gaze refocused on Velvet and she shrugged. "That's it I'm afraid. I tried to See more, but that's all that you're supposed to know. I think even that may be too much information. I'm sorry, Velvet, I wish I could be more helpful. But I can only See what I am supposed to See."

Velvet patted her friend's hand. "You have helped. I understand a little more now. Thank you, Magenta. It was good of you to make the time to see me."

Magenta smiled. "I did See one more thing."

"Yes?"

"You're going to be late."

*   *   *

Velvet never hurried. But as she straightened her robes after rushing from her office to the main hall, she had to calm herself and recollect her thoughts. She could have just clicked her fingers and moved to the main hall instantly, but she preferred to do as many things she could as humanly as possible. She felt it set a good example.

She took a deep breath and entered the main hall; she held her head high and swept in as if she were on time. All of the teachers were standing on stage; Linen was standing at the front, trying ineffectually to calm the excited crowd of celestial beings. He looked pathetically grateful when she appeared at his side and took over. She clicked her fingers and everyone went silent. Her face appeared behind her on the wall.

"Welcome back to the main hall, Earth Angels! I trust that you have all found your rooms, met your room-mates and had

- 27 -

fun making the place your own. I would like to introduce you to the professors we have teaching here." She waved to the first one in line, an owlish-looking, bespectacled man, dressed in red tartan robes. He stepped forward and nodded at the beings, a grimace of a smile on his lips "This is Tartan. He is an Old Soul and is our Professor of Human Culture." She nodded at him and he stepped back. The next professor, dressed in light blue robes, stepped forward. "This is Cotton, she is also an Old Soul and is our Professor of Patience." She waved at the class and smiled. "This is Indigo, another Old Soul and Professor of Human Emotions." The third in line, dressed in purple batik robes and a frown on his face inclined his head slightly.

The fourth professor floated forward in a cloud of wispy orange fabric. "This is Chiffon, she is an Old Soul, but has spent a few lives in the Elemental Realm and is our Professor of Manifestation." The fifth professor stood out from the rest. The gold highlights of her feathered wings sparkled in the bright light. "This is Athena. She is our only Angel Professor and is also the Head of all Guardian Angels." Athena blushed a little and waved. "She is our Professor of Free Will." Velvet smiled at her, then gestured to the next soul in line. "This is Corduroy." Even without the help of the flames, he still managed to look menacing. Velvet swallowed a giggle as he glared out at the trainees. "He is an Old Soul and our Professor of Death," she said in as serious a tone as she could muster.

A hushed murmur went around the trainees as they took this information in. Velvet caught a glimpse of his face on the wall behind her; he really did look terrifying. She groaned inwardly, she just knew there would be a few fainters and screamers in his class this term.

"And finally, this is Suede, an Old Soul and Professor of Cause and Effect." The last professor stepped forward. He was dressed in heavy bottle green suede robes. He nodded at the trainees.

"There will be other guest professors teaching many other

classes and I too, teach some classes." She consulted her mental list. "Now that the introductions are done, our first task here today is to divide this large group into smaller groups, so that a class schedule can be arranged. There will be seven groups and they will consist of between thirteen and twenty beings. The groups will be a little smaller than that today, as the Starpeople have still yet to arrive. So, if you could all raise your right palm towards the stage, you will receive a number. Once you have a number, please make your way to the professor with that number above them."

The professors all raised their right hand and clicked their fingers at the same time. Giant purple glittery numbers one through seven appeared above each of them. They all clicked their fingers again and vanished from the stage. They reappeared, dotted around the large room. There was a collective gasp then a round of applause. Velvet raised her palm to the class and in return they all raised their palms towards the stage. Velvet clicked her fingers. Purple glittery numbers appeared instantly on each palm and the beings all made their way to the corresponding professor. When everyone had found their group, Velvet called for their attention once again.

"The professor that you are with right now will be your guidance professor for the duration of your stay here. If you need to talk to someone, they should be your first port of call. They will now take you to their classrooms so you can get to know the other members of your class. Your schedules will be posted in your rooms by the time you return to them. After the session with your guidance professor, you are free for the rest of the day. Please consult your schedule and be at your first class promptly at nine o'clock tomorrow." She looked around and saw some confusion on the faces staring back at her. "Before we leave here now, are there any pressing concerns or questions?"

Everyone looked at one another, seemingly too afraid to ask what was puzzling them. Finally, sensing that no one else would, an Angel with long blue robes and pale blue feathered wings lifted his hand into the air.

"Yes?" Velvet asked.

"I do believe that some of the beings here may be unfamiliar with the time scales you have mentioned and are using in the class schedules," he stated, his deep, beautiful voice ringing out across the room. There were several nods in agreement, particularly from the Faeries and Merpeople.

"Of course," Velvet said calmly. Mentally, she berated herself. How could she have forgotten that explanation from her welcome speech? Granted, she was a little distracted by the whole situation with Linen, but still, time was one of the most important things she had to explain and she had forgotten it completely! She shook herself back to the present moment. Everyone was waiting expectantly for her answer. She nodded at the Angel. "Thank you, Angel. What is your name?"

"Sapphire."

"Thank you, Sapphire, for raising this issue. It is indeed an important matter. Obviously, being in this realm, time isn't something that we think about, for the only thing that exists is the present moment in which we are currently in. In terms of cause and effect and manifestation, everything happens instantly." She clicked her fingers and her long white hair turned into a dark brown bob and her robes turned bright pink. "Appearances can be changed instantly, décor can be changed instantly, etc. On the Earthly plane however, this is not the case. On Earth, there is such a thing as the past, the present and the future. To humans, time passes in a linear fashion and everything moves from the past towards the future. So, in order to make it easier for you to acclimatise to being human, here at the Academy, we run things according to the human time scale. For example, time is measured in seconds, minutes, hours, days, weeks, months and years. There are sixty seconds in a minute. Sixty minutes in an hour and twenty-four hours in a day. There are seven days in a week, roughly four weeks in a month and twelve months in a year" She paused for a moment and saw that some of the Faeries' mouths were wide open in dismay. She clicked her fingers again and her white hair and purple robes reappeared.

"Do not fear - I won't be testing you on this, and this information is available at all times to those who need it - remember, any questions you have, write them on the notice boards in your rooms and the answers will be given. Anyway, the class schedule is set according to a typical human day. You will learn how to tell time as you go along; we do not expect everyone to get it right straight away. There are plenty of Angels and Old Souls in this class also. I'm sure they won't mind helping you with it, as they are quite familiar with the human way of time." Sure that she had now completely confused them all, she decided it was time to quit while she was behind and send them off to their first session.

"Okay, Professors, please take your groups, I will be making rounds of the classes tomorrow morning, I hope you all have a pleasant evening." She swept from the stage; Linen trailed after her.

Once out of the main hall, he asked her quietly, "Are you okay?" He glanced at her profile as he tried to keep up with her long pace. "You seemed a little, well, off-balance up there."

She shook her head. "I'm fine, Linen, just got some of my schedule messed up, that's all, and I think my explanation of time was a little confusing, but I'm sure it will be rectified by the professors."

Linen nodded. "Okay, well if you need to talk you know where I am."

Velvet grimaced. "Thank you, Linen, I will keep that in mind."

Chapter Four

Amethyst could barely understand the little green Faerie as she chattered excitedly on their way to the classroom with their guidance professor. She smiled politely at the other beings in their group and was looking forward to meeting some new people. She really liked the green Faerie, but it would be good to have some calm conversations to complement the ultra-excited crazy Faerie encounters.

"It's so amazing that we're room-mates and now we're in the same group! Do you think that means that we'll be placed near each other on Earth too? Oh! I'm just so excited!"

Amethyst smiled and nodded at the Faerie, wincing at the high-pitched squeals of excitement.

They reached the classroom with their guidance professor and Amethyst silently read the gleaming gold sign on the door a second before it vanished to let them in.

"Prof. Orange Chiffon. Manifestation 101."

They filed into the classroom and sat on the orange seats. Amethyst managed to grab a seat next to another Angel and the green Faerie sat across the room with some other Faeries.

"Welcome, class! My name is Chiffon, and I will be your guidance professor for the duration of your stay here at the Academy. I know there has been a lot of information to absorb today, so this afternoon we will just do some fun activities to get to know one another a little better and then you will be free to socialise and explore the grounds for the rest of the day. I am the Professor of Manifestation, and you will have some classes with me, as well as your guidance sessions. Why don't we go around the room and introduce ourselves to the group?" The soft-voiced orange wispy cloud drifted towards the closest being, an Angel, and gestured for her to stand.

The Angel smiled shyly. "My name is Amber. I am an Angel and I love to sing."

Chiffon smiled at her and gave her a hug. "Welcome, Amber. I look forward to hearing your beautiful voice around the Academy." Amber sat down and stared at the floor, blushing.

Chiffon moved on to the next being, who seemed to float upwards on an invisible current. "I am a Mermaid," the fishtailed being said in a very high-pitched voice. "I do not have an individual name."

Chiffon smiled at the Mermaid, then turned to address the class. "That is another purpose for our session here today. I know that in many realms, beings do not have individual names, but for the duration of your stay here, it makes things a lot easier for us if you do. Humans also have individual names, so when you get there you'll be used to it. So," she said, turning to the Mermaid. "What did you do in your realm? What was your occupation or favourite activity?"

The Mermaid thought for a moment. "I used to love swimming alongside the dolphins, especially when almost asleep, I would hold onto their fins and be swept along. It made for the most amazing dreams."

"That does sound lovely. I think," she paused for a moment, deliberating. "That Dreams-with-dolphins would suit you perfectly. Maybe Deedee for short."

The Mermaid smiled and nodded happily. "I like that very much."

Chiffon hugged Dreams-with-dolphins and drifted to the next being.

The little green Faerie bolted out of her seat, her green dragonfly wings fluttering faster than the eye could see. "I don't have a name either!" she squealed, barely able to contain herself.

Chiffon smiled patiently. "That's okay, little one. What did you do in the Elemental Realm?"

"I helped grass to grow!"

Chiffon chuckled. "I bet your grass grew to be at least ten foot tall, with that much enthusiasm! Well, little one, there are a couple of options, you could choose a descriptive name, like Deedee, or you can choose a Latin name after your favourite flower."

The Faerie bounced a few times in the air, thinking. "What are the descriptive names?" she asked.

"There are a few variations I can think of, maybe Grassgrower, or Grasswhisperer, or Growsgrass."

The Faerie nodded, considering. "My favourite flower is a pretty little one called Honesty. What would my name be in Latin?"

Chiffon thought for a moment, then smiled. "That would be Lunaria."

The little Faerie's eyes widened. "I like that! Lunaria." she repeated, smiling.

Chiffon nodded and attempted to hug the Faerie, but missed. She chuckled again. "Lunaria it is. Excellent choice." She started to move on, but Lunaria tapped her small hand on Chiffon's orange-clad shoulder.

"Would it be okay if I shortened it to Aria?"

Chiffon patted the little Faerie on the head. "It is your name, little one, it is yours to do with as you wish."

The Faerie flew around in a happy circle before finally resting back on her chair. She whispered loudly to Amethyst across the room. "Amethyst! I have a name! Isn't that amazing?" Amethyst laughed quietly and a few others in the room joined in.

They continued around the room. Each being introduced themselves, and if they didn't have a name, they chose one that best fit their personality.

Amethyst looked around at each of them, committing their faces to her memory while silently repeating their names: Amber, Dreamswithdolphins (Deedee), Lunaria (Aria), Onyx, Quartz, Waterglider (Glider), Shellfinder (Shelly), Leontodon (Leon) and Filix.

"Okay. Now that everyone has their own individual name, it's time to name the class. Seeing as you will be going to Earth when you graduate, and there are seven groups, we've decided that each class will be named after a continent. Now, for those of you who don't know, a continent is a large mass of land. On Earth, there are seven of them. They are: North America, South America, Africa, Antarctica, Australia, Asia and Europe. Our group will be called -" She turned to the front of the room and clicked her fingers. A picture of the Earth appeared, spinning on its axis. She clicked her fingers again and it stopped. A bright red arrow appeared, pointing at large mass of land.

"North America!" Chiffon declared. "As well as being our group name, there is the possibility that you will be called to live on Earth within this continent, therefore you will focus on the culture of this continent in several of your classes. I have personally spent several lifetimes in America and they were very enjoyable indeed." She coughed a little. "For the most part anyway." She shook herself out of her memories and smiled at the class. "Right, for the last part of this session, I want you to talk to three new people in this room that you have yet to meet properly, and find out something about them that is unusual." She clicked her fingers and a large clock appeared where the map of America was before.

"You have thirty minutes. Go!"

*   *   *

Velvet was wandering through the incredible gardens within the Academy when she heard footsteps behind her. She sighed. It seemed she would never get rid of Linen. He was worse than a bad smell. She took a deep breath and tried to stay calm.

Then she turned to face the being intruding on her peace.

"Oh! Velvet! I mean, Miss, I mean Ma'am, er, oh, I do apologise, I didn't mean to disturb you."

Velvet smiled at the stuttering Old Soul. "Please, just call me Velvet. And you are?"

"My name is Cerise, Cerise Silk."

"That is a beautiful name. With beautiful robes to match. Is there anything I can do for you, Cerise?"

Cerise shook her head. "I just came out here for the peace and quiet; I have a rather noisy room-mate"

Velvet smiled and gestured for Cerise to join her on one of the beautiful golden benches lining the luminous green grass. They both sat.

"Let me guess, a Faerie?"

Cerise laughed. "Actually, my other room-mate is a Faerie, but he's a very quiet little thing, called Leon. He just sort of stares off into the distance for a while, then draws pictures in his tiny notebook."

"Leon. Short for Leontodon?"

"Yes, he was named this afternoon after his favourite flower, the dandelion."

"He must be a Faerie Seer. A little unusual, but not totally unheard of. His name means 'Oracle'. Excellent choice." Velvet frowned at Cerise. "So if you have a quiet Faerie, who is the noisy one?"

"Her name is Coral, short for Coralsinger. She hasn't stopped singing since she arrived, and though I got a short break from her this afternoon, she's been in our room all evening, screeching away. I hate to be rude and ask her to stop, but it's like nails on a black-board. I'm sure it sounded amazing underwater, but here, well, it's not so great." She suddenly realised that moaning about her room-mate on the first day to the Head of the Academy was probably not the best thing to do, and hastily added, "But the room is really great. It was so amazing to be able to decorate it the way we wanted; we had so much fun with that. And my group is the South America group. They're all very interesting souls. I can't wait until we begin our classes tomorrow."

"You do realise that you can manifest anything you want by saying it three times? Did you read that on the notice board?"

"Yes, yes I did."

"Then why don't you manifest an invisible sound proof wall between you and Coral?" She winked. "I'm sure that will make things a whole lot easier."

Cerise looked relieved. "That's a brilliant idea! Thank you, Velvet. I would never have thought about doing that. I would have just put up with it."

Velvet sighed. "I know what it's like to have to listen to something annoying and not be able to block it out." She tilted her head to the side, consulting her mental schedule. "Speaking of which, I have a meeting to go to." She stood up and Cerise stood with her. She gestured to the bench. "Stay here as long as you wish; enjoy the gardens. Tomorrow, the hard work will begin." She smiled, then clicked her fingers and vanished.

*   *   *

Amethyst was reading through her class schedule on the notice board when Aria came careening into the room.

"Am!" she practically screamed. "The aliens are coming!"

Amethyst turned to the Faerie, who was moving so quickly she was practically a green blur. "I thought they didn't arrive for another day or two?" Amethyst wondered.

"According to an Angel called Sapphire who seems to know everything about everything, some of them are arriving tomorrow, but there are a few who are on their way right now! Isn't that exciting? I wonder if our room-mate is one of them. Do you think we should do something special to welcome them?"

Amethyst was thoughtful for a moment. "Considering

they've come such a long way, I'm sure that the best thing we could do to welcome them is to provide a calm, restful environment so that they can be fully rested before classes start in the morning."

Aria paused for a moment, looking quite disappointed. "So you don't think we should decorate the room and have a party?"

Amethyst smiled. "Maybe we should let them adjust first. After all, this environment will be completely new to them. We don't know if they're going to be a little overwhelmed."

Aria sighed. "Okay, I guess you're right." Then she looked at Amethyst hopefully. "We can still go and welcome them though? In the main hall?"

"I think that would be a lovely idea."

"Cool! Let's go!" Before Amethyst could agree, the Faerie had already flown out of the room, the door barely had time to vanish before she whizzed through it. Amethyst chuckled to herself at the little Faerie's excitement and followed at a slightly slower pace.

"I hope the aliens know what they're letting themselves in for."

*　　*　　*

"Linen, did you put the message out through the boards that there are Starpeople arriving tonight?"

"Yes, Velvet, I even added music to it so that people would see the new notice."

"What music did you use?"

"There was this programme on TV on Earth that I liked watching, and it was all about aliens and spaceships, so I thought I'd use the theme music to that."

"What was it called?"

"Flash Gordon."

"Hmm, sounds interesting. Good choice, Linen."

Linen smiled. "Um, you do know what a TV is, right?"

Velvet raised an eyebrow. "Though they weren't invented the last time I had a life on Earth in this age, I have been on Earth for thousands of lifetimes spanning all thirteen ages. So yes, Linen, I do know what a TV is. I also happen to watch Earth from time to time. I have to keep up-to-date with the current events and developments."

Linen blushed. "I'm sorry, Velvet, I didn't mean to be patronising. I forget that you Old Souls know everything."

"Yes, we do, and don't you forget it." Velvet winked at Linen to show she was teasing. "Right, the first group of Starpeople will be arriving very soon and I want to get to the main hall to brief whoever has seen the notice and come to welcome them. So we'd better get going." Velvet straightened her robes and started for the door.

"Velvet?" Linen asked before she reached the exit.

"Yes?"

"Why don't you just click your fingers to get to the main hall?"

Velvet shrugged. "I just never got into the habit of doing that I guess. Besides, I try to be a good role model and do things as humanly as possible."

"Oh, I see."

"Why?"

"Well, I really miss being able to fly everywhere, and I kind of hoped you would show me how to do the clicky trick thing."

Velvet rolled her eyes. Did the Universe really think that this lazy Faerie could ever run her Academy? The idea was ridiculous.

"One day, Linen, I will show you how to use the Old Soul Magick. But not right now."

"Okay, Velvet. Thank you."

Velvet nodded and left the room. As she glided down the hallway, her mind was already on welcoming the Starpeople. The ones arriving that night had come from the star Zubenelgenubi. They had only had a few souls from there attend the Academy before, and for some reason, their arrival always made Velvet feel nervous. Each new group seemed to be different to the one before, making it impossible to know what to expect. Velvet didn't like the feeling of not being in control.

They reached the main hall and could hear the babble of excited voices chattering away inside. Velvet paused for a moment outside the hall, and Linen, so absorbed in reading his notes, walked into her.

"Oops, sorry, Velvet! Didn't realise you'd stopped."

"That's quite alright, Linen." Velvet took a deep breath. Though he'd been there less than a day, she was wondering if it would be possible to convince him to go back to the Elemental Realm. Having him as her constant shadow was seriously beginning to irk her. *Oh well*, Velvet thought, *concentrate on the matter at hand.*

She entered the main hall and went immediately to centre stage and clicked her fingers.

"Thank you all for coming to welcome our dear friends, the Starpeople. I have been informed that they will be here very shortly, and I'm sure we can give them a very warm Earth Angel Training Academy welcome."

Over the clapping and cheering, Velvet heard the faint sound of wind chimes. She nodded in acknowledgement, and then heard Beryl's voice in her ear.

"They will be arriving in one Earthly minute." Velvet nodded again and heard more wind chimes. She raised one hand to quiet the babbling Angels, Faeries, Mermaids and Old Souls.

"I have just been informed that the Starpeople will be here momentarily. So if we could keep the noise to a minimum that would be excellent." The din was replaced with hushed whisperings as Velvet's internal time-keeping system counted down the seconds to the arrival of the Starpeople. She wasn't entirely sure how they were arriving; they seemed to do something different every time.

"Three...two...one..." Velvet muttered to herself as she glanced around the main hall.

Suddenly, there was a flash of glittering light and the crowd gasped. They seemed to be staring at something behind Velvet. Calmly, with a welcoming smile fixed upon her face, Velvet turned slowly and gracefully. She kept the surprise from her face as she greeted the human-sized and shaped beings of pure light. Shaking hands or hugging was clearly out of the question, so she bowed her head to them in greeting.

"Welcome, Starpeople of Zubenelgenubi. I hope your journey was pleasant. Some other beings here at the Academy have come to welcome you." She gestured out at the sea of awed faces.

The pure light figures seemed to look out at the crowd, and though it was difficult to tell, as they had no real faces or features, they seemed to be pleased.

"We have a translator here, who can communicate for you." She looked to the side of the stage where Bk stood. A Starperson of Zubenelgenubi himself, he had come to the Academy some time ago, and so had assumed a human form. He had never received the call to Earth and therefore decided to stay on as staff, serving as a translator for the first few weeks or months of each new class. He came forward now, smiling at the beings of pure light. He telepathically welcomed them and made sure they had understood what Velvet had just said, then he read their thoughts and translated them to Velvet.

"We are very happy to be here among such beautiful beings. We are so very pleased to be afforded the privilege of training with you to become humans on Earth, and to help in any way we can."

The crowd of trainees clapped and cheered, and the beings seemed to glow even brighter, making it difficult to look at them directly.

"I assure you that the privilege is ours, dear souls, and I think I speak for everyone at the Academy when I say that we are very excited that you could be here with us," Velvet replied. "Bk will give each of you your room allocations, and will take you to them so that you can settle in. Tomorrow, classes will begin. Your class schedules will be posted on the notice boards in your rooms." Velvet bowed to them again, and out of the corner of her mouth muttered to Bk; "Did they get all of that?"

Bk turned to the Starpeople and asked them if they understood, then translated their thoughts and smiled at Velvet. "Yes, they got it all. They can also sense your feelings of awkwardness and stress, and hope that you will relax; they assure me that they come in peace." He chuckled.

Velvet smiled at the beings and glared at Bk. "Thank you for your assistance, Bk, if you could now show them to their rooms?"

Bk raised his eyebrow. "That would be a whole lot easier if I knew which ones they were."

Velvet shook her head. She really was off-balance today. She clicked her fingers and a small scroll of ethereal paper appeared in Bk's hand.

"Thanks." Bk led the beings from the stage and out of the main hall. Velvet turned back to the trainees.

"Thank you, everyone, for coming to welcome the Starpeople. We have had a very long and busy day, and tomorrow will be busier still; so I would suggest you all get some rest. I will see you all back here at nine o'clock tomorrow morning. Good night."

Velvet sighed in relief as the trainees dispersed quickly. She headed out of the hall, with Linen, her evil shadow, hot on her heels. She walked too quickly for him to pepper her with questions. Back in her office, she sank gratefully into her plush velvet chair.

"Wow, that was so cool! There were only a couple of Starpeople here at the Academy when I was here, but they didn't look like that. I've never seen anything glow so brightly before. I can't wait to see what the Starpeople arriving tomorrow are like. Do you think they'll be as amazing?"

Velvet had her eyes closed and was letting Linen's babble wash over her. When he paused for an answer to his question, the best she could manage was, "Mmm, probably."

Seemingly satisfied with this, Linen started whistling and sorting through his notes in his little notepad.

His whistled tune was actually quite restful, and Velvet found herself drifting into a very pleasant daydream. She was strolling across a sandy beach, right at the water's edge; the waves were lapping at her bare toes. The sun beamed down, warming the skin on her arms. Up ahead, a lone figure stood. She squinted in the sunlight, trying to make out his features, but he was too far away. She walked a little faster, hoping to catch a better glimpse of the figure, when suddenly-

"Velvet!"

Velvet sat bolt upright in her chair, the beach and the mysterious figure vanished. She opened her eyes and blinked in confusion at the face right in front of her.

"Are you okay?" a voice belonging to the face asked. She frowned, then nodded.

"Linen, what the hell was that all about?" she asked, finally finding her voice.

"I thought you were dead! You weren't moving! And you were so still and cold, I didn't know what to do."

Velvet stared at Linen for a full minute before she could muster a reply. "Linen - where are you right now?"

Linen looked around, confused. "Um, your office? The Earth Angel Training Academy?" Velvet gestured for him to continue. "Umm, Heaven? The Other Side? The Fifth Dimension?"

"So you're absolutely certain this is not Earth then?"

Linen nodded hesitantly.

"So if this is Heaven, how the hell would I be dead? We're on the Other Side! Technically, in Earthly terms, we're already dead! In fact, if you want to be precise, I've been dead for more than a hundred years! So excuse me for not being a cosy thirty-seven degrees Celsius!" Velvet gritted her teeth and cut off her angry outburst. She looked at the cowering Faerie in front of her and sighed. "Linen, I think now may be the best time for a rest, don't you? It's been a very long, very odd, very eventful day, and I think I've just about reached my patience limit."

Linen nodded quickly and gathered his notes. He practically ran out the room, almost tripping himself up.

Velvet tried to relax back into her chair, but the sensations of the warm sand and the cool ocean that were so vivid only moments ago had gone. She sighed and resigned herself to a dreamless rest. The first day of the new class had completely worn her out. She couldn't even begin to imagine what the next day might bring.

*   *   *

"Am, what do you think it's trying to tell us?"

Amethyst looked from Aria to the glowing, pulsating being of light.

"I have no idea, Aria. Maybe we should let it read the notice board - the welcome sign is back, explaining about the décor. Perhaps he or indeed she could read it?"

Aria nodded. She looked at the Starperson. "But how do we tell it to read the board?"

"Umm, sign language?" Amethyst suggested.

"Sign what?"

Amethyst sighed. "Like this:" She pointed at the being of light. "You," she said. The she pointed at the board. "Read the board." She mimicked reading the notice board.

The being of light moved to the board and stayed in front of it for two seconds before shooting around the room in all directions. Aria and Amethyst tried to keep up but it was too fast for them to watch. Finally, it came to a halt and they both blinked, trying to get the blobs out of their eyes.

Aria regained her sight first. "Wow!" she breathed.

"Wow, indeed!" Amethyst echoed. They both turned in circles to take in the whole room. The Starperson had turned their room into the most beautiful galaxy, with clouds of stars moving about, their beds were now planets and the colours were unimaginably beautiful.

Aria was the first to find her voice once they'd taken it all in. "I've always wanted to live on another planet!" She flew over to her revolving planet bed. "This is so wicked! Do you think this is what it looks like in Zebblenubblegenoobi?" She jumped into the bed and snuggled under the star-dust blanket, laughing. A few rotations later though, she began to turn as green as her dress. Amethyst went over to her bed and touched it. "Stop revolving," she said firmly. The planet came to a standstill and Aria looked relieved.

"Thanks, Am!" She turned to the being of pure light. "Thank you, alien room-mate!"

Amethyst chuckled and went over to her own planet. She touched it and murmured for it to stop. Then she laid down on it and closed her eyes. Seeming to get the idea, the Starperson retired to their own planet, their glow dimming slightly.

"Good night, Angel," Aria whispered. "Good night, Alien."

"Good night, Faerie."

Chapter Five

When the wind chimes sounded, Velvet could have sworn that she had closed her eyes only a moment before. That was the problem with being on the Other Side, when you 'slept' there were no dreams. Nothing to make you feel like you had been resting for hours. And nothing pleasant to ponder while you went about your day. Velvet sighed and opened her eyes. The office was bright in the morning sunlight, and thankfully, empty. She shifted in her chair to face the wall.

"Yes, Beryl?"

Beryl's round face appeared, smiling her usual angelic smile. "Good morning, Velvet, I hope you had enough rest. I have Elder Damask waiting to speak with you."

Velvet groaned inwardly. Yesterday had started off in a similar way to this, and it did not turn out as well as she had hoped. *Please Goddess*, she whispered silently. *Please let it be good news this time. I don't need any more crazy Faeries.*

"Very well, Beryl, put him through." Beryl nodded and her face faded.

A moment later, Elder Damask's face appeared. "Good morning, Velvet."

"Good morning, Gold. What can I do for you?" *Uh oh*, she thought to herself, *his right eye is twitching again. Please Goddess no, not another Faerie!*

"Well, ahem, I have another rather unusual request."

Velvet kept her smile on her face and nodded for Gold to

continue.

"Um, yes, well, it seems that young Mikey, I mean Dictamnus, um,"

"Linen. His name is now Linen."

"Yes, well it seems that Linen has begun a kind of a trend."

Velvet raised her eyebrows; her smile vanished. "A trend?"

"Yes, it seems that the other Earth Angels who have made early exits in the last few weeks have heard that he has returned to the Academy, and they, too, wish to return."

"As trainees? But isn't it our policy that they must have a proper break between their Earthly lives? What would be the point in sending them back so soon?"

"Well, erm, they believe that it would be different this time."

"How so? The classes and professors are the same. The Academy hasn't changed. The Earth hasn't changed that dramatically. So how do they think it will be different?"

Gold's twitching eye was working overtime. "They have requested to be taught only by you. Like Linen, they believe that they are meant to be your apprentices. And because they have just recently left Earth, they believe they do not need to be taught about being human by the other professors."

Velvet sat back in her chair and considered this. Then she frowned. "Gold, what is going on? What do these souls believe that I can teach them? I only teach two classes here at the Academy, and that's only because there was no one else to do the job. Do you understand any of this?"

Gold shook his head a little too quickly to be believable. "I really don't know, Velvet. But these souls are rather adamant. I've not seen this kind of passion in a long time."

Velvet sighed. "I think I need a little time to think about this. Term is just starting, things are extremely busy. And Linen, well, he can be useful at times but it's taking a little while to get used to having him around constantly. I need to think about whether I could seriously take on a whole other group of Earth Angels when I'm already so busy."

Gold nodded again. "Indeed, it is entirely your decision. I can give you some time to think about it."

Velvet smiled gratefully. "Thank you, Gold, I promise I will get back to you as speedily as possible."

"I appreciate that, Velvet, I really do. I hope today goes well." Elder Damask nodded once, then his face began to fade.

"Oh! Gold!" Velvet said quickly, before he completely disappeared. "How many souls want to come?"

His voice replied faintly, "Thirty-four."

*   *   *

"Twice in two days!" Magenta exclaimed. "I don't think even I could have predicted this!"

Velvet sank down onto the golden sand and buried her head in her arms.

"What's wrong, Velvet? Are you okay?" Magenta sat gracefully on the sand next to the Old Soul, her soft robes billowing out around her.

"Magenta, I have no idea what's going on," Velvet replied, her weary voice muffled.

Magenta rubbed her back soothingly. "Oh, darling, it can't be that bad, surely."

Velvet looked up, her eyes focused on the gentle waves rolling in. She shook her head. "I've never felt like this before. Like I have no control over anything. Honestly, there is something going on, and I feel like the only one who cannot see the bigger picture. I feel like all the pieces are there, but I'm unable to put them together." She turned to her friend, her ancient, wise eyes sad. "Why can't I see it, Magenta? Why must I wander blindly right now?"

Magenta was silent for a moment. Her gaze left Velvet's eyes and focused off into the distance. "I don't think you are blind right now. I just think that you don't want to open your eyes." She continued to stare into the distance, past Velvet's shoulder.

"The Earth has begun its downward spiral. Right now, the effects are not disastrous, but it won't be long before the decline increases rapidly. The Earth Angels who are already there are doing the best they can. And some will ultimately excel at spreading the word of Awakening, reaching thousands through their inspirational lives and words. But there are many who feel too ill-equipped to be of any use, and they are now returning to the Other Side. They are in need of more counsel, more teaching." She smiled.

"They wish to return to Earth with more wisdom and information, so that they can Awaken more beings. They believe that we can stop the decline, and move into the Golden Age."

"The Golden Age?" Velvet asked. "I thought that was a myth. In all the worlds and ages, no planet, no civilisation has ever reached that time. They have always woken up too late."

"The Golden Age is not a myth. It is a promise. One that many souls believe will be kept this time. It is similar to what we live here. But on Earth. Indeed it is what the prophets have always predicted - a true Heaven on Earth."

"And the Earth Angels believe that I have the wisdom they need to make this happen?"

"Yes."

Velvet shook her head. "Their faith is a beautiful thing. But I don't know if it is true. I don't know if I have the wisdom they are looking for."

"I believe you do. Velvet, you do an amazing job running the Academy; I don't think anyone could do it as well as you, but you are a teacher. An Awakener. You have the ability within you to truly bring out the best in people. To help souls to realise their true potential. In all the years you have been the Head of the Academy, I believe you have let many of your talents and abilities lie dormant. It is time to wake them up. It is time to truly use what the Goddess and the God have given you."

Velvet tilted her head and looked at her friend. "Is this a reading or is this your own opinion?"

Magenta smiled. "It is both, my dear friend. It is what the Universe and I both want you to know. It is about time that you realised your own true potential."

Velvet looked back out to the ocean, lost in thought. Her mind cast back over the time she had been running the Academy. So lost in the organisation and the planning and the scheduling, she realised that her own thoughts and messages had indeed been buried. But why was this becoming clear only now? Why hadn't it been made apparent to her before? She voiced her thoughts to Magenta.

"You started the Academy fifty Earthly years ago, when I, along with my fellow Seers, told you our predictions of the demise of the planet Earth. You felt that with some help from the other realms and from the Old Souls of Earth, we could change the path of the current human civilisation. So you set up the Earth Angel Training Academy and it has accomplished amazing things. There are more humans awake now than ever before in this age. But like I said, your own talents have not been utilised, and though the humans are stirring, remembering, it is not happening fast enough. At the current rate, the world will end before the humans truly understand what life is all about. And so, something needs to happen. Something big."

"Something big?"

Magenta was quiet for a moment. "Can you tell me why, every time you visit me, we sit on a beach?"

Velvet frowned at her friend. "What do you mean? I come to look for you and find you here."

"No, when you find me, my location always changes to a beach. You see, every soul who visits me brings their own location. Mostly it's a small, poorly lit room with a round table, complete with a crystal ball and incense, because that's their own vision of where a psychic should be. But with you, it's always a beach. This exact beach, to be precise. Can you tell me why?"

Velvet looked around her. "I don't know. I mean, I certainly don't recognise it." She looked down the shoreline and for a moment, thought she saw a figure standing there. But when she blinked, it was gone. Unconsciously, she stood and took a step towards the shore.

Magenta stood with her, following her gaze. "What is it?" she whispered.

"I do know this beach," Velvet replied softly. "It has appeared in my daydreams. I am walking along the water's edge." She walked towards the waves and they lapped over her bare feet. The sensation was the same as her daydream.

"Then I look up and there's a figure in the distance. But it's hazy and I can't quite make out who it is. So I start to walk towards it, to see who it is, when I am usually brought back to the present." She remembered the last occasion, with Linen. "Usually rudely."

"And you saw this figure again, just now?"

"Yes. Though it was slightly different this time. Clearer, somehow. I'm almost certain now that the figure is a man."

Magenta was thoughtful. "How many times have you had this vision?"

Velvet looked at Magenta, surprised. "Vision? You think it is prophetic?"

Magenta smiled. "As I said before, you have suppressed your abilities for way too long, my friend. Do you honestly think that you are unable to See as I do?"

"But I'm not a Seer. Why would I come to see you if I were?"

"Because you do not trust yourself. Again, I do not think you are blind. Only unwilling to open your eyes. So how many times have you seen this beach, other than when you visit me?"

Velvet thought back over the past few Earthly months. "About six times, I think. But only…" Her voice trailed off.

"Only what?"

"Only since I began to prepare for this new class. The Academy has been fairly empty since the last few souls of the previous classes heard their calls, so I had more time to myself, more time to meditate and sit in silence. And that is when I have had these... visions."

"And they are the same each time?"

Velvet nodded. "The same thing happens, but the last time, it was more vivid somehow. I could actually feel the warm sand under my feet and the cool water lapping at my toes. Rather like I feel it right now. Whereas in the previous visions it had more of a surreal, dreamlike quality."

"What was happening around you when you had the more realistic vision?"

Velvet raised her eyebrows in surprise as she remembered. "Linen was there. He was whistling a tune."

"Linen? The one with the flame-red hair? The Faerie who is pretending to be an Old Soul?"

"Yes, that very one."

"What was the tune?"

"I have no idea, but it was quite beautiful. Do you think I should ask him?"

"Yes, I think any extra information would be helpful."

Velvet agreed. Faintly, she heard the sound of wind chimes on the breeze. She checked her mental schedule. "Oh Goddess, I have to go."

"Were you late last time?" Magenta asked cheekily.

"Of course not. Everyone else was just a little early that's all."

Magenta chuckled. "I'll see you again soon. Good luck with the first day of classes."

Velvet smiled. "Thank you again for all your help." She hugged her friend, then went to click her fingers but stopped herself suddenly. "Wait. I have to make a decision. Do I say yes to these Earth Angels coming back to the Academy? To teaching them myself?"

"What do you think?"

"Oh, Magenta! You're the psychic one; can't you just tell me what I should do?"

Magenta looked off into the distance. "I See…"

"Yes?" Velvet asked eagerly.

"That you have already decided," Magenta concluded, looking at her friend with a smile. "I also see that if you don't get your butt moving, you're going to be late again."

Velvet sighed. "You really think I will make the right decision?"

"You always do."

Velvet rolled her eyes. Realising that her friend would be offering no more counsel, and hearing the wind chimes a second time, she clicked her fingers and vanished, leaving Magenta standing alone on the beach.

"Good luck, my friend." Magenta whispered into the ocean breeze. "Good Luck."

*   *   *

"Velvet!" Linen squawked in relieved surprise. "There you are! I was about to send out a search party! Where have you been?"

"Might I remind you, Linen, that I may do as I please without having to explain myself to you?"

Linen's face turned as red as his hair. "Oh, um yes, Ma-erm, Velvet. I didn't mean any disrespect; I was just concerned that's all."

Velvet straightened her already perfect robes. "Very well, Linen. I had some important business to attend to, but I admit, had I known it would take so long I would certainly have left you a note."

"Oh, no don't worry. It's fine. I overreacted. I apologise."

"Apology accepted. Now, I have a very important question to ask you."

Linen's eyes widened. "Yes?" he asked timidly.

"Yesterday, before you thought I was dead, you were

whistling a tune. Can you tell me what it is you were whistling?"

Linen looked relieved at the simple question. "Oh, I'm not sure exactly what it's called, it's something that I heard on Earth. It's a piece of classical music, my mother used to play it on the piano." He smiled at the memory. "She was teaching me how to play it, just before I decided to leave."

"Hmm, there is a professor who may be able to place it. Do you think that if you had a piano here you could play it for him?"

"Um, possibly, I might need to practice a little; my human memories are already slightly hazy."

Velvet clicked her fingers and a gleaming white grand piano appeared in the middle of the office. "Excellent. That will be your sole task for today. Practice the tune, then later I will ask Tartan to listen and see if he can name it."

"But don't you need me today? I mean, it's the first day of classes and the next group of Starpeople are arriving, won't you need some extra support?"

"Linen, I have coped quite well on my own for the last half a century. I'm sure I will be just fine." She gestured to the piano bench. "Now, if you please. I will see if Tartan can come by later."

Linen nodded and sat at the piano, he tried a few scales, and the sound filled the room. "Wow," he whispered. "It sounds amazing here."

Velvet smiled. "Happy practising. I will see you later."

Chapter Six

Feeling lighter and much happier now that she faced a whole day without Linen, Velvet swept through the gleaming white hallways, smiling brightly at anyone who crossed her path.

She was about to enter the first classroom on her rounds, when she heard the wind chimes again. She stopped and answered. "Yes, Beryl?"

Beryl's voice spoke in her ear. "I'm very sorry to interrupt; I know you have a busy schedule today."

"That's fine, Beryl, what is it?"

"I have Elder Damask here, he seems quite anxious to speak with you again."

"Already? But he has barely given me any time to make the decision."

Beryl was surprised. "Oh. He seemed quite certain that you had already made the decision. Shall I tell him that you need more time?"

What is it with people knowing I've made a decision before I do? Velvet wondered. She shook her head. "No, it's okay, Beryl, you can put him through." A small screen appeared in Velvet's vision with Gold's face on it.

"Velvet. I am so very sorry to trouble you, I know how busy you are, but I was wondering if you could tell me what you have decided."

"That's quite alright, Gold. Today is already turning out to be an even busier day than yesterday." She paused for a moment. "I have decided. Quite honestly, I cannot see any other option. You must send the souls here, and I will create a new programme for them."

Gold looked relieved, and for a moment, his eye was still. "Oh, I am so pleased, Velvet. I knew you wouldn't let me down."

Velvet frowned. "Let you down? Gold, are you going to tell me what your involvement is in all this?"

Gold's eye twitch started up again. "I don't know what you mean, Velvet. Anyway, I won't keep you any longer; I know you have much to do. I will send the souls to the Academy by this afternoon."

Velvet nodded. "Very well, Gold."

Gold nodded and the tiny screen disappeared.

Velvet sighed and called Beryl.

"Yes, Velvet?" Beryl's voice asked in her ear.

"Beryl, we have another new group of Earth Angels arriving this afternoon. Could you please ensure that their rooms are sorted out? It would be preferable if they could be accommodated all together in a wing by themselves. And could you ask Linen to be there to greet them if I am unavailable when they arrive?"

"The rooms are sorted and ready. I have put them in the Mediterranean Wing. And I will ensure that there will be someone to greet them. If Linen is unable to, I will greet them myself."

"Thank you, Beryl. You're an Angel."

Beryl laughed. "So I've been told. Is there anything else you need me to do?"

"No, that's all for the moment. Thank you, Beryl."

"You're welcome." The wind chimes sounded softly in Velvet's ear.

Velvet focused on the hallway in front of her and realised that she had an audience. The Mermaid flipped her fins nervously and stared at the floor.

"Can I help you at all, Mermaid?" Velvet asked kindly,

she wondered if the sight of her seemingly talking to herself had scared the poor soul.

"I am so sorry to have eavesdropped, Ma'am. I was just trying to find my first class. I'm terribly lost and terribly late." A crystal shaped tear fell from her luminous blue eyes.

Velvet smiled reassuringly. "Don't get upset, my dear Mermaid. What is your name?"

"Shelly, Ma'am."

"Shelly, first of all, call me Velvet. Second of all, it's the first day of classes; there are always a few hiccups. We don't penalise trainees for lateness. I probably should have mentioned this in the beginning, but there is no such thing as punishment here. You are here because you choose to be, and because of that, you will try your hardest because you want to, not because you will be punished if you don't. Now, I know things work a little differently on Earth, and we will have to become a little stricter so that everyone can get used to it. But on the first day? No one will be mad, I promise."

Shelly smiled and wiped the tear from her cheek.

"Now then, what is your first class?"

"Death 666."

Velvet sighed. Of all the classes to be sending this pure, sensitive soul to on the first day. She plastered a smile back on her face. "Okay, that class is with Corduroy, and his room is right..." She reached out to hold Shelly's hand then she clicked her fingers and suddenly they stood in a different hallway. "There," she finished, pointing at the door in front of them with Corduroy's name engraved on the shining gold plate.

Shelly moved towards the door. "Thank you so much, Velvet."

"You're welcome. In fact, seeing as I'm here now, why don't I come in with you?"

Shelly nodded eagerly.

They entered the room just in time to hear the screams. Shelly shrank back in horror at the gruesome sight before them.

There were bloody corpses everywhere. Gunshots rang out from all directions. The Faeries were flying around in shock, not knowing what to do. The Angels were hovering to the side, watching the scene sadly. The other two Mermaids were crying and holding each other. There were two Starpeople in the far corner, their lights dim, and their forms shrunken. Suddenly, a huge man appeared wielding a machine gun.

"Welcome to the end," he said in a deep voice. He let off a round of bullets, then laughed maniacally. The Faeries screamed again and shot to the other side of the room.

Shelly was now cowering behind Velvet, whimpering.

Velvet sighed. Corduroy meant well, but his classes got more sickening every term. She clicked her fingers and the corpses disappeared, along with the blood, guns and creepy background music. The room instantly lightened and the Faeries finally stopped screaming.

Corduroy blinked and looked around the room. He smiled when he saw Velvet.

"Ah ha! Hello, Velvet! Welcome to Death 666."

"Corduroy. I am sorry to disturb your first class. Though I do believe that your trainees are rather relieved that I have."

Corduroy chuckled and went over to Velvet. "I thought they were rather enjoying it actually." He glanced around at his trainees, all in varying stages of distress. He scratched his head. "Hmm, or maybe not." He turned back to Velvet. "So what brings you here? I didn't think you were going to drop in until the second lesson."

Velvet raised her eyebrow. "I take it you had something tamer planned for the second lesson?"

Corduroy grinned. "You take it right."

Velvet shook her head. "I found one of your trainees lost in the hallway, so I thought I would show her where to find you and make sure that you went easy on her, seeing as I explained that we don't punish souls for lateness."

"I see." Corduroy looked around. "So where is this

trainee?"

Velvet stepped to the side to reveal the Mermaid hiding behind her. Velvet pushed her towards Corduroy. "This is Shelly," she said.

Corduroy extended a hand to Shelly. She looked at it suspiciously. "Welcome to Death 666, Shelly." Shelly very slowly and cautiously took his hand and shook it.

"May I speak with your class briefly?" Velvet asked.

"Please, be my guest."

Velvet went to the front of the room and clicked her fingers. Chairs appeared in front of her in a circle. She gestured to the chairs. "If everyone could just come and sit for a moment."

The Merpeople, Starpeople and three of the Angels came forward to sit in the chairs. The fourth Angel went over to the corner where the three Faeries were hiding, and coaxed them out. "Come on, Aria, Leon, Filix," she said gently. She led the tiny shaking beings over to the chairs, then sat down herself. Velvet smiled at her.

"Thank you, Angel. What is your name?"

"Amethyst," the Angel replied.

"Lovely to meet you, Amethyst. Now," Velvet said, turning to the whole class. "The purpose of me dropping in this morning was so that I could get to know you all a little better, learn your names, and also answer any questions you may have. I know this isn't the whole group, the Starpeople who are missing should be arriving this afternoon. So, let's start." She pointed to the Angel on the far right of the circle. "What is your name Angel?"

"My name is Onyx," the male Angel replied, his beautiful voice ringing out clearly.

"Welcome, Onyx. Tell us all one thing about yourself."

"I am an Angel of Protection. I have spent my entire existence keeping humans and other beings safe. I decided to go to Earth because I hope to help keep humans on Earth safe in person. Being a whisper in their ear is no longer good enough. They don't seem to hear us anymore."

The other three Angels nodded in agreement and Velvet felt a little sad. She hoped that he would be able to help on Earth, but she wondered if he realised that it would be just as difficult to get them to listen in person as it had been as an Angel.

"Thank you, Onyx. What is your name?" she asked the female Angel sitting to Onyx's right.

"My name is Amber," the Angel replied. "I am an Angel of Evolution. I, along with many fellow Angels, have helped the humans evolve to their present consciousness. Now I wish to join the human race and help their evolution to accelerate. Like Onyx, I have found it difficult to get through to them at times; I hope to have a better chance among them than outside of them."

Velvet nodded. "Thank you, Amber, and welcome. Your name, Angel?"

"My name is Quartz. I am an Angel of Time. My speciality was the past. I helped humans to overcome it, and to free themselves of the shackles of guilt they felt for their past actions."

"That must have been quite some task."

"Yes, the human race is the only civilisation I have ever come across who are so intent on holding onto their past mistakes. They seem unable to let go and let themselves grow. Some seem to prefer the past to the present, but when they do finally wake up, they realise how much they've missed. I hope to help them let go now, and not when it's too late."

"I wish you luck with that, Quartz. What is your name little Faerie?"

The small grey winged Faerie seemed to have recovered from the earlier horror. "I am Leon," he said, sitting tall in the too-big chair.

"Leon, I have heard about you, welcome to the Academy."

"What have you heard?" he asked curiously.

"Just that you are a very quiet Faerie. I understand from

your name choice that you are a Seer?"

Leon nodded. "Yes I am. That was what I did in the Elemental Realm. I mostly predicted the weather, but occasionally I would get visions of major things, like the humans unknowingly destroying our homes and land. I would warn everyone and we would move on."

"It sounds like you were very much needed in the Elemental Realm, why did you choose to come to the Academy?"

"We ran out of land. The humans destroyed it all. We were surviving inside a lone tree when we met the recruitment souls from the Academy. We saw no reason to stay there. My entire family and all of my friends are here at the Academy right now. We hope to change the way humans see nature. To make them realise that they're not just chopping down a tree, they're destroying a home."

"We are very glad to have you and all of your kin here at the Academy, and I wish you luck with your mission." She moved onto the next Faerie, who spoke before she even asked.

"My name is Aria!" she blurted out. "I lost my land too. I helped grass to grow. But after moving on several times, there was no more grass to help."

Velvet smiled at the tiny green Faerie, remembering Corduroy's comment the day before about whispering to grass all day. This little Faerie did seem a little ditsy.

Aria looked at the Angel called Amethyst, who nodded at her encouragingly.

"I want to stop the humans from destroying all the grass, so that I can stop other grass growing Faeries from losing their jobs, like me."

"That is an admirable mission, little Faerie. I wish you well."

The third Faerie was still looking a little shell-shocked.

"What's your name?" Velvet asked gently.

"Filix," he whispered, his pale silvery blue eyes wide, his wings fluttering nervously.

"Welcome, Filix, would you like to share anything?"

He shook his head silently.

"Okay, then. That's fine." She smiled at the Mermaid next to him. "Hello, Shelly, are you okay now?"

"Yes, thank you."

"Good. Would you like to tell us anything about yourself?"

"There's not much to tell, I'm afraid. I am here so that I can go to Earth and hopefully help humans realise how precious the ocean is and to stop polluting it with chemicals and waste that are killing the ocean life." She smiled sadly. "I have lost too many friends now, and though I now know that the Other Side is a beautiful place, and that they are probably now Earth Angels on Earth; I'm sure that they would have liked the option to have stayed in the waters, in their homes. I came here by choice, in the hope that my family will stay safe."

"Thank you, Shelly."

"I'm here for the dolphins," the Mermaid next to her said. "My name is Deedee, and I lost many dolphin friends to man-made pollution. I couldn't stop it as a Mermaid. But as a human, I know I can make a difference."

"I didn't come here by choice," the next being said, his deep voice a little sad. He looked at the other two Mermaids. "I admire your choices, and I agree that the Merpeople should have the choice to stay. If it hadn't been for the chemicals that were dumped in the ocean near my home, I would still be alive. When I got here, I was told about the Earth Angel Training Academy, and I thought that maybe I too, could make a difference. Although I must admit, I do feel a little bit of anger towards the ignorant humans on Earth."

Velvet nodded. "I don't blame you for feeling that way. But I will say this - your anger will hurt no one but yourself. Release your anger and turn it into passion. Not only will you make a difference to your people, but you will make a difference to humans too. By helping those who hurt and anger us, we take one step closer to healing the planet."

The Angels nodded in agreement.

"I couldn't have said it better myself," Corduroy said.

"What is your name?" Velvet asked the Merman.

"Glider."

"I'm sorry that coming here was not your own choice, but I'm glad that you have decided to join us, Glider. I have a feeling that you will make big waves as an Earth Angel." She winked at him as everyone groaned at the terrible joke.

"And last, but not least, we come to you, Amethyst. Would you like to share anything?"

"Yes," Amethyst said in her gentle, melodic voice. "I, among many other fellow Angels, requested to come here because the humans seem to have become deaf to our whisperings. Though each time we failed to reach them, a beautiful addition was made to Heaven, it hurt to think that Earth was losing yet another precious soul."

She looked around the class, her gaze coming to a stop when she met Velvet's eyes.

"I also came here because not only are there large numbers of humans leaving Earth; but Earth Angels don't seem to be able to stay there for too long either. I'm hoping that I can somehow persuade them to stay there by explaining to them why they are there in the first place."

"What do you mean?" Aria asked. "Earth Angels choose to go to Earth to help humans. Why would they need someone to explain that to them?"

Amethyst looked at Velvet apologetically. Velvet smiled reassuringly. "It will all be explained in the later classes," she said to Aria. "But basically, when an Earth Angel, or indeed any soul is born on Earth as a human, they remember nothing of their previous existence. When you are born, the slate is wiped clean."

Aria's eyes were wide in shock. "You mean, I won't remember that I was a Faerie? That I was here?"

Velvet shook her head. "I'm afraid not, little one."

Aria looked at Amethyst. "I won't even remember my friends?"

Amethyst smiled sadly. "No, Aria. But that's why I want to go to Earth. So I can help people to remember who they are. Because I believe that if they remembered, they would realise their purpose and their mission and they would stay on Earth, making it a better place for all."

"So it is possible to remember then? The memories aren't lost forever?"

"Nothing is truly lost. Souls just have to remember that they are all one. That everyone and everything is connected. Then they begin to catch glimpses of what they used to be, of what their aim was for this life," Velvet explained. "But the number of Earth Angels who remember has been quite small in recent times. We have done all we can at the Academy to help them, and once they are on Earth, the Angels do their best from their realm to wake them up, but, well, sometimes it's just too much for them." She gestured at Corduroy. "Though you may think that he was teaching a harsh lesson earlier, I'm afraid that sometimes Earth really is that grim. Many of the souls who try to be human are just too sensitive and pure to deal with it. And some are simply overwhelmed by the idea that they went there to make a difference. In such a vast planet, how could one person make a difference?"

There were a few moments of silence. Aria still looked upset. She kept glancing at Amethyst. Finally, she spoke up.

"If we forget everything, what is the point of all the training? Why take all these classes only to forget them as soon as we're born?"

Amethyst replied. "Because although you may not consciously remember this experience, your soul remembers. If you are able to listen to your soul, you will remember the training. Then you might Awaken, and realise that there is so much more to being human than sleepwalking, stumbling blindly through life from birth to death."

Aria nodded. "So does that mean there are no exams here?

Seeing as we're going to forget everything anyway?"

Everyone laughed and the tense atmosphere lightened. Velvet chuckled. "Don't worry, little Faerie, there are no exams, tests or anything too stressful. We are training you simply to increase your chances of remembering your mission, and hopefully to help you out when you need it." She looked up at the Starpeople, noting that their light seemed much brighter than before. "I'm afraid I haven't got Bk with me to translate, so we'll have to get the Starpeople to introduce themselves later." She nodded at them, hoping they would understand, then took a deep breath. "Now then, I need to continue with my rounds of the classes, but does anyone have any pressing questions they would like to ask me before I leave you in Corduroy's capable hands?"

Leon raised his hand.

"Yes, Leon?"

"I was just wondering, I know there are none in our group, but I did notice that there are some Old Soul trainees in the new class. Surely Old Souls do not need training in being human, seeing as they have been human so many times before?"

"That's an excellent observation. Yes, there are a few Old Souls in the trainee class, and this is because their last lives on Earth were so very long ago. They have opted to join the Academy as trainees to refresh their memories of what it is like to be human."

"Where have they been all this time then, to have forgotten how to be human?" Aria asked, her curiosity piqued.

Velvet smiled. "I'm afraid you would have to ask them that. They could have been anywhere in the Universe. And as you know, it's a rather large place."

Aria nodded, but was dissatisfied with the vague answer.

"Now then, any more questions?"

Everyone shook their heads except Filix.

"Filix, do you have anything you'd like to ask me?"

Filix snapped out of his daze and looked up at Velvet. He

shook his tiny head.

"Okay, then, I will leave you to get back to the lesson." She noticed the Faeries all looking at each other in horror and stifled a smile. Corduroy walked her to the door.

When they reached it, she put her hand on his arm. "Go easy on them, won't you?"

"Of course," he replied, smiling. She nodded and stepped through the vanishing door. The door hadn't even had the chance to reappear when she heard a scream.

She paused, then sighed and carried on.

Chapter Seven

"Are you okay, Aria? You've been terribly quiet since our first class this morning. Did Professor Corduroy really frighten you that much?"

Amethyst and Aria were sat in the Elemental Garden, enjoying a midday break between classes. After Death 666, they had attended Manifestation 101, with their guidance professor, Chiffon. The class had been fun and very enjoyable, but Aria had remained silent and withdrawn throughout.

"I'm fine," Aria responded quietly.

"You know you can tell me anything? I hate to see you so upset."

Aria nodded, a tiny tear hanging on the edge of her dark eyelashes. "I know."

"When you're ready, I'm here for you, okay?"

Aria nodded again, and the tear left a glittering trail down her pale cheek.

They sat in silence for a while, listening to the chatter of fellow trainees relaxing around them.

"I'm afraid."

Amethyst looked down at the tiny Faerie next to her.

"Afraid of what?" she asked gently.

"Of forgetting."

"That was a bit of a shock for you wasn't it? Finding out that we forget all that we know previous to our Earthly life?"

Aria nodded. "The thing is, if the percentage of Earth

Angels that remember really is that small, then I have no hope of remembering anything at all."

"Why do you say that my friend?"

"Because my memory is already terrible!" She held out her left palm for Amethyst to see. "Velvet said our room numbers would fade once we had them committed to memory." The 409 shone brightly on her palm in purple glitter. "Thing is, even with it written on my hand, I've still ended up on the wrong floor and in the wrong corridor at least twice, and it's only the second day! If I can't remember a simple number, how on Earth am I going to remember all of the lessons I learn here? And you! How am I going to remember our friendship? I've never had a proper friend before, and now that I've finally found you, I'm going to forget you completely!" The little Faerie buried her face in Amethyst's robes and sobbed.

"Shhh, little one, shhh," Amethyst said, patting the Faerie lightly on the shoulder. "It's okay to be afraid. But that fear mustn't stop you from continuing on this journey."

The Faerie carried on crying, her tiny shoulders heaving.

Amethyst was thoughtful for a while. "Aria, do you think you would feel better if there was something that increased your chance of remembering me when you are born on Earth?"

Aria looked up at Amethyst, her face stained with tears. "Do you know of such a thing?" she asked hopefully.

"It is likely that we will be placed near one another on Earth, seeing as we are in the same group. If we decided on something now, something that would help us to recognise each other when we are on Earth, we may also have a better chance of remembering all that we learnt here too, as well as our previous existences as Angels and Faeries."

Aria perked up. "Do you think we could come up with something like that? That we could really find each other on Earth?"

Amethyst smiled. "I think it would be a good idea to give it a try, don't you?"

Aria smiled shakily and wiped the remaining tears with the hem of her green dress.

"Yes," she agreed. "I think it's a wonderful idea." She put her tiny hand on Amethyst's. "Thank you, Am. You truly are the best friend anyone has ever had."

"Likewise, little Faerie, likewise."

*   *   *

Velvet was feeling quite drained by the end of the day. She had visited each group in all their different classes, and had had some very in-depth discussions. Everyone's names were neatly recorded in her memory, connected to an image of their face. She entered her office and stopped suddenly, taken by surprise at the beautiful melody that came spilling out when the door vanished. For a few moments, she stood still and listened. This was the song Linen was whistling the day before. It was so haunting, so beautiful, that incredibly, for the first time in half a century, a tear escaped from Velvet's eye. Surprised at the sensation on her cheek, she raised her hand to wipe it away and accidentally caught Linen's attention. His hands stopped on the keys and the last strains of the music faded away.

"Are you okay, Velvet?" He stood up and took a step towards her. He tilted his head, confused. "Are you… crying?"

Velvet rubbed her cheek and cleared her throat. "Um, no, of course not," she said unconvincingly.

Linen frowned, but accepted this. He gestured at the piano. "I've remembered the song. Do you want to hear it?"

Velvet nodded and went over to her desk. She sank into her chair and relaxed. Linen returned to the piano stool and began to play.

Velvet sighed in bliss and closed her eyes. The melody washed over her, and completely against her will, another tear trickled down her cheek. Why did this song have such a profound effect on her? She was certain that she had never heard it before, not on the Other Side or in her many thousands of lives as a human. And yet, at the same time it was utterly familiar. Almost like the musical expression of her very soul. She took a deep breath and as she relaxed further, found herself in a deep meditative state.

The soft splash of cool water at her ankles made her laugh out loud in surprise. She looked all around her and instantly recognised the beach, with its long stretch of golden sand and deep aquamarine waves rolling in gently. She walked along the shoreline, enjoying the sensation of the cool water in contrast to the heat of the sun soaking into her bare skin. Then she remembered why she was here. She looked up and squinted down the beach, but there was no one there. She turned to look all around her, but she was completely alone. She sighed and her shoulders drooped slightly. Where was he?

Faintly, she could hear the most beautiful music, drifting along on the breeze. She closed her eyes and smiled. She decided to follow the music, and see where it led her. With her eyes still closed, she turned to the direction of the music and began to walk. After a few steps, she opened her eyes in surprise. The water was now lapping at her knees. She realised that she had been walking directly towards the ocean. She tilted her head to listen to the music, closing her eyes again to concentrate. *Yes*, she thought, *it was definitely coming from the ocean*. How odd. She paused, uncertain. What did that mean? Was she supposed to swim towards it? She wasn't entirely sure if she could swim. It had been so long since she'd been in the ocean.

As she pondered what to do, she noticed the music becoming louder, almost as though it was reaching the final crescendo. Enticed by its beauty, she began to wade forward again, desperate to see where the music was being created.

The water had just reached her waist when suddenly; the music began to fade and then stopped altogether. Velvet strained to hear it, but the only sound was that of the waves lapping around her. She felt the loss of the music so deeply that her face crumpled and she let out a wail.

"No!"

"Velvet!"

The panicked shout and the two hands shaking her shoulders brought Velvet back to the present with a thump.

She opened her eyes and felt a sense of déjà vu as she stared into Linen's bright orange eyes.

"What?" she asked, irritated.

Linen stepped back and raised an eyebrow. "What? First you fell asleep while I was playing the song for you, and then, when I finished the song and looked over at you, you had this awful look on you face, then you started crying and you shouted 'No!'."

Velvet's cheeks heated up. "I did?" she asked, wondering how she was going to explain this one.

"I thought that souls didn't have dreams on the Other Side? I thought that when we rest, there's just silence? Because well, it seems to me like you were having a nightmare of some kind."

Realising that she wasn't going to explain this away, Velvet decided to be honest. "I was having a vision."

"A prophetic vision?"

"I'm not entirely sure. I'd had it several times before you arrived, but it was always quite vague and unreal. But then yesterday, when you were whistling that tune, I had the vision again. This time, it was incredibly vivid and detailed. Which is why I asked if you could play the tune. I need to find out why it seems to have such an effect on me."

"So what happened just now? Did you have the vision again?"

"Yes I did, but this time, it was a little different and even more real if that's possible. I felt compelled to follow the music and felt that if I did, I would find what I was looking for. But when I listened, the music seemed to be coming from the ocean. I was just wading in, to find the source of it, when it stopped." She laughed a little. "I guess that's when I yelled. I didn't want the music to stop."

"So what do you think it all means?" Linen asked curiously; glad that Velvet was finally talking to him like an equal and not like an idiot.

"I have no idea. And that's what I find irritating." Velvet smiled at Linen. "As you may have noticed by now, I like to be in control, I can't stand it when I don't know what's going on."

Linen grinned back. "Yeah, I had noticed."

Velvet shook her head and laughed at herself. "Thank you for listening, Linen. And thank you so much for remembering how to play the song, it truly was beautiful."

Linen blushed. "You're welcome. When do you want me to play it for Tartan?"

Velvet hit her forehead with the heel of her hand. "Goddess! I knew there was something I meant to ask him earlier. I'll have to go see him this evening and find out when he's free." She thought for a moment. "Do you know any other songs?"

Linen shrugged. "Sure. Somehow, playing here is really easy, it's like I sit at the piano and my fingers just know which keys to hit."

"Do you think you would mind playing for the trainees in the Academy? I'm sure we have some other musicians here too, maybe we could have some kind of concert as one of the evening activities?"

Linen smiled shyly. "Do you really think I'm good enough?"

"Linen, I think you are incredible. But don't let the compliments go to your head; I need your feet on the ground to help me right now, not your head in the clouds."

Linen nodded, still grinning. "I think a concert would be brilliant. A great way to relax and wind down after all those boring – I mean, interesting classes." His cheeks turned a brighter shade of red.

Velvet chuckled. "I agree completely. I will organise it

with some of the professors. I'm sure Tartan will definitely be interested. I think he can play the bagpipes."

"You know, that doesn't surprise me at all."

Wind chimes sounded loudly, making them both jump a little.

"Yes?" Velvet asked.

Beryl's face appeared. "Oh! Velvet you're back, that's good. The Starpeople from the distant galaxy of Pyrydia have just arrived."

Velvet jumped up. "Oh Goddess, why didn't they call ahead to warn us?" She straightened her robes and smoothed back her long white hair. "Where are they?"

"They are in the main hall. I believe that Bk is on his way there now to see them, they arrived literally moments ago."

"Okay, thank you, Beryl, I will be there very shortly." Beryl nodded and faded into the wall. "I wish they would stick to the protocol and call ahead," she muttered.

Linen had gathered his notebook and pen and stood ready to go at the door.

Velvet frowned. "There's not enough time to walk. I don't want them wandering off before we get there."

Linen smiled hopefully. "Does this mean...?"

Velvet rolled her eyes. "Yes it does, now get over here."

In his haste to get to her side, Linen tripped over the piano stool, causing Velvet to roll her eyes again. When he finally stood next to her she turned to him. "Just make sure you close your eyes okay?"

Linen looked confused. "Why? Is it a secret, how you do it?"

"No silly, if you keep your eyes open during transition, you'll feel sick."

"Oh! Okay." He obediently closed his eyes.

Velvet sighed, took hold of the back of his bright yellow robes, and clicked her fingers.

*   *   *

They reappeared just outside the stage doors of the main hall. Velvet looked at Linen and smothered a laugh. He still had his eyes scrunched tightly shut.

She released her grip on his robes and shook his shoulder gently. "You can open your eyes now, we're here."

Cautiously, Linen opened one eye at a time. When he managed to focus he gripped his stomach and groaned. "Ugh, I think I prefer flying."

Velvet chuckled. "Maybe next time I'll let you walk, eh?"

Linen grimaced. "Maybe that would be best."

Still laughing, Velvet led the way into the main hall. For the second time in two days, her abrupt halt made Linen crash into her back. He peered over her shoulder to see what the problem was. Expecting a scene of chaos, his mouth dropped in shock at the incredible sight before them.

A giant golden pyramid hovered a foot or so off the ground. It was so big, the main hall ceiling had actually adjusted its height to fit the structure in. It shimmered and glowed, giving off an ethereal aura.

Velvet and Linen stood side by side and stared at it.

"Is that their ship?" Linen whispered.

Velvet lifted her shoulders. "I have no idea," she whispered back.

They both jumped a little at a noise behind them.

"Hey," Bk said. "The Pyrydians have arrived then?"

Velvet and Linen nodded in unison. Velvet cleared her throat. "Uh, yes, we were just waiting for them to exit their ship so that we could welcome them."

Bk frowned. "Their ship?"

Velvet looked at Bk, perplexed. "Um, yes, the giant pyramid in front of you that has come from a distant galaxy."

Bk laughed. "That's not their ship." He walked towards the pyramid and stopped a foot away. He reached his hand out to it, palm first, and spoke telepathically. Within seconds, the pyramid split apart into ten smaller pyramids and they formed a line, each hovering a few feet off the ground.

Velvet blinked at the sudden transformation. "They're pyramids?"

"Yes," Bk nodded.

"But they're all identical, how are we supposed to tell them apart?"

"Oh, that's easy." Bk turned back to the pyramids and spoke to them. In another second, each one turned into a different geometrical shape.

"Okay, I guess that does make things a little easier," Velvet muttered to Linen. In a louder voice, arms open, she spoke to the beings. "Welcome to the Earth Angel Training Academy! My name is Velvet, and I am the Head of the Academy. This is Linen, my assistant. You have only missed a day of classes, so I am sure that you will have no problems in getting up to speed. This is Bk, as you probably already know, and he is our resident Starperson translator. So, in the first few weeks, if you have any problems, please speak with him and he will relay them to me. Alternatively, if it's possible, you can use the message board in your room. I don't want to bombard you with too much information right now; so if you would like to follow Bk, he will take each of you to your rooms where you can settle in, meet your room-mates, and see your class schedule. If you can try to be at your first lesson at nine o'clock promptly, that would be excellent. I hope you have a pleasant rest, I will try to get round and see you all tomorrow." Slightly breathless, Velvet turned from the hovering shapes that had remained still and unchanging during her entire speech to Bk. "Did they understand all of that?"

After a pause Bk turned to Velvet and nodded. "Yes they did, they are grateful for the warm welcome and are looking forward to learning all there is to know about being human."

"Excellent." Velvet clicked her fingers and an ethereal scroll of room numbers appeared in Bk's hand. "For now we shall name them after their shapes, it'll make things a little easier in the beginning. If they wish we can always rethink their names when they receive their human form."

Bk nodded and scanned the paper in his hands. "Sounds good to me." He tilted his head for a moment. "It sounds good to them, too."

"Perfect. Thank you, Bk, please come to see me if there are any problems, otherwise, I will see you tomorrow for the next and last arrival."

"Oh yes, the Synapsians. I'm looking forward to them arriving."

Velvet raised an eyebrow. "Yes, the last group from that planet were quite, erm interesting. I just hope this new group aren't quite so..."

"Mad? I wouldn't hope too hard," Bk laughed. He turned to the shapes and spoke to them. They all formed a line behind him and they moved silently and effortlessly like a family of ducklings as he led them out of the hall.

"Wow," Velvet muttered to Linen. "If only all aliens could be so obedient."

Chapter Eight

"How are you feeling now, Aria?" Amethyst asked as she arrived back at her room after a long conversation with a fellow Angel about their personal missions. When there was no immediate answer she searched the swirling galaxy for her Faerie friend. She found her tucked away in the corner, sat at a tiny desk that she must have manifested. She was furiously scribbling away, occasionally letting out a frustrated sigh and crossing things out. Amethyst watched her for a while, then after the fourth crossing out, she rested a hand gently on her friends' shoulder.

"Aria, are you okay?"

Aria jumped a little, and looked up at the Angel. "Oh, Am!" She smiled, but it seemed strained. She looked down at the paper in front of her that was covered in angry black lines. "Yes, I'm fine; I was just trying to come up with some ideas."

"Ideas for what?"

"For what we talked about earlier. You know, something to help us recognise each other when we're on Earth."

"I see. You do know that we have plenty of time don't you? It's only the second day; we'll have many more days to work something out before we're called to Earth."

"I know," Aria said quietly, "I just wanted to make sure we came up with something before we have to go."

"We will. I promise you. I will not go to Earth until we have figured something out, okay?"

Aria smiled and balled up the piece of paper. "Okay." She rose up and threw it into the overflowing bright pink rubbish bin.

Amethyst smiled at the little Faerie. "So, what shall we do tonight before we rest?"

Aria flew over to her planet bed and bounced up and down excitedly. "What are the options?"

Amethyst went over to the notice board and scanned the evening activities poster that had appeared earlier in the day.

"'Snow White and the Seven Dwarves, a fairytale film by Walt Disney.' In the main hall." Amethyst read.

"What's a film?"

"It's a moving picture with words and music. Humans make them, they're stories that you watch on a screen."

"Ooh, that one sounds good. What else?"

"'Bingo. In the Games room.'"

"Bingo? What in Heaven's name is that?"

"It's a game that humans play, to win prizes."

"Prizes? Let's do that one!"

Amethyst turned and smiled at the Faerie, still bouncing tirelessly. "You sure you don't want to hear the rest of the options?"

"I'm sure! Let's play Bingo!"

"They might do it differently here; it doesn't say for certain that there are prizes."

"That's okay, I just want to know what it is. Besides, they're trying to show us how the humans do it, right?" Amethyst nodded. "So there must be prizes! Otherwise it wouldn't be teaching us anything!"

Amethyst laughed. "I like your logic, little one." She glanced at the clock and back at the poster. "We'd better get moving if we're going to make it on time, it starts in five minutes."

Aria sped to the door, then she turned back to Amethyst and grinned. "Wanna race?"

Amethyst joined her at the doorway. "You're on."

"Ready... go!" Aria shouted, flying as fast as her dragonfly wings would take her. Amethyst's powerful, feathered wings flapped at a more sedate pace, but she still managed to keep up with the tiny green blur. They arrived at the games room and Aria reached the door a second before Amethyst.

"I win! I win!" She flew around Amethyst in circles. "I bet I win a prize tonight too!"

"I wouldn't doubt it, little Faerie."

They entered the room together and found a small gathering of beings milling around, chatting to one another. Aria flew around a geometrical shaped structure that hovered a couple of feet from the floor; unsure if it was part of the décor or if it was some kind of being. She pointed at it and mouthed to Amethyst, "What is that?"

Amethyst shrugged.

"Hello, all! Welcome to the evening activity of Bingo!"

Amethyst and Aria looked up to see Athena, the Angel professor at the front of the room.

"For those of you who know how this game works, I warn you now, we do it a little differently here, so I would suggest just going with the flow. Now then, I see we have a few of the latest Starpeople here, is Bk here too?"

"Yes, I'm here," Bk replied from the centre of the crowd. He went up to the front of the room and stood next to Athena.

"Excellent! Right then, if everyone could just move to the edges of the room, and we'll set up the boards."

Everyone shifted to the outer edges of the room. Seeing as the hovering shape moved too, Aria figured it must be some kind of alien. When she reached the wall she turned to find herself right up close to it. "Hello," she said to it. "I'm Aria." There was no response or change in the hovering cube in front of her. She frowned. At least the Zubenelgenubi aliens glowed brighter when you spoke to them; these ones didn't seem to have any kind of reaction at all.

"Um, can I have your attention for a moment?" Bk called

out. Everyone was quiet. "The Cube Pyrydian says "Hello, Aria, I'm very well, thank you, how are you?"

Aria laughed and her cheeks turned pink. "Fine, thanks!" she squeaked. A few beings around her laughed. She looked at the cube. There was still no change. So that she wouldn't embarrass herself further, she turned away from the odd cube-alien and focused on what was happening in the room. Athena was flying around, her golden wings glittering in the bright lights. She seemed to be flying at random, but when Aria looked at the floor, a very neat grid was drawn in golden light.

Once finished, there were three grids on the floor. Athena clapped her hands once and numbers appeared in a kind of formation within the boxes.

"Okay, now if everyone could come forward and each stand or hover above the squares with numbers in." There was a slight commotion as everyone moved forward to occupy the spaces. Once everyone was in place, Athena got their attention once again.

"The object of the game is simple. Numbers from one to forty-nine will be called out at random. If the number you are standing on is called, you sit down," She paused. "Or, well, hover closer to the floor. Then, once a whole line of you is sitting, the last one to sit yells out 'Line!' and everyone in that line will win a prize! Then we continue to call out numbers, and when everyone within your bingo board is sitting down, the last one to sit calls out 'House!' and then everyone in that board wins a prize. Is everyone clear?" There was a chorus of yeses and lots of nodding. Athena glanced at Bk and he nodded for the Zubenelgenubis and Pyrydians. "Right then! Let the games begin!"

*   *   *

"Is there anything else you need me to do?" Linen asked later that evening.

Velvet shook her head. "No, you go and get your rest.

You'll need it before the Synapsians arrive."

"Are they really that bad?"

"There weren't any in your class were there?" Linen shook his head. "You were lucky then. They're not so bad when they are in human form, but in their own form..." Velvet sighed. "Let's just say that dealing with them has been known to cause headaches."

Linen chuckled. "Okay, I guess I'll see for myself." He headed to the door, stopped halfway and turned back to Velvet. "Is it even possible to get headaches here?"

Velvet smiled. "It's avoidable, for certain, but here, on the Other Side, all things are possible. The good and the bad - there are no exclusions."

Linen considered this. "But why would anyone want to experience the bad if they have the choice to choose only good?"

"For the same reasons that humans choose the bad, though it may be an unconscious choice. If we don't experience the bad, how could we possibly know the good? If we don't experience down, how do we know what's up? Everything has an opposite, black, white, up, down, hot, cold. If we know only one, then how do we know the other exists? If we wish to be whole as beings on this side and as humans on Earth, we must know both. There is no way of being a balanced soul with only one side of the story."

Linen smiled. "You may want to use that in one of your lessons. You made a very good point just then."

Velvet groaned. "Oh, Goddess, have the new Earth Angels arrived yet? I didn't even think to have a welcoming session - honestly, all the changes this year have totally thrown off my internal schedule."

"Yes, they arrived a little while ago. I assigned Corduroy to take care of them."

"Oh, great. That's bound to ensure a good deal of chaos to sort out tomorrow."

Linen headed for the door again. "That's okay, after all,

how could you know orderliness and perfection without chaos?" He turned and winked, then disappeared through the vanishing door.

"Smart ass," Velvet muttered, a small smile on her face. It had taken a full forty-eight hours, but Linen was actually becoming tolerable. It wasn't like her to warm to someone so quickly. Especially someone who had irritated her so much initially.

Sighing, she tapped her fingers on her desk, thinking. Then, when she decided it was pointless to put it off any longer, she called Beryl.

"Yes?" Beryl answered, her face appearing on the wall along with the sound of wind chimes.

"Could you put a notice on the boards of the new arrivals who got here this afternoon for me, Beryl?"

"The Starpeople or the new apprentices?"

"The apprentices, though we're going to have to come up with a new name for them. Having one apprentice looks bad enough, but thirty-four? The trainees will wonder what the hell is going on."

Beryl's face fell a little.

"What is it?" Velvet asked.

"I was hoping Linen would tell you, but it seems he's chickened out."

"Tell me what?" Velvet frowned, thinking that this sounded particularly ominous.

"There aren't thirty-four apprentices. Word got round, and I'm afraid the number increased."

Velvet held her breath. "How many are there now?"

Beryl grimaced. "Seventy-five."

"Seventy-five!" Velvet practically shouted. "Please in Goddess' name tell me you are joking."

"I never joke, Velvet, you know that," Beryl answered timidly, her wings fluttering nervously.

Velvet took a few deep, calming breaths. "I know," she told the nervous Angel. "I'm not angry with you, Beryl. You just took me by surprise. Seventy-five? Do you think this is it now? Or do you think there will be more?"

Beryl lifted her shoulders. "I don't know, Velvet, word of your new class has been spreading through the dimensions like wildfire."

Velvet frowned for a moment. "Are they all former Earth Angel Training Academy graduates?"

"Actually, no, they're not. Some are graduates of other training schools in other dimensions."

"So if they're not former trainees of my Academy, how do they know that they want me to teach them?"

"I don't know, Velvet, but they're all extremely excited." She paused. "So, what notice did you want me to put on their boards?"

"Oh, yes, the notice. Hmm, well I think I should meet with them all at the same time, so let's have a welcome meeting. Then I can work out a schedule to do classes with them. I don't like teaching classes that are too large, and seventy-five is way too large, so maybe we should have a morning class and an afternoon class. I haven't even begun to work out a lesson plan." She laughed humourlessly. "I can't even work out *why* they want me to teach them, let alone *what* they want me to teach."

Beryl smiled kindly. "I'm sure you will do just fine. So, shall I tell them to be in the main hall at nine o'clock tomorrow morning for the official welcome meeting?" She consulted the schedule. "The main hall is free until eleven o'clock - will two hours be long enough?"

"Yes, that sounds perfect. I will just do some exercises with them tomorrow so they can get to know one another, and see if I can get out of them what sort of things they're expecting. Then I guess I'll figure out a lesson plan of some sort." She looked up at Beryl, suddenly aware that she was rambling to herself in front of her secretary. "Okay, Beryl, that will be all, I will see you in the morning."

Beryl nodded and faded with a soft: "Good night, Velvet."

"Good night," Velvet echoed, knowing for certain that this would not be a good night, but a very long one. It was time to see her old friend again. She needed some help, fast.

*　　*　　*

"Well hello, Velvet, long time no see," Magenta joked as she walked up the sandy beach to greet her friend.

"I know, I know, this is becoming a rather regular meeting, I do apologise for taking up all your time."

Magenta waved her hand dismissively. "No need to apologise, my dear old friend. I always have time for you. Besides," she gestured at the surroundings. "I really quite enjoy being here on this beach, it's very relaxing. It gets stuffy in that tiny, dark, incense-filled room."

Velvet smiled tiredly. "Always glad to be of service."

Magenta reached Velvet and stopped. "What's it to be, a walk along the water or sitting on this beautiful sand?"

"I need to sit."

Magenta sat gracefully on the sand, folding her soft jersey robes around her. "So, let it all out, what's troubling you now? Is it the vision still?"

"No, I don't know what the song is yet, but Linen is able to play it on the piano, so I am going to get Tartan to see if he can identify it for me. I'm thinking it must be a classical tune, hopefully he's come across it in one of his many lives."

"That's good progress. Have you had the vision again?"

"Yes, while Linen was playing the piano actually. I was here on this beach. This time I could hear the music, and I decided to close my eyes and follow it. But it was coming from the ocean. I waded in, trying to find the source, when the music stopped." She omitted the part where she had yelled out.

Magenta looked to the water. "It was coming from the ocean?"

Velvet nodded, staring out at the waves.

"Hmm, that's interesting."

"What do you think it means?" Velvet asked.

"I'm not sure. But I will think about it for you. Did you see the figure again?"

"No, no figure this time. But I felt that if I followed the music, I would find him."

"I see." Magenta was quiet for a while, thinking. "So why did you come to visit me? If it wasn't about the vision?"

Velvet groaned. "It's this new group of Earth Angels that want me to teach them. It's getting completely out of control."

"How so?"

"There are now seventy-five of them. Seventy-five!" Just saying it again made it seem even worse.

Magenta frowned at her friend. "Is the number really that big a problem? Surely if you're teaching one it's the same as teaching a hundred?"

"But I don't know what to teach them!"

Magenta smiled. "Yes, you do." She nudged Velvet with her arm. "Remember what I said last time about opening your eyes?"

Velvet nodded.

"Now would be a good time to do just that. Look at everything that's happening here; think about what you know about the Earth's future. What do you think it's all adding up to mean?"

Velvet sighed. "Can't you just tell me what it means?"

Magenta laughed. "Don't you teach the Earth Angels that being human means figuring things out for themselves?"

Velvet smiled sheepishly. "Yes, we do. But I'm not an Earth Angel. I'm the Head of the Earth Angel Training Academy." She smiled. "Which means I can cheat a little."

Magenta shook her head, smiling. "No dice, my friend. This time, I'm afraid you need to figure this one out for yourself."

Velvet made a face at Magenta, then turned to stare at the waves again. She took a deep breath. "Okay, so let's see. First of all, we're getting close to the predicted end of the human world. This year is the biggest class of Earth Angels we've ever had. An Earth Angel Faerie hears an unknown internal call to return to the Academy to be my apprentice, so he wilfully leaves Earth to learn from me. I keep having visions of this beach, which sometimes include a figure of a man and which is linked to a piece of music. And finally, a huge group of former Earth Angels have just arrived at the Academy to be taught solely by me." She finished her summary and looked at Magenta. "And you somehow seem to think that I do in fact know the meaning of all this, but I am refusing to open my eyes and see the bigger picture."

Magenta nodded thoughtfully. "I think that just about sums it up."

Velvet sighed. "Can you at least tell me when I'm going to finally open my eyes and figure out what the hell is going on?"

"You really want to know?"

"I wouldn't ask if I didn't."

"You will work it out when you need to. And not a moment sooner."

Velvet let out a frustrated groan. "Magenta! Don't do this to me! Don't be one of those irritating psychics who knows all and tells very little! You're my friend, we've known each other forever, please help me out here."

Magenta smiled infuriatingly. "I'm sorry, Velvet, but I'm following my intuition on this one."

Velvet sighed. She loved her friend, but she was beginning to feel impatient. "I could always just grill Linen or Gold for more information. I know they know more than they're letting on."

"They won't tell you either. You know how it works, everything happens for a reason and everything happens in the perfect sequence. When you are supposed to know all that is happening, you will."

Velvet stood up abruptly. "I have to go."

Magenta nodded silently, staying where she was.

With another irritated sigh, Velvet clicked her fingers and

vanished.

Magenta sighed too. She hated to be so secretive. To know what her friend was desperate to know, and to keep it from her, was extremely difficult. This time, she only had to wait a few moments before she sensed the soul approaching her. She patted the sand next to her and called out: "Come and sit with me, Gold."

The Elder's beautiful robes rippled in the breeze as he moved slowly yet gracefully towards Magenta. He eased himself down onto the warm golden sand.

"Don't fret, my dear Magenta, she will forgive your covertness, you know that."

"I know," Magenta said quietly. "It still pains me though."

"Yes, well, I'm afraid that difficult times like these create some difficult circumstances."

"Do you honestly believe that she will be able to leave? To return to Earth? It's been such a long time since she was there, don't you think she will just choose to exit early like the many other Earth Angels have done?"

"I believe she is stronger than that."

"Yes, she is strong. But I think her strength will work against you." She looked into Gold's eyes, noticing a slight twitch in his right eye.

"She will fight to stay," Magenta continued. "The Academy is her whole reason for existing. And you think she will just give it up without a fuss? Just accept the call and return to Earth to become a human again for the three thousand, three hundred and thirty-third time?"

Gold smiled a little at Magenta's assessment of the situation. "I agree it is a lot to ask. But it is all for a very good reason."

"It's always for a good reason. I don't doubt the reason. But I do know what I have seen." She shook her head. "Gold, even if she accepts, even if the future that you have seen with her as a human on Earth actually happens, you know that it might not prevent the demise of the human world. I don't think the Golden Age is going to happen this time. Maybe it really is a myth."

"My dear Seer, listening to you lose heart like this is very saddening. Do you honestly not think that the future can change? Do you not think that maybe, if we just at least try, we can perhaps lengthen the current human age, and maybe even make their lives more pleasurable and enjoyable?"

Magenta shrugged. "I know that of all the possible futures, we have seen but a small handful. It is possible, as are all things possible, that Velvet's return to Earth could change the human age for the better, and the Golden Age could finally be experienced. But is it likely? I would say not."

"Likely or not, calling Velvet back to Earth is our best hope." He nodded to himself. "And she will come to understand that. She has done an amazing job of preparing the Earth Angels for their human incarnations. But now it is time for her to help them to endure Earth. We cannot afford for many more Earth Angels to leave Earth. If it gets any worse, there will not be enough there to help with the shift. And if the humans don't Awaken in time, well, their world will be ending even sooner than our conservative predictions."

Magenta sighed and looked at the scene around her. "It's beautiful here, isn't it?"

Gold smiled and looked out at the ocean. "Yes, it is. I've always loved this beach. Takes me back to the beautiful times we had in Atlantis."

Magenta looked at him sharply. "You know this beach?"

Gold's eye twitched. He sighed. "Who else do you think started off the visions?"

"You? You're the one giving Velvet the visions? You're the figure on the beach?"

"Oh my dear, no, I am not the figure. The figure is her soulmate."

Magenta frowned. "Her soulmate?"

"Yes." Gold sighed again. "This goes no further?" Magenta nodded quickly. "The visions are an encouragement of sorts. I wanted to give her a reason to go back."

"And you think she would go back willingly if there was a soulmate relationship there for her?"

"Not just any soulmate, though she will encounter many of them. No, this one is her Twin Flame."

Magenta's eyebrows shot up. "You are reuniting Flames? Then you must believe that the world will soon end."

"We know for certain that the Earth is not going to stay in its present state for much longer, so we held council, and have come to the decision to reunite as many Flames as possible. It is time for those on Earth to experience love in the way that it was intended. To be with the other half of their very souls." He sighed. "We are hoping that this kind of love will produce the miracles that the world so desperately needs."

"You still believe in true love?" Magenta asked wistfully.

"Yes. In fact, that's one of the reasons I am here to see you."

Magenta frowned. "I'm listening."

"Your Twin Flame has asked to return to Earth."

Magenta's breath caught. "But he's on the uppermost guidance level. I thought once you were there, you could not return?" she whispered.

"My darling, don't you remember the concept of free will? Every soul in existence has the right of free will. He has asked to return, and his request will be granted. But he asked if we could find you, and see if you would also be interested in returning."

Magenta's eyes widened. "You're asking me to return to Earth?"

"No, I'm asking you if you would like one last human incarnation with your Twin Flame."

"Wow," Magenta whispered. "I did not see that one coming."

"Of course not, dear, we so very often are blind to our own futures. It is the way the Universe works."

Magenta was quiet for a while. "Do I have time to think

about this?"

"Of course, my dear Magenta. This is not a decision that you make in an instant. We would not expect that of you."

"What about you, Gold? Are you going to return to Earth? Or will you watch the end from here?"

Gold smiled at her cynicism. "I'm afraid that I am needed here; with all of our best going back for the final battle, I'll be needed here to hold down the fort."

"The final battle," Magenta whispered.

"And perhaps the most love you have experienced in many, many lifetimes."

Magenta nodded. "I will let you know when I have made my decision."

"I have no doubt that you will, my dear," Gold stood slowly. "I will see you again soon."

In a swirl of golden dust, Gold was gone, leaving Magenta to her thoughts. She sighed heavily. Another life on Earth. A chance to be with her Twin Flame. The possibility of being able to help one of her oldest friends in Awakening the humans. And maybe, just maybe, an opportunity to experience the incredibly elusive Golden Age.

Magenta lay back in the sand and stared up at the blue sky. She waved her hand above her, turning the day into night. Stars sparkled brightly from the deep blue sky above her.

"Stars, what should I do?" she whispered. "Show me the way. Please."

Chapter Nine

The main hall was once again filled with the sound of excited chattering. The new arrivals had all gathered for the nine o'clock meeting that Velvet had announced the night before.

Emerald shifted from one foot to another. She looked down at her right hand, which was intertwined with her soulmate's.

"Are you okay?" Mica asked her.

Emerald smiled up at him. "Yes, I'm just excited I suppose." She looked around at the other beings. "I can't believe so many others answered the call."

Mica nodded in agreement. "Yes, it is good to see that so many still have faith in the power of the shift."

"Let's hope our faith proves true."

Just then, the voices around them hushed and a tall Old Soul in beautiful purple velvet robes swept onto the stage, with a wiry looking Old Soul dressed in bright yellow, trailing after her. She came to a stop in the centre front of the stage and held up her hand.

"Welcome, all," she said, smiling. Her gentle voice reached every corner of the massive hall. "My name is Velvet, I am the Head of the Earth Angel Training Academy and your professor for this course. Due to an unexpected increase in numbers, I will have to split the group into two, and have a morning class and an afternoon class. There will be various evening activities, and there will also be plenty of time to relax and meet other souls in your group. Now, as you have all retained your human appearance, I would appreciate it if you could keep yourself separate from the souls on the training course here. It may confuse them, and I don't wish to explain the situation to them at this point. They will be changing into human form within the next few weeks. After that, it won't be noticeable that you are all on a different course to them." She paused and consulted her notes.

"I have your names here, and to make the split easier, I have decided to just split you up alphabetically. So, those with names beginning with A to M, please step to my left, and those with names beginning with N to Z, please step to my right."

There was a great deal of shuffling around as everyone moved to the correct group. Emerald and Mica stood in the left-hand group, pleased that they had not been separated. They looked around at their fellow group mates and smiled.

Velvet was looking at both groups, seemingly doing a quick head count. "I see that there are about fifty in the A to M group and about forty-five in the N to Z." She looked down at her list. "I only have seventy-seven names on my list, so do we have some new additions to the original group here? If you think your name won't be down, could you please raise your hand?"

About twenty hands went up into the air. Emerald thought she saw a look of dismay on Velvet's gently lined face, but it was gone so quickly she couldn't be sure. When she spoke next though, her voice was definitely strained.

"Could all those not on the list please see my assistant, Linen," she gestured to the bright red-haired man beside her. "Before you leave the hall this morning." She looked back down at her notes again.

"The morning group will be called the MorningStar group, the afternoon group will be called the EvenStar group. The morning session will run from nine o'clock to one o'clock, the afternoon session will be from two o'clock to six o'clock." She looked up from her notes. "I thought that this morning perhaps we could have an informal discussion on why you are all here and what you expect from this course." She clicked her fingers and a hundred seats appeared in front of her, with a gap dividing them down the middle. She gestured to the seats. "Please all be seated, and if you would like to speak, please raise your hand."

While everyone sat, she clicked her fingers and two seats appeared behind her, one for herself and one for Linen. She sat down heavily.

Emerald and Mica found two seats together, their hands still intertwined in the small gap between them. Mica squeezed her hand gently. "Are you going to speak?" he asked.

Emerald nodded. "I will speak for us both," she replied softly. She looked back at the stage, where Velvet was looking around the room for the first soul to speak.

"So first of all," Velvet began, "I would like to know the reason why you think you are here at the Academy." She looked around the room. "Anyone wish to start?"

There was a silence as everyone looked around them, waiting for the first soul to raise their hand. Feeling bold, Emerald raised hers, much to Velvet's relief.

"Yes, the soul in the third row wearing green. What is your name and what realm are you from originally?"

Emerald stood, still holding onto Mica's hand for support. "My name is Emerald. I am from the Angelic Realm, and this is my soulmate, Mica, who is also from the Angelic Realm."

"Welcome, Angels," Velvet said. "What do you believe is your reason for being here?"

"We believe that our purpose is to help humans to meet their soulmates." She smiled down at Mica. "But not just their soulmates. We believe that it is time for the fiery passions that have lain dormant for so long to Awaken." She took a breath. "We wish to return to Earth to reunite the Flames."

There was a small collective gasp from around the room. Velvet looked at Emerald with interest.

"That is a remarkable mission, Emerald. But I am unclear

as to why you feel the need to be here before returning to Earth. Surely you could have just returned there immediately to fulfil your purpose?"

Emerald smiled. "I thought so too. But after asking the Elders for guidance on our mission, we were told to listen to our intuition for the answers. And when we heard that there was a new course here, taught by the Head of the Earth Angel Training Academy, one of the oldest souls in existence, we felt intuitively that we needed to come here first, before returning to Earth."

"What do you think you can learn from me that would help you?"

Emerald shrugged. "I'm afraid I do not know. All I know is that we would more than likely fail our mission on Earth without your wisdom."

Velvet nodded but looked a little frustrated. "Thank you, Emerald." She turned back to address the rest of the group. "Would anyone else like to share their thoughts on why they are here?"

After a moment a very tall, slim soul stood up.

"Yes, the soul in the very back row, dressed in silver. Your name and realm of origin?"

"My name is Al, and I originally came from the Zubenelgenubi star. I was actually about to re-enter my own realm when I heard about this new class. As soon as I heard, something within me clicked into place, and I realised that I was needed here."

"So you have no clear idea why you are here?" Velvet asked, even more desperately, Emerald thought.

Al shook his head. "No, I only felt deep within that it was my purpose to return to Earth, to help with the shift, but that I should come here first."

Velvet nodded, her face looking weary. "Thank you, Al, welcome to the Academy. I hope you find what you are looking for."

Al nodded and sat back down.

"Does anyone have any other questions about the course? Or would like to add any thoughts as to why you are here?"

All over the room, tentative hands raised. Velvet sighed and chose the first soul she saw.

"Yes, the soul in pink, fifth row back to the right..."

*　　　*　　　*

After the meeting, Emerald and Mica left the main hall, still hand-in-hand. Without a word, they both headed for the expansive gardens within the Academy. They came to the golden benches in the Angelic Garden and sat, facing a beautiful waterfall that shimmered in the midday sun.

"Are you thinking what I'm thinking?" Mica wondered.

"I usually am," Emerald replied, smiling.

"Tomorrow's first class should be interesting shouldn't it?"

"Well, considering Velvet doesn't seem to have any idea what we've all come here for, it should be very interesting." They watched the waterfall in silence for a while, enjoying the soothing sound of the running water.

"It's not our place to say anything," Emerald said abruptly, sensing what Mica was about to say. "I already said more than enough this morning, but she was not open to the information. I think we should hold back from giving anything more away. Everything must unfold at its own pace."

Mica nodded. "You're right, as usual. I just hate to see people struggle unnecessarily."

Emerald leaned against his arm. "I know you do," she said softly. "But it is quite necessary."

"I guess we will see."

"Yes, we will."

*　　　*　　　*

"Are you still glowing from your win last night, Aria?" Amethyst asked the still rather overexcited little Faerie, as she zoomed along the hallway on their way to the gardens during the midday break.

"Uh huh! Didn't I tell you I would win? It was so much fun! Can we do it again tomorrow?"

Amethyst shook her head. "I think the evening schedule changes every day. We can do it again next week though."

"How long is a week again?"

"Seven days."

"Aww, we have to wait seven whole days 'til we can play again? That sucks. I hope they're doing something fun tonight."

"Me, too. Although my mind is still reeling from what we learnt in class this morning."

Aria slowed up to fly alongside Amethyst. "I know what you mean! It's so weird to see how everything is connected to everything else. To think that a butterfly flapping its wings could be the cause of a typhoon on the other side of the planet is just incredible. It makes you really think about what effect you could be having."

"Yes, I think humans in particular do not realise that everything they do and say has an effect, whether they witness that effect or not. I think if more of them realised it, they would realise that each and every one of them can help to change the world. Even the smallest of actions can make the biggest changes."

"Even the smallest of people can make the biggest differences!" Aria chimed in, zipping round in happy circles.

"Well said, little one. Well said. Even the smallest of candles can brighten the darkest of rooms."

"Wow, we're getting good with these little quotes aren't we? We should write a book."

Amethyst chuckled. "Who knows, maybe that will be one of the missions we choose to pursue on Earth, to spread our message through the written word."

Aria smiled at her. "You would be so good at that! You should definitely choose to be a writer."

"We will see."

They arrived at the gardens and headed for Amethyst's favourite area, the Angelic Garden. Aria let out a little sigh of disappointment when she realised their usual golden bench was taken. Two beings sat there, holding hands. Aria headed for a nearby bench and sat down. Amethyst settled next to her.

"Hello, there!" Aria called out to them. "Hope you don't mind us joining you. This is our favourite part of the gardens."

"Not at all," the male replied. "We were just on our way, anyway."

He stood gracefully and the female stood with him. She smiled sweetly at Aria and Amethyst, and they glided away, their robes rippling in the breeze. Amethyst watched them go, a slight frown on her face.

"What is it?" Aria asked her friend.

"Have you seen them before?"

Aria shook her head. "I don't think so, but then our class is awfully big. Weren't they Old Souls? Maybe they're visiting professors or something."

"That's the thing. They looked like Old Souls, but I honestly felt like they were really Angels. But no one has changed into their human form yet, so it doesn't make any sense."

"Changed into human form?" Aria frowned at Amethyst. "What do you mean?"

Amethyst looked at the little fluttering Faerie. "I'm beginning to wonder if you listened to a single word the recruitment souls said."

Aria turned red. "I may have been daydreaming while they were talking."

Amethyst shook her head. "Oh, Aria, what am I going to do with you?"

"For starters, you can explain the human form thing."

Amethyst took a breath. "We're here to learn how to be human, right?" Aria nodded. "In order to do that effectively, it's not enough to just learn the theory of being human, we have to experience it physically too. Before we're called to Earth."

"Which means we're going to look human soon?"

"Yes."

Aria looked over her shoulder at her beautiful, iridescent green wings. "I can't imagine being without wings." They drooped slightly and her tiny shoulders slumped.

"That's why you need to experience being in a human body for the first time now, and not when you are born on Earth. Otherwise it will be too much of a shock."

Aria nodded. "That makes sense. I'll just miss them, that's all."

Amethyst glanced back at her own feathered wings. "I know, I will too."

"Do we just get given bodies or do we get to choose what we look like?"

"I'm not certain, but I think you get to choose."

Aria's wings lifted and her face brightened up. "Do you think I could choose a tall body? I mean, without wings I would be trodden on all the time. Last thing I want is to be a short human."

Amethyst laughed. "No one could possibly tread on you, little one, you're much too loud."

"I am around you, because I know you. But around big crowds, I don't know," she shuddered. "I get all shy and tongue-tied. I would definitely get trampled on."

Amethyst was still chuckling. "Perhaps you should choose self-confidence as one of your virtues."

"We can choose virtues too?" Aria asked excitedly, her little wings fluttering once again.

Amethyst sighed. "I tell you what, I'll have a word with someone in the office and see if I can get a brochure for the Academy, then you will see exactly what's to come during our training course."

Aria smiled. "That would be brilliant. You really are a wonderful friend. I would never have thought about doing that."

The sound of a choir filled the air around them suddenly.

"Oops, we're going to be late for class," Amethyst said, getting to her feet. "Wanna race?"

Aria grinned. "Always! Ready, set, go!"

*   *   *

The sound of swishing robes was too distracting for Linen to concentrate on sorting his notes.

"Velvet, is there anything I can do to help?"

Velvet paused mid-pace and glanced at him distractedly. "What?"

"Is there anything I can do to help?" Linen repeated patiently.

Velvet resumed her pacing and shook her head absently. "No, no, I just need to think."

"Still no ideas on what to do with your apprentices?"

"No, none at all."

"I'm sure you'll figure it out. Did you ask Tartan about listening to the song yet?"

"Oh, yes, I did, he'll be here this evening, is that okay for you?"

"Of course. I'm free whenever."

Velvet stopped suddenly. "Actually, there is something you could do for me right now."

Linen jumped up, happy to be of some use. "Anything."

Velvet gestured to the gleaming white piano. "Could you play me something? Not the song you played the other day, just something relaxing."

Linen smiled. "Sure, I actually remembered a couple more songs when I was practising." He set his pen down and went over to the piano. He played a few scales then launched into a beautiful melody, which instantly relaxed Velvet. Her hunched up shoulders un-knotted themselves and her pacing slowed. She took a few deep breaths and tried to let the music clear her mind.

She knew that the solutions were right in front of her. She knew that she was making this whole situation way more difficult than it needed to be, but still, she felt like she couldn't get her mind around it all. Feeling much better as the music washed over her, Velvet went over to her chair and sank into the purple cushions. She closed her eyes and went into a meditative state. She needed to take her focus off of the problem and open her mind to receive the solution.

She wiped all thoughts that were threatening to overwhelm her and concentrated on the music. The notes of the song rose up around her, engulfing her with a feeling of peace.

There was a slight pause in-between notes and then a different piece started. The tune was more soulful and haunting. Still deep in a meditative state, Velvet was dimly aware of a tear escaping down her cheek.

Suddenly, she felt a cool breeze across her face, and then felt the shock of cold water lapping at her feet. She opened her eyes and found herself on the beach again. The music continued to rise and fall around her as she adjusted to her surroundings. She squinted in the bright sunlight, her bare skin instantly warmed. Involuntarily, she smiled. Though she was certain it was impossible, the scene around her seemed even more real than ever before. She let the waves wash over her feet, making her feel calm and happy.

She took in a deep breath of salty air and then almost screamed when she felt a hand on her shoulder. She whipped around and found herself staring into the deepest green eyes she had ever seen. Her fear dissipated and she felt herself melting under the steady gaze of the green eyes. She wanted to take a step back to see who it was, but instead found herself stepping forward. The green eyes got closer until she felt soft lips touching her own. She closed her eyes then, and lost herself in the stranger's embrace.

Though it was merely seconds, to Velvet it seemed like entire lifetimes had passed by before she opened her eyes and leant back a little. The green eyes were sparkling, and the smile was mischievous.

"Who are you?" she whispered.

The deep pink lips smiled. "Your destiny." His voice was rough, but so sweetly gentle at the same time. She smiled back, completely mesmerised by his incredible emerald green eyes. Velvet suddenly became aware of the music when he looked out to the ocean and she caught a glimpse of his long, tangled blond hair. The notes were reaching a crescendo, and he frowned. He looked back at her and the frown melted into another heart-stopping smile. He leant forward and whispered in her ear.

"Listen to your heart, and you will always find me."

"You're leaving?"

He nodded and stepped back. He gave her hand a squeeze, then released her, waded into the water and dove into the waves.

"Wait, where are you going?" she called after him, wading into the water. She squinted, the sunlight almost blinding her. "Please don't go yet!" As the notes of the song drifted away, she lost sight of the man with the deep green eyes. Just as the last note sounded, she thought she saw a green fin disappear into the waves.

"Velvet?" a voice called softly. "Velvet, are you okay?"

Velvet opened her eyes and saw a bright orange pair of eyes stare back at her with concern. She lifted her hand to her face and found that it was wet.

"Velvet?" Linen said again.

Velvet was torn between wanting to appear professional and needing to express the feelings of grief and despair that were ripping her to shreds inside. She choked out, "I'm fine, Linen, could you just leave me be for a moment?"

Linen nodded, still very concerned. "I'll just be in my room. Call me if you need anything."

Velvet nodded, unable to speak anymore. Linen left quickly, glancing at her once over his shoulder as he went through the vanishing door.

As soon as the door reappeared, Velvet let out the sob she'd been holding in. How real it had felt, being in his arms. How incredible it was, to be held, to be kissed, and to feel so utterly loved and cherished. It had been so long since Velvet had let herself go. Had given in to her instincts and felt so... *alive.*

More sobs followed the first and soon her shoulders were heaving and her vision was blurred with tears. She had never cried so hard before, not even in any of her many, many lifetimes as a human. Watching him leave was like losing a piece of herself, a very important, vital piece.

She took in a jagged breath and blinked several times. She clicked her fingers and grabbed a wad of tissues from the box she had just manifested. She wiped her face and blew her nose. The feeling of being wildly out of control hit her again, and she glanced around her to make sure that there really was no one there to witness her breakdown. After several calming breaths, her tears began to slow up.

Her thoughts collected themselves and she tried to go back over the experience. She recalled his incredible green eyes and smiled. She felt such an immense feeling of love when she thought about him. Like she had been lost, alone and living in a dull, grey world when suddenly, she looked into his eyes and everything exploded with colour.

It was the song again. The song had taken her to him. So, she reasoned, the song was linked to finding him. And he was clearly linked to the ocean, seeing as the music had led her into the waves last time, and he had disappeared there when the music stopped. She got up and began to pace again, trying to piece the fragments of the puzzle together. Long blond tangled hair, deep green eyes, linked to the ocean, beautiful rough voice... she paused suddenly when she recalled what she thought she saw glinting in the sunlight before it disappeared into the waves. A fin.

"A Merman?" she wondered out loud. She quickly flicked

through all the information she kept in her mental files about the physical characteristics of Merpeople incarnated on Earth as humans. The stranger on the beach fit the bill exactly. She frowned, puzzled. She had met many Mermen at the Academy, but none of them had made her feel the way she did in her vision. She recalled the few words that he had uttered.

"My destiny," she whispered. She laughed at herself. It seemed that even the stranger in her vision knew more of what was going to happen in her future than she did. Yet again, she felt like she had been given all of the pieces but was incapable of putting them together to create the bigger picture. She knew that the answers were all within her visions. She knew that once she figured it out, she would know exactly what to teach her new class. She would also know the significance of the beach and the blond stranger on it. But until it all fell into place, she would have to wing it.

She grabbed some more tissues and wiped away the remaining tears. Then she clicked her fingers and checked herself in the mirror. Her face looked like she had been through a terrible ordeal; yet it was incredibly calm at the same time. She clicked her fingers again, and for the first time in fifty years, used the Old Soul Magick to make herself look bright and happy. She couldn't have her trainees see her in the state she was in right now. She checked her internal schedule and realised that if she left now, she would be on time to meet with Corduroy in the gardens as they had arranged.

She took one last look at her happy mask in the mirror, straightened her already perfect robes and clicked her fingers again. The mirror, the box of tissues and the used, wet bits of tissue all disappeared, leaving the room clean and tidy again. She nodded in satisfaction and straightened up. She took a deep breath, plastered a smile on her face and swept from her office.

Chapter Ten

"Velvet!" Corduroy called.

After a quick glance around the Angelic Garden, Velvet spotted her friend through the archway, sitting in the Atlantis Garden. She nodded in return and gracefully glided towards him.

He stood to greet her, and pulled her into a quick hug. He stepped back and looked at her more closely.

"Wow, you look amazing today."

Velvet laughed. "Thank you. You look old and haggard as usual."

Corduroy bowed. "Why thank you, your kindness is much appreciated."

They both laughed then settled down on the bench. Corduroy looked around the stunning, crystal encrusted garden, and sighed.

"God, I miss our life in Atlantis. Don't you?"

Velvet nodded. "It certainly is very beautiful here, though my memories of that time are hazy, it was such a long time ago."

"My memories of that time are so clear. Sometimes I come here just to pretend that I'm still there."

"I'm glad for you; sometimes it is good to imagine being somewhere else, an escape of sorts. Thank you again for creating it."

"As I have said before, you are very welcome. It was a

kind of selfish thing for me to do though; I just wanted somewhere to remember that lifetime."

Velvet smiled. "Sometimes the most selfish acts are also the most beautiful."

Corduroy frowned. "Did someone famous on Earth say that?"

Velvet nodded. "Yes, a very wise sage called Janelle La Taime. In the tenth age."

"What did she do?"

"She was a writer and philosopher."

Corduroy nodded. "You knew her then?"

Velvet chuckled. "I was her."

Corduroy looked at Velvet and shook his head. "Why didn't you just say so in the first place?"

Velvet shrugged. "I like to have a bit of fun every now and then."

"What else did Janelle say?"

"Oh, many, many wise and important things. But that's not the purpose of our meeting here today."

"There's a purpose to this meeting? And here I was, just thinking that you wanted to spend some quality time with your old pal."

"Of course I enjoy spending time with you, Corduroy, but I did want to speak with you about an important matter."

"In that case, please, enlighten me."

"Well," Velvet started. She looked out over Atlantis, and something caught her eye. Without thinking, she stood and took a step towards it.

"Well?" Corduroy repeated. He looked up at Velvet, amused. "Is there an end to that sentence?" When he got no reply, he stood up next to Velvet and followed her gaze. Unable to see why she seemed so spellbound, he put his hand on her arm gently.

"Velvet? What is it?"

Velvet's gaze never wavered from the statue in front of her. She walked towards it, seemingly looking at its jewel green eyes. When she stood just a foot away, she reached up to touch the golden arm of the man.

Corduroy followed her, now a little concerned about his friend. He had never seen her act so strangely before.

After a moment, she finally spoke. "Corduroy, who is this?"

"You mean you don't know?" Corduroy asked in surprise. "You don't recognise him?"

Velvet shook her head. "Did I know him in Atlantis?"

"Everyone knew him in Atlantis, Velvet. He was one of the wisest souls in the whole land. Have you never noticed him in the garden before? He was one of the first statues I put in here, for you."

"For me? I didn't know that. And I guess I did see him, but it just didn't mean as much to me before."

"So why does it mean something now? Have you remembered that he was your soulmate?"

"What did you say?" Velvet asked, startled into turning to look at Corduroy.

"Your soulmate. Velvet, don't you remember? That was the last lifetime you spent together. When Atlantis fell and the people moved on, he became a Merman and became the leader of the Merpeople. That's how Merpeople came into existence, they are souls who escaped the fall of Atlantis." Corduroy looked into Velvet's surprised eyes. "You've forgotten all of this, haven't you?"

Velvet blinked a few times then looked back at the statue. She noticed for the first time that he had a tail instead of legs. She looked back up at the emerald green eyes. Suddenly, her memories became clearer and she found herself transported back to those beautiful times in Atlantis. The streets were paved with crystals; everything sparkled. The people who passed her were smiling and laughing. She looked around, searching for someone. This time, the tap on her shoulder didn't frighten her. She turned to face those beautiful green eyes. She smiled, and threw herself into his arms.

"I'm so sorry I forgot about you," she whispered. She felt his deep chuckle.

"Don't worry; I remembered enough for the both of us."

"Velvet?"

The change in the voice was enough to make Velvet lose the vision. She looked at Corduroy.

"Yes?" she asked, wishing she were still lost in her beautiful daydream.

"What just happened?"

"I saw him. I was on the main street in Atlantis, as it was then."

"Wow, when did your visions return?"

Velvet tilted her head at Corduroy. "Return? What do you mean?"

"You really have forgotten so much. Perhaps your soul is getting a little too old to remember everything. Ever considered getting an upgrade?"

"I used to get visions before?"

"That was what you did, in Atlantis. You were the Seer that everyone went to. You would See the future and your soulmate, Laguz, would advise them on the present." He looked at Velvet seriously. "You're the reason why we survived the fall of Atlantis. You saw the end and did all you could to save us all. You also saw that you would not survive it, and that's when you told Laguz he would have to leave without you. It was the last lifetime you ever spent with him."

Velvet looked up at the golden statue. "Laguz. How could I have forgotten him? Perhaps my soul felt it would be too painful." She looked back at Corduroy. "Thank you for bringing back the memories."

Corduroy smiled a little sadly. "I'm pleased to help, as always. The only thing I'm not sure about is why this is all coming to the surface now. It's been lifetimes since you were with your Twin Flame, why the sudden interest?"

A shudder went down Velvet's spine. "My what?"

"Your Twin Flame. Everyone has many soulmates, but

just one Twin Flame." He gestured at the statue. "Laguz is yours. You know that usually Flames are only united on Earth when the world is coming to the end of its current phase. You were with Laguz in Atlantis because that world was coming to its end."

"Twin Flame," Velvet whispered, her mind whirling with all the new possibilities this revelation brought. "Reuniting the Flames. The end of the current phase. Laguz. The beach." Her eyes widened. "I think I'm finally beginning to understand."

Corduroy frowned. "I'm glad one of us is. Care to enlighten me?"

"I'm sorry, Corduroy, but there's someone I need to speak to urgently. Raincheck?"

"Of course, Velvet. You know where to find me."

Velvet smiled and patted his arm. "Thank you." She clicked her fingers and vanished.

Corduroy sat back down on the bench and looked up at the statue of Laguz.

"Do you think she'll ever realise how I feel? Or are you always going to be the wedge between us?" He nodded as if the statue had replied. "Yes, that's just as I thought. You're never going to give me a chance are you? You fishy-tailed bastard."

*   *   *

"Magenta!" Velvet called the instant the beach appeared around her. She searched the beach for a glimpse of her friend's bright robes.

"What's wrong, my friend?" Magenta's voice answered. Velvet spun around to face her.

"I think I can see the bigger picture. I think I understand what is happening." She frowned. "Most of it, anyway, some of the reasons and outcomes are still a little vague." She looked at Magenta with interest. "Did you know that I was a Seer in Atlantis?"

Magenta laughed her throaty laugh. She waved her hand and a big floral couch appeared on the sand. She sat down, still laughing, and gestured to the empty seat beside her.

Velvet sat, and waited patiently for her laughter to subside.

"My dear friend, I am so glad that this is all coming to light. You have no idea how hard it was to watch you struggle so. But it wasn't my place to tell you." Her twinkling eyes looked into Velvet's more serious ones. "You were my mentor. Everything I know about Seeing came from you. You were the most famous Seer in Atlantis, which is quite something, considering how many Seers there were. You Saw the end before anyone else. It was you who saved the lives of thousands of Atlanteans. It was you who saw the beginning of the Merpeople and who helped those who were supposed to, to make the transition from land to water."

Velvet shook her head in wonder. "I can't believe I blocked out all of those memories for so long."

"The important thing is that you remember now. So what's the bigger picture then, what do all these seemingly random things mean, do you think?"

"I was listening to Linen play the piano in my office, and I told him not to play the piece of music that gives me the beach visions, but he did anyway, and I saw him." She smiled at Magenta, her eyes bright. "He was so beautiful, Magenta! I've never felt so loved and so amazing. I asked him who he was, but he wouldn't tell me. Then the music was coming to an end, he said he had to go. So he turned and dove into the waves. Though the sun was bright, I was sure I saw a fin disappear into the waves."

Magenta nodded, looking out to the ocean. "A Merman. That makes sense, considering your earlier visions and what happened in Atlantis."

"I can't describe how I felt when he left. It was like I'd been torn to shreds inside." Velvet shook her head, shaking away the feelings of despair. "A little after that, I went to meet with Corduroy in the Atlantis Garden, and I noticed a statue there, a golden one of a man with emeralds for eyes. It was him. It was the man from my vision. That's when Corduroy told me all what I had forgotten about our lives in Atlantis. Which triggered another vision, this time I was in Atlantis. I turned around and he was there. We hugged and I apologised for forgetting him."

She looked at Magenta, her eyes full. "Corduroy told me that his name was Laguz, and that he was my Twin Flame." She shook her head. "The Passion of the Flames is something that I haven't thought about in centuries. That's why I didn't see it straight away. That's what my visions were trying to show me, they were trying to help me remember what it felt like to be with the other half of my soul." She took a deep breath. "It's beyond words. It's truly indescribable how wonderful it is." She paused, lost in the memory of the feeling.

"So that's what the bigger picture is. The Reunion of the Flames. The Angels in my meeting this morning were trying to tell me as much. The world is coming close to the end of its current phase, and it's time for an infusion of Earth Angels who will help to reunite as many Flames as possible."

Magenta smiled. "I think you are finally opening your eyes, my friend."

"I'm going too, aren't I? That's why Linen has come to take over isn't it? Will Laguz be going too?"

"What do you think?"

Velvet smiled. "He'll be there."

They sat in silence for a while. "I'm going to miss you, Magenta." Velvet placed her hand on her friend's. "You truly have kept me sane all this time."

Magenta sighed, then smiled at her friend. "There will be no need to miss me. You don't really think I'd let you go without me, do you?"

Velvet's eyes widened. "Seriously? You're going back too? But I thought you always swore that you would never leave this realm."

"Never say never, eh? Even I was blind to this one. But I have decided that I should give it a shot. Besides, it's going to be pretty boring up here without you knocking on my door every five seconds. I might as well try and help you down there instead. Also," she smiled and her whole face lit up. "My Twin Flame is going to be there too."

"Wow. That's so amazing!" Velvet shook her head. "I honestly never thought I would return to Earth. But the idea of being with Laguz again…"

Magenta nodded. "I know, the idea of another life with my Twin is what really made the decision for me. But I have to admit, having Seen some of the world's possible futures, it's a bit of a scary idea, going back. This life will definitely be tougher than any of our past lives."

Velvet thought of the deep green eyes. "It'll be worth it though. I'm so glad that you will be with me! It makes it all seem so much easier."

They sat for a while, each lost in their own thoughts.

"So you've worked out what you will be teaching your new class then?"

"Yes. I think my central theme will be love. Even if the Earth as it is now cannot be saved, at the very least we can send an army of Earth Angels to bring the message of love and peace, Awaken as many souls as possible and reunite the Flames. We can make these last few decades the most enjoyable of the entire thirteenth age. And who knows, maybe the high levels of love in the world could work miracles and the Golden Age might finally be experienced."

"It seems the mists have lifted, your eyes are wide open and you are finally Seeing clearly."

"It took me long enough, didn't it?"

"Yes."

Velvet nudged her friend in the side with her elbow. "Thanks."

"You're welcome." Magenta smiled cheekily.

Velvet heard the faint sound of wind chimes on the cool

breeze. "Oh Goddess, what time is it?"

Magenta stared into the distance over Velvet's shoulder. "Time you got going. I can't see what it is, but you're definitely late for something."

Velvet got up from the sofa. "It might be a bit before I get the chance to see you again; my new classes start tomorrow, morning and afternoon, but if you get a chance, pop by my office in the evening okay?"

"I certainly will do that, yes."

Velvet smiled. "Thank you, again, for everything."

"Again, you are most welcome. Now scoot, otherwise you're going to be very, very late."

Velvet nodded and clicked her fingers, leaving Magenta sat on the floral sofa on the beach, lost in her thoughts once again.

*   *   *

Velvet arrived just outside the door of the main hall, when she suddenly realised what she was late for.

"The Synapsians!" she muttered. She called Bk. "The Synapsians have arrived in the main hall, will you be able to join me?"

"I'm already on my way," Bk replied.

Velvet sighed in relief. She tried to mentally prepare herself to welcome the new Starpeople, but honestly, she felt so drained from all the new developments over the past couple of days that it was difficult to concentrate.

Lost in her thoughts, she jumped when Bk touched her elbow gently.

"Sorry," Bk apologised. "But I can sense that they're getting a little agitated." He nodded to the main hall door in front of them.

"Hmm, we don't want a bunch of irate aliens on our hands; let's get in there and welcome them."

Bk opened the door and Velvet stepped through. The sight

was just as odd and breath-taking as the one yesterday, but it was a whole lot less organised and still. Where the giant pyramid had stood just hours before, there was a giant mass of what looked like cords. These cords were transparent, with different coloured lights shooting around them. The constant movement of light, though mesmerising, hurt the eyes if looked at for too long. After just a few seconds, Velvet wrenched her gaze away and looked at Bk.

"Shall I just talk to it as it is now, or is it going to split up first?"

Bk spoke telepathically to the tangled mass of moving light. He turned back to Velvet.

"They would like to thank you for finally showing up." He rolled his eyes at their impatience. "They also wish to stay in their current form while you speak with them."

Velvet nodded. She turned to the mass, trying to find a fixed point to look at, then opened her arms wide to it.

"Welcome, Synapsians! I hope your journey here was a pleasant one, and that you are well. I am Velvet, Head of the Earth Angel Training Academy, and I am available to help you at all times. This is Bk, and as you probably already know, he is our resident Starperson translator. So if you need help, it's probably best to find him and he will relay the message to me, or my assistant, Linen. I'm afraid Linen couldn't be here to welcome you, but he is the Old Soul with bright red hair." She paused and glanced at Bk, who nodded for her to continue.

"I'm sure you would like to have some time to settle into your rooms, you will each be sharing with two other beings. You have missed a couple of days of classes, but I'm sure that won't be a problem for Starpeople as intelligent as yourselves." She blinked a few times and looked away quickly; she was beginning to go cross eyed with all those moving, flashing lights. She glanced at Bk who seemed to be listening. He smiled and turned to Velvet.

"The Synapsians thank you for the kind welcome, and assure you that they will indeed have no problems with catching up, after all, they are a superior race. In fact they have developed their communications since the last group that arrived here. All anyone needs to do to speak with them is to hold onto one of the cords, and they will hear your thoughts and you will hear theirs."

Velvet's eyebrows raised. "You have indeed evolved it seems. That will certainly make it easier for you to communicate with the other beings, which is excellent."

"They want you to try it."

"Me? What, now?" Velvet asked.

"Yes, now."

"Can they see all of your thoughts? Or just the ones you are currently thinking?"

"Just the current ones."

"Oh," Velvet said, marginally relieved. "That's okay then, I guess I can try." She took a few steps towards the wriggling mass and tentatively held her hand out towards it. One of the many cords extended out to her, and she gripped her fingers around it. Suddenly, it was as though she could see what they were saying on a large screen in front of her. She blinked and read their thoughts. Then pictures began to appear on the screen. They showed her their home galaxy, their journey to the Academy, and how they were feeling at that moment. Velvet smiled. She had no idea that aliens could get nervous.

"Of course we can get nervous, we have feelings too you know." The thought shone out to her, loud and clear.

"Oops," she muttered. They really could read your thoughts. She glanced at Bk, who was grinning. He too, was listening to the exchange between them.

"How many of you are there?" she asked them.

"We are as many as is needed."

She frowned. "You mean you could split up into any number of beings?"

"Yes. We have no limits. We could be three beings as easily as we could be three thousand beings."

"Wow, that's quite incredible. I must say, you seem

different to the last group that came, you seem... calmer."

"Like we told you, we have evolved. The calmness comes from knowing that we will have to fit into the human race without causing too many problems. The last group to come here relayed all the information to us so that we could evolve."

"That's amazing. I'm pleased that you take this all so seriously."

"We still know how to have fun." The thought came back. Suddenly the mass of cords lit up in rainbow colours, all shooting outwards like fireworks.

Velvet chuckled. "Of that I have no doubt, dear Synapsians. Now then, I cannot accommodate as many as three thousand, but it would be nice to have a decent number of intelligent beings to send to Earth this time, so how about twenty?"

"That would be fine. If you let go for just a moment, we will perform the separation."

Velvet let go of the cord, pleased to have her thoughts to herself again. She turned to Bk. "That was certainly interesting."

Bk smiled. "You can't stop an alien from evolving. It's like how breathing is to a human. Absolutely necessary."

Velvet nodded. She looked at the writhing mass of transparent cords. They were moving, transforming, slowly splitting into equal amounts. Soon, twenty smaller bundles of cords all with bright lights still shooting about hovered in two rows in front of Velvet.

The one in the middle of the front row held a cord out to Velvet, and after carefully blanking out her mind, she reached out to hold it.

"We would very much like to settle in, meet our room-mates and prepare for classes tomorrow."

Velvet nodded. "Yes, of course. Bk here will take you to your rooms-"

"Unnecessary, just tell me the room numbers and we will find them with ease."

"Oh, okay then, hang on." Velvet clicked her fingers and a sheet of paper with purple glittery writing on it appeared in front of her. She read out the room numbers where there were still beds available.

"Excellent. We go now to our rooms. Thank you for your welcome and your patience."

Velvet smiled. "It was my pleasure; we are very pleased to have you here." Before she could stop herself, her mind flashed to the conversation she'd had with Linen the day before.

Suddenly the Synapsian's lights dimmed and stopped moving so quickly.

"We will do our best to not cause any distress or pain to the beings at the Academy. We apologise for the problems that our previous kin have caused you."

Velvet blushed. "I'm sure things will be just fine this time." She took her hand off the cord before any more errant thoughts could enter her mind. She took a step back towards Bk, but he held out a hand to stop her.

"They have one more thing they want to tell you."

Sighing, Velvet turned back and held on to the outstretched cord once more.

"Soon. You will understand everything very soon."

*   *   *

Later that evening, still dazed from her meeting with the Synapsians, and intrigued by their knowledge of the bigger picture she still hadn't grasped completely, Velvet arrived in her office and blinked in surprise.

"Tartan!" She suddenly remembered the meeting. "I'm so sorry! I completely lost track of time today, I don't quite know where the day went!"

Tartan nodded seriously. He tried to smile, but it didn't quite reach his eyes. "That's fine, Velvet. Linen and I were just waiting. He hasn't played the piece for me yet, he said he wanted to wait for you."

"Excellent. Linen, if you wouldn't mind." She clicked her fingers and an armchair appeared. She ushered Tartan into it then she went behind her desk and sat in her chair. Linen took his place at the piano and started to play. Velvet sat as upright as possible and wouldn't let herself blink. The last thing she wanted was to fall into a meditative state and have the vision again while Tartan was there to witness it.

The haunting melody filled the room and the notes rose up and fell around them like a blanket. Tartan was nodding in sync with the rhythm, a genuine smile replacing his usual grimace. Velvet fought to keep herself in the present moment as the music threatened to whisk her away to her beach and into Laguz's arms.

A few minutes later, the song reached the crescendo and the last few notes trailed off into nothingness. Furtively, Velvet wiped the tear that had escaped down her cheek then she clapped. "Thank you, Linen, I think it was even more beautiful that time." She turned to the professor. "So, Tartan, do you think you recognise the song from current human culture?"

"It's not too recent, but it is of the current age. The song is called Piano Sonata No. 14 in C-sharp minor. It was composed by Ludwig Van Beethoven, in 1801. It is a classical piece, and might I just say that Linen here plays it beautifully. Tell me, Linen," Tartan said, turning to him. "How many lifetimes have you been able to play the piano?"

"I learnt in my last life on Earth. Which was my only life, actually," Linen replied, failing to notice Velvet shaking her head wildly behind Tartan.

"I'm sorry, did you say your only life?" Tartan frowned. "How can an Old Soul only have had one life on Earth?"

"Oh, I'm not really on Old Soul, I'm a Faerie."

Velvet dropped her head into her hands, and finally, Linen noticed. But it was already too late.

"You're a Faerie?" Tartan repeated, a scowl of disgust

settling on his face.

Linen nodded hesitantly, taking in his expression and Velvet's reaction.

"I see. I had better get on." He stood and turned to Velvet. "I hope I was of help to you."

"Yes, thank you, Tartan. I shall see you tomorrow."

"Mmmhmm," Tartan mumbled, heading quickly for the door. When the door reappeared behind him, Linen turned to Velvet.

"Um, what was that about?"

Velvet sighed. "Tartan hates Faeries. Some time ago, a group of Faeries got together and played a joke on Tartan, and he's never forgotten it. I know in the beginning I was more interested in keeping your origins from the trainees, but I was hoping to keep it a secret from the staff too."

Linen winced. "Sorry, Velvet, I didn't realise. I would have kept my mouth shut if I had."

"Oh, don't worry about Tartan; he'll get over his jealousy sometime within the next millennium."

Linen frowned. "Jealousy? If he hates Faeries, why on Earth would he be jealous of me?"

"Ever since he joined the staff here, he has wanted to become Deputy Head of the Academy. But I've always insisted that I didn't need any help, and yet, here you are, working as my assistant in the head office."

"So not only have I got the job he wanted, but I'm also a Faerie. Wow, he really must be hating me right now." Linen glanced at the door, half expecting Tartan to come back and shout at him.

"Like I said, he'll get over it someday. Maybe." Velvet shrugged. "There's not much we can do about it. And to be perfectly honest, even if I had needed any help all these years, Tartan would have been the last person in the Universe I would have chosen to work with me."

"If you had been allowed to choose your assistant, would you have chosen me, do you think?"

Velvet thought for a moment. "Probably not, no."

Chapter Eleven

"Aria?" Amethyst called out as she entered their room that evening. She looked around and saw that the moving galaxy was empty of life. "Where has that little Faerie gone now?" she muttered to herself. She turned around to head back out the door on a Faerie hunt when Tm arrived. The glowing being flowed into the room, his light shining brightly.

"Oh, hello there, Tim, have you had a good day?" Amethyst asked. Tm moved up and down, which was their agreed sign language for yes. They had realised quickly that he could understand them perfectly, but had no way of replying verbally. So they had agreed on some simple signs to use for communication.

Amethyst smiled. "Oh, good. I was wondering, have you seen Aria this evening by any chance?"

Tm moved side to side, the sign for no. Amethyst sighed. "Okay, thanks. I'm going to go and find her; I'll see you a bit later, okay?" Tm moved up and down again, his light glowing brighter.

Amethyst waved goodbye and exited the room. She paused in the hallway and looked up and down, trying to decide where she might find the wayward Faerie. Giving up on a methodical plan of action, Amethyst decided to try the gardens first, knowing how attached Aria was to all things green and growing.

As she flew down the hallway, she smiled and said hello

to the Mermaids, Faeries and Angels that she passed. Occasionally inquiring whether they knew where she could find her tiny green friend. No one seemed to have seen her since their afternoon class had finished a couple of hours before. Amethyst arrived in the gardens, and decided to fly up over them, to see if she could spot the small green blur from above.

She flew over the Angelic Garden, their favourite spot, and found only fellow Angels and a few Starpeople. She tried the Elemental Garden, the Planetary Garden, the Underwater Garden, and even the Atlantis Garden, yet she saw no sign of Aria. Feeling slightly desperate now, Amethyst saw the two Old Souls that she had met earlier that day, sitting quietly in the Atlantis Garden, and decided to see if they had any ideas how she could find her friend.

She flew down and landed softly on her feet behind them. They were sat on an ornate, crystal encrusted bench in front of a large statue of a Merman who had emeralds for eyes. They were talking quietly to one another, but as with most places in this realm, the sound carried in the quiet environment. Amethyst intended to clear her throat and make herself known to them, but stopped when she heard some of their hushed conversation.

"...think that she may be finally seeing the bigger picture," the female was saying to her companion.

"Well, Emerald, I do truly hope so. Without her presence on Earth, I think our mission to reunite the Flames may well be impossible." He smiled at Emerald. "Though I know we would still do our very best."

Emerald smiled back then looked up at the statue. "I think once she realises that she will have the chance of another life with her Flame, there will be no problems in convincing her that she must return."

"Yes. I remember watching them in Atlantis. I don't think I'd ever seen two souls so intertwined with one another. So in sync. It was as if they were one."

"I remember too. I remember hoping that I would one day experience what they did while in human form."

"We will, I promise you from the very depths of my soul that when we reach Earth I will find you. I won't rest until we are together again."

Emerald smiled and leaned her head on his shoulder. "Oh, Mica. If you retain even an ounce of your romantic nature when you reach Earth, I have no doubt that we will indeed be together again."

"Hey, Am, what are you doing? I've been looking for you everywhere!"

Amethyst whirled around at the shrill sound of Aria's tiny voice. She put a finger to her lips.

"Shhh!" she hissed. She looked back over her shoulder at the two on the bench, but they seemed to be oblivious to the disturbance. She grabbed Aria's tiny hand and flew her to the nearby Underwater Garden.

"What's going on?" Aria demanded, yanking her hand from Amethyst's. "First I can't find you anywhere, then I find you eavesdropping on two Old Souls in the garden and then you practically yank my arm off!"

Amethyst's cheeks coloured slightly. "I do apologise, little one, I didn't mean to hurt you." She patted Aria's arm. "Are you okay?"

Aria crossed her arms over her chest. "I'm fine. I just want to know what's going on."

Amethyst frowned. "I'm not entirely sure. I was looking for you; in fact, I'd searched almost the entire Academy looking for you. I had just arrived here and noticed those two Old Souls. So I decided to ask them if they had seen you at all and if they had any ideas on how to find you, when I overheard some of their conversation, and to be honest I couldn't stop myself from listening."

Aria looked slightly mollified. "Oh. You were really looking for me everywhere?"

"Yes, little one, I had been to the reception and got you a

brochure, and when I couldn't find you in any of the usual places, I got worried."

"I'm sorry, Am." Aria looked down at the floor. "I was with Myrt, Rosa and Flora from the Australia group, we were playing BugScotch."

Amethyst shook her head, smiling. "Don't worry, little Faerie, I'm not mad at you. I don't know why I got so anxious; of course you don't have to stick to me like a shadow at all times. I'm glad you are making friends with other Faeries. You need to have some fun friends to laugh with."

"I do have fun with you, Amethyst! I love spending time with you. But I kind of think you should be making other friends too. Maybe with some other Angels. Then you'd be able to have more serious conversations."

"You mean more boring conversations."

Aria grinned impishly. "Well, yeah." She bounced up and down impatiently. "But anyway, what were the Old Souls saying then? What caught your attention?"

Amethyst blinked. "Oh, yes, their conversation. You know how I said they seemed to be more Angelic than human?" Aria nodded. "I think I was right. I think they are Angels."

"How do you know?"

"Their names are crystals. Emerald and Mica. And they spoke of watching over humans during the times of Atlantis."

"Okay, so what does that mean?"

"It's unusual to have beings at the Academy who already have human appearances for one, and I also don't think they're in our normal classes. But they were talking about someone finally seeing the bigger picture, and they were also talking about reuniting the Flames. Whoever they were talking about was in Atlantis, and her Twin Flame was the soul whose statue is in the Atlantis Garden."

Aria put her hands up. "Whoa, now, I think you may have completely lost me. What is a Twin Flame? And why would we be reuniting them?"

Amethyst gave a detailed explanation about the Flames. And about how they were usually only reunited on Earth when the world was in its last stages of the current age.

"So does that mean that Earth is dying?" Aria asked, her tiny features scrunched into a frown.

"No, little one. The planet Earth itself will carry on regardless. It is the human race that is in danger. The current age of humans is reaching a critical point right now, and if nothing is done, then it might not last much more than a few more Earthly decades."

"What's a decade?"

"Ten years."

"So by the time we hear the call, humans could already be dying out?" Aria was aghast. "What's the point of us going then?"

"To help. That is why I am going. The more souls who are Awakened, the more chance we have of turning things around. We need to wake people up to the real reality, and shake them out of the Maya, the illusion that they have currently buried themselves in."

"And if we do that, humans will survive? Earth will continue as it is now?"

"That is what I was hoping. That is why I chose to become an Earth Angel. But this talk of reuniting the Flames is making me think that perhaps the situation is worse than I thought."

"Because they only do that when the age is ending? Why do they wait until the end of the world before bringing Flames together? Surely if they brought them together earlier, the passion and the love they create could prevent the world from getting into such a bad shape to begin with?"

"That's an interesting question and a very good point. It has been a topic of much debate for many, many aeons now. And you may be right; perhaps they have finally decided that the Flames should be reunited regardless of when the current age is ending." Amethyst smiled at the Faerie. "But if I know the Elders as well as I think I do, I think that theory is quite unlikely."

Aria's tiny shoulders slumped. "I really wanted to make a difference. I honestly thought that by becoming a human, I could change things, make things better."

Amethyst put her finger under Aria's chin and lifted the little Faerie's face. "And you will, little one. Remember, even the smallest person can make a difference. Just because there are those who have predicted the end, it doesn't mean that the future is set in stone. Things can be changed, and I promise you, we Earth Angels will be in the very centre of those changes. If we can bring love, light and peace to just one human being, we will have made a difference."

Aria smiled. "Thank you, Am. I'll promise I will try to stay positive about this. Thank you for always picking me back up again."

"What are friends for, eh?" Amethyst realised she was still holding the long-forgotten brochure in her hand. "Hey, this is for you. I picked it up at reception." She handed the tiny, Faerie-sized glossy colour brochure to Aria.

"Wow, did they really give us one of these before we joined the Academy?"

"They did, yes. What happened to yours?"

Aria shrugged. "I have no idea." She flicked through the brochure, pausing to look at the colour pictures. "I don't even remember receiving one, to be perfectly honest."

"Oh well, just look after this one. Perhaps if you read it cover to cover you might actually have an idea of what's to come."

"Mmmhmm. I'll give it a go anyway." She tucked the brochure under her arm and straightened up. "So what's tonight's activity then?"

"I can't be sure, but I think that tonight is a sports night, so they'll be teaching us how to play all sorts of human sports. Rugby, tennis, golf, football, basketball, baseball, cricket-"

"Ooooh! I love crickets! They're the best bugs! Can we play that one? Please? Pretty please?"

*   *   *

"Welcome to the first class, MorningStars! I hope you have had time to settle in and relax, please, take a seat, and we will begin with some introductions. Though considering the size of the group, they will have to be very short I'm afraid."

The MorningStar group all took their seats in the large classroom that had been manifested especially for the new classes. The room was set out like a lecture theatre, each row a little higher than the previous one, so that they could all see Velvet as she paced up and down the front of the room. Once everyone was seated, Velvet spoke again.

"Before we begin, are there any questions you'd like to ask, or problems that have arisen in the last twenty-four hours?"

One hand went up, belonging to a pixie-like soul with deep red hair and freckles. Her light, iridescent blue robes rustled as she stood to address Velvet.

"My name is Delis. I am originally from the Elemental Realm. I'm afraid that I was unsuccessful in staying away from the trainees, and some of the Faeries guessed my origins. I responded with the first thing that came to mind and I told them I was a second year Earth Angel. They seemed to accept this explanation, and did not question me any further." She bowed her head. "I apologise if I have caused any complications."

Velvet shook her head. "Delis, I do believe that you have provided the perfect explanation, and from now on, I advise all of you to do as Delis has done. If you encounter the trainees and they question why you are here, just tell them you are a second year, which is why you already have a human appearance." She smiled at Delis. "Thank you, Delis, I'm very glad you were able to think of such a good explanation so quickly."

Delis sat down, looking pleased. Velvet looked around the class.

"No more questions? Okay then, just so you can acquaint yourselves with one another, please turn to your neighbour and tell them your name, your realm of origin and your occupation in your previous life on Earth. Then ask them to tell you the same in return." She clicked her fingers and a clock appeared on the wall behind her. "You have two minutes. Begin."

There was a cacophony of voices in all different pitches as each soul introduced themselves. Velvet took advantage of the time and went through her notes for the class. Though she felt she was finally beginning to see the bigger picture, she still felt a bit apprehensive about what she was meant to teach these souls. So she'd decided to keep it all quite informal, and invite plenty of interaction and feedback from the Earth Angels. In many ways, she felt that they had as much to teach her as she had to teach them. After all, they had all been to Earth much more recently than she had, and as she had discovered in the last couple of days; her memories really weren't as accurate or complete as she had thought they were. Aware of a lull in the chattering, Velvet looked up at the class to find fifty pairs of eyes staring at her. Refusing to feel daunted, Velvet straightened up.

"I hope you all now know at least one other soul in the class. Every day we will be changing where you sit, so that you can get to know a different soul every day. I'm not entirely sure how long this class will run, seeing as this is all entirely new - we haven't ever had Earth Angels return to the Academy before. I assume that once you have gained the necessary wisdom and knowledge, you will be called to Earth. Which means of course, that the number of souls in this class could start decreasing very quickly. But nevertheless, I would like for you each to try and get to know one another, for I feel it could be very useful for when you return to Earth. Recognition of fellow Earth Angels is quite a useful tool in Awakening." Velvet looked up from her pacing back and forth to see them listening keenly.

"For those of you who attended other training academies,

I teach the classes here on Awakening and Remembering."
Mentally, she chuckled. How was it that someone who taught
others how to remember had forgotten so much herself? "And
the best way to Awaken on Earth to the reality, and see beyond
the illusion that will attempt to smother you; is to recognise
other Earth Angels, who will help you immensely. Especially
if they themselves have already remembered and started the
Awakening process." Velvet paused her pacing and addressed
her class. "Did anyone here manage to recognise any fellow
Earth Angels in their last Earthly incarnation?"

Everyone looked around at each another. Only two hands
went up.

"How many Earth Angels did you two recognise?"

"One," the blond-haired male soul replied.

"One," the brunette female soul echoed.

"So, out of a class of fifty, only two souls managed to
recognise other Earth Angels while human. Who were those
Earth Angels to you? Were they relatives?"

Both souls nodded.

"And how did you recognise them as Earth Angels?"

The brunette soul shrugged. "The Earth Angel was my
aunt. She always listened to me, even when I spoke of unusual
or magickal things. She encouraged me to be creative, and she
treated me like an adult, like an equal. She had a love of nature,
animals and spoke of small winged beings helping her to keep
her garden beautiful."

Velvet nodded. "An Elemental. A Faerie, most likely.
What about you?" she asked the male.

"It was my father. He also listened to me. Treated me like
a well-respected friend. He loved water. We always had to live
near the sea. He seemed to diminish when we were too far
away from a large body of water. He encouraged me to swim
and to connect with the natural world. I too, was a Merperson
originally; therefore his passions were aligned with my own.
Though neither of us ever admitted that we felt like we were
from the water, we had a deep bond with one another and with

the sea."

"Thank you for sharing, dear souls. On Earth right now, humans have yet to reach the stage where it is acceptable to be different. The hardest part about being an Earth Angel is that from the very beginning, you are different. You don't feel like you fit in. You feel like an outcast, an oddity. There has not been a large number of Earth Angels on Earth all together at the same time. And those who are there tend to keep to themselves because they fear that their uniqueness will be seen as something wrong or evil and they will be persecuted." Velvet sighed.

"Of course, this has happened many times in this human age, and many of these Earth Angels watched the persecutions from their realms. So they have legitimate reasons to be fearful. However, choosing to be an Earth Angel means that you are choosing to go to Earth to bring peace and love to humans and help them to Awaken to the reality. That is a near impossible task if you keep to yourself and refuse to step out into the spotlight." Velvet grew tired of pacing and clicked her fingers. Her favourite purple chair appeared and she sat down, taking a moment before she continued speaking, to gather her thoughts.

"As you may have noticed, the class of new Earth Angel trainees this year is the biggest we have ever had. And as you can see, we have almost a hundred souls who have decided to return to Earth to try once more to help with the Awakening. This means, hopefully, that humans will begin to understand that being different is not only acceptable, but it is something to be proud of. The Earth Angels who will be going to Earth in the next few years will hopefully have a better reception than those who have come before them. And because there will be so many of you, you are more likely to find one another, recognise your similarities, and no longer will the Earth Angels feel isolated and that they are outcasts. When you begin to come together, show the humans who you really are, and let them know that you have come to help them; that's when the Awakening will really take off, spreading like wildfire throughout the globe." Velvet paused, surprised at how effortlessly all of these ideas were coming together. It actually sounded like she knew what she was talking about and wasn't just making it all up as she went along. She noted with satisfaction that she had their rapt attention.

"I understand that you all heard a calling to be here, and that most of you are unsure as to why exactly you feel the need – the desire – to go back to Earth." Velvet looked around the room, her face serious. "What I am about to tell you now, does not leave this room. I will be giving the same information to the class this afternoon, so you will have no need to discuss the matter outside of this session. I would rather that the trainees did not hear about this." She took a deep breath; every soul was still hanging on to her every word.

"The Earth has begun a downward spiral. If it continues to go the way it is for much longer, then there will be nothing we can do to prevent the end of the current human age."

Low murmurs filled the room, but no one seemed overly surprised at this revelation.

"Now, though the predictions aren't very positive, as you well know, there are several different possible futures, all of which could happen - it all depends on the decisions made by those on Earth in the next few decades. Which is why, despite everything, I really believe that you all, and the new trainees, working together, could actually make a difference. Change the world." Velvet smiled, "I even believe that the Golden Age could be experienced, finally."

The murmurs this time were more excited, as the souls looked at each other, smiling.

"So, does anyone have any questions? Or anything they'd like to add?"

A tall male soul with light brown hair raised his hand, then stood when Velvet nodded at him.

"I understand that the Earth's population is growing rapidly, and by the time we are all called to Earth, it will have reached an extremely high number." He gestured around the room. "I don't like to underestimate my fellow Earth Angels here, but there are only a hundred of us. And a hundred trainees. Two hundred Earth Angels scattered around the world in a population of billions seems like a drop in the ocean. Do you honestly think that we can make that much of a difference?"

"Thank you, that's an excellent observation, er…"

"Mo," the tall soul supplied.

"Mo. Does anyone have any thoughts on Mo's question?" Velvet looked around the room, her gaze settling on a familiar face.

"Yes, Emerald isn't it?"

Emerald nodded and stood to address Mo and the rest of the class. "I agree that it seems as though our numbers will be incredibly small in comparison to the population of the world. But we must remember that this is not the only training academy in this dimension; there are several others, who will also be sending many more hundreds of Earth Angels to Earth in the next few decades. And we must remember that every drop creates ripples that spread outwards, reaching far and wide, despite its small original size. Each of us will be a single drop, but the ripples we create will hopefully reach many, many humans, connect us to other Earth Angels, and help the ripples to reach every corner of the Earth." Emerald sat down, and smiled at Mica, who was sat next to her as always.

"I completely agree, Emerald. Does that answer your query, Mo?"

Mo nodded and sat back down.

"I know it may seem that our mission is hopeless. That all of us going back to Earth may not change anything at all. But I think the point is that we try. And besides, could any of us stay here, and watch the Earth decline, knowing that we could have at least attempted to help?"

Velvet paused and a hand was raised. "Yes?"

"I apologise if I am mistaken," the dreamy looking soul

dressed in pink said as she stood. "But from the way you are talking of the return to Earth, it sounds as though you will be coming with us?"

Velvet smiled. "Very observant of you, dear soul." She stood and began to pace again; she needed to keep moving to stay calm. "I will indeed be returning with you all to Earth."

A gasp went around the room. Velvet continued. "It seems as though my soul's path has changed its course. After all these many years of running this Training Academy, I will be returning to Earth to help my dear Earth Angels in their missions." She ran her hand through her long hair nervously.

"I only hope that my wisdom and knowledge may be used more effectively there than it has been here." She chuckled. "That is of course, provided that I Awaken."

"Surely there is no doubt that you will Awaken," a soul called out from the front row, "you are one of the oldest souls in existence."

Velvet smiled at the outspoken one. "My dear, I appreciate your vote of confidence. But you must know that even the oldest of souls are not infallible. There is every chance that I will fail to Awaken. There is every chance that I will make no difference at all. But I cannot ask you all to try, and then stay here and do nothing myself."

The soul in the front row nodded. "I understand that you may have doubts, but you should know that I, and many others from the Angelic Realm, have complete faith in you."

Velvet stopped pacing and turned to the soul, a sad smile creasing her lined face. "Thank you. What is your name, dear Angel?"

"Ruby."

"Well, Ruby, I do hope that I manage to meet you when we are both on Earth, I'm sure I will need many beautiful gems like you in my life in order to Awaken."

Ruby smiled, her cheeks matching the colour of her deep red robes.

Velvet heard the faint sound of wind chimes. "It seems

that time has run away with us class. I'm afraid we shall have to conclude our first session now, I hope the rest of your day goes well. I will see you all here at nine o'clock tomorrow."

*   *   *

"It seems that maybe we should have had more faith. I feel quite sorrowful that we doubted Velvet even for a moment," Emerald murmured to Mica as they left the classroom later.

"I agree. I think perhaps we should take a leaf out of the book of our fellow Angel, Ruby. She seemed to have complete and utter confidence in Velvet's knowledge and wisdom."

"I never doubted her wisdom. I only worried that she would not be able to step back and consider the whole situation. She seemed too close to the details."

Mica squeezed Emerald's hand as they walked silently through the glistening white halls of the Academy. "It seems that she has managed to do so. And I have to say, I feel a lot more confident that we will be able to attempt our mission of reuniting the Flames. It's interesting she did not mention the Flames today. I assume one of the reasons she is returning to Earth is because she knows her own Flame will be there."

"We did run out of time. I'm sure the subject of the Flames will be discussed in the coming days."

"How long do you think it will be before we hear the call?" Mica wondered.

"Not long, I'm sure. I think the only reason we had to come here was so that we would realise that we aren't going to be alone on Earth. That the very best of every realm will be there with us, helping us. And maybe we also came so that we could be of some help to Velvet, too."

"Let's enjoy the time we have here together then. Which garden would you like to go to today?"

"I heard from some other Angels that there's a garden that was created by the Leprechaun, but you have to go through a series of tasks before you are given the secret password and the door to it appears."

"Sounds intriguing, lead the way!"

*   *   *

"So what do you think?" Amethyst asked when Aria finally set the brochure down, later that evening.

Aria sat up on her planet bed and frowned. "I think maybe I should have listened a little better before I agreed to come here."

Amethyst chuckled. "There is a lesson to be learned there, don't you think? What is troubling you?"

"I'm still dreading the day I lose my wings, but aside from that, I guess there's nothing really in the brochure that worries me. I just can't get out of my head what happened last night."

"I'm sorry that cricket doesn't have anything to do with bugs, I should have explained that to you."

Aria shook her head. "No, no. I don't mean the sports part. I mean what happened before the evening activity. With the Old Soul-like Angels in the Atlantis Garden. I guess I never thought about the possibility that by the time I get to Earth and try to get humans to respect nature, to save as much grass for my fellow Faeries as possible; there might not be any grass left. There might not be any humans left!" She sighed. "I guess if I had known, I might have decided to stay in the Elemental Realm until the world ended. At least I knew who I was and I had friends there. On Earth I will forget everything and everyone I know, have no wings, and from the sound of this human emotion lark, be completely miserable all the time!"

"Oh, my dear little Faerie!" Amethyst exclaimed as she flew over to Aria and sat next to her. She put her arms around the tiny Faerie and stroked her hair gently as she cried quietly.

"You mustn't lose hope! It sounds bleak and I know that the human world is filled with despair, sadness and anger." Aria's sobs got louder. "But it is also filled with wonder and joy and love and happiness. On Earth, as it is here, there is

- 137 -

everything. The good and the bad. The only problem is that right now, most humans find it easier to experience the bad than the good. And that's where we come in. We have to retain as much love and light as we can, so that when we're on Earth, we can shine brightly, and encourage others to shine too."

Aria's sobs subsided into sniffles. She wiped her face with the hem of her green dress. She was quiet for a while before she spoke. "Will you do me a favour?" she asked in a small voice.

Amethyst nodded. "What is it, little one?"

"Will you promise me that you will choose writing as your occupation on Earth? Because I think I might just make it as a human if I had books written by you to guide me through."

Amethyst chuckled. "If you think it will help you, then yes, I promise to write when I am a human. Who knows, maybe my writing will even help others like you."

"Thank you, Am. You'll be famous, I just know you will."

"With you as my biggest fan, how could I not be?"

Chapter Twelve

When Velvet returned to her office after the afternoon class had finished that day, she was surprised to hear piano music as she stepped into the room. It wasn't the soft, melodic, classical music that Linen had been playing for her these last couple of days; it was almost harsh and painful. So it wasn't much of a surprise when she realised that it wasn't Linen sat on the piano stool, but Corduroy. She stood in the doorway for a while, wincing at the hard tones as he pounded away at the ivory keys.

Finally, after several minutes and a particularly harrowing ending, Corduroy stopped playing and noticed Velvet.

"Hey!" he said, getting up to greet her. "I didn't know you had a piano. What have you been playing?"

Velvet stepped forward to hug Corduroy, then she moved to her desk and settled into her chair. Corduroy sat back on the piano stool, but turned to face her.

"Nothing, I'm afraid. I manifested the piano for my assistant, Linen. I have to admit I had no idea that you, uh, were a pianist."

Corduroy grinned. "I have been known to play a tune or two."

"What can I do for you, my friend? I'm afraid I am quite tired after a full day of teaching, so please excuse me if I am not entirely coherent."

"I was kind of hoping to continue that rather odd, yet

interesting conversation that we were having in the Atlantis Garden. But if you're too tired for me to call in the raincheck, I can come back at a more convenient time for you." He began to rise from the stool, but Velvet gestured for him to sit.

"No, no, please stay. I will be teaching all day every day for the foreseeable future, so I will be even more tired tomorrow and the next day. We can continue the conversation now if you wish."

"Okay, all I know so far is that somehow Laguz is involved, that you mentioned reuniting the Flames, and that there are a large number of Earth Angels at the Academy right now who are not trainees."

Velvet sighed. "Where to begin? It took me a while to see what it all means too; I suppose I should start with my meeting with Gold, on the very first day of term…"

*   *   *

"I've called you all here, because I felt that after my discussion with Corduroy this evening, it is only fair that I tell you all what he now knows." Velvet looked around the cavernous classroom at her staff members.

"It seems I am to return to Earth. Not immediately, but along with the new trainees and the second year Earth Angels who have joined the Academy recently."

"You're leaving?" Beryl blurted out amidst the shocked gasps of the staff.

"Yes, I will be leaving the Academy in the good care of yourselves, and the new Head – Linen." She gestured to her red-haired assistant, who blushed when everyone turned to stare at him, eyebrows raised, mouths open in shock.

"A Faerie? Run the Academy?" Tartan said harshly. "Please tell me you're joking."

"Linen is a very capable soul, who, yes, happens to be an Elemental. I trust him implicitly, and I have no doubt that he will be an excellent Head of the Academy."

Linen went an even deeper shade of red at Velvet's praise and compliments.

"This is utterly ridiculous." Tartan crossed his arms over his chest. "And I, for one, won't work for a Faerie."

"Tartan, I know you teach Human Culture here, but please, can we not resort to the separation that humans cling to? We are all one. Fairies, Merpeople, Starpeople, Angels, Old Souls - we are all the same. There is no separation between us: we are all just individual drops in the same ocean. Therefore, if you can work under my direction, you can work under Linen's."

Tartan remained silent, a look of disgust on his rough features.

"Are there any other questions?"

"Are you the only staff member allowed to leave?" Everyone turned to look at Athena.

"You are all, of course, under no obligation to stay - you are free to come and go as you please."

"Then I will return with you."

Velvet looked shocked, then she smiled at her friend. "My dear Athena, are you quite sure that is what you wish?"

"I have felt, for quite some time now, that my efforts here to help humans are not enough. I want to be on Earth, and live as a human. I want to help you in any way I can."

"Me, too."

Everyone turned to look at Cotton, who stood to emphasise her point. "I wish to return to Earth with you, Velvet."

"As do I." Chiffon stood, her wispy orange robes fluttering.

Velvet looked around the room, rendered speechless by their moving declarations of support.

Beryl, Indigo and Suede all stood simultaneously. Wordlessly adding themselves to the rest.

A tear rolled down Velvet's cheek. She cleared her throat. "I don't know what to say, I cannot believe that you would all do this for me, that you would return to Earth, to complete uncertainty, to help me."

"We can't have you wandering alone, can we?"

Velvet turned to the door where Corduroy stood. "I'll be right behind you too." He grinned. "I know you were looking forward to getting away from me, but no such luck I'm afraid." He came to stand next to her and put his arm around her shoulders. He turned to Linen. "Um, no offence meant towards you, of course, Linen. I don't want you to think that I wouldn't work for you." He glanced meaningfully at Tartan, who still sat, arms crossed. "Because I would, it's just that, well, Velvet and I, and all of us, we're a team. And teams only work well when they work together."

"Hear, hear!" Athena chimed in, her round cheeks pink and her eyes glowing with excitement.

Velvet looked around the room. The only staff member still seated was Tartan. "Tartan," she said softly. "Do you want to stay, or do you want to go to Earth?"

Tartan uncrossed his arms, looked at Linen distrustfully, then declared in a rough voice. "I will go to Earth."

Velvet nodded. "I don't quite know what to say. Thank you, all of you, for supporting me like this. You do realise though, that we now need to find replacements for all of you, to continue teaching the classes when we all leave. So, I propose that-"

"Actually, there's no need," Linen cut in softly. Everyone turned to him. Velvet raised her eyebrows.

"I'm sorry, Linen, what did you say?"

Linen stood and gestured to the seats. "Perhaps you should all sit down and I'll explain what I can."

The staff sat back down, looking puzzled. Tartan continued to look annoyed.

Velvet clicked her fingers and two more chairs appeared for herself and Corduroy.

Once they were seated and he had their attention, Linen cleared his throat and began.

"Velvet hasn't really explained about how I came back to the Academy, so I will begin there. Until very recently, I was on Earth. I had been there for eight years when the Elementals began to talk to me. Being young, I accepted this without question. It seemed perfectly natural to talk to the small winged folk who lived in the huge oak tree in the yard. I tried to tell my parents a few times, but their only response was to give me boyish toys like trucks and guns. They didn't want anyone to know that their son thought he could talk to Faeries." Linen laughed sadly.

"I talked to some other kids about it, and even they didn't believe me. They too, had been told by their parents not to be so ridiculous, to stop pretending and making things up. They had very quickly stopped believing. I asked the Elementals, well, begged them really, to tell me what I could do to help them. To change the way people thought about them. They began to tell me about the changes that the human race would be going through. About the shift in consciousness that would see humans not only openly discuss and accept that Faeries existed, but even admit that they too were able to speak to them." He shook his head, smiling.

"At this point in time, I didn't believe them. I saw the cynical adults around me, the kids with their eyes closed tight to the magick around them, and I couldn't understand how on Earth this shift would ever happen." He sat down on his chair and continued his tale.

"So they began to tell me, and show me, how it was all possible. They told me that not only would there be massive changes on Earth, but that there would be a major overhaul on the Other Side too. That there would be a huge number of Earth Angels coming from the Other Side, to assist in the shift, to Awaken people to the magick. To breathe life back into their weary souls. Over two Earthly years, they continued to tell me about the shift, but one thing that they were never quite sure of, was when exactly the changes would take place."

Linen paused and stared into space, lost in memory. "The

rest of the information came to me in a dream. An Angel, with wings that sparkled like they were studded with stars, came to me and told me that I would be the one to initiate the changes. But not the changes on Earth - the changes on the Other Side. I would be the one to start the shift on the Other Side that would filter through to Earth. She told me that I had to leave Earth as soon as possible, and that I would know when and how, because a beautiful voice in my head would tell me to do something. All I would have to do is the exact opposite of what she said." He looked up and caught Athena's eye. "I did hear you, Angel. And I'm sorry that I disobeyed your requests. But it was the right thing for me to do."

A tear rolled down Athena's cheek. "Oh, Mikey," she whispered. "Oh, Dictamnus."

Linen nodded. "I know you tried really hard to save me, but I was determined. I knew I needed to be here."

Velvet cleared her throat softly. "When you first arrived, you said you didn't know why you were here. But you knew all along."

Linen looked down at the floor, unable to meet her eye. "Yes, I know I said that. I was told to. I wasn't meant to tell anyone why I was here."

"So tell me now, why don't we need replacements for my staff, is the Earth Angel Training Academy no longer going to exist?"

"It will of course exist, but not exactly as it is now; there will be some big changes. It will still be an Academy of sorts. But not for Earth Angels."

There was silence as everyone took this in.

"Then who will be taught here?" Cotton asked softly.

"The Children of the Golden Age."

Velvet's eyebrows shot up. "The what?"

"The last class of Earth Angels, the staff here, and the returnee Earth Angels will all go to Earth to bring about the great Awakening. To educate the humans there now on the changes that will happen. All of you will help to make way for the Children." He nodded at them all. "The Golden Age is still a possibility. That future still exists. And the Faeries want to see it happen. As do the Angels, Starpeople, Old Souls and Mermaids too, I'm sure."

"So the Earth Angel Training Academy will be turned into the School for the Children of the Golden Age?" Velvet asked.

"Yes. The mentors will be mostly Faeries and Angels who have been brought directly from their realms. The main education that will be given to these pure new souls will be about love and wonderment and magick. Which is what the Angels and Faeries embody in their own realm. No offence meant to you wise Old Souls, but the idea will be to send the Children to Earth with their innocence and pure energy and beauty as intact as possible. Any contact with lower vibrations will deaden their joy and weigh them down."

"They'll be crushed on Earth by the heavy energies if they have not been properly prepared," Tartan interjected. "They won't last a day as humans."

Linen looked Tartan in the eye. "They will make it just fine if you guys do what you set out to do on Earth. If you fail, then yes, they will not survive." Tartan dropped his gaze from Linen's. "And then the possibility of the Golden Age will disappear."

There was a moment of silence as they all took in the implications of them failing on Earth.

"How long do we have?" Chiffon asked. "When will the Children begin to arrive on Earth?"

Linen shrugged. "When they believe it is the right time. But the Elementals gave estimates on how long the human race has left before the decline begins and the possibility of the Golden Age becomes dimmer."

"When will that be?"

"The human race, if not sufficiently Awakened by then, will begin to see the first stages of decline by the last decade of the century."

"Which century are you talking about?" Corduroy asked,

frowning.

"This one."

"But there's less than fifty years left in the current century," Velvet said, confused. "The Seers said we had about a hundred Earthly years before the decline."

"The Seers are taking into account that you will do what you set out to do on Earth. If none of you went back, then the human race would most likely become almost extinct by the turn of the millennium."

"Wow," Athena breathed. "Do you honestly think that we could change the way humans think, act and feel in such a short amount of time?"

"I think you ought to try," Linen answered. "The alternative is to stay here and do nothing. Leave them to their demise."

"That would never happen," Velvet declared. "We will go to Earth, and we will pave the way for the Children of the Golden Age. We will teach the latest trainees all that we know as quickly as possible, so that they will be called to Earth as soon as they're ready to begin the changes. I think we should introduce some new sessions that incorporate all this new information. I don't think they should be kept in the dark on these new developments. They need to know the challenges that face them." Everyone was nodding in agreement.

"Linen, thank you for sharing with us tonight, I, for one, am glad to finally know what is going on, and I feel that if we truly do work together, as a team," she glanced at Corduroy. "Then the Golden Age could be the future for the humans on Earth right now."

Linen smiled. "I have no doubt that you will succeed. With some of the oldest and wisest souls on Earth making the changes necessary, I feel confident that we will indeed be the first age of humans on Earth to live in the Golden times."

Velvet opened her mouth to speak, then stopped, tilting her head to the side, listening. "Does anyone else hear that?" she whispered. Everyone was still, listening hard.

"It sounds like some kind of… aircraft?" Corduroy guessed quietly.

Velvet frowned. "Beryl, are we expecting anyone?"

Beryl shook her head, a frown on her angelic features.

Velvet stood up and the noise got louder. "Linen, do you have any ideas who it is?" she asked, raising her voice over the rapidly increasing noise.

Linen shook his head quickly, his eyes darting around, trying to figure out where the sound was coming from.

Velvet turned to Corduroy. "Would you come with me?" she practically shouted. He nodded and gripped her wrist. She closed her eyes and clicked her fingers.

*   *   *

"What's going on?!" Aria shouted to Amethyst, her hands clamped over her ears. Amethyst shrugged back, wincing as the noise reached an intolerable level.

All around them, beings were stood still throughout the gardens, hands clamped over their ears. Aria looked at Amethyst closely. She seemed to be mouthing something.

"What?" Aria shouted, thinking that Amethyst was trying to say something to her. Suddenly, the noise completely vanished.

"Oh!" Aria squeaked in shock. She shook her head to clear the ringing in her ears and looked at Amethyst. "It stopped! What was it?"

Amethyst smiled. "It hasn't stopped, my dear Faerie; we're just in a protective bubble, so we can't hear it." She gestured at their fellow beings who were still wincing and apparently shouting to each other.

Aria raised her eyebrows. "How on Earth did you do that?"

"I was talking to an Old Soul called Cerise, earlier. She told me about a problem she had with a noisy room-mate, and how Velvet told her to manifest a soundproof wall between them by saying it three times."

"Wow. I'm so glad I'm your friend! That noise really was unbearable. So what do you think it is?" Aria looked around, feeling bad for her fellow souls. "Can't we manifest a soundproof bubble for all of them?"

"It's more difficult to affect others with our manifestations. It was hard enough to include you in the bubble just now." Amethyst took Aria's hand. "Come on, let's go see what all the commotion is about." They left the gardens and flew towards the gleaming white Academy building.

"How are we going to find it if we can't hear it?" Aria wondered.

"We'll just follow our intuition," Amethyst answered, flying purposefully down the white hallway. "Also, I think we can follow the vibrations. Let me just…" She reached out and touched the shimmering white wall. "Yes, the vibrations feel stronger here. Let's go this way." She flew down the hallway, beating her heavy, feathered wings. Aria flapped her dragonfly wings as fast as she could, trying to stay in Amethyst's soundproof bubble. Every few seconds, Amethyst touched the wall, nodded and continued on. Suddenly she stopped and Aria bumped into her.

"Oomph! What's wrong?"

Aria looked over Amethyst's shoulder and saw Velvet with the Professor of Death. The two of them looked up at Amethyst and Aria as they arrived in the hallway.

Velvet seemed to be saying something to them, but they couldn't hear her through the protective bubble. Amethyst muttered something under her breath three times and concentrated. Suddenly, all four of them were within the bubble and Velvet blinked in surprise. "It stopped?" she asked.

Amethyst shook her head. "No, I just extended our soundproof bubble."

"Oh!" Velvet exclaimed. "Why didn't I think of that? That noise was just about bursting my eardrums."

"Yours and everyone else's in the Academy," Amethyst

- 148 -

replied.

"Oh, Goddess, I hadn't thought of that either. Let me fix that." She thought for a moment then clicked her fingers. "There, now everyone should be soundproofed." She turned to Amethyst. "Thank you, Angel." She squinted at her. "Amethyst, right? Now Corduroy and I need to go and investigate the origin of the noise."

"Would you like some help?" Amethyst asked.

Velvet smiled. "Thank you for the kind offer, but I'm sure we'll be fine. Please, feel free to resume whatever activity you were doing before you were disturbed."

Amethyst nodded and flew back the way they'd come, a perplexed Aria flying by her side.

"Am, are we really leaving?" she whispered in the Angel's ear.

Amethyst flew around the corner and stopped. "No," she whispered back. "But I didn't want to appear to interfere." They both peered back around the corner, just in time to see Velvet and Corduroy enter the door on the right.

"What do you think is going on?"

"I don't know," Amethyst said grimly, flying quietly back down the hall to the door that had just reappeared. "But judging by the look of strain on Velvet's face, it can't be good." She put her ear up to the wall near the door, not wanting to get too close otherwise the door would open, giving them away. Aria did the same. After a few seconds she shrugged. "I don't hear a thing," she whispered.

"Me neither." Amethyst sounded frustrated. "What could we manifest so we could see what was happening?"

"Invisible walls?" Aria suggested jokingly. Amethyst's eyebrows shot up.

"Excellent idea! Though only one way, the walls need to appear solid to those on the inside of the room. How to word it…" Her eyes lit up and she began to mutter under her breath again. After repeating it the third time, the wall in front of them became completely transparent.

"Wow!" Aria whispered. "I've really got to try this manifestation lark more often, this is brilliant!" She turned to Amethyst. "They can't see us though, right?"

"No, they can't, it's only invisible to us. It's still solid to them." She peered into the dimly lit room. "What is that?"

Aria squinted through the murky shadows. "I can see Velvet, and Corduroy, well, their backs anyway. But I can't quite see what they're looking at, it's too dark."

Suddenly, as if in response to Aria, Velvet clicked her fingers and the room became brighter. Amethyst and Aria gasped in unison as they took in the sight before them. It appeared as though there was an entire city inside the room, and that Velvet and Corduroy were standing a few feet from the edge of a cliff, looking out over an entirely different world. The buildings were made of gold, as were the streets and everything on them. Spheres of blue light moved around at great speeds through the city, seemingly unaware of their audience. They saw Velvet turn to Corduroy and say something, then she clicked her fingers and began to speak. Her voice boomed out, echoing off the walls of the golden city buildings.

"May I speak with the one in charge, please?"

The light beings all stopped moving and seemed to turn towards the voice. Aria's breath caught. "Am, do you think they're friendly?" She watched anxiously as the beings all moved towards where Velvet stood. She turned to Amethyst, wondering why she hadn't replied, and she saw that the Angel was crying silently, a smile on her face.

"Am, what's wrong?" Aria whispered, moving to her side. "Are you okay?"

Amethyst nodded, her tears falling like crystals from her blue eyes.

"Then why are you crying?" Aria asked.

"It is the Children of the Golden Age. They have come."

*   *   *

Velvet squinted slightly as the bright blue lights came closer. Corduroy shifted slightly towards her, probably trying to be protective, but Velvet did not need protecting. She could tell, just from being in their presence, that these beings of light meant no harm. When they were just a few feet away, the spheres of bright blue light changed form. Suddenly, Velvet and Corduroy were faced with a line of the most radiant, beautiful Children they had ever seen.

Corduroy gasped. "The Children of the Golden Age."

Velvet nodded in confirmation. She smiled at them, and held her arms out.

"Welcome, Children. I apologise for the poor reception, but we were unaware of your imminent arrival."

The smallest Child in the line stepped forward and bowed her head. "We are very sorry that we didn't let you know we were coming," she said, her tiny voice ringing with quiet authority. "But when we heard the call, we answered immediately. We are the Indigo Children."

"The call?" Velvet inquired.

"Yes. We were told by a beautiful Angel with wings of starlight that we were needed immediately at the Earth Angel Training Academy, which would soon become the School for the Children of the Golden Age," she looked up at them, her innocent face confused. "Have we come to the wrong place? Or have we come at the wrong time?"

Velvet shook her head. "You are in the right place, my dear child. As for the timing, I'm afraid that we ourselves did not know you would be arriving so soon, but that is not a problem. Will you need accommodation? Or any other services?"

The Child shook her head; her waist-length blonde hair rippled in waves around her. "We have no needs whatsoever. Everything we desire is within our Golden City."

Velvet smiled. "If you do ever need anything, I'm Velvet, the current Head of the Earth Angel Training Academy. This is Corduroy, one of our professors. Please do not hesitate to call on us at any time. I will send Linen to meet you as soon as possible; he will be the Head of the School for the Children of the Golden Age."

The Child nodded. "You are most kind. We look forward to meeting Linen. For now, we shall stay here, within the city; we shall not be any bother to you at all."

Velvet bowed her head slightly. "As you wish. We will leave you be now." She took Corduroy's arm and they headed for the door.

They reached the vanishing door and Velvet looked back, just in time to see the Children turn into bright blue lights again, moving around the city like ghostly, yet beautiful orbs.

As they exited, Velvet thought she saw the hem of lilac coloured robes whipping around the corner at the end of the hallway, but she couldn't be sure.

"I can't believe they're here already. What do you think this means? In terms of the time frame?"

Velvet shook her head. "It means that we have much less time than we first thought. I don't think even Linen knew this would all be happening so soon. He would have told us tonight if he had."

"Do you think everyone is still waiting for us to report back?"

"Probably. Give me your hand." Corduroy held out his hand and Velvet grasped it firmly before clicking her fingers.

*   *   *

"What was it? Are we being attacked? Was it aliens?"

Velvet blinked and focused on the scene in front of her. Most of the staff had remained, waiting for news. It was Tartan who was firing questions at her.

"Calm, Tartan, calm. We are not being attacked. There is no trouble. Although now I really do have to tell the entire population at the Academy about the changes that are taking place."

Tartan huffed and continued to pace.

"Please, everyone just sit back down for a moment. Then Beryl, we will need to put up a notice about the noise, otherwise we will have many confused souls wanting to know what's going on." Beryl nodded.

Velvet sat down, and looked at Linen. "It seems that we were all wrong about the time frame we were working to."

Linen frowned. "I don't understand, what has the noise got to do with our time frame?"

"The Children of the Golden Age have arrived."

There were gasps and a shocked "Oh my!"

"Already?" Athena asked. "But that's so soon! I thought we would have longer on Earth to change things before they were incarnated as humans?"

"I assumed there would be more time too," Linen spoke up. "I am deeply sorry now that I was not honest from the beginning."

"Now Linen, don't beat yourself up; you've been here less than four days, I'm sure if we'd known all this four days ago, we still wouldn't have been any more prepared," Velvet said kindly. She turned to the staff. "This means though, that we need to step up the game. We need to cut out the less important curriculum and focus on the most important. We need to condense all the information that we can into as small amount of time as possible. I know we usually ease them into things a bit slower, taking it week by week, but I think we need to go right ahead and give each trainee Earth Angel their human appearance."

"Are you sure?" Cotton asked worriedly. "They've barely been here a few days, we don't usually turn them into humans for at least a couple of weeks."

"Considering our time frame has become so much smaller, I think the quicker we move through the necessary material, the better. And for the Starpeople to progress more quickly, they need to be able to communicate more effectively with the professors and their fellow Earth Angels. Which they can only do by being human." Cotton nodded uncertainly.

"Yes, it will be more difficult this way," Velvet continued. "There will be much that the trainees will have to adapt to in a short amount of time, but I think it's best this way. We all need to get ready to go to Earth to pave the way for the Children." She smiled tiredly at Linen. "We need to do the best job we can to ensure that these Children enter the Earth at the right time to bring about the massive changes that will make the Golden Age a certain future for the humans."

Chiffon rose to her feet. "We had better get started. I will work on my lesson plans tonight, making it a more intensive course."

Velvet nodded. "Yes, I think that would be a good idea for everyone to do. Linen, the Indigo Children are currently in room 333, I told them I would send you along to introduce yourself. The rest of us, I think, should retire now to our offices and do our best to condense our lessons. I will put out a notice tonight to the entire Academy for all to meet in the main hall at nine o'clock tomorrow, and I will address the issues we are currently facing. Then," she continued, looking exhausted already. "We shall give the trainees their human appearances so they have time to get used to the dense human body."

Everyone nodded and stood, then made their way to the door. When all had left but Linen and Corduroy, Velvet let out a deep sigh. "Linen, do you know you way to classroom 333?"

Linen gathered his notebook and pen and shook his head.

"Corduroy, would you mind?" Velvet asked.

Corduroy nodded and reached out to grab Linen's robes. Too late, Linen realised what he was about to do and started to protest.

"Oh no, please, I hate-"

Corduroy took no notice and clicked his fingers.

Linen's facial expression the second they vanished was priceless. Velvet chuckled to herself, then tried to haul herself out of the chair. After her second attempt, she gave up and clicked her fingers. The chair turned into her purple velvet office chair. She clicked her fingers again, and both she and the chair disappeared.

Chapter Thirteen

"Am! There's a new notice up!" Aria bounced up and down in the air in front of the notice board in their room. Amethyst turned from her signed conversation with their alien room-mate to listen.

"What does it say?"

"It says that the noise was nothing to worry about, and that there's a meeting tomorrow at nine o'clock for the whole Academy! Trainees and Second Years!" She turned to Amethyst. "Do you think they'll tell everyone about the Children arriving? And their Golden City?"

Amethyst lifted her shoulders. "I don't know, little one. I think perhaps they might. The Children arriving is certainly unexpected. It means that Earth is closer to the possibility of experiencing the Golden Age than I thought."

Aria flew over to her bed and sat on it cross-legged. "But that's a good thing right? I mean, if the Golden Age really is coming, doesn't that mean that the world isn't going to end?"

"It would seem so. Though I wonder what has changed to make the Children so sure that it will happen this time?"

"Maybe we'll find out in the meeting tomorrow!" Too excited to sit still for long, Aria flew around the room, touching things and changing their shapes and colours. Their room-mate, Tm, whizzed around after her, changing things back to the way they were. Amethyst shook her head at the pair of them.

"I think perhaps we need to get some rest before tomorrow. Something tells me that it is going to be quite an eventful day."

Aria paused briefly and nodded, then continued doing mad laps around the room. Amethyst sighed. "I think I will go to the gardens for a while to meditate. I will be back in a bit to get some rest."

"Okay!" Aria cried out, competing with Tm over the room décor.

Amethyst shook her head once more at their antics, then went through the vanishing door.

*   *   *

Amethyst flew slowly to the gardens, enjoying the cool breeze rushing past and the low murmur of voices coming from the rooms in the Pacific wing. She reached the entrance to the gardens and paused momentarily. She decided to revisit the Atlantis Garden, to take a better look at the statue of the Merman.

At the entrance to the Atlantis Garden, Amethyst paused again. There was already someone on the bench in front of the statue, and she would have recognised the long white hair and bright purple robes anywhere. Unsure whether she should announce her presence, Amethyst hesitated before opening her mouth to speak.

"I wish you were here already, Laguz. I wish you would help me through all this craziness." Velvet said. "I wish I could know with absolute certainty that we will be together on Earth. How will I find you? I have seen so many people on Earth miss meeting their soulmate by mere minutes or inches - how do I know that it won't be the same for us?" She sighed. "With all the uncertainty of the future of the human race, I wish I could be certain about being with you."

Amethyst closed her mouth. She didn't want to intrude on what was obviously a very personal monologue. But something held her in place, and refused to let her leave.

Velvet was quiet for a moment, then she began to hum a tune. It was vaguely familiar to Amethyst, but she couldn't place it. She looked down at her feet, which were hovering silently a few inches off the ground. She knew she should leave, but she felt incapable of moving right then. The humming got louder and Amethyst looked up. She silently clapped a hand over her mouth to contain her gasp of surprise. The Merman statue had come to life! Amethyst was in shock. Velvet seemed to be oblivious; she was still humming the tune. *She must have her eyes closed,* Amethyst thought vaguely, still in shock. The man seemed to see her standing there, agog, and he winked at her. She blinked and held a hand up in apology, then started flying slowly backwards out of the garden. She bumped into the archway, but she couldn't pull her eyes away from the Merman with the long blond hair and jewel green eyes.

Once he was out of her view, she turned and flew quickly to the hedge surrounding the garden, and though she knew she shouldn't, she looked through to see what happened next.

*   *   *

"Velvet, my love."

Velvet stopped humming and slowly opened her eyes. She blinked once, then three more times in quick succession.

"Laguz?" she whispered.

His heart-stopping smile made her catch her breath. She wrenched her eyes from his to look at where his statue stood, but it was gone. She looked back at him, her eyes wide.

"Is this a dream?" She stood and reached out to touch his face gently, and when her fingertips met his cheek, it was like she'd been given an electric shock.

"You're real," she breathed. "How is this possible?"

"You wanted me to be here. You wanted certainty. So here I am."

"It's that simple? All I had to do was to say that I wanted you here, and you would come?"

"Yes."

Velvet leaned forward and her lips met his. She closed her eyes and ran her hand through his long hair. He responded passionately, drawing her closer to him.

After a few minutes, she pulled back, slightly breathless. "Can you stay?"

"There's nowhere else I would rather be."

Velvet smiled and grabbed his hand. "There is somewhere else I would rather be," she said, her eyes sparkling. She raised her other hand, clicked her fingers, and they both disappeared.

*   *   *

Amethyst returned to her room later that night, having spent some time meditating in the Angelic Garden after the scene she witnessed in Atlantis. She was slowly piecing together all of the information she had, and it seemed that maybe she and Aria had been a little too optimistic about Earth being saved by the Children. Because, to her knowledge, if the Flames were being reunited, then the end must be near. None of it made sense, and she hoped that the morning meeting would bring some clarity to everything. She smiled to herself. Of course, she should know better than to eavesdrop and spy on others. That was what led to confusion. But if she and Aria hadn't been keeping their eyes and ears open, they would be completely oblivious to all of the goings on at the Academy. And if there was one thing that Amethyst really did not like - it was being kept in the dark.

She arrived back at her room and stepped through the doorway. Aside from the dim glow of Tm, and the glittering stars, it was dark, and blissfully quiet. Amethyst could just about make out Aria's tiny form under the star-dust covers; resting peacefully. Amethyst flew silently over to her own planet bed and stretched herself out under her covers. She emptied her mind of all thought, which even after aeons of practice, was difficult tonight, and then finally she drifted into a deep, peaceful rest.

*   *   *

Velvet could not stop smiling. She lay on her purple velvet bed and stared into the eyes of her one true soulmate, her Twin Flame. Her face ached from smiling so much.

She reached out to touch the wooden rune that hung around his neck on a worn leather cord; and marvelled at the electric current that ran between them when her finger brushed against his skin.

"What I don't understand is why you didn't stay with me on the beach, in my vision. When the music stopped, you left me there." She didn't want to sound pitiful, but she was unable to stop the pain she had felt in that moment from creeping into her tone of voice.

"I didn't stay because it wasn't real. And because it wasn't the right time."

"What about when Corduroy told me about you? About us in Atlantis? Why didn't your statue become alive then?"

"Because you didn't ask me to come then. It's very simple, you manifested my presence."

Velvet shook her head. "I'm sorry. I guess I've been alone for too long. I've forgotten what it's like to be with someone - but to think, all these years, all I had to do was ask you to come to me."

"I know. It's extremely frustrating to find out that what we yearn for all our existence is ours - all we had to do was ask for it, then be open to receiving it." His voice was gentle as he traced figure eights on her bare arm.

"Are you saying that I was closed off to you before?"

"Until just a couple of days ago, you'd forgotten I even existed."

Velvet blushed. "I did, didn't I?" She bit her lip. "I'm so

sorry, Laguz. I never meant to shut you out, I didn't even realise what I was doing."

Laguz reached out and put his finger to her lips. "Shhh, it doesn't matter now. We both just need to concentrate on the matters at hand," he grinned. "And enjoy being together right now, of course."

Velvet grinned back and moved forward to kiss him. Suddenly, she heard the distant ringing of wind chimes. She jerked back and checked her mental schedule.

"Oh Goddess!" she muttered. She threw back the covers and stood up from the bed. Laguz looked at her, amused.

"Something I said?"

Velvet clicked her fingers and was instantly clothed in her usual purple velvet robes. She leant back down to kiss him once more.

"No, it's those matters you were just talking about, I'm running late for them."

Laguz smiled. "You're the Head of the Earth Angel Training Academy; you're never late, they're just early."

Velvet laughed. "That's what I always say." She gestured around the room. "Take your time, make yourself at home. If you want to join the meeting, we're in the main hall from, well now, 'til about eleven."

Laguz nodded. "I'll be right there," he promised.

Velvet grinned again and pulled him into another quick embrace. The chimes sounded again and she groaned.

"Gotta go!" She clicked her fingers and she was gone.

*   *   *

Amethyst and Aria had arrived at the main hall early the next morning, to find that it had magickally trebled in size. The screen behind the stage had been enlarged and there were now at least five hundred seats facing it.

"Wow," Aria said, looking around the hall. "Does this mean that even more people have joined the Academy?"

Amethyst shook her head. "I don't know. It's quite possible. Shall we get seats down near the front?"

Aria nodded and they made their way to the front, smiling and saying hello to friends as they passed them. They settled down where they could see the stage clearly, and within minutes, the seats filled quickly with souls. Most of them, Aria noticed, had human appearances.

"Do you think they're all Old Souls? Or more second years?"

"Most likely more second years. I think word must have spread throughout the dimensions that there was a new class for Earth Angels who had returned from Earth in the last century."

Aria bounced up and down in her seat, eager to find out for sure what was really going on.

Amethyst sighed and turned to Aria. "I think you need to find a way to work off some of your excess energy. You wear me out just by being near."

Aria became still. "Sorry, Am, I just can't help it when I'm excited. Do you really think that Velvet's going to tell everyone today about the Children?"

"I don't see how she has any other choice. It's not going to help anyone, keeping it a secret."

The seats were now completely full, and the clock on the giant screen chimed softly at nine o'clock. Aria squinted at the stage and could see Velvet's assistant pacing back and forth, looking a little stressed. He kept glancing at the clock, then glancing at the door.

"Velvet's late again," Aria whispered. "Do you think there's a problem?"

Amethyst recalled the scene in the Atlantis Garden the night before and smiled. "No, I don't think there's any problem. I think Velvet's just been a little, er, busy. That's all."

Aria frowned. "I hope she gets here soon, I'm just dying to know what's going on!"

Everyone in the room was talking quietly, but considering

the volume of souls in there, it was quite noisy. Aria was sat silently, staring at the door to the stage, when finally at six minutes past, it opened and someone stepped out onto the stage.

"Oh," Aria said, surprised. "I thought it would be Velvet, but it's not…" she trailed off, squinting hard. The soul nodded to a very relieved Linen and stood centre stage. With a click of her fingers, her smiling face replaced the clock on the giant screen and she cleared her throat gently to get everyone's attention.

Aria gasped, her eyes wide. "Is that Velvet?" she sputtered.

Amethyst nodded silently. *Wow*, she thought, *it's amazing what one night with a soulmate can do to someone.*

The Velvet before them had perfect skin; every last wrinkle had gone. Her cheeks were rosy and her eyes sparkled like a mischievous Faerie's. But the most startling change was her hair. It was still very long, cascading down her back, but it was now a deep shade of mahogany. If it weren't for her signature purple velvet robes it would have been difficult to recognise her. Still smiling widely, she spoke.

"Good morning, Earth Angels! I hope you are all well on this wonderful day." She looked around the room. "I see that we have many newcomers, I want to welcome you all, and thank you for coming to join us. I know that even though this is only the first week of term, things have been, well, rather hectic to say the least. I just want to thank the trainees for their patience, and apologise for all the many distractions. It has never been like this in past years, which is the reason why I have called this meeting this morning. There are some things that I need to inform you of, because it affects all of us, though in different ways." She took a deep breath before continuing.

"Earth is on the verge of either choosing a path of destruction, or a path that will lead to the Golden Age. Because of this, we here on the Other Side have to make rapid changes. We can no longer work with our usual time frame; things on

Earth have become too desperate. So the course that we are now on, will see everyone here, staff and trainees included, incarnated on Earth within the next five to ten Earthly years. Most of you will be incarnated within the three. Some may stay here longer, we're not entirely sure. What this means is-" Velvet stopped mid-sentence when a hand shot up in the air right in the front row.

"Yes?" she asked.

"I'm sorry to interrupt," the Faerie said, hovering above her seat. "But it sounded like you said that the staff would be leaving to go to Earth too?"

"I did, yes. The staff have decided unanimously that we will all return to Earth."

"But who will run the Academy? Who will be teaching?"

Velvet smiled at the young Faerie. "Patience, little one, I will get to all of that in just a moment, I promise." The Faerie nodded and sat back down.

"Now then, as I was saying, all of these things mean that there will be massive changes to our usual trainee program. The professors and I have decided to condense the lessons as much as possible, and move through everything more quickly. We feel that the trainees could be called to Earth at any moment, and we do not want to send anyone there unprepared. So trainees, please report back here this afternoon at one o'clock, so you can select your human appearances."

Aria looked at Amethyst, her eyes wide. "My wings!" she whispered. "I didn't think I'd lose them this quickly!" She glanced over her shoulder at the fluttering iridescence and looked as though she would start crying. Amethyst put her arm around her tiny friend and whispered:

"Shhh, little one. I will be there with you. It won't be so bad, I promise."

"By doing this," Velvet continued. "The Starpeople will be able to communicate more easily with us and so progress quicker. You will all also get a good idea of what it is like to be in a human body, and get used to not being able to fly or swim everywhere."

"It sucks," the second-year next to Aria muttered. Aria frowned at him and leant closer to Amethyst, seeking comfort.

"There will be some very big changes happening very quickly, and again, I apologise to the trainees, we usually try to do this all as gently as possible, but like I said, the time frame has changed dramatically. The belief at the moment seems to be that if we can send enough Earth Angels to Earth as soon as possible, then we can make sure that the humans are on the path that will lead to the Golden Age. Now, the Golden Age hasn't ever been experienced before, so the protocol for the events leading up to it are entirely unknown to us." Velvet smiled. "We are very much making things up as we go along. What we do know for sure, is that once all of you and the staff have been called to Earth, this Academy will no longer train Earth Angels."

Hushed whispering broke out around the massive hall, and Velvet held up a hand for silence.

"It has become clear to us, that this Academy is to be the School for the Children of the Golden Age. For those of you who are unfamiliar with this term, these are the pure souls who will be incarnated on Earth with much of their innocence intact. They will come to Earth once it seems we have managed to bring about the Great Awakening within the humans and other Earth Angels already there. The Children will be the ones to lead us into the Golden Age. Now, we originally thought we would have plenty of time in which to do all of this, but we were wrong. The Indigo Children have already arrived at the Academy. The noise that could be heard last night was their city being transported into this realm. They have come from a much higher frequency and it interfered with the frequency here. I do apologise for the unpleasantness of the noise." Velvet looked up to her left then, and smiled at the soul who entered and quietly sat in a spare seat at the front.

Amethyst didn't need to see his face to know that it was the statue that had come to life the night before, Laguz.

"Who's that?" Aria whispered, trying to get a look at him.

"I'll explain later," Amethyst replied, turning back to concentrate on what Velvet was saying.

"The other major change that will be happening on Earth in the coming few decades will be the reunion of the Flames. Now I know that many of you associate the reunion of the Flames with the end of the current age on Earth, but I believe that it will be different this time. I believe that this time, the Flames are being reunited to bring the love to the world that will be needed to keep us on the path to the Golden Age. I don't believe that it means the end of the current age, but merely the end of the current way of thinking. I believe that the shift in consciousness will make humans more spiritual, more aware than they have ever been before. Each soul finding their other half will also heighten this awareness. Part of our mission when we are incarnated on Earth will be to seek our own Flames," she flicked a glance to her left. "And to also help both Earth Angels and humans find their Flames and soulmates too. I honestly believe that the unions between souls will bring more love to the world than has been seen for the last two thousand years of this human age."

Aria smiled up at Amethyst. "So the world isn't coming to an end after all," she whispered, hope shining in her green eyes.

"Not if we have anything to do with it," Amethyst replied, smiling.

"So, now, we will continue lessons with the trainees as normal, though the material will be taught more quickly. The rest of you, who have recently joined us, will have to join me here, in the main hall every day, and I will do my best to lecture to you all at the same time. There are too many of you to have the smaller classes that I would prefer, and there's not enough time to teach you over a longer period. As I explained to my groups just yesterday, I believe that you will all be called to Earth quite quickly, so the number will decrease, which will make it easier." She paused and tilted her head to one side as though she was listening.

"Oh," she said. "It seems that we could actually be increasing in number. I have just been informed that new groups of souls will be arriving daily to join us." She smiled. "It seems we will be sending an army of Earth Angels to aid the humans in the shift. And I, for one, am glad there will be so many of you there." She chuckled. "It's a good thing we're not on Earth now though; it would take months to build the whole new wing that we need to accommodate you. As it is, all we need to do is click our fingers, and it's done." She clicked her fingers and the staff all appeared behind her. She turned to them.

"I'm going to need some help here. If each of you could please take a group of forty, and show them to their rooms. They can share a room with whomever they wish." Velvet turned back to the Earth Angels and smiled. "Welcome again to the Academy, I hope to get to know some of you before you are called. If you have any problems, just let me or a member of staff know. Trainees, please meet me back here at one o'clock. I hope you all have a very pleasant day!"

She walked off the stage to the left where the blond soul was sat. They spoke quickly to one another, then Velvet reached out for his hand, clicked her fingers and they disappeared.

Aria turned to Amethyst, her eyebrows raised. "Okay, now you really need to fill me in on what's going on. Velvet's younger, relaxed and trying to be funny? Has she been taken over by a pod person?"

Amethyst chuckled. "No, no she hasn't. Not unless there is a pod person called love."

*   *   *

Velvet sighed happily. She rested her head on Laguz's arm and looked up into the glittering green pools of light. "You are definitely the best cure I have ever found for stress."

He laughed; the deep rumbling vibrated through his chest, jostling Velvet.

"Glad to be of service." He touched her cheek gently. "I've missed you."

Velvet frowned. "Where have you been exactly? Since Atlantis?"

Laguz raised an eyebrow. "You want me to account for my whereabouts for the last six ages?"

Velvet smiled. "Not for the entire time, but I mean, have you been back to Earth? Were you in another dimension? Were you still a Merman at sea?"

"I was a Merman for a considerable amount of time. Until the end of the age after Atlantis in fact."

"Wow, that is a long time. I had no idea that Merpeople lived so long."

"Merpeople have no particular life span - they can essentially live forever. The only thing that kills them is the environment around them. And at the end of that age, the oceans heated to such a degree that we all agreed to leave, and enter heaven together."

"Like the Mayans?"

"Yes, just like them."

"But how did the Merpeople repopulate the oceans in the next age? Surely some of you would have had to have remained behind?"

"No, they had to start over again, the way Merpeople started after Atlantis."

"How did they start after Atlantis? How did you go from being a man to a Merman?"

Laguz smiled. "I cannot believe how much you have forgotten."

Velvet shrugged. "My soul is so old, that there are far too many memories for me to remember them all."

"That's not true. I'm not much younger than you, and I remember everything. Every life, every age, and every time in-between."

Velvet frowned. "Are you saying that I blocked out Atlantis on purpose?"

"It would seem so. Although why you would do that, I don't know."

"Perhaps it was because I knew I'd miss you too much if I remembered you. Anyway, stop changing the subject, how did the Merpeople start?"

"By magick. Not the illusionary kind, the real kind. Where you imagine something, and then request it from the Universe."

"And who made such a request?"

Laguz squeezed her gently. "You did."

"I did?" Velvet was learning more about her forgotten past every minute.

"Yes. You saw it in a vision. You knew that Atlantis would soon come to an end, that the age would be over, but that ocean life would survive. You saw human bodies adapt to life underwater. And so you requested from the Universe guidance on how to bring about that future. You helped every soul in Atlantis who wished to make the transition, become a Merperson."

Velvet thought about this for a minute. "Corduroy said that I knew I wouldn't survive the fall of Atlantis. What happened to me? Did I at least even try to go with you?"

Laguz's eyes clouded over and his arms tightened around her. "When you told me your vision, I tried to convince you that just because you had seen one possible future, it didn't mean that it would be the future you would experience. But you were adamant. You said you could feel, quite clearly, that you would not accompany me to the waters."

"What happened, did I just stay and die on my own? Or did I go before the end? Before you left?"

Laguz was quiet for a while. Velvet looked up and noticed a tear escape from his jewel green eye. He made no move to brush it away, so Velvet kissed it away. "I'm sorry, my love. We should be enjoying our time here together now, not lamenting over our last life together on Earth. I don't want to make you sad."

Laguz closed his eyes and held her even more tightly to him.

"Remember I said it was magick that changed us?" Velvet nodded. "You were the channel for that magickal energy. When your vision was realised, and it was time for us to change into Merpeople, you would meditate with each of us, touching our feet and necks. One by one, our feet turned to fins, gills appeared in our necks and we left Atlantis, taking the jewels of the city with us to start our underwater Atlantis. Within no time at all, aside from a few who had decided to stay, you and I were the last ones there. The amount of energy running through you to change everyone had left you weak and had aged you beyond repair." He ran a hand through her now dark and glossy hair. "You were fading away right before my eyes. I wanted to stay with you, live with you until Atlantis was no more. But you wouldn't let me." His voice broke. "I was stood on the sand, begging you to let me stay with you until the end, and I thought you had finally given in, when you reached forward, kissed me once on the lips, and hugged me. But it wasn't an embrace of surrender; you were giving me the final energy needed for me to change." Tears now fell silently down his cheeks, dripping onto the pillow

"You died right there, in my arms. On our beach." He looked at her, his green eyes glistening. "The same beach from your visions."

Velvet felt her own tears making trails down her smooth cheeks.

"I'm sorry," she whispered.

"You have nothing to apologise for. You saved us all. I'm only sorry it has taken this long for us to be together again. I have to admit, that's partly my fault."

Velvet frowned up at him. "Why do you say that?"

Laguz sighed. "I was afraid that you wouldn't want to be with me. I think the fact that you made me leave made me think that maybe it was because you didn't want us to be together."

Velvet sat bolt upright. "I have never heard anything so ridiculous. Though I don't remember those times well, I know that the only reason I would ever have sent you away would be because I had no choice. If I hadn't done what I did, everyone would have perished. I could never have had that on my conscience. And I obviously loved you more than anything, how could I not? You are my Twin Flame. If I knew there was a way to save you, keep you alive, then of course I would have chosen that course of action."

Laguz smiled. "So are you saying that I have spent the last six ages alone for no reason?"

Velvet shook her head. "I would never say there was no reason for it. There is a reason for everything. I'm just saying that I wish you hadn't spent the last six ages doubting my love for you."

"Doubt kills dreams. Kill doubt, not dreams."

Velvet frowned. "That sounds familiar, who said that?"

Laguz reached up and pulled her down to him. "You did," he murmured, placing his lips on hers.

Chapter Fourteen

"Please, Am! Please don't make me go!" Aria was hiding behind her planet bed, begging Amethyst not to make her go to the one o'clock meeting.

"Come on now, Aria. If you don't come this afternoon, then we won't get to choose our appearances together. It occurred to me, that when we are born on Earth, we might actually end up having similar appearances to the ones we choose today. So you know what that means, don't you?"

There was a moment of quiet. Finally, Aria asked sullenly. "No, what does it mean?"

Amethyst flew around the planet to face Aria. "It means that if we get to know what each other looks like here, then we may recognise each other easier when we get to Earth."

"Really?" Aria asked, brightening for a moment. Amethyst thought she may be finally winning, but then the moment passed and Aria frowned again.

"Am, I'm not sure I want to go to Earth anymore. It doesn't sound like a very fun place." She looked at Amethyst, her wide green eyes sad. "I don't want to lose my wings."

Amethyst sighed. "Me neither, little one. But I am going to Earth, regardless of what it costs me. It is my purpose now to help all those who need it there." She smiled at the sad green Faerie. "And I really think it would help me so much if you were there too."

Aria thought about this. "Would I really be helping you,

being on Earth too?"

Amethyst knew she'd finally won her over. "Of course, little one. While the changes are big and the work will be hard, we will certainly need to play and rest plenty too. And who will remind us to do that if you and all of your fellow Faeries aren't there? The world needs you, Aria. I need you."

Aria sighed. "Oh, Am, if you really need me that much, how could I possibly let you down?" She took a deep breath and extended a hand, which Amethyst took.

"Let's get this over with." They left the room and slowly headed to the main hall. Amethyst tried to speed up their pace, worried that they would be very late, but Aria was dragging behind. Struck with an idea, Amethyst smiled suddenly and turned to Aria. "How about it, one last race, just for fun?"

Aria grinned. "You know I'll beat you."

"Maybe." Amethyst shrugged. Then she shot off down the hall, faster than Aria had ever seen her fly before. "Maybe not!" she called over her shoulder as Aria flapped her tiny wings furiously to catch up with her friend.

"That's cheating!" she cried out, then burst into giggles.

*   *   *

The main hall was filled with chattering Angels, Faeries, Merpeople and silent Starpeople when Aria and Amethyst finally arrived, breathless and only five minutes late. Aria was still beaming – she had beat Amethyst by a hair.

"See? I told you that Faeries are always faster than Angels."

"I guess you were right, little one," Amethyst replied, smiling. She was glad to see her friend happy again. They entered the noisy hall and found themselves a couple of seats. Aria glanced at the giant clock.

"Velvet is late, again." She scrunched up her nose. "Do you think they're at it?"

Amethyst chuckled. "Probably. They have been apart for

- 174 -

a very long time. They've got a lot of catching up to do."

"Ewww," Aria complained.

"Just wait until you get to Earth. When you fall in love, I'm sure you'll be exactly the same."

"I don't think so," Aria retorted. "I'd rather have animals than a man."

Amethyst was still chuckling when Velvet wandered in, a dreamy smile on her face, five minutes later.

She got to the centre of the stage and her face appeared on the screen behind her.

"Welcome, Earth Angel trainees! I apologise for the delay, I, uh, had some important business to attend to."

Aria rolled her eyes at Amethyst. Amethyst bit her lip to keep a giggle from escaping.

"Now then, I have asked Corduroy to help me with the proceedings here this afternoon," she gestured to the very sullen looking professor, who was sat off to the side. "We will split you into four groups. Two groups will begin; one with me, one with Corduroy and the other two will just watch. Then we will swap around. So, group one will consist of Europe and Australia, the second will be North America, the third will be Africa and Antarctica, the fourth will be South America and Asia. Please find your classmates and form the groups now."

There was a lot of shuffling about as the groups formed. Amethyst and Aria found their fellow North Americans, and sat near the front. Amethyst noticed Velvet had snapped out of her dreamy state and was talking to the irritated Corduroy. Though their voices seemed to get louder at times, with all the noise in the hall, Amethyst couldn't tell what they were arguing about. Finally, everyone settled down, and Velvet turned back to them, a confused look replacing the earlier dreamy one.

"Right," she said, seemingly trying to gather her thoughts. "If Europe and Australia could go with Corduroy on that side," she gestured to the left of the stage where Corduroy still sat, a scowl on his face. "And North America can come over here with me."

The groups moved forward to join them; Amethyst had to practically drag Aria down to the stage.

When they joined Velvet, she took a deep breath and looked around them.

"Now then," she said. "I know this is all very sudden. We usually give trainees a little more time to adjust, but as you know, we don't have the luxury of time right now. So the best advice I can give you is this - go with your instincts and intuition. Don't over-think your choices too much, just go with what feels right to you, okay?"

Everyone nodded; some more confidently than others. The Zubenelgenubi Starpeople glowed more brightly, and the Synapsian Starpeople looked like miniature firework displays. Aria looked away from their lights and hid behind Amethyst, trying not to be seen.

"The first thing we will take care of is your human appearance. You will each choose the human features that you want from the choices in front of you, then we will put the features together. If it looks the way you want it to, you will assume the appearance you have created. If there is something you would like to change, that is the point at which to change it. After assuming the form, there won't be a chance to change it, as we will be introducing Earth laws to the Academy, such as gravity and the delay between cause and effect and manifestation."

"Do you mean we won't be able to manifest things anymore?" Filix asked.

"No, you will be able to manifest, but only in the way you have been taught in Manifestation 101 - instant manifestation will no longer work."

"So we have to think of something, hold the thought and vibration of it, then it might possibly happen at some point in the future?" Filix asked unbelievingly.

"Yes, I'm afraid that's how things work on Earth. The energy and vibrations there are so dense that it takes a considerable amount more time than you are used to, to create things that we want and need."

Filix looked dismayed and Velvet chuckled kindly. "You will get used to it, little one. With a little practice you can still manifest, I promise. Now then, would you like to be the first to choose your human appearance, Filix?"

The Faerie brightened a little. "Okay." He flew towards Velvet. She clicked her fingers and a row of what looked like different coloured wigs of different hair length and styles appeared. Filix considered each one, then chose a dark brown, short style, with flecks of red in it. Velvet clicked her fingers twice, and the wigs were replaced with faces. Filix jumped a little when he saw all the bodiless faces staring at him, causing the others to laugh. He again considered each one before choosing a serious looking face, with dark brown eyes and dimples. Velvet clicked her fingers again twice and different bodies appeared this time, with different physiques - short, tall, muscular, rounded, wiry. The Faerie chose a tall, muscular body, and Velvet clicked her fingers twice again. This time all the features he chose were assembled to create the whole human appearance. Filix blinked at the human he had created.

"Wow," he said. "I'm really good-looking."

Everyone laughed at that, even Aria, who was watching with open curiosity now.

"I think there's something missing," Velvet said thoughtfully. She studied the human then smiled. "I know." She clicked her fingers and a pair of glasses appeared on the face.

Filix grinned. "Yes, that's perfect. Now I'm good looking and intelligent."

Everyone was laughing uproariously now, causing the other group working with Corduroy to keep glancing over. Corduroy kept barking out instructions for his group to pay attention to what he was saying.

Velvet turned to Filix. "Are you ready then?"

Filix nodded. He took a deep breath and Velvet clicked

her fingers. The group all blinked in surprise. Filix vanished in a cloud of sparkling silver dust. A second later, the human opened his eyes and came to life. Filix blinked a few times, as if adjusting to the human's eyes.

"Wow," he said. His new human voice came out several octaves lower than his old Faerie voice. He cleared his throat and moved his arms and legs. "This body is so heavy!" he exclaimed, in his new deep tones. He walked around a couple of steps. "It's no wonder humans cannot fly, they weigh a ton!"

Velvet smiled. "You will get used to it in time, Filix." She turned back to the group. "Now, who's next?"

*   *   *

One by one, the members of the North American group chose their features, all giggling when combinations created odd looking humans. Soon there were just two left; Amethyst and Aria.

Amethyst looked down at her small green Faerie friend. "I'll go next," she said.

She stepped forward and went through the process, choosing long blonde hair, blue eyes, a kind face and a curvaceous body that was an average height. When assembled, she nodded in satisfaction to Velvet.

"I'm ready." She glanced back at Aria and smiled.

Velvet clicked her fingers and Amethyst disappeared in a cloud of feathers.

"Am!" Aria squeaked, her wings fluttering, her hand over her mouth.

"It's okay, Aria," the blonde human said, holding out her hand. "I'm here."

Aria shook her head wildly. "You're not Amethyst! You don't even sound like her! Amethyst!" she screamed, flying around their heads madly. "They killed Amethyst!"

"Aria!" Velvet called gently. "No one has been killed, Amethyst is right here."

"They killed my friend!" Aria wailed, still flying around crazily.

Velvet clicked her fingers and Aria was pulled to the ground unwillingly by an unseen energy.

"No! They're trying to kill me! Help me someone! Please help me!" She struggled uselessly against the energy, trying to break free. Amethyst looked helplessly at Velvet.

"What do we do?"

Velvet smiled calmly. "This happens at least once every new class. Don't worry, she will be fine." She clicked her fingers and Aria seemed to fall asleep.

"I will send her to my office. We can chat to her there."

"Chat about what? She will have to change soon anyway won't she?"

"You can come too. We will talk to her together." Velvet clicked her fingers again and the sleeping Aria disappeared. "I've sent her to my office; Beryl will look after her for us. Now then, that's all of North America done now, how do you all feel?"

She looked around at the group of human-looking Earth Angels in front of her. They all nodded slowly.

"I feel very heavy, like Filix said," Leon, a former Faerie said. "I hope I will still be able to See in this human body."

"You should be able to," Velvet said thoughtfully. "But it may require a little more concentration. There is no reason why you should not retain your Seeing ability when you are on Earth – but it may take a while to master again. Or even to realise you are able to do so at all." Leon nodded. "Anyone else have any questions or thoughts? Because I need to move onto my second group."

Everyone shook their heads.

"You are all free now for the rest of the afternoon. Amethyst, if you would like to meet me in my office at three o'clock, we can talk to Aria then."

Amethyst nodded, her new features set in a concerned frown. Velvet touched her arm reassuringly.

"She'll be fine, I promise."

Amethyst nodded. Then she and the rest of her group left the main hall to make way for the next group.

*   *   *

Amethyst wandered through the gardens for a while, lost in thought. She hoped that Aria would be okay. Perhaps the Faerie shouldn't have come to the Academy after all. Amethyst doubted that she would be very happy on the human plane. It was a dense place, filled with anger, sadness and disease. Of course, there was the other side of it too, the joy, happiness and beauty of the Earth. And of course, the feeling of love. Amethyst smiled. After watching the humans on Earth all her long existence, she looked forward to the love most of all. The simple pleasure of meeting someone, falling in love and spending every moment possible in their embrace. She knew it wasn't always that simple, but the difficulties of being human were always so much easier to bear, it seemed, when you were loved by another.

Amethyst wondered what it would feel like. She had heard it described as butterflies in the stomach, tingling sensations and the heart beating furiously. She touched her now human hand to her chest, and felt the heartbeat there. It felt both wonderful and alien at the same time. Speaking of aliens, it was so strange to see her room-mate, Tm, the former flowing, pulsing light, as a human. She would be able to talk to him now and receive a longer reply than yes or no.

Things would be quite different at the Academy from now on. No more races down the halls, or beautiful beings fluttering about. Amethyst sighed. Everything changed. The only certainty there was, it seemed, was change. She supposed she should get used to it. Humans experienced more changes than the beings in this dimension, and so many more than the Angels in the Angelic Realm.

Amethyst came to a stop and realised that she had

wandered into the Atlantis Garden. She sat on the bench that now faced an empty space where the statue of the Merman had stood. She realised now that the blond soul was Velvet's Flame. She sighed and wondered where her own Twin was. She wasn't exactly sure if every soul had one, or if it was just a few. She hoped that hers was out there, maybe even already on Earth, waiting for her. She sat for some time, staring at the empty space. It wasn't until a loud laugh nearby startled her that she realised she'd been lost in a deep meditative state. She shook herself and decided to head to Velvet's office to wait. She wanted to be there when Aria awoke.

She got to her feet, already feeling the weight of her new body. She walked slowly through the gardens, feeling, somewhere in the pit of her stomach, that the conversation she was about to witness would not have the outcome she hoped for.

*   *   *

"Aria," Velvet called softly. The little Faerie stirred and slowly opened her eyes.

"What?" she muttered, blinking her eyes sleepily. She focused on the faces around her and a scowl appeared. "You're not Amethyst," she said to the blonde lady across from her.

The lady smiled. "Aria, it is me. I promise you. It's me. My soul is now living in this human body."

Aria crossed her arms across her chest. "Prove it."

Amethyst raised an eyebrow. "Okay. You used to be a grass-growing Faerie in the Elemental Realm, before the humans destroyed all the grass and you were out of a job. You didn't read the brochure before coming, you love crickets, have a ladybug friend called Larry and you like playing BugScotch," Amethyst continued. "You're terrified of losing your wings and you were with me the day the Children arrived, I stopped the noise from hurting our ears."

Aria uncrossed her arms slowly, and peered at Amethyst

uncertainly.

"Am?" she whispered.

"Yes, my little Faerie friend, it is me."

Aria flung herself into Amethyst's arms. "Oh, I'm so glad you're okay!" she cried.

Amethyst chuckled. "I'm fine, little one, I just look different, that's all."

Aria leant back and bit her lip. She looked over at Velvet who was sat behind her desk. "I'm sorry I kind of lost it in there."

Velvet smiled kindly. "Don't worry, Aria, it happens every time. And you have had less preparation time than most. Now that you are calmer, you face a decision that needs to be made."

"A decision?"

"All souls have free will. You are here of your own will. If you wish, right now, to remain a Faerie, and to not become human, then it is your right to choose that."

Aria's eyebrows shot up. "I can go back to being a Faerie?"

"Yes. You can be reincarnated into the Elemental Realm instead of as a human on Earth."

"Wow." Aria looked over at Amethyst. "I had no idea we could change our minds."

Amethyst shook her head. "You still didn't read that brochure properly did you?"

Aria blushed and shook her head.

"I should have guessed." Amethyst rolled her eyes, then became serious again. "What do you think, Aria? Are you going to come with me, or are you going to go home?"

Aria shrugged her shoulders. "I don't know, Am. I want to be where you are. But I want to be a Faerie. But not just any Faerie, I want to still be me, as I am now."

"Well, in that case, there is a third option." Aria turned to Velvet expectantly. "The Earth Angel Training Academy will soon become the School for the Children of the Golden Age, and they are currently recruiting teachers from the Angelic and

Elemental Realms to work here."

Aria's eyebrows reached her hairline. "Teach? Me? What on Earth would I teach the Children? They know way more than I do. I don't know anything."

Velvet chuckled. "I'm sure you know more than you give yourself credit for."

"You could teach them about nature. About how humans need to have respect for it, about how to care for plants and animals," Amethyst added softly. She looked at Aria. "It's what you planned to do on Earth. You could do it here instead. Then you wouldn't have to worry about forgetting it all when you get to Earth."

Aria was thoughtful for a while. Then she turned to Amethyst. "Am, I'm really sorry, but I think-"

"-that you should stay. I know." Amethyst smiled sadly and reached out to hold the Faerie's tiny hand. "I think you should too."

"You really are the best friend in the whole Universe."

Amethyst laughed. "I know that, too."

Chapter Fifteen

Velvet was sat at her desk, staring into space and lost in her thoughts, when Laguz peered into her office.

"What are you doing sat here in the dark?" he asked, walking in. He clicked his fingers and a warm glow lit up the room.

Velvet smiled up at him. "I was just thinking."

"You do know that too much thinking is harmful to your health?"

Velvet chuckled. "Yes, it would seem so. I wasn't thinking about anything particularly taxing. I was just trying to imagine all the changes that will happen as a result of the shift in consciousness. I mean, I haven't been to Earth in a very long time, and I know there have been many changes since my last visit, but I imagine that there will be even more significant changes in the next few years."

"That sounds like some fairly serious thinking to me. But yes, there will be some big changes. Humans are evolving much like they did in Atlantis."

"Will they make it this time do you think?"

Laguz sighed and sat in the chair on the other side of her desk. "I sure hope so." There was a moment of silence, and Velvet sensed something change in Laguz's energy. She looked at him more closely and realised that his face looked a little strained.

"What is it?" she asked.

Laguz sighed again. "I'd forgotten that you could read my mind."

Velvet smiled. "I can't read your mind as such, but I did sense just now, that something... changed. Your energy shifted slightly."

Laguz looked into her eyes. "They're calling me."

Velvet frowned, confused. "Who's calling you?"

"The Angels. To Earth. I heard it a little earlier. It was quiet at first, but it's become progressively louder throughout the day. I heard it again just then."

Velvet stared at him for a moment before she could speak. "You're being called to Earth? Already? But when do they want you to leave?"

Laguz reached across the desk and grasped her hand. "Now."

"Now," Velvet repeated in a whisper. "Please tell me you're joking. Please tell me this is some practical joke that you and Corduroy have cooked up and that he's watching right now, laughing."

Laguz shook his head. "I wish it were."

Velvet jumped up and started to pace. "But how could they do this? You just got here! I only just got you back and now you have to leave? I can't come with you because I can't leave yet! Until the trainees and the other Earth Angels have been called and until Linen has taken over the Academy, I can't leave! And all of that could take years! By then you could be old enough to be my father!" Her voice was becoming more hysterical as her robes whipped back and forth.

"What are the Angels thinking? I thought the whole idea of the shift was to reunite the Flames, not separate them by vast chunks of time so that their union is considered illegal in most parts of the world!" Laguz stood up and took hold of her elbows.

"Velvet, calm down. This could still work. We could still be together."

She looked up into his jewel green eyes. "How? I don't

want to be on Earth without you, but I think it would be even harder to be on Earth at the same time and not be able to be with you."

Laguz swallowed. "It can still work," he repeated. "It is not up to us to figure out how, only to have complete faith that the things that we wish for will happen. You know that."

Velvet buried her face in his chest, her hand resting upon his rune necklace. Laguz clung to her tightly, breathing in the scent of her dark hair.

"How long do we have?" she asked, her voice muffled.

"I should leave tonight. So about an hour or two."

Velvet pulled back and looked up at him, a tear shining on her pale cheek.

"Then let's not waste a single moment of it." She leant forward to kiss him, and at the same time clicked her fingers.

*   *   *

Later that evening, the beach was quiet but for the waves gently lapping onto the sand. Velvet and Laguz walked hand in hand along the shore, lost in their own thoughts. The sun was setting, painting a vivid backdrop to their quietness. As though something had suddenly occurred to him, Laguz stopped abruptly and turned to Velvet.

"Promise me something," he said, an urgency in his rough voice.

Velvet nodded. "Anything."

"Promise me you will come to Earth, no matter what. I want to go there knowing, with absolute certainty, that you will be following me. That one day, you will find me."

"I promise. I will listen to my heart."

Laguz nodded, then he blinked. "It's getting louder," he whispered.

"What does it sound like?"

"It starts off as one voice, calling your name, then it's two, then three, then soon it sounds like a million Angelic voices, all calling out your name."

"Have they explained why you have to leave so soon?"

Laguz shook his head. "No, but I think that things are developing at a rapid pace right now. I guess they need as many souls to help with the shift as possible." He stared at her face, trying to memorise every detail. "I wish I didn't have to leave you."

Velvet bit her lip. "They need you. I don't know if they need you as much as I do, but it seems they shout louder." She attempted a smile but it turned into a grimace.

He traced the outline of her cheek with his thumb softly. "I'll wait for you."

Velvet shook her head. "No. You will live your life to the fullest. You will do what you need to do to help with the shift. If you meet someone else before I get there... well, we can cross that hurdle when we get to it. Whatever you do, don't put your life on hold. Live." She took a breath and a tear slid down her cheek. "I'll check in on you from time to time."

"I love you," he whispered, a tear sliding down his own cheek. His green eyes glistened in the dim light of the sunset. "I'll love you for eternity."

Velvet caught her breath suddenly. "I remember," she said, a look of wonder mixed with pain on her face. "I remember the last time we said goodbye. You said exactly that. And I replied-"

"'Our love will outlast eternity itself,'" he said. Velvet nodded.

"Why must it always end this way? Why must it end at all?"

"So it may begin again. Besides, it's not the end this time, not really." Laguz smiled. "We'll be together again soon." He grimaced slightly. "It's time."

Velvet leaned forward and kissed him hard on the lips. He responded passionately, lifting her up so that her toes barely touched the sand.

With great reluctance, they parted and Laguz set her

down. He took the leather cord from around his neck and fastened it around Velvet's. "So you don't forget me again," he whispered.

Velvet touched the wooden rune. "Thank you."

Laguz looked out to the ocean. He shook his head. "Well, we may as well make this little scene of déjà vu complete." After one last final hug, he waded into the water. He faced the sunset, but kept glancing back over his shoulder as he got further away from Velvet.

The tears flowed freely down her cheeks now, as she longed desperately to wade in after him, and beg the Angels to take her as well.

Finally, the water was waist deep. He turned one last time and waved. Then he dove into the water. The glint of a silvery green fin shone in the fading sunlight.

Velvet, now aged and haggard, clutched the rune pendant as she sank to her knees in the sand, her salty tears mixing with the waves as her heart broke into a million pieces.

*   *   *

The soft voice calling her name made no impression on Velvet as she lay on the damp sand, feeling completely drained.

"Velvet, oh my dear Velvet," the voice said, coming closer. A haze of pink filled her vision as she tried to focus on her friends' face.

Magenta sat beside her and gathered her up in her arms. Velvet lay there limply. All of her spirit seemed to have left her. Magenta rocked her back and forth, smoothing back her white hair, murmuring soothing words. None of it seemed to affect Velvet. Her eyes remained dull, her wrinkled face creased in a permanent grimace of pain.

They stayed like that for some time, until Magenta realised that no amount of comfort would heal her friend's pain. After a period of silence, Magenta winced then said softly; "Velvet. I need to talk to you about something. I know that now is not the best time, but I'm afraid it cannot wait."

Velvet's eyes focused on Magenta's for the first time. After a moment they narrowed. "You're leaving me too, aren't you?"

Magenta nodded, her features twisted in a frown. "They've been calling me all day. I can't ignore it much longer."

Velvet's face crumpled. Her body heaved with sobs but there were no more tears left. "I don't understand. How do they think I can do this on my own?"

"I believe in you. You can do this. And you will. You'll be on Earth with us in no time at all, you'll see."

Velvet looked up at her friend; her heart ached. "I'm going to miss you. In all this time, I don't think I've ever truly told you how much I love you."

Magenta smiled. "Me neither. So let's say it here, now. I love you, Velvet. I'm going to miss you. I can't wait to see you on Earth again."

"I love you too, Magenta. I promise I'll work as quickly as possible here to get to Earth to help you all."

Magenta nodded then winced again.

"You shouldn't keep them waiting," Velvet said. She reached out and pulled Magenta into a hug. "Good luck."

"Thank you. I'll see you soon, okay?"

Velvet pulled away and nodded.

Magenta looked up to the skies. "Good bye," she whispered.

Velvet blinked and her friend was gone. She looked all around her. The sun had completely set, huge storm clouds had rolled in. The beach was no longer warm and inviting; it was cold and threatening. Velvet drew her knees up to her chest, put her arms around herself and shivered. In no time at all she had gone from being blissfully happy, with her Twin Flame by her side and a best friend not far away, to being completely alone and facing some of the biggest challenges she'd had in over a hundred years. *If only death were possible here,* she thought wistfully. *If only it were possible to wade into the ocean and drown myself in blissful ignorance.* Maybe humans were right to believe that death meant falling into a void of non-existence. Velvet would have given anything at that moment to not exist. She lost track of time as she sat huddled in the unrelenting chilly breeze. She wanted to stay there and never face another soul again.

Drifting towards her on the breeze was the faint sound of wind chimes. She sighed and tried to ignore them. But like the Angelic call to Earth, they only got louder and more persistent. Feeling a thousand years older than she had a few hours previously, Velvet stiffly got to her feet and carefully tucked Laguz's necklace inside her robes, so that it rested close to her heart. Then she clicked her fingers.

*   *   *

"Aria, like I have said a million times before, there's no need to apologise. You're doing what you feel you need to." It was early the next morning, and Amethyst and Aria stood outside Velvet's office.

Aria frowned. "But I feel so bad! I should be coming with you; I should be on Earth with you."

"There is no such thing as 'should', Aria. There is only what your heart desires to do."

Aria stopped in front of the Head Office door. She stared at the gold nameplate bearing Velvet's name.

"Thank you, Am. At least by staying here I know for certain that I won't ever forget you."

Amethyst smiled. "And for that, I am glad." She nudged Aria closer to the door. "Now, go in there and get yourself hired."

Aria nodded, her face was a similar shade of green to her dress.

"Wish me luck," she said a little nervously.

"Good luck, my little Faerie friend. I will be waiting in the gardens for you. We have the day off, so we may as well enjoy it."

Aria nodded and knocked on the door. A male voice inside called out for her to enter. The door vanished and Aria took a deep breath before flying into the room.

Amethyst turned and slowly walked down the hallway towards the gardens.

*   *   *

"Can I help you?" Linen asked, glancing up from his notes.

"Um, yes, I um, spoke to Velvet and she said you were looking for Faeries to teach the Children and I thought maybe you would hire me to teach them even though I don't know what I would teach them but I thought I would ask because -"

"Whoa!" Linen held up a hand. "Slow down there! I have plenty of time to chat. Why don't you sit down?" He gestured to the piano stool in front of his desk. Aria nodded, flew to the stool and sat. She smiled at Linen, a slightly puzzled look on her face.

Linen noticed. "What is it?"

"Are you really an Old Soul? Because you don't really seem like one, but your name is Linen and you look like one."

Linen smiled. "Actually no, I'm not. I'm a Faerie. My name was Dictamnus."

"White Dittany," Aria said, thoughtfully. She looked at his bright red hair, orange eyes and yellow robes and smiled. "A fire Faerie. Cool! I always wanted to learn how to create fire, but I was a little clumsy, I probably would have set myself alight."

Linen chuckled. "I did that a few times. You were a grass-growing Faerie, I assume?" He nodded at her green attire.

Aria nodded. "Yes, it was a much safer occupation for me. Not too many chances of injuring myself. Though I did manage to fall off a toadstool once."

Linen laughed again. "It's a pleasure to meet you- what did you say your name was?"

"Aria. Short for Lunaria. My favourite flower is Honesty."

She blushed. "I'm also pretty forgetful."

Linen smiled. "Okay, Aria, getting back to the reason why you came to see me, I think it would be an excellent idea for you to become part of the new teaching staff here at the Academy. I assume that you have definitely made up your mind that you will not be going to Earth?"

Aria nodded vigorously. "I can't bear the thought of losing my wings. Flying is everything to me."

Linen sighed and looked over his own shoulder. "Tell me about it. I'm afraid I had no choice in the matter of losing my wings."

"Oh, that's awful! You should demand them back! Can't you do that, now you're going to be Head of the Academy?"

Linen shrugged. "I have no idea, though I may bring up the subject with Velvet when she returns."

Aria glanced over at the empty desk. "Where is she?"

"I'm not sure. I haven't seen her this morning. She's often out on important errands. Though she's been quite busy with a new visitor just recently."

Aria made a face. "You mean her Twin Flame?"

"Yes, I do." Linen made a face of his own. "I'm quite fortunate they've kept themselves to Velvet's room mostly, but I did walk in on them in here yesterday."

"Oh, eww! That's so gross. Seriously, are humans really like that on Earth?"

Linen grimaced. "Actually, on Earth they're even worse."

"Even worse? Wow, I'm so glad I decided to stay here!"

"Indeed. I suppose that rather than continue to attend the Earth Angel classes, it would be better for you to spend time with myself, talking to the Children and maybe you could even come with me to the Angelic and Elemental Realms, recruiting new teachers."

Aria grinned. "That sounds brilliant! I'd love to! Thank you so much, Dictamnus, I mean, Linen. I promise you won't regret this! We'll make an excellent team!"

Linen smiled at all the exclamations. "I'm sure we will.

Velvet and I are supposed to be having a meeting soon," the sound of wind chimes filled the room. "Ah yes, she should be back any second. So if you don't mind, we can meet here tomorrow morning at say, nine-thirty?"

Aria nodded and flew up off of the stool. "That sounds great! I will be here to-"

A loud click made her jump and they both turned in time to see Velvet appear next to her desk. Her robes were covered in sand, her long hair was tangled and white again and her face was more ancient and haggard than it had ever been before. Her pale cheeks were stained with tears and she looked as though she was about to faint.

"Velvet!" Linen exclaimed in shock. He rushed towards her and helped her into her chair. She seemed quite unresponsive. Linen looked up at Aria who was staring at Velvet, open-mouthed. He nodded at the door. Aria mouthed "Sorry!" and flew quickly out of the room.

Linen turned back to Velvet.

"Velvet. Can you hear me? Are you okay?"

Velvet remained mute, her gaze fixed on the grain of the wooden desk.

Linen looked around the room, seeking inspiration. His gaze rested on the grand piano, its stool standing off at an angle. He looked back at Velvet; her face was still set in the same blank stare.

He moved towards the piano, righted the stool and sat. He glanced at her again; still no response. He rested his fingers lightly on the keys and very softly began to play the Sonata, the piece of music that he had started to call Velvet's Song. Lost in the melody, he'd forgotten that Velvet was sat there until midway when he noticed a sound over the music. He looked over to her and his fingers became still. She was hunched over in the chair, arms wrapped tightly around her chest as she sobbed. Her shoulders shuddered as she gasped for air.

Linen sat uncomfortably for a moment. He remembered

how she had sent him away the last time she was upset, and wondered if he should leave the office. But his caring Faerie nature took over and he moved slowly to her side. He carefully wrapped an arm around the distraught Old Soul and murmured soothingly. Instead of the rebuff he was expecting, Velvet buried her head in his chest and continued to sob. He smoothed her hair and tried to project a calming energy towards her. Gradually, her cries subsided into sniffles, and she clicked her fingers to manifest a box of tissues. She wiped her face and took a few deep breaths. She pulled back a little and looked into Linen's concerned face.

"Linen, I-"

"What the hell is going on here?" a voice interrupted loudly.

Startled, Linen jumped back from Velvet and lost his balance, tumbling to the floor. He picked himself up and peered over the top of Velvet's desk.

"Corduroy! You scared us, I didn't hear you knock." Velvet straightened up and tried to sort out her wildly disarrayed hair.

"What's going on?" Corduroy advanced towards Linen, who stayed behind the desk. "You don't hang around do you? Laguz has only been gone two minutes and you've already moved on to the next guy!"

Velvet blinked in shock. She looked at Linen, still hiding, and laughed tiredly. "Oh, Corduroy, keep your pants on. It's nothing of the sort. I was just a little, well, in quite a bad way after Laguz's departure, then Magenta also left. Linen was just comforting me, that's all."

Linen bobbed his head in agreement, still looking a little scared of the stormy-looking Professor of Death.

"Comforting you," Corduroy scoffed. "It looked like a hell of a lot more than that to me."

Velvet frowned at Corduroy; she was beginning to get annoyed. "I'm sorry, Corduroy, if you cannot believe me, but I assure you, it's the truth." She stood and gestured for Linen to stand too. She clicked her fingers making the box of tissues vanish and she suddenly looked a little more presentable. "I don't see how it is any of your business, anyway."

Corduroy glared at Linen as he quickly scurried past. He grabbed a few things from his desk and hurried out the door.

"What can I do for you Corduroy? I assume you came here for a better reason than to spy on me?"

"I came to see how you were, after losing Laguz. But I can see that you're just fine now."

He turned and strode out of the room. Velvet sighed and dropped heavily back into her chair. She recalled their tense conversation in the main hall the previous day and frowned. Something was definitely up, but what? Normally she would follow him and talk to him, find out what his problem was, but she had no energy left to bother. She closed her eyes and recalled Laguz's face as he'd turned away from her. A tear slid down her face, and she brushed it away. She swore to herself that she would picture his face every single day, so that there would be no chance of forgetting him this time. After all, he was waiting for her.

Suddenly, without warning, another long-lost memory surfaced. She could see Laguz very clearly. His back was to her; he was looking out to the ocean from their home in Atlantis. His beautiful body was framed by the red sun setting over the horizon. She was sat at a beautiful piano, and was playing their song. The one she had written especially for him.

Velvet's eyes snapped open and the scene faded. As if still in the dream, she stood and moved towards the piano. She sat on the velvet-covered stool and placed her long, creased fingers on the keys. She closed her eyes and began to play. As the music enfolded her in its embrace, she understood. Her heart filled with joy as she realised that this song would always link them together, and that if only she could remember it when she got to Earth, it would bring them together again.

*   *   *

Long after the last note faded away, Velvet was still sat at the piano, her fingers just resting on the keys. A soft chime brought her back to the present moment. She wiped her face with the back of her hand and answered.

"Yes, Beryl?"

Beryl's face appeared on the wall. "I'm sorry to intrude, Velvet, but I have several messages from the second years, it seems that some of them are already hearing the call to Earth and would like some guidance before they go. What should I tell them?"

Velvet took a breath. "Tell them to meet me in the main hall. I will be there in ten minutes."

"Of course, Velvet. I will do that right now." Beryl paused, then bit her lip. "Are you okay?"

Velvet sighed. "Not yet. But I'm sure I'll be just fine."

Beryl smiled kindly. "If you need me…"

"Thank you, Beryl." Beryl nodded and her face faded away.

Velvet looked down at the gleaming ivory and ebony keys in front of her. All this time, she had forgotten that she used to play in Atlantis. She was never concert material, but creating simple melodies had brought her an immense amount of joy. It was amazing that she had managed to suppress it for so long. And to think, if it wasn't for Linen, she might never have remembered! She sighed. She had better go find him and apologise for Corduroy's rudeness. She should also thank him, too. Despite her misgivings at the beginning, she felt he would make an excellent Head of the Academy.

She stood slowly and concentrating on Linen's face, she clicked her fingers.

*   *   *

"Linen," she said softly. The poor soul just about jumped a mile at the sound of his name. He looked around and relaxed when he saw it was Velvet. He patted the bench he was sat on in the Angelic Garden.

"Come, join me."

Velvet sat next to him, and they sat quietly for a moment.

"Linen, I wanted to apologise for Corduroy's behaviour, I have no idea what's got into him recently. But he has been extremely rude and it's unacceptable."

Linen shrugged. "Don't worry about it. I'm sure he meant no harm." Despite his flippant tone he glanced furtively around him.

"Nonetheless, I'm sorry. I also want to apologise for being such a mess. But I'm very grateful for your comfort; I hope though, that we can keep my little breakdown between us."

Linen nodded, thinking about the Faerie, Aria. He would have to speak to her, make sure she didn't go round telling everyone what she had seen.

"And finally, I wanted to thank you. For coming back to the Academy, for helping me remember my past through your music. If it weren't for you, I wouldn't have even met Laguz once more before he was called to Earth. So thank you. I think you will be a wonderful Head of the Academy, and I think the Children will flourish under your instruction." Velvet glanced at Linen, whose cheeks were the same bright red colour as his hair.

Velvet patted his hand and stood. "I must go. Some of the second years have been called already; they are awaiting some last minute counsel before they leave."

Linen looked up in surprise. "Already? They only just got here."

Velvet smiled sadly. "Yes, it seems that things are moving ever more rapidly with each passing day. I believe that we will be losing and gaining Earth Angels every day. Once the final class of trainees have been called, I believe then, that the Academy will be turned over to you, and I too, will return to Earth." Velvet looked down at the shimmering path. "I just hope it's not too late," she added in a whisper.

She took a deep breath and smiled through her uncertainty.

"I will see you later."

Linen nodded and she disappeared.

Chapter Sixteen

"Do you think she's okay then? Do you think we should do anything?" Amethyst asked, concerned.

Aria shrugged. "I don't know. She looked a complete mess! Her white hair and wrinkles are back too. Do you think that means he's left already?"

Amethyst shook her head. "I'm not sure. It would seem likely though, considering her state. Losing a Twin Flame after such a short reunion must be quite devastating." She was thoughtful for a moment. "It seems cruel that he would be called away so soon after them finding one another again."

Aria shook her head vigorously. "If that's what happens to you when you find your Flame, I think I'd rather not."

Amethyst smiled sympathetically. "I know it must be hard to believe that the pain could possibly be worth it, but it is, my dear Faerie. Without knowing great pain, we cannot know great love."

Aria stopped bouncing up and down on her bed, which was currently a giant toadstool with fresh flowers as the bedding and looked at Amethyst curiously.

"Have you met yours then? Your Flame?"

Amethyst shook her head. "No. I haven't, though I hope to when I get to Earth."

"How can you believe in this 'great love' if you've never experienced it?"

"Faith, little one. I have faith that it is true. And that I will find it," she smiled. "Or it will find me."

Aria raised an eyebrow. "All this Flame business seems way too much hassle to me. I think if I were going to Earth, I'd join a convent."

*   *   *

The chattering voices quietened as Velvet entered the main hall and stood centre stage. She looked out at the crowd of faces, a little sad to see that so many of the second year Earth Angels had already been called. Still, it seemed that Earth needed them more than Heaven did right now.

"First of all, I would like to thank all of you for coming back, and for giving life on Earth another chance. I hope that you will all succeed in Awakening in your next life, and that you will help with the shift in consciousness. I know we haven't had long together, but I hope that the information you have gained in this short time was sufficient enough to be of use to you." She glanced around the room and her gaze rested on Emerald, who was clutching the hand of another Angel with a worried look on her face.

"Does anyone have any pressing questions to ask before you leave?"

Emerald's hand shot up and Velvet nodded at her.

"Is there anyone we can speak to about the calling? I believe there has been a mistake."

"What is the mistake, dear Angel?"

"I have heard the call, but my soulmate, Mica," she nodded to the Angel at her side, "has not. And I can't imagine that the Angels would separate us now. We are Twin Flames. We are two parts of a whole."

Velvet smiled sadly. "I'm afraid that there has been no mistake. It seems that Flames who are together in this dimension are indeed being called to Earth at different times. I do not know the reason why, though."

"How do you know this? Are you sure it isn't a mistake?"

Emerald asked, a little desperately.

"I know this because my own Flame, with whom I was reunited just a day ago has already been called to Earth. He left just last night."

Emerald's mouth opened in dismay. "I'm so sorry," she whispered.

Velvet smiled at the Angel. "It was difficult. But I'm hoping that in time, the reasons will become clear. As I understand it, you will not be able to ignore the call for long. When it's your time to go to Earth, you must go. And hope that your Flame won't be far behind you."

Emerald nodded, her eyes glistening with unshed tears. Mica tightened his hold on her and they seemed to melt together into one.

Velvet turned to the others. "Does anyone else have any questions?"

Another hand was raised. "Do you have any advice on how we can Awaken faster?"

Velvet thought this over for a moment. The music from earlier filled her mind. "I guess the best thing I can tell you is to listen. Listen to yourself. Listen to the Angels whispering to you. Listen to music and listen to the sounds of nature. All of the answers you seek can be found if you just ask the right question, then listen for the answer. Listen. And you will Awaken. Listen, and you will find yourself again." She looked at the distraught Emerald. "Listen, and you will find your Twin Flame, your soulmate." She thought of Linen. "Listen, and you will always find your way home again."

There was a silence as they all took in her words, trying to commit them to the memory of their very cores.

Velvet sensed a shift in energy then, much like she had with Laguz.

"I wish you all the very best of luck. May you live fully, love fully and hopefully even see the Golden Age." She took a step back, and before she could even blink, the entire group of Earth Angels disappeared. All except two.

Emerald was clinging onto Mica, wincing at the loudness of the call in her mind, but desperate not to let go. Velvet looked down at the hem of her robes, not wanting to intrude on their last moment, but not wanting to leave in case she was needed.

She could hear Mica whispering urgently to Emerald, and then there was a pause.

Velvet looked up in time to see Emerald finally let go of Mica, and with an anguished cry, disappear.

Mica stood there for a moment, staring at the space where his love had stood just moments before. Then he crumpled to the ground.

A tear slid down Velvet's cheek as she recalled the incredible pain that she had felt at the exact moment that she had let Laguz go. She stepped down from the stage and reached out to the Earth Angel, hoping to help ease his pain.

*   *   *

Aria and Amethyst were on their way to the gardens to meet some other friends when they bumped into Linen.

"Oh! Aria! I was hoping to see you," Linen said, looking a little stressed.

Amethyst looked at the little Faerie and noticed how she blushed at this.

"I was hoping that perhaps you could keep what you saw in the office earlier to yourself." He glanced at Amethyst, unsure of how much to say. "You know, when Velvet returned."

Aria looked at Amethyst a little guiltily then nodded. "Of course, I, uh, won't tell anyone else. I promise."

Linen nodded distractedly, glancing about him. "Good, good. I'll see you in the morning then."

Aria nodded. "Yes, nine-thirty. I'll be there."

Linen smiled then hurried past them down the hallway.

"Join a convent, huh?" Amethyst said cheekily as Aria

stared at Linen's retreating back.

Aria turned to Amethyst, frowning. "What?"

Amethyst laughed and continued towards the gardens.

"No, seriously, Am, what did you say?" Aria asked, flying after her friend.

Amethyst shook her head. "Doesn't matter. Let's go, we'll be late for meeting Rosa and Cerise otherwise."

"Oh, Am! Tell me! Please!"

Amethyst sighed. "I was just commenting that perhaps you did believe in love after all."

Aria frowned. "What are you talking about?"

"I'm talking about how you went bright red when a certain Faerie spoke to you."

Aria's eyes widened. "You think I fancy Linen? Oh please! I do not!" She shuddered. "Nope, that is most definitely not going to happen."

Amethyst smiled at her vigorous protests. "We'll see," she muttered to herself.

They arrived in the Elemental Garden, and found their friends already gathered by the unicorn statues.

"Guess what?" Aria exclaimed, flying up to them. "I'm staying here! I'm going to teach the Children!"

"Oh, Aria, that's wonderful," Rosa said. She looked at the little Faerie's wings. "I'm quite envious, I must admit. I miss my wings already." She shifted her weight from one foot to the other. "This body takes some getting used to."

Aria smiled sympathetically. "I'm sorry, Rosa. I didn't mean to make you sad."

"No, no. This is good news, Aria. I'm very pleased for you." Rosa smiled. "I'm still happy to go to Earth. Honestly, I'm very much looking forward to finding my Twin Flame."

Aria rolled her eyes. "Oh Goddess, not you too!"

Amethyst smiled at Rosa. "I'm very excited at the prospect too. I was wondering though, do you think that all souls have one, or is there just a select few?"

Tiring of the conversation, Aria flew off by herself,

leaving the newly human souls to talk of meeting their other half.

"Twin Flames. Honestly. You'd think they'd have better things to do when they go to Earth," she muttered. She was so lost in her own mutterings that she hadn't noticed where she was. She glanced around and saw the jewelled city of Atlantis. She was about to turn around and go back to the Elemental Garden, when she heard Velvet's voice. She stopped and decided she'd check to see if she was okay.

Aria flew quietly towards where she'd heard Velvet speak, then stopped short of intruding. She could see Velvet standing next to the bench facing where the statue of the Merman had once been. Sat on the bench was Corduroy.

"You called, Corduroy?"

Unable to help herself, Aria moved closer until she could hear the conversation clearly, while remaining invisible to the two Old Souls.

*   *   *

"I'm surprised you came," Corduroy said a little bitterly. He looked up at Velvet's confused face and softened slightly. "But I'm glad that you did," he added. Velvet sighed and sat next to him.

"What's going on, Corduroy? Why have you been acting so strangely recently?"

"Isn't it obvious?"

"Honestly? No, it isn't. You need to spell it out for me here."

Corduroy turned to face Velvet. He lifted a hand and stroked Velvet's cheek.

Suddenly aware of their close proximity, Velvet shifted uncomfortably. Unaware of her discomfort, Corduroy gripped her chin softly and leaned down to her. Their lips met and he kissed her, hard.

Velvet wrenched herself out of his grip and leant back,

shocked.

"What the hell are you doing?" she asked, blinking rapidly.

"I'm spelling it out for you." Corduroy reached out to pull her to him again, but she resisted.

"No, you're kissing me. What on Earth is going on, Corduroy?" She shifted backwards on the bench out of his reach and crossed her arms across her chest.

Corduroy frowned. "I can't believe it's not obvious. Velvet, I love you. I always have. During all of the lifetimes we have known each other, and during the entire time we have been at the Academy together. I have been in love with you."

Velvet's eyes widened. "How was I supposed to know? Why didn't you say anything? I thought we were just friends. I had no idea."

Corduroy shrugged. "I didn't know how to. You know me; I find it difficult to express how I feel."

"Why now? Why tell me after all this time, when I've finally rediscovered my Twin Flame? I mean he only just left! Did you honestly think I would just forget him again and jump into your arms?"

"You jumped into Linen's quickly enough."

Velvet stood, outraged. "I have already explained that it was nothing of the sort. I cannot believe you, Corduroy! You have never given me any indication of your feelings for me. I am not a mind reader!" She took a deep breath. "And I have no intention of being with anyone but Laguz. So I'm afraid that's the end of this conversation." Velvet turned away to leave.

"I might as well go then," Corduroy said sullenly.

Velvet stopped and looked back at him. "Go? Where?"

Corduroy looked up at her, his face pained. "Earth. They're calling me already."

Velvet felt a flicker of surprise and sadness, but dismissed it. "Perhaps you should. I don't think it would be wise for us to work together now anyway. I will teach your class myself."

Corduroy sighed. "You're not even going to miss me, are you?"

Velvet softened slightly. "I will miss our friendship, Corduroy. I wish we weren't parting like this, but I can't change that now."

Corduroy was silent as he stared at the paving stones beneath his feet.

"Goodbye, Velvet," he whispered.

Before Velvet could reply, he was gone.

*   *   *

Aria watched Velvet's shoulders slump as she stared at the now empty bench. She tried to process all of what she had witnessed, but as much as she hated to admit it, the part that stuck most in her mind was Corduroy's accusation that Velvet had jumped into Linen's arms. She couldn't help but wonder what he had meant by that. It irked her that it bothered her so much. She hoped that Amethyst wasn't right, and that she wasn't really falling for the wiry, red-haired former Faerie.

Shaking the thought from her mind, she watched Velvet for a few moments, then blinked as she too, disappeared suddenly. Aria hoped that Velvet would be okay; she seemed to be having a pretty tough day. Aria flew slowly back to the Elemental Garden where she had left her friends. She found them all laughing uproariously about something, and she did her best to join in the light-hearted banter, but found herself struggling to keep the images of Velvet and Corduroy's embrace from her mind. Not to mention her own mental images of Velvet and Linen getting cosy with each other.

Amethyst noticed that Aria seemed distracted and made a mental note to ask her later what was wrong. She wondered what else could possibly have happened. Amethyst didn't get the chance to speak to Aria until much later that night, just before they were retiring for the day.

"Aria, are you okay? You seemed a little distracted earlier, after you came back to join us."

Aria sighed and snuggled under the flowers that covered her bed.

"I went for a wander, and I saw something that I really shouldn't have."

Amethyst frowned. "What did you see, little one?"

Aria did her best to describe the exchange between Corduroy and Velvet, leaving out the part about Linen.

"Oh dear," Amethyst clucked sympathetically. "Poor Corduroy. I hope he made the transition to Earth okay."

"At least now you don't have to put up with his awful Death classes." Aria shuddered.

Amethyst smiled. "Yes, I suppose every cloud has its silver lining."

"What cloud? If you ask me, there are no bad points at all to Corduroy leaving!"

"Now, Aria," Amethyst said reproachfully. "He was a good professor. I wonder who will replace him?"

"Oh, Velvet is. She said she would be teaching his classes. Though with all the new Earth Angels arriving daily, I can't imagine that she will have the time to."

Amethyst sighed. "It can't be easy, keeping on top of all the changes taking place right now."

"No, it can't," Aria agreed. "I wouldn't be able to do it." There was a silence as they listened to the gentle snoring of their room-mate, Tm.

"Are you excited about tomorrow?" Amethyst asked.

Aria pulled her cover of flowers up to her chin and turned her head away from Amethyst. "Uh huh," she mumbled. Amethyst would have bet anything that her Faerie friend's face was a brilliant shade of red.

"That's what I thought."

"Good night," Aria mumbled, faking sleepiness.

"Good night, little Faerie," Amethyst replied, smiling into the darkness.

*　　　*　　　*

Velvet lay in her bed later that night, and went through the days' events in her mind. It seemed unbelievable that she had shared her bed with Laguz just yesterday evening. The rapid changes were leaving her head spinning. She couldn't even dream of what the next day might bring. She sighed and shifted about. Somehow she didn't think she'd get much rest tonight. After laying there in the dark for a while longer, Velvet couldn't stand her thoughts any more, and clicked her fingers.

She reappeared in her office. Without bothering to light the room, she sat at the piano and began to play very softly. She played her song for Laguz first, then she played some of the other melodies she had written while in Atlantis. Each one brought back other lost memories of her time in the jewelled city.

Helping the people of Atlantis through her visions of the future. Walking hand in hand with Laguz down the streets to the local market. Stargazing on the beach while the waves crashed onto the sand. In every memory she could see Laguz, and felt how it had been to be so close to him, to be with him all the time. No matter what happened, they were inseparable, until the end.

The music changed suddenly, and Velvet found herself playing a sad mournful song filled with longing and pain. The melody brought back another lost memory of when she'd had the vision of the fall of Atlantis. She saw herself telling Laguz her idea, of changing them all into ocean people. She saw herself become weaker with each transformation.

The notes became slower then, and each one struck a chord deep in her soul.

She remembered the moment that she gave Laguz all she had left; when her soul left her body in Atlantis, and arrived on the Other Side.

When Velvet played the last note, a tear fell and hit a key. She knew then that it would be her last tear. She would be strong now. She would do the best job she could in getting the Earth Angels to Earth, then she would join them. And she would find Laguz. She thought briefly of Corduroy and shook her head. She was sad to lose another friend, but there was nothing she could do to stop it. She hoped that one day he would forgive her for not returning his feelings.

Lost in her thoughts, she hadn't noticed Linen's presence until she felt his hand on her shoulder.

"I had no idea you could play," he said softly. "The music was so beautiful, I just came back to pick something up and I felt compelled to listen. Why didn't you tell me?"

Velvet shrugged. "Until earlier today, I had forgotten that I could play. I used to play in Atlantis. I wrote the song that you played for me, it seems."

Linen frowned. "I thought Tartan said that the piece was only written recently."

"Yes, well, almost everything from Atlantis was lost to the human world. Perhaps the music was channelled later on by another soul. After all, music comes from the universal source, humans and musical instruments are merely the channels that the music is heard through."

"So all music that exists in this age existed in the age before? And maybe even in ages previous to that?"

"Yes, most likely."

"Wow. I guess I'd never really thought about it before."

Velvet took a deep breath. "There are many things that exist that are never thought of, Linen. That's what makes our Universe such an interesting one to exist in."

Linen patted her shoulder. "Well, I think I've done enough thinking for one day. I'm going to rest. Are you going to be okay?"

Velvet nodded and looked up at Linen. "Yes, thank you. I think now that I may be able to rest too." She stood up and surprised Linen by giving him a hug. "Good night, Linen."

She clicked her fingers and vanished.

"Good night, Velvet," Linen said to the empty room.

*　　*　　*

Velvet was already sat at her desk, organising her busy schedule for the day when there was a knock at the door.

"Come in," she called. The door vanished and Aria flew in. She looked at Linen's desk and her face fell a little.

"Oh, I was supposed to meet Linen here at nine-thirty?"

Velvet smiled. "You're a little early, my dear Faerie. It's only eight-thirty, Linen isn't up yet I don't think."

"Oh!" Aria squeaked, embarrassed. "This whole time thing is taking a little while to get used to; I must have read the clock wrong."

"No worries dear, you're welcome to wait here for Linen; he's usually in before nine. Or you can come back in an hour if you wish."

Aria thought for a moment. "I'll wait," she said, flying over to the piano stool and perching there lightly.

Velvet nodded and went back to her paperwork. She was almost done when Linen arrived, whistling a jaunty tune. He stopped short when he saw Aria waiting.

"Oh!" He looked at the clock on the wall, confused. "I'm not late am I? What time did we say we would meet?"

Aria shook her head. "No, no. You're early. I read the time wrong, I was an hour out." She blushed, and hoped that Linen wouldn't think she was an idiot.

Linen chuckled. "Easily done. Not to worry." He went over to his desk and pulled out a list. "We have two options for today. We can either go to the Angelic Realm to recruit new teachers or the Elemental Realm."

Aria bounced up and down. "The Elemental Realm!" she said excitedly. "I'd love to go back to visit."

Linen smiled. "The Elemental Realm it is." He took out some new brochures he'd made for the School for the Children of the Golden Age, and tucked them into a briefcase. He looked up at Aria. "Ready?"

Aria nodded then looked around, a little confused. "How do we get there?"

"Ah," Linen smiled. "Magick, of course." He turned to

Velvet. "Would you be so kind?"

Velvet smiled. "Of course. If you can hold hands it would make it easier for me."

Linen nodded and held his hand out to Aria. A little shyly, she flew forward to grab hold of it. Velvet smiled a little when Aria blushed brightly when their hands linked together.

"When you wish to return, just click your fingers, okay?"

Linen nodded and turned to Aria. "You might want to close your eyes for this."

"Why?" Aria asked.

Linen squeezed her hand gently. "Just trust me on this."

Aria nodded and closed her eyes tight shut.

Linen smiled at Velvet and did the same. She clicked her fingers and they both vanished.

*　　*　　*

Velvet arrived at the main hall early. She felt very organised and in control, a feeling that had eluded her since the beginning of term. She was sticking to her decision from the night before and concentrating on the tasks at hand. The main one being to prepare the Earth Angels for their most difficult mission yet.

She stood centre stage at exactly nine o'clock and welcomed the Earth Angels. The number had yet again increased, despite the fact that a large group had left for Earth the day before.

"Good morning! I'm glad to see that you have remembered that we are combining the two groups. Now we know that we are on a very limited time scale, and due to the fact that I am now teaching several classes to the trainees, I thought it best to just have all of you here each morning and evening. I assume that some of you will be leaving each day, and so I hope that I impart the right information to help you along the way." She paused to look around the sea of faces.

"Today, I wanted to talk to you all about fear. This is

something a pure being would know nothing about. But seeing as you have all spent at least one lifetime on Earth recently, I thought it might be useful to hear your ideas on fear. Did you experience it? Were you taught it? Was it an instinctive thing as a human to be fearful? Did it prevent you from doing anything?" She gestured around the room. "I would like to hear your thoughts. So, if you would like to share something, please, raise your hand."

Despite the large number of souls, only six put their hands up. Velvet nodded to one of them.

"The soul in the third row, wearing black."

The soul stood up, and spoke in low, yet ringing tones. "My name is Obsidian. And I was on Earth for just twelve years. In my time there, though my family tried to drum fear into me, telling me what to do, what not to do, I never developed the sense of fear. I got told off for being stupid and reckless quite often. But to me, nothing terrible could possibly happen because I knew that death wasn't terrible. Dying was simply a way to get home. And so I did not fear anything that could hurt my physical body. Which, of course, is why I ended up leaving so quickly. My lack of fear led to my physical body dying." He shrugged. "What twelve year old boy doesn't love climbing trees in thunderstorms?" There were a few scattered giggles around the room.

"I think that a small amount of fear can be a good thing – for your physical body, anyway," Obsidian continued. "Fear causes us to be more careful, to look after ourselves. Fear stops us from being stupid and reckless. But there is also the other side of it. Too little fear may cause the physical body to die, but too much fear causes the spiritual body to die. Trapped by fear in a boring life, our spirits die, and so our bodies go through the motions without experiencing anything. As Earl Nightingale quite rightly said: 'Most people tiptoe through life, hoping to make it safely to death.' Once fear overtakes a soul, and shuts the love and light out, then that person is merely tiptoeing through life so that they can die from old age.

Life is to be experienced, to be filled with joy and happiness. Not wasted by being dull."

"Life is either a daring adventure or nothing!" a soul called out.

Obsidian nodded. "Indeed."

"I think your observations of fear are excellent, Obsidian. It is true that fear can save a human as well as paralyse them. The objective then, is not to rid humans of fear completely, but to help them to use fear to their own advantage. Use it to keep their physical bodies safe, but help them to control it so they can experience an eventful and exciting life. Does anyone else wish to share their thoughts on fear?" Velvet nodded at another soul with their hand raised. "Yes, the soul in the back row, also dressed in black."

"My name is Lacy," the soul said, her quiet voice ringing throughout the main hall. "I am an Old Soul, and so experienced the burning times of the current age. Even though I myself was not persecuted, in every life since those times, the fear has prevented me from living fully. In each life, I have let fear rule me. I have dampened any feelings of intuition, from fear of being seen as different. I have refused to allow myself to Awaken. In many of those lives, that fear may very well have saved me. If I had continued the practice of channelling energy and healing people, then I may well have been persecuted. But in my last life on Earth, I Awoke to some degree. I felt the healing energy trying to make itself known through me, but I refused to use this ability. I ignored it as much as I could. Even when I saw people in pain or distress, I feared people's judgement so much, that I did not help them." Lacy sighed, the pain of her previous life etched on her wise face.

"In my last life, my husband, my dear love, my soulmate, became very ill, and was beyond the help of traditional medicine. I knew, in my heart, that I could help him; that the healing energy that I could channel would make him feel better, perhaps even cure him. But because of my fears, I did nothing." A tear trickled down her face as she smiled sadly. "He died. But not before he suffered greatly. And the pain of losing him, the sorrow of the emptiness in my life and the sheer guilt of having stood by and done nothing, killed me too. I could not live with myself. I know now, that I would have been accepted if I had allowed myself to Awaken, for humans are beginning to understand that there is so much out there that is unknown and even magickal in nature, that they are more accepting. I hope to go to Earth once more and this time, live purely in the present. I do not wish to carry the old experiences, guilt and resentments from past lives with me into the next life. This time, I hope to not only Awaken and remember, but also help others to do the same. This time, I will use the channelled energies to help others."

"Thank you, Lacy. I'm sure that many other souls in the room have had similar experiences to yourself. Awakening can be a difficult process. And because it is human nature to crave acceptance and love, being openly different can be a painful and terrifying thing. If you manage to remember one thing, let it be this – do not crave acceptance from others, only wish to understand and accept yourself. Be yourself, and you will be a success. Try to become someone else, and you will have forgotten your own soul."

Velvet took a deep breath and looked around the room once more.

"Would anyone else like to share with us before we finish for the morning?"

A soul in the front row put his hand up. Velvet nodded at him.

"I have a question, for you, Velvet."

"Go ahead."

"What do you fear the most? When you get to Earth, what do you think will be your biggest fear? And do you think you will allow it to paralyse you, or do you think you could overcome it?"

Velvet was thoughtful for a few moments. "That's an

excellent question. It has been quite some time since I was on Earth, but fear is something that I am quite familiar with. Even here, in this dimension, where love is the most prevalent emotion, I experience fear. Usually in small amounts, therefore it does not affect me too much. But I think that when I get to Earth, my biggest fear will be that I might never find my Twin Flame. That I might spend my whole life alone, searching, hoping and wishing for my Twin, yet never finding him. Or that I might live my whole life in relationships that are wrong for me, all the while knowing that there is more to life than that. Or, actually, I think my biggest fear would be to find my Twin, and yet for whatever reason – society, circumstances – we cannot be together. I don't know if I would be able to ignore those fears, or if they will work for me or against me in my quest to find my Twin. But I know I am likely to have those fears, because they are fears that I have right now." She looked at the soul in the front row who had asked the question, and noticed that the soul sitting behind him was Mica. He was nodding in agreement with what she had said, and looked to be on the verge of tears.

"I know that many of you possibly have this same fear," she said quietly, looking at Mica. "And I would tell you not to worry, that the Universe will bring you and your Flame together, that you will of course spend a good part of your life with your Twin, but the truth is, I don't know that. I can only hope that it will indeed happen. For myself and for each of you. I guess in some way, though our union cannot be certain, at least we have the comfort of knowing that the other half to our soul is actually out there. That they are not a figment of our imagination, but that they do exist. And that they too, are looking for us."

Velvet smiled at Mica, who smiled back through his tears.

"Thank you all for joining me for this discussion this morning. I hope that what has been said will be of some use to you. Please join me here tonight, at seven o'clock. If you hear the call to Earth and you leave before then, I wish you all the love and happiness possible in your next life. May you remember and help others to remember too. Be confident and allow your wise soul to shine through. You have nothing to fear, you are already amazing in God's eyes."

Chapter Seventeen

Amethyst sat in her morning classes and found herself glancing over to where Aria normally sat. She missed the little Faerie. She always made classes more exciting and interesting. For some reason, Amethyst didn't have the patience to listen to the professors, let alone take in what they were saying. By the time she got to the midday break, Amethyst realised that she had not taken in a single word all morning. She was gently berating herself when she walked into someone in the hallway.

"Oh!" she exclaimed. "I'm so sorry, I wasn't paying attention."

The soul turned around and Amethyst was suddenly rendered speechless by his beautiful smile.

"Don't worry," he said. "I shouldn't have stopped so suddenly. I just realised I was going in the wrong direction."

Amethyst stared at him for a full minute before managing to find her words.

"Oh, uh, well, where are you trying to go?"

The soul consulted the purple glitter on his hand. "Room 510. I've only just arrived, and I thought I'd get settled in and relax before the session later this evening."

"You must be a second year."

"If that's what they're calling us, then yes, I guess I am," he replied, his smile even more glittering than before. He held his palm out to Amethyst. "Do you know where it is?"

"Where what is?" Amethyst asked, still slightly awe-struck.

The soul chuckled. "The room. Number 510?"

"Oh!" Amethyst smoothed her robes nervously. "Yes, I er, think I do. I mean, I'm in room 409, so it's probably not far from there. I mean, it's probably in the same sort of place one floor up." She paused. "Would you like me to take you there?" She held her breath, hoping.

The soul grinned. "That would be perfect. Thank you. Though I do hope I'm not taking you away from anything important?"

"Oh, no, I was just going for a walk to the gardens. It's well, this way." She gestured to the hallway to their left, and started slowly in that direction.

"Lead the way," he said, following her steps. "My name is Cobalt. What's yours?"

"Amethyst," she replied, her heart fluttering. "You're an Old Soul?"

Cobalt tilted his head. "I guess that would be an accurate label. I have had many, many lives on the Earthly plane over several ages. But I started out in the Angelic Realm actually."

Amethyst smiled. "I should have sensed that. I have only just left the Angelic Realm myself."

"Is that so? And yet you seem quite comfortable in a human body. When did you lose your wings?"

"Just yesterday actually."

"Yesterday? You have adjusted very quickly. I'm sure you will have no problems adjusting to human life on Earth. The heavy body is quite possibly the worst part." He smiled reassuringly.

"I hope so. I am looking forward to my first human life." She looked up at him and found herself melting in his gaze again. "Is that naïve of me, do you think?"

Cobalt shook his head. "I think it is admirable. If you manage to keep your optimism and innocence when incarnated on Earth, you will be much further ahead of the others when it comes to the Awakening process." He smiled when Amethyst blushed at the 'innocence' part.

All too quickly, they arrived at the door of his room. Amethyst stood awkwardly while Cobalt went in and surveyed the room. He scanned the notices on the board, and Amethyst was just thinking she should leave, when he came back out.

"I have a few hours until tonight's session, would it be okay if I tagged along to the gardens with you?"

Amethyst nodded quickly. Then in an attempt to erase her eagerness she added. "I have classes this afternoon from two, but I'm free until then." She calculated quickly. A whole hour and a half with him. She inwardly sighed happily.

"Excellent!" Cobalt fell into step with Amethyst again as they headed to the gardens. "So what has been the most memorable part of your time at the Academy so far?"

Amethyst smiled. "Well, on the very first day, I met this crazy little Faerie called Aria…"

*   *   *

When Velvet entered her office early that afternoon, she was in high spirits. The morning had gone well, and she was looking forward to the afternoon classes with the trainees and the evening session with the second years. More Earth Angels had been arriving all day; it would be interesting to see how many would be there at seven. As she swept in, she hid a smile at the sight that greeted her. Aria and Linen were sat, close together, talking about something. When they saw her, Aria jumped backwards and had she not had wings, would have toppled to the floor.

The two of them make quite a pair, Velvet thought, remembering Linen's many clumsy moments.

"Good afternoon!" she said cheerfully, making her way to her desk as though there was nothing amiss.

Linen cleared his throat. "Uh, good afternoon, Velvet." Aria just nodded mutely.

"Have you had a good time in the Elemental Realm?"

"It was brilliant!" Aria enthused, overcoming the awkwardness. "It was so cool going to see a different part of the Elemental Realm. We even bumped into some Leprechaun!"

Linen smiled at Aria's enthusiasm.

Velvet raised an eyebrow. "I trust that you weren't recruiting them as teachers for the school?"

Linen laughed. "No. Luckily I managed to get Aria to hold her tongue around them. I told her what happened the last time the Leprechaun attended the Academy."

Aria's eyes widened. "I knew they could be a little mischievous, but I never thought they'd be that much trouble."

"Yes, well, neither did we," Velvet remarked wryly. "But never mind, lesson learnt. Did you recruit any Faeries or other Elementals?"

Linen nodded. "Yes, we have several who are interested. We're going back there for second interviews once we've been to some other areas of the Elemental Realm and once we've been to the Angelic Realm too."

"Sounds great, Linen. I'm glad things are moving along nicely. I think the changes are occurring rather more rapidly than we assumed."

"Yes, they are. I've scheduled a meeting with the Indigo Children later to discuss their thoughts on the time frame we are now working to, and to see if they have any ideas of what will be happening on Earth in the coming years. I thought it might be useful to you in your lessons to have some idea of what is to come. Especially now that Magenta has left."

Velvet smiled warmly at the former Faerie. "It would be incredibly helpful to know as much as possible about what the Earth Angels will be facing. Thank you, Linen, I would love to know what the Children have to say. I'm afraid I won't be able to attend the meeting myself, I have a session this evening with the second years. But I wish you both luck with it."

"Ooh!" Aria exclaimed. "Am I coming with you, Linen?"

Linen chuckled. "I thought you would probably insist

anyway. Besides, you were brilliant in the Elemental Realm today, so yes, I think you should be at the meeting with me."

Aria beamed at the praise. "I better go and straighten myself up then! I'll meet you back here at six?"

Linen nodded and Aria practically floated out of the room. Linen watched her go with a bemused yet smitten look on his face.

"-don't you think?"

"Huh?" Linen asked, turning to look at Velvet, realising that he had no idea what she had just said.

Velvet smiled patiently. "I said Aria seems to be more suited to this environment than she would be to Earth, don't you think?"

"Oh yes, definitely. There's no question that she should stay here. Earth would be much too harsh a place for her."

Velvet bit back a laugh. Linen's tone was so definite; it was obvious that he was as taken with Aria as she was with him.

"I must be on my way; I have to teach Corduroy's classes this afternoon."

"You will let me know if there's anything I can do to help, won't you?"

Velvet smiled as she stood and straightened her robes. "Of course, Linen, I appreciate all of your help. But actually, I have managed to get things under control now. In fact, I don't think I've ever been so organised."

"Excellent. I'm glad that all of the drastic changes haven't thrown you off course."

Velvet paused by the piano, and turned to Linen. "The only thing constant in this Universe is change, Linen. Big changes, small changes, they all happen for a reason." She smiled. "I trust the reason. I trust the Universe."

Linen nodded thoughtfully. "Indeed. I know that I personally have changed a lot in the short time I have been here at the Academy," he smiled wryly. "In more ways than I thought was possible."

Velvet swept towards the door. "I think we all have."

*   *   *

"Amethyst? Amethyst? Are you with us?"

Amethyst was suddenly jolted out of her daydream and she blushed furiously when she realised that her classmates were all staring at her.

Velvet tried again. "Amethyst?"

"Yes?" Amethyst answered, having no idea what class she was even in, let alone what she had just been asked.

"I was just asking each soul for their thoughts on death. Taking into consideration what you have learnt here at the Academy," Amethyst noticed that she avoided saying Corduroy's name. "And what you knew previous to your training."

"My thoughts on death?" Amethyst repeated, straightening up. Velvet nodded. "Um, well, in the Angelic Realm of course, we do what we can to prevent humans from dying before their time. We try to keep them safe by whispering to them. Not because we fear death, or think it's a bad thing, but because we know what each human has gone to Earth to do, and we want them to accomplish their missions. Death is, well, quite beautiful actually. The shedding of the heavy human body, then the shedding of all worries, troubles, fear; it's like being reborn as a beautiful divine spark of light. It is being reunited with the Universe, the illusion of separation is shattered and you feel whole again. Death is the discovery of pure love. And the realisation that you may just be one drop in the ocean, but you are a very beautiful drop."

Everyone in the class was nodding; the Starpeople looked a little awed.

One of them, Rectangle, looked a little confused. He raised his hand.

"If death is so beautiful, then why do some humans fear it so? Why do they avoid it all costs? Do they really believe what

Professor Corduroy taught us, that death is a hideous, painful black hole of non-existence?"

"Yes, it is true that some humans believe that. Many believe what they are taught through religion, science and other sources. They do not make up their own minds; they follow what has already been taught. But it is my belief that this will be changing. Humans are beginning to look at their lives, and indeed death, and they are beginning to wonder if there is more to it than what they have been taught. That maybe there is something that has been suppressed until now. It is the beginning of the Awakening."

"You know," Quartz, another former Angel spoke up. "I always watched humans and wondered why they fought with one another. I wondered why wars were started, why they would invent things that could cause mass deaths, and now I'm beginning to think that those who engage in such behaviour, are more aware than we assumed. Maybe they know, deep in their soul, that death is a beautiful thing. And that they want to experience it. Because life, as a human on Earth, is not always a beautiful experience. Some of it is ugly and painful."

"That may be very well," Amethyst interjected. "But what about the innocent people that wars kill who were quite happy on Earth? They didn't choose to go to war; they just were in the wrong place at the wrong time."

Velvet smiled. "My dear Angel, after all you have seen on Earth, do you really believe there is such a thing as being in the wrong place at the wrong time? Or indeed being in the right place at the right time? Everything that happens in a human's life happens because of his or her own choices. There is no such thing as chance, fate or luck - just choices."

Amethyst frowned. "But there are some cases, where the human really doesn't seem to have a choice in the matter. Are you saying that people choose to be sick, to die in wars or to lose everything and everyone they love?"

"I'm not saying that they have chosen to experience these things consciously, in fact they may not even have made the choices in their current lifetime. But everything in their lives was chosen by them at some point in their existence. The beauty of free will and choice though is this – when a human is experiencing something undesirable in their life, they get to choose how they experience it. They can choose to be upset, angry or miserable, which is perfectly acceptable, or they can choose to see it as an opportunity to grow, to realise their own strength or as a time to end what they knew before and to begin again."

Amethyst smiled. "I guess I can see that," she said to Velvet. "I hope that I will remember that when I am on Earth."

"It's something that more humans are beginning to realise. Another choice that we make, when it comes to the death of our human incarnation, is made before we even get to Earth. I don't know if this was covered yet, but before your soul enters humanity, you decide when you will be making your exit. Now, when you become human, you do not remember this, so it's not like you will be counting down all your life until you reach the agreed upon age. But in your deep subconscious, this number will be known, and your soul will endeavour to accomplish all that you set out to before that time comes."

"How do we know, before we're even born on Earth when we should return to this dimension?" Leon, the Faerie Seer asked.

"You will discuss this with your Guardian Angel before your departure. I'm a little unclear as to the exact process, but you will discuss what you will do in your life and between you, you will come up with a rough age that you will exit at."

"What if you change your mind? What if you want to stay longer or come home earlier?" Onyx wondered.

"Then you can choose to do so," Velvet replied. "You have free will, dear Angel. Exactly as you do here. The age that you choose before your incarnation is an estimate, so that your soul has some kind of guideline to work to. For example, if you decided to exit at around the age of ninety, then your soul would know to pace itself, for if the body tries to do too much too quickly, then it will burn out long before that age. Whereas if you decided that your incarnation was to be a short one, then your soul would work hard to do as much as it wants to as quickly as possible."

"I was talking to a second year earlier," Amethyst said, her cheeks becoming a little rosy at the thought of Cobalt. "And he mentioned that Earth Angels are exiting Earth in large numbers right now. Why is that?"

Velvet thought for a moment. "In all honesty, I'm not certain why this is happening, but I do have a theory."

The class waited patiently for her to continue, as she gathered her thoughts.

"I believe that the Earth Angels have been exiting en-masse recently, because they have sensed the shift. At first I thought that the situation must be so dire, that they can't bear to be there, but seeing as all of these Earth Angels are coming back to the Academy in order to return to Earth immediately, I have changed my mind. I think that they have exited, to reborn in these times, so that they can help with the huge shift that is occurring. If they had remained on Earth, they would have been quite old at the time of the shift, and therefore maybe less able to help. Also, if the Golden Age does indeed happen, then they would have passed into spirit before they were able to experience it. By coming back now, and then being reincarnated on Earth during this time, they will be in a better position to help the Children. Also," she added, suddenly realising something. "I think that many of the Earth Angels returning to Earth now will be the parents of the new Children who are going to be entering Earth in the years to come."

"That would make sense. If the parents are Earth Angels, and they are Awakened, they will help the Children in their own Awakening," Onyx said.

"Yes, I think that is why we are seeing these patterns emerging. The Children will need all the help they can get. This was an excellent class everyone, I look forward to seeing you all next time." Velvet dismissed them then, and began to prepare for the next class. She looked up after a few minutes and saw Amethyst hanging back.

"Is everything okay? You were a million miles away earlier."

Amethyst nodded and blushed slightly. "Yes, I'm fine. I just wondered, well, I wondered if you were okay?"

Velvet's eyebrows lifted in surprise. "Me? Why yes, of course, I'm fine. Do I appear to be otherwise?"

Amethyst shook her head. "No, not now, but before, you seemed a little, well, sad."

Velvet smiled. "I will admit that there have been some recent changes that I have found a little difficult to get used to, but I'm doing very well now." She tilted her head to one side. "Thank you for your concern, dear Angel. I appreciate it. Now you'd better get going. Otherwise you'll be late for your next class."

Amethyst smiled and left the room. Her feet, like her heart, felt just a little lighter as she hurried along to her Human Culture class. She thought about Cobalt and her smile widened. They had agreed to meet later, after his evening session with Velvet. She couldn't wait to see him again. She slid into her seat just one minute before a grouchy Tartan began the class. Smile still fixed on her face; Amethyst tuned out his monotonous voice and slipped into another beautiful daydream.

*   *   *

"Come in!" Aria called out. She was flying excitedly around her room, trying to use up some of her excess energy before meeting Linen at six when someone knocked on the door.

The door vanished to reveal a very handsome soul in bright blue robes and a glittering smile. Aria stopped suddenly in her circles and stared.

"Uh, yes?" she stammered.

The soul smiled. "You must be Aria."

Aria's mouth formed a surprised 'o' shape. "How did you know that?" she asked, still mesmerised by his smile.

"An Angel told me," he replied cheekily. "Speaking of which, do you know where Amethyst is?"

"You're friends with Am?" Aria asked, a little jealously. "How come we haven't met?"

"I only met Amethyst early this afternoon, when I arrived from Earth. She did tell me all about you though. Said you were the most memorable part of her experience at the Academy."

Aria beamed, her jealousy forgotten. "She did? Oh bless her! She really is the best friend ever. Well," Aria flew over to the notice board and scanned the class schedule. "She'll be finished for the day in about five minutes. She has Human Culture 101 with Tartan in room 295. If you go there now, you'll be able to catch her as she leaves."

Cobalt nodded. "Room 295? That's by the gardens right?"

Aria shook her head. "No, it's near the main hall."

"And the main hall is near..." Cobalt grinned. "I'm afraid I'm not very good with directions."

Aria giggled. "Me neither. But I do know where the main hall is. Shall we go and surprise Amethyst together?"

"I think that sounds like a fine idea."

Aria looked at herself once more in the mirror, smoothed down a few wild hairs and joined Cobalt at the door. "Let's go!"

*   *   *

"Am!" Aria called out as soon as the Angel stepped through the door of the classroom. Amethyst blinked in surprise when she saw Cobalt standing next to Aria.

"What are you two doing out here?" she asked, smiling.

"Aria was kind enough to show me where I could find you. I thought we could go for a walk in the gardens. Aria has been telling me about the secret Leprechaun Garden."

"I thought we were meeting later?"

"We can meet then if that's better for you. I just thought-"

"No, no, now is fine," Amethyst cut in. "Um, Aria, will you be joining us?"

Aria was looking at the two of them a little suspiciously. "No, I have a meeting with Linen at six." She frowned. "What time is it now?"

"It's five after six."

"Oh!" Aria squeaked, flying away as quickly as her tiny wings would take her.

"Bye, Aria," Amethyst called out, chuckling. "She sure does make me laugh that one."

"Yes, she is quite entertaining. I understand that she won't be coming with us to Earth?"

Amethyst loved the way he used the word 'us'. Already she was finding it hard to imagine existing without him. She wondered how she had managed all these aeons.

"Amethyst? Are you okay?"

Amethyst snapped to attention, caught, for the third time that day, lost in her own daydreams.

"Oh! Yes, I'm fine. I was just thinking. No, Aria isn't coming with us. She has decided to stay here. And honestly, though I will miss her unbelievably, I do think she has made the right choice. She has been so happy since making the decision."

"Then it must be the right one. Shall we?" Amethyst nodded and they walked at a leisurely pace towards the gardens.

"We've never managed to get into the Leprechaun Garden, you know. You have to do all manner of tasks and solve lots of riddles before you can get the secret password, which makes a door appear. I've heard that even Velvet doesn't know the password."

"Well that sounds like a challenge. Shall we give it a go?" Cobalt asked, his smile lighting up his face again.

Dazzled by his smile Amethyst managed a nod and an uttered "uh huh," in response.

"Excellent. I love a good adventure."

*   *   *

"Yes, Beryl?" Velvet said in response to the sound of wind chimes.

Beryl's face appeared on the wall in the office. "I have Elder Damask here; he wishes to speak to you."

"Oh, sure, no problem. Put him through please, Beryl."

"No, he's not on the line; he's here, in person."

Velvet's eyebrows rose. "I see. Well, show him in then." Beryl nodded and faded from the wall. Velvet tried to straighten her desk and herself the human way but gave up. She clicked her fingers and everything fell into place just as the door vanished and Gold walked in.

Velvet stood to welcome him. "Gold! Welcome. Please, come in and make yourself comfortable." She gestured to the seat in front of her desk and Gold made his way forward slowly.

Once seated, there was a pause in the quiet room. Velvet noticed with slight apprehension that his nervous tick seemed to be back in action. She was just about to ask what he wanted when he cleared his throat.

"I just wanted to drop by to see how you were doing, after, well, all that happened with Laguz."

Velvet frowned. "I didn't realise you were aware of the situation with Laguz."

Gold smiled, his creased face tinted with sadness. "My dear Velvet. We Elders know all that happens within our dimension."

"If you know everything, then you must also know that I am fine. That I am now concentrating on getting the Earth Angels prepared and ready for their call."

Gold shifted a little uncomfortably in his seat and the out

of control tick was driving Velvet a little crazy.

"What are you really here for, Gold?"

"Ah, well, yes, I guess I did know you were okay," he said, stalling. "The thing is, Velvet, is that the Elders and I, we have decided, and this was after much debate and discussion, I might add-"

"Gold, please, just spit it out," Velvet said gently. She tried to dampen her impatience and her feeling of dread.

"We are going to alter your time."

Velvet frowned. "I'm not sure what you mean by that."

"In the past, at the Academy, you have always existed in the same time as the humans on Earth - minutes, days, weeks, years - they're the same as what is passing on Earth, yes?"

Velvet nodded. "We work to the same time scale so that Earth Angels can get used to it. It's not such a shock when they reach Earth. The only difference here is that we can still manifest instantly without the time delay."

"Yes, well, as I'm sure you are aware; things are changing very quickly in the Universe. And to accommodate these changes, it's been decided that time should slow down here."

"Slow time down?" Velvet shook her head, still confused. "I'm sorry, Gold; it has already been a long day. I'm afraid what you are saying still makes no sense to me."

Gold sighed. He wasn't the best when it came to explaining difficult things. "Okay, well, in the time it takes to experience one day here, a year will have passed on Earth."

Velvet blinked. She calculated this in her mind. "So after one week here, seven years will have passed on Earth? After one month, thirty years will have passed?"

Gold nodded. "Yes. Which is why Earth Angels are arriving and leaving every day."

"But that's ridiculous! The trainees can take up to ten years to graduate. By the time they get to Earth," Velvet did the maths quickly, "More than three thousand years will have passed! There might not even be any humans by then! Oh Gold, this is completely crazy, surely you can convince the others that this is a terrible idea?"

"Well, actually, this last class of trainees you have, they will be graduating in the next week or two. We will have to accelerate their training."

Velvet narrowed her eyes. "You mean, you aren't even going to try to stop this?"

Gold sighed and rubbed his eye. "I have been trying to do so for days. They cannot be swayed. This is the way it shall be."

Velvet leant back in her chair and considered this. "What about me? Will I be returning to Earth in the next couple of weeks?"

"I cannot say for sure. It may be a little longer."

Velvet shook her head. "Do you really think this is going to work? When will the new time come into effect?"

Gold cleared his throat nervously. "Ah, well, that's the thing. It already is in effect."

"Since when? When did it begin?" Velvet asked anxiously.

"Seven days ago. At the beginning of the new term."

"Seven days ago. So each day that's passed, it's been a year on Earth?" Gold nodded.

"I see. Well, I'm glad that you have come to tell me, though it would have been nice to have known sooner, I'm sure you did your best to change their minds." Velvet stood and Gold hastily did the same. "I have a session now, with the second years. So if you could see yourself out..."

"Yes, yes of course." Gold bowed his head slightly and retreated from the room. Velvet sat heavily back in her chair. One year for each day. She sighed and quietly did the maths in her head. It had already been two years since Laguz had reached Earth. In another week, it would be nine years. In two weeks it would be sixteen years. Another week again, it would be twenty-three. She rested her chin on her hand and fought to hold herself together. When she realised that things were changing rapidly, she had begun to hope that she would be going to Earth within a few years, and so the age gap between herself and Laguz would be manageable. It would be possible to be together again. But now, with the time slowing down here, it seemed that her dream of being in his arms again was becoming a very dim possibility.

Wind chimes sounded and Velvet stood. "Yes, Beryl?" she asked, gathering her things and filing her thoughts away for later.

"It is nearly seven, Velvet. Just thought you might need a reminder," Beryl said, her kind face appearing on the wall.

"Thank you, Beryl, I am on my way there now." Beryl smiled and the wall faded to white again.

Velvet took a deep breath to steady herself. Then she clicked her fingers.

*   *   *

Her thoughts too scattered to be wholly coherent, Velvet welcomed the Earth Angels who had arrived during the day, did general notices, then invited them to talk in small groups about what they hoped to accomplish in their next life on Earth.

She sat in her chair on the stage and wondered whether to inform the souls at the Academy about the change in the time difference. She certainly wished that she hadn't been told about it. Her earlier cheerful mood had completely evaporated and showed no sign of returning. She sighed and hoped Linen had more uplifting news to report from his meeting with the Indigo Children.

She tried to think of some good points that would come from the time change, so that if she did announce it to the Academy, she could point them out. But in her current state of mind, it was difficult to think of any. She supposed that it would at least feel like less time to her before she went to Earth. She wouldn't have to wait so long to be with Laguz again. But then, if he were more than twenty years older than her, would they even get to be together? Surely by then he would be married with children, settled in his life and doing well for himself? The last thing Velvet would want to do is appear in his life and disrupt things.

She sighed again and tried once more to think of the good points. But after an hour, she had come up with nothing. She refocused her eyes and glanced around the room. Most of the Earth Angels were still busy talking, but some seemed to be meditating or just sitting patiently, waiting for her to speak again. Making a snap decision, she decided to tell them about the time change. She noticed a soul sitting quietly to the side, a look of longing on his face, and she almost changed her mind. She was sure that Mica would be just as distraught as she was at the news. But she felt it was important for everyone to know as much as possible. It might just help them in some way. She took a deep breath and stood stiffly, her body feeling older than it did that morning.

"Earth Angels," she began, getting their attention. "I hope you have enjoyed learning from others what they hope to do on Earth, as well as perhaps refining your own missions for your next human incarnation. Now, just before this session, I had a meeting with an Elder, who has informed me of a rather big change that has occurred. I wish to tell you about it now, rather than keep you in the dark about it, as I was for the last few days." She took in another deep breath and began to pace slowly, gathering her thoughts.

"The time here has been greatly slowed down. The changes are happening so rapidly, that the Elders felt that the time scales needed to be changed to accommodate this. Basically, now, when twenty four hours pass at the Academy, a whole year will have passed by on Earth." She looked around the room and saw many dismayed faces. She couldn't even bring herself to look at Mica. "This is why we have been gaining Earth Angels and losing them to Earth daily; there aren't large groups of Earth Angels being born every day on Earth, but rather every year." Velvet paused and nodded as though a question had been asked. "I know this will be quite upsetting to those of you whose Twin Flame or soulmate has already left for Earth. I can only say that I feel the same way. And that I hope you will be called soon too. For it is my greatest wish, and I believe, the wish of the Universe, that you shall be together again."

She finally looked at Mica, and saw the tears steadily making their way down his cheeks.

"For now, we just have to look at the positive side of things and work hard to get you all on your way." She looked around the room again. "Are there any questions?" No one raised their hand. "Has anyone heard the call today?"

To this, about twenty people raised their hands. "I would like to wish you all the love and happiness in the Universe. May your human lives be everything you hope them to be. I will see the rest of you tomorrow morning, at nine-thirty, back here. I hope you all have a pleasant evening."

She turned and walked quickly from the stage. As soon as she exited, she clicked her fingers and reappeared in her bedroom. She tried to hold it in, but as she recalled the look of devastation on Mica's face, she crumpled onto her bed and sobbed.

Chapter Eighteen

"Wow, I didn't see that one coming," Amethyst said later, as she and Cobalt walked to the Angelic Garden. He had just filled her in on the evening session with Velvet.

"Yeah, it was a bit of a shock. I mean, it makes sense, when you really think about it. Earth Angels who have just left Earth would be returning so quickly, you'd have people remembering past lives and the people they knew in those past lives would still be alive. I can imagine it could cause a lot of déjà vu and confusion."

Amethyst nodded. "But I imagine that Velvet was probably thinking more about the fact that in just a few weeks' time, her Twin Flame, who is already on Earth, will be so much older than her, that they might not be able to reunite."

"Okay, now I get the look on her face," Cobalt said soberly. "Wow, I had no idea that was why she seemed so upset by the time change. When did he go to Earth?"

"Two days ago, I think."

"So he's already two years old." Cobalt shook his head. "That must be awful. Knowing that your soulmate is there, waiting for you, but that you might be too late getting to them." He stopped walking and looked at Amethyst, his usual smile replaced with a serious expression.

"Amethyst, I know we only met a few hours ago, and this may sound completely crazy, but well, I feel like there's a connection of some kind between us-"

Before he could finish his sentence, Amethyst stood on the tips of her toes and kissed him. Though shocked, he put his arms around her and pulled her in closer. Their kiss deepened and there was a sense of urgency in their embrace.

When they finally pulled apart, Cobalt's dazzling smile returned. "I think you said it better than I ever could have."

Amethyst smiled back. "I've been dreaming of doing that all day." She shook her head. "I didn't know that I had the courage to do it until just now."

"I, for one, am glad that you found the courage, Angel. I would also be quite happy if you found the courage to do it again."

"I'm sure I could just about manage that." Amethyst reached up and this time Cobalt met her halfway. She was so deeply wrapped up in him that she was oblivious to their surroundings.

"Am!"

Amethyst pulled back from Cobalt and quickly turned to find Aria hovering there, her hands on her tiny hips. Her eyebrows were raised; she did not look happy.

"Hey, Aria, meeting finished already?" Amethyst asked nonchalantly. She smiled a little as Cobalt wound his arms around her waist.

"Yes, it finished a few minutes ago. I thought we were going to hang out tonight, seeing as we haven't seen each other all day, but if you're busy…"

Amethyst smiled at the little Faerie. "Of course we can hang out. Cobalt and I were just, um, walking."

"Walking? Okaaaaay." Aria sighed. "I can hang out with Rosa and Myrt if you want to be alone."

"Actually," Cobalt cut in, "I should be going. I need to get some rest. It's been a long day."

Amethyst turned to him and they kissed once more. "I'll see you tomorrow?" Amethyst murmured.

"Of course," Cobalt replied. "I'll be at your room at twelve, if that's okay."

"Yes. I can't wait."

"Me neither." Cobalt squeezed her hand and gave Aria a little wave as he left the gardens.

"Oh my God, Am! You only met him a few hours ago and you're already sucking face!"

Amethyst sighed. "Oh, Aria, where's your sense of romance? It was love at first sight."

"Gag me. I think everyone around here has gone mad with all this Twin Flame stuff. Love at first sight? Oh, please! Everyone just wants to get some!"

"Aria! Honestly! It's not like that. And believe me when I say - when you meet your Twin Flame you will see for yourself what all the fuss is about."

"That's not likely to happen is it?"

Amethyst frowned and sat on the nearest bench, suddenly exhausted. "And why do you say that, little one?"

"Because I'm not going to Earth am I? The whole Twin Flame reunion nonsense is an Earthly thing - the miracle of love will save the world and all that stuff?"

Amethyst chuckled at the little Faerie's cynicism. "I thought Elementals were meant to believe in fairytales? Don't you believe in happily ever after, Aria?"

Aria frowned. "It's a nice theory, yes, but in practice, I don't know."

"Since when did you get all practical on me? Aria," Amethyst turned to her friend. "It's okay if you do believe, you know. No one will think you're mushy or soft or sappy because you believe in soulmates. It's a beautiful thing, to find your other half, your one true mate. And you're wrong about the Earth thing. Twin Flames can be found in any dimension at any time. So you never know, even one of the teachers you recruit for the Academy could be your Twin Flame. Anything is possible, Aria. Anything."

Aria was quiet for a while. "Do you think Cobalt is your Twin Flame?"

"I think there's a strong possibility that he is, yes."

"How do you feel when you're around him?"

"I feel..." Amethyst took a deep breath of the cool night air. "Complete. Like my soul is filled with love and joy and light. I feel like I want to sing and dance and just hold him all night and all day." Amethyst chuckled. "I have to admit, I loved the idea of Twin Flames and soulmates, but I had no idea it would be like this. I had no idea it would be quite so, well, magickal, I guess."

"Magickal," Aria repeated quietly. "Do you think it will be like that on Earth? I mean, humans don't even believe in magick do they?"

Amethyst bit her lip. "I hope it will be like that. I think that in the next few years, people will begin to believe in magick again. They will come alive again, and shake off the illusion they've been trapped in. I think some people on Earth have already achieved this."

Aria sat on the bench next to her friend, and leaned against her arm. "I'm going to miss you, Am. I'm so glad we get to be together here for a few years before you leave."

Amethyst swallowed. "Aria, about that," she turned to look at her friend, "I'm afraid things have changed a little."

*   *   *

Velvet had no concept of how much time had passed since she had collapsed onto her bed. She lay there still, face down on her purple velvet covers, and wondered what would happen if she never got up again.

Distantly, she heard wind chimes, but chose to ignore them. She sighed; she knew she was being pathetic. She knew that she had broken her steely resolve after just one day. But the black storm clouds that hung over her head were unrelenting. She wished they would just get it over with, and rain down all they had. Lightning, thunder - a damned good storm, that's what she needed. Clear the air around her. It was so heavy it was suffocating her right now.

Maybe there was something she could do about that. She shifted a little, held her arm up and clicked her fingers.

The ocean was calm when she reappeared on her beach. The sky was bright blue, not a cloud in sight. Velvet clicked her fingers and she was picked up by an invisible force to a standing position. She lifted her arms, and recalled a memory that had been locked away for four ages. She waved her hands in a complicated formation, and uttered the harsh words that were nearly painful to say.

Instantly, the sky turned an ugly black and purple. The ocean became turbulent and the waves grew, crashing onto the beach ferociously. The clouds roiled and shifted. As her hands moved faster, the first bolt of lightning struck, just feet away from her. She smiled as she felt the electricity whip around her. The crack of thunder that followed was deafening. Her hands danced in the strong winds that blew in from the ocean, and the lightning struck the sand repeatedly in a tight circle around her, making her hair stand out on end. Tears now accompanied her manic laughter. She shouted out more ancient words, their sound ugly and harsh on her tongue. In an ear-splitting crescendo, the thunder cracked louder until the final bolt of lightning hit Velvet's outstretched hands.

As she crumpled to the sand, the thunder rumbled away into silence.

* * *

"Beryl, have you seen Velvet this morning?" Linen asked, pacing around the office.

Beryl's concerned face appeared on the wall. She shook her head. "No, Linen, I haven't, I'm afraid. She's already late for her morning session, too. I've sent Tartan to tell the second years to come back in an hour."

Linen frowned; he glanced at the clock. "She's never this late. Not since Laguz left anyway. Have you checked her room?"

"I tried her room and got no answer. Do you want me to go in a check to see if she's there?"

Linen sighed, unsure. "I don't want to pry, but I'm worried about her, Beryl. She didn't turn up for our meeting last night, and now she's missing this morning. Yes, I think perhaps checking her room would be a good idea, could you?"

Beryl nodded and faded away.

Linen continued to pace up and down until she reappeared moments later.

"Her room is empty, Linen. It looks like she might have slept there last night, but she's not there now."

Linen shook his head. "I don't know where to look; do you have any idea where she usually goes?"

Beryl thought for a moment. "Mostly she used to just go visit Magenta, but she has left for Earth now, so I don't know where else she might be. Besides, to get there you would need the Old Soul Magick."

Linen nodded, and turned suddenly when he heard a sound from the doorway.

"Good morning!" Aria flew into the room and noticed the agitated look on Linen's face. "Am I late?" she asked.

"No, no, you're fine. We just have a slight problem that's all."

Relieved that he wasn't angry with her, she relaxed a little. "What kind of problem?"

Linen glanced at Beryl and she shrugged.

"We haven't been able to get a hold of Velvet. We're not sure where she's gone."

"Oh dear, was she still upset from yesterday's evening session?"

Linen frowned. "What happened yesterday?"

Aria recounted what Amethyst had told her. "Cobalt seemed to think she looked quite upset when she told them about the time change. Amethyst thinks it's because she might not get to be with Laguz anymore."

Linen sat on the edge of Velvet's desk. "I didn't know

about any of this. Beryl, when did Gold come here?"

"Just before the evening session yesterday, around six forty five, perhaps?"

"I'd already left then. That's why she didn't tell me," Linen said thoughtfully. "And no one has seen her since the end of the session last night?"

Beryl shook her head, and so did Aria.

"Right. I need to do something. Aria, could you stay here in case Velvet does return, so you can let us know?"

"But how will I contact you?"

"You just say my name three times and I'll be able to hear you."

"Wow, really? Okay, I can do that. Hang on, why don't you just do that to get hold of Velvet?"

"I already did," Beryl cut in. "She didn't answer."

"Right, I'm going to call Cotton or Chiffon to use their magick, maybe I can find her that way," Linen said.

"Cotton is in class, but Chiffon is available right now." Beryl said, checking the schedules.

"Right. Let's try it. Chiffon. Chiffon. Chiffon."

"Yes, Linen?" Chiffon's voice replied in his ear.

"Could you come to Velvet's office immediately, please?"

"Of course." There was a loud click and Chiffon appeared in the office, like an orange cloud descending from the heavens.

She took in their expressions and frowned. "What's wrong?" She looked around the room. "Where's Velvet?"

"That's what we're trying to find out. Chiffon, if we concentrate on Velvet should we be able to find her even if we don't know her location?"

Chiffon nodded. "It'll take a fair bit of concentration, but it should work, yes."

"Excellent." He walked over to Chiffon and grasped her hand. Aria looked on a little jealously. He turned to Aria. "I'll keep in touch." She nodded and Chiffon clicked her fingers.

*   *   *

It took a few moments to take in their surroundings. When Chiffon and Linen arrived on the beach, the black and purple clouds had receded but the sky was still a steely grey. The winds whipped around them and they looked up and down the beach. It was difficult to see much with sand blowing in every direction.

"Where are we?" Linen all but shouted, coughing as he got a mouthful of sand. Chiffon shook her head and concentrated. She clicked her fingers and the winds died down, the sand settled and suddenly it was quiet enough to hear the waves lapping gently on the shore.

"I don't know," she replied, still looking around them. Suddenly, something caught her eye. She squinted at something by the edge of the water. Linen followed her gaze.

"What is it?" he whispered. Slowly they walked towards the sand-covered object, unsure of what they were about to find. Just a few yards away, Linen broke into a run. He dropped onto the sand and began brushing the sand off of the purple velvet that was now visible. Chiffon joined him and together they uncovered a very still Velvet. Linen brushed the sand and hair from her face and called her name.

"Velvet. Velvet? Can you hear me?" He refused to panic like he had the first time he thought Velvet had died, that day in her office. "Come on, Velvet. Time to wake up now."

He reached for her hand and recoiled when he saw her blackened fingers.

"What the hell?"

Chiffon looked at them and then looked up at the skies. "Weather magick," she muttered.

"Weather magick?" Linen asked. He shook Velvet gently, trying to bring her round. "What does that mean?"

Chiffon shook her head. "I think it means she has left us."

Linen stopped shaking Velvet and looked at Chiffon. "Excuse me?"

Chiffon gestured at Velvet's prone form. "Her soul has left this ethereal body."

"Left?" Linen looked down at Velvet's closed eyes. "But we're in Heaven, the Fifth Dimension, the Other Side. You can't die here! We're not human, essentially, we're already dead!"

Chiffon placed a hand on Linen's arm. "What you say is correct. Velvet has not died." Linen sighed in relief, and Chiffon continued. "Because death, after all does not exist. Her soul, however, has left this body; therefore she is no longer with us here in this dimension."

Linen frowned. "I don't understand. How can she leave us now? Why would she leave? Where has she gone?" He dropped his head into his hands. "What are we going to do? We can't run the Academy without her. How am I supposed to tell her trainees that she just left them? When they need her the most?"

"I don't know the answers I'm afraid," Chiffon whispered. "We should get back to the Academy; they'll be waiting to hear from us."

Linen nodded. "Do we take her body with us?"

Chiffon shook her head. "There's no need. It will be taken care of." She stood and held a hand out to him. After one final look at Velvet's sleeping face, he took Chiffon's hand and let her pull him up. After a moment, she clicked her fingers and they vanished, leaving Velvet's body behind.

*   *   *

"Linen!" Aria squeaked when they reappeared in the office. "What happened? Are you okay?" She flew over to him and peered, concerned, into his drawn face. He seemed to have aged greatly in the last twenty minutes, looking more and more like the Old Soul he was pretending to be.

"We found her," he said heavily. "Actually, we found her body."

Aria frowned. "What do you mean?"

Linen walked slowly to his chair and sat. "I mean she has

left us. Her soul has left this dimension."

Aria shook her head. "But why would she leave us?" She looked at Chiffon, who stood by the door, her face pained. "Where has she gone?"

"We don't know, little one." Chiffon shook her head. "And I'm not sure if there is a way to find out. Magenta is no longer here, neither is Corduroy. Out of anyone, they might have had an idea." She lifted her shoulders. "I'm afraid I don't have the magickal strength to search the Universe for her."

"But there is someone who does," Linen said suddenly, jumping up out of his chair. "Beryl?" he called. Beryl appeared on the wall, looking worried.

"Oh, Linen! Did you find her?"

"Beryl, we need to get Gold here immediately, can you do that?" he asked, ignoring her question.

Beryl nodded. "Yes, of course. Give me a moment."

Her face faded away and two minutes later there was a knock at the door.

"Come in!"

The door vanished and Gold appeared. He swept into the room and looked around at the three of them stood there and Beryl's face on the wall.

"What's going on?" he asked.

"You're an Elder, you know everything that's going on, please don't pretend otherwise; we need your help."

Gold frowned and his right eye began to twitch. "I see. Let me rephrase that. How can I help you?"

"Velvet has left. We need to find her soul, immediately. She needs to come back to the Academy." Linen started to pace. "Everything is changing right now, and we need her to help us here. Who will teach the second years what they need to know before they leave for Earth? Who will teach her classes to the trainees? We can't do this without her, Gold. I don't care why she left, we need her back."

Gold shifted his weight from one foot to another uneasily and cleared his throat. "I'm afraid that getting Velvet back here is not something I can do."

"Who can then? There must be a way Gold! Where is she?"

"She... she is with the Angels right now," Gold replied hesitantly.

Linen turned to Beryl. "Get Athena in here, now." Beryl nodded.

"We cannot interfere!" Gold's raised voice made Aria and Chiffon jump. "She has free will. She chose to run this Academy, she can choose not to just as easily. If she wishes to remain in the Angelic Realm then that is up to her."

There was a knock at the door and Gold and Linen glared at one another.

"Come in," Aria called out.

Athena entered and quickly took in the scene. "Someone called?"

"I did." Linen said, narrowing his eyes at Gold and then turning to Athena. "We have a situation, and we need your help."

"Of course. What is it?"

"Velvet has left her body here and her soul is currently in the Angelic Realm. We're not entirely sure why she has left, but we're guessing it has something to do with Laguz and the change in time."

Athena frowned. "What change in time?"

Linen shook his head impatiently. "I'll explain it later. Right now, we need someone to go to the Angelic Realm and get her to come back. Seeing as you are the Head Guardian Angel. I think it should be you."

Athena frowned and looked at Gold who still had a hostile expression on his face.

"I cannot do that," she said softly. "She has free will, she can do-"

"Damn free will!" Linen shouted, making them all jump. "She has to come back!"

Athena went over to Linen and put a hand on his arm.

"Calm, Linen, calm. I can go to speak with her, but I cannot force her to do anything she does not wish to. I will try my best to make her see how much she is needed though."

Linen took a deep breath and made himself relax. "Thank you, Athena." He glanced at Gold. "I guess that is all I can ask of you."

Athena nodded and stepped back. "Can you take care of my classes for the rest of the day? I don't know how long I might be." Linen nodded.

She smiled, closed her eyes, and vanished in a golden cloud of feathers.

*   *   *

"Athena. What are you doing here?"

"Hello, Pearl, how are you?" Athena asked the brunette Angel.

Pearl smiled. "I am doing well, thank you. We weren't expecting you?"

"No, this isn't a planned visit. I have come because I believe that there is an Old Soul here, and I need to speak with her."

Pearl smile disappeared. "You mean Velvet? I'm afraid that she isn't available to speak with anyone right now."

Athena sighed. "Pearl, you know I don't like to be authoritative, but you will take me to see Velvet now."

Pearl looked up at the Head Guardian Angel and nodded. "Just, well, be careful. She's in a very delicate state right now."

Athena put her hand on Pearl's arm. "Velvet is one of my oldest and dearest friends. Don't worry, it will be fine."

Pearl smiled and turned from Athena. She walked through the gates and down a long winding path to a huge glassy lake. She gestured down the shore to a figure on the sand at the water's edge.

"She hasn't moved from that spot since she got here," Pearl whispered. She glanced sideways at the Head Guardian

Angel. "Is it true?"

"Yes it is. It will be happening quite soon, in fact. But don't worry, Pallas has been doing such a good job of running the Angelic Realm while I have been at the Academy teaching; I'm sure she will continue to do a fantastic job while I am on Earth."

Pearl sighed. "Will you come to say goodbye?"

Athena smiled at the Angel. "My dear, you know there is no need." She leant forward and hugged Pearl. "I will see you again, my dear. But right now," she looked down the beach. "There is someone I need to see."

Pearl nodded and stepped back. "Peace, love and light be with you always."

"And with you," Athena replied softly, before making her way slowly and cautiously down the beach towards her friend.

When she was just a few feet away, Velvet turned to look at her, a sad smile on her face. Her soul, no longer in a body, shifted and shimmered, giving the impression of what Velvet looked like in Atlantis.

"Velvet. My dear friend," she called out gently as she approached her.

"It didn't take you long. I guess Linen is more intelligent than I gave him credit for."

"He is extremely worried about you, Velvet. As we all are." Athena said softly, sitting on the sand next to her. "Are you alright?"

Velvet looked back at the lake and Athena followed her gaze. It became apparent then, why she was there. On the glass-like surface, Athena could see a young boy, a toddler, playing on the beach with a little girl. They were digging in the sand and squealing with laughter.

"Who's that?" Athena asked, though she thought she already knew the answer.

Velvet smiled, her shimmering face lighting up as she watched the boy. "Laguz."

They watched in silence for a while, as Athena considered

what to say.

"I know what you're going to say," Velvet said suddenly, breaking the silence. She sighed. "I know I'm acting quite ridiculously human right now, giving in to my emotions, being heart-broken and all that. I guess after thousands of human lives, it's hard to know how else to act."

Athena nodded silently, allowing Velvet to continue.

"It was selfish of me. To leave. I made a commitment to the Academy, and I intend to see it through." She looked at Athena and smiled sadly. "I hope I have not caused too many problems?"

Athena shook her head. "My dear friend, we all lose it occasionally. Just because you are the Head of the Academy, doesn't mean you have to be in control all of the time. Look at me!" She smiled. "Every time a human doesn't listen and dies before their time, I can't help myself; sometimes the grief is too much."

Velvet nodded gratefully. "I know. I just wish I were stronger. I mean, I've been alone for many lifetimes now, and have done just fine. How is it possible that a mere twenty-four hours with my Flame is enough to derail me?"

Athena smiled. "Because all of the love you have hidden within you in all those lifetimes was revealed when you were reunited with Laguz. It is a difficult thing, to forget such love."

"I did it once," Velvet whispered. She reached out her hand towards the water, as though to touch the now sleeping child. "I forgot everything. Even who I was back then."

Athena said nothing, and waited patiently.

"I don't want to forget this time. But I don't know how to handle the pain. I don't know if I can exist without him."

"You can, Velvet. I know you can. And I wish I could give you some kind of promise, or guarantee that you will be with him on Earth in your next life, but I'm afraid I can't. Even if I could though, it wouldn't do much to fill the hole he has left in your heart."

Velvet nodded. "I know. And despite my supposed ability

to See, I too, cannot predict whether we will be together. Things keep changing too often. The future is quite uncertain right now."

"One thing is certain; you know that you can check on him whenever you need to? You don't have to leave your body behind in the Fifth Dimension."

"Yes. Coming here wasn't my intention when I did what I did. I just kind of lost control. The Angels came to me then, and said they could ease my sadness."

They were quiet while they watched the little boy playing with his sister.

"What will you do now?" Athena asked softly, aware that there was an office full of souls anxiously awaiting her return.

There was a moment of silence. Velvet reached out and touched the cheek of the little boy, who had grown considerably even in the short time they had been watching him. The picture disappeared and only the bottom of the clear lake could be seen. Velvet turned to Athena.

"Shall we?" she asked, holding out her hand. Athena nodded and took it. Velvet clicked her fingers.

*   *   *

They appeared a moment later on the beach where Velvet had worked the weather magick. Athena glanced around, sensing the charged energy around them.

"This is how you left?" she asked. She looked around and spotted Velvet's body by the shoreline.

Velvet nodded and moved towards her body. "Yes, it is. It was irresponsible of me, I know. It's been a long time since I have worked weather magick."

"Wasn't the last time when you were on Earth?"

"Yes. It is how I exited a life I hated. And before you ask, no, I would never do it on Earth again. I shouldn't even have done it here, but I needed an outlet. I needed a way to express everything that was burning inside me."

They reached her body and both stared down at it.

"I think it's time to make a few changes. I look a complete state." She looked at Athena. "You're my friend, why didn't you tell me how awful I looked?"

Athena looked at her. "I think you look beautiful. I've always thought so."

"Hmm. I think a new look is in order." She clicked her fingers and she disappeared. Athena looked down at the body on the sand and with a slight cough, Velvet opened her eyes.

"Ugh, gross, sand." She clicked her blackened, burnt fingers to rid the sand from her mouth, then stood. "Now, let's see." She closed her eyes and clicked her fingers.

As Athena watched, new, clean robes replaced the sand-covered ones, her hands were renewed to their former state and the sand disappeared from her face. Where her long, white matted hair was previously, there was now a glossy mane of waist-length silver hair. Velvet clicked her fingers and a mirror appeared. She surveyed her new appearance then turned to Athena.

"There, do I look like I'm in control again?"

Athena nodded then put her hand on Velvet's arm. "But next time you're not, please come and find me."

Velvet clicked her fingers and the mirror disappeared.

"I will," she said, smiling at the Angel. "I will."

*   *   *

"This is taking way too long," Linen said, frustrated. He paced back and forth while Aria, Gold and Chiffon all waited patiently.

"I'm sure they'll be back soon," Chiffon said softly. A moment later there was a loud click and Velvet and Athena appeared at the doorway.

Velvet looked around the room. "What's this?" she asked. Aria jumped up guiltily; she had been sat in Velvet's chair. "A welcoming party? Linen, you really shouldn't have."

Linen sighed in relief and rushed over to her. "Oh, Velvet!" He threw his arms around the Old Soul. "I'm so glad you're back!"

"Erm, well, thank you, Linen, I uh, missed you too." Velvet extricated herself from the Faerie's embrace, but not before she noticed Aria's upset expression.

"I'm sorry I have worried you all. It was selfish of me and I do apologise. Beryl," she turned to the Angel on the wall. "Could you please inform the second years that the evening session tonight will still be running?" Beryl nodded. "Is there anything that happened today I should know about?"

Linen blinked at her efficiency. He still couldn't quite get the image out of his head of her lifeless body slumped on the sand.

"We cancelled the morning session, and we also cancelled your afternoon classes. We told the second years that you had been called away unexpectedly on important business," Linen reported.

"Excellent. I'm sure you all have things you should be doing; please don't let me keep you all any longer."

She went over to her desk and sat, straightening out some papers. Everyone in the room stared at her for a moment, then made a move to leave. As the room cleared, Gold went over to her desk.

"I'm sorry, Velvet."

Velvet looked up at Gold, a frown on her face. "For what, Gold?"

"For not warning you about Laguz. I knew that the reunion would be a short one, I should have told you. Perhaps then, we could have avoided this."

Velvet shook her head and smiled. "Don't worry yourself, Gold," she said, noticing that his nervous tick had begun again. "If you think about it, this is just a little preparation for me. I need to get used to being human again. After all, humans don't have anyone to tell them what's coming or what to expect, do they?"

Gold shook his head. "No, they don't. But in the next few decades, that will be changing. Divination will become more popular, and humans will seek the counsel of Seers to know their future."

"Really? Do you think that means that Magenta will become one of those Seers?"

Gold smiled. "I would be surprised if she doesn't. Did you check up on her while in the Angelic Realm?"

Velvet shook her head. "No, I only looked for Laguz. It didn't occur to me to check on her too. I will do though."

"But if you watched Laguz, you must have surely seen Magenta too."

"Why is that?"

"She is his twin sister."

Velvet's eyebrows raised in surprise as she recalled the little girl, who appeared to be a similar age to Laguz.

"I will leave you to your thoughts." Gold smiled and disappeared in a cloud of gold dust.

Velvet leant back in her chair and closed her eyes. Though the events of the past couple of days had been quite draining, her time in the Angelic Realm had left her feeling quite peaceful. She felt a fleeting pang of jealousy that Magenta got to be with Laguz on Earth right now, but she was relieved to know that two of the souls she loved most in the Universe were together. There was no doubt in her mind that they would Awaken. She was glad that they would be together, supporting one another while experiencing the shift.

Later in the afternoon, Velvet was playing the piano quietly when she became aware of another presence in the office. Her fingers paused and she glanced towards the door to see Athena hovering there.

"Athena, my friend. Please, come in."

Athena flew into the office. "Please don't stop on my account," she said as Velvet rose from the piano stool.

"That's okay, I have much preparation to do. I should be working." She stepped towards the Angel. "But I would like to thank you, for what you did, for bringing me back. You have been a true friend to me, and I want you to know just how much I love you."

Athena smiled, and moved forward to engulf Violet in a hug. "You are most welcome, my dear Old Soul. I love you too, with all my heart." She pulled back a little. "Which is why it saddens me that the reason I have come to see you, is to say goodbye."

Velvet's breath caught in her throat as she looked at Athena. "You have been called?"

Athena nodded. "I was hoping to stay a little longer, but it is not possible. I must go as soon as I can."

Velvet nodded. "I won't lie, losing you after losing Laguz, Magenta and Corduroy seems harsh. I feel like I am being punished in some way, losing all my loved ones so suddenly."

Athena shook her head. "Oh, my dear Velvet, you know that is not the case. Not at all. All of your loved ones are just leaving for Earth a little earlier than you, that's all. We'll try and get everything ready for you."

"So you believe we will meet again?"

"Velvet, I know we will." Athena reached out and hugged Velvet one more time. "I'll see you there."

Velvet nodded. Suddenly, she was hugging empty space. Her arms dropped to her sides and she looked down. A single golden feather lay on the floor where Athena had stood moments before.

"I'll see you there," Velvet echoed.

Chapter Nineteen

When Velvet arrived outside the main hall for the evening session, there was a blur of silvery black and she found herself being embraced tightly.

After a moment, she pulled back a little and looked up at the face of Mica.

"Mica! What was that for?"

Mica grinned, his first smile since Emerald had left.

"I've been called! I wanted to tell you this morning, but class was cancelled. So I thought I would wait here to tell you. You don't mind if I don't stay for this session do you? Only the quicker I go the less of an age difference there will be between Emerald and I."

Velvet laughed and shook her head. "Of course I don't mind!" She pulled Mica back into another hug. "I'm so, so happy for you, Mica. I knew the two of you would be together. There's only a couple of years between you, I'm sure it won't keep you apart." She pulled back again and smiled warmly at the Angel.

"I hope you, too, are reunited with your Flame."

Velvet nodded. "Thank you. Now go. Get to Earth, find Emerald and help as many souls find their Twin Flames as possible."

Mica grinned and did a mock salute. "Yes, Ma'am."

Velvet laughed and he disappeared. "Bye, Mica," she said, still smiling.

The chattering died down as soon as she entered the main hall. She stood centre stage and smiled at the souls gathered in front of her.

"Good Evening! First of all I would like to apologise for my absence this morning. I was gathering research for this session with you. Tonight, I would like to start a discussion on the topic of running away from pain, fear and negativity, rather than facing it head on and working out your problems." She looked around the room as the souls took this in and tried to decipher the meaning of her absence. "Death, it seems, is no way to escape. Would anyone like to start?"

*   *   *

Amethyst's eyes were wide as Aria described all of the events of the day back in their room later that evening.

"Wow, she actually left her body? She was going to leave the Academy?"

Aria nodded. "It seems so, yes. You should have seen Linen, he was beside himself. It didn't matter what any of us said, he was distraught."

Amethyst picked up on the hint of jealousy in Aria's tone. She smiled at the Faerie.

"I'm sure he would have been even more devastated if it were you who were missing."

Aria's face lit up. "Do you think so?"

"Yes, I am quite certain," Amethyst replied. "Speaking of Twin Flames, have you got any friends you could meet up with tonight? I promised I'd meet Cobalt in the Elemental Garden at nine."

Aria frowned at the suggestion that Linen was her Twin Flame, but decided not to comment. "I've made plans with Rosa. We're going to the evening activity."

"Oh good. What is the activity tonight?"

Aria flew over to the notice board. "Something called 'Clubbing'." She frowned. "You don't think it involves hitting each other with clubs, do you?"

Amethyst chuckled. "Anything is possible, little one. I hope you have a good time with Rosa. I'll see you later, okay?"

Aria smiled. "Don't do anything I would do."

Amethyst left the room, still laughing.

Aria sighed. She flew a few circles around the room to pass the time and was just about to leave when Tm came back to the room.

"Oh! Hey, Tim! How's your day been?" she asked politely.

Tm frowned. "Oh, hi, Aria. It's been fine, except for this really annoying voice that keeps shouting my name. I keep replying and asking what it wants, but it won't tell me."

Aria frowned. "Huh, that is weird. And annoying. Well, I'm off to meet a friend now, I hope it stops."

"Yeah, me too." Tm sighed. He lay down on his revolving planet bed and closed his eyes.

Aria watched him for a moment, and he grimaced suddenly, put his fingers in his ears and groaned in frustration. She bit her lip, wondering if she should do anything to help. But what? Stumped, Aria decided to go to the evening activity, and maybe ask one of the professors there if they knew what was wrong with him.

She flew out of the room and went to the main hall where the activity was to be held. She entered the large room and was almost blasted backwards by the noise.

"Whoa!" she shouted. The room was dark, with bright lights shooting around it, and the music was so loud that the air thrummed and everything seemed to be vibrating. She squinted into the darkness and spotted some of her classmates dancing on a wooden platform in the middle of the room. Fingers in her ears, she flew to them and shouted.

"What is this?!"

"Clubbing!" Myrt screamed back.

"Why is it so loud?" Aria shouted, her tiny voice already hoarse.

Myrt shrugged. "This is how the humans like it! It's going to be a very popular thing to do on Earth in the future!"

"Okay!" Aria replied, looking around at the other souls who had joined them and were dancing to the odd music.

"Who's running it?"

Myrt pointed to the front of the room, where Cotton and Tartan were throwing themselves around in time to the beat. Aria raised an eyebrow at the sight of the usually very stiff and serious professor thrashing about; his tartan robes clashing with the flashing lights.

She nodded to Myrt and flew over to the professors. She didn't fancy staying here too long; her eardrums would be completely shot after a few more minutes. But she did want to try and help Tm.

"Cotton!" she shouted. The professor paused mid-beat and looked at the hovering Faerie.

"Yes?" she shouted back. Aria gestured to the side door and Cotton nodded. They left the main hall and when the door reappeared it was suddenly quiet. Aria shook her head, her ears ringing in the silence.

"Yes, Aria?" Cotton asked. "What is it?"

"It's my room-mate, Tim. He's an alien, I mean, a Starperson, and he's having some trouble."

Cotton frowned. "What kind of trouble?"

"He says that someone is calling his name, but there's no one there. And he keeps answering, and asking what they want, but they won't answer."

Cotton looked shocked. "Where is he now?"

"He's in our room. Room 409. What's wrong with him?"

"We need to see Velvet. Would you like to accompany me?"

Aria nodded. "Sure."

Cotton reached out, took the Faerie's hand and clicked her fingers.

*　　　*　　　*

They reappeared in front of Velvet's office door and Cotton knocked.

"Come in," Linen called out.

They entered and found him in there on his own, playing the piano. He stopped when he saw them.

"Hey, Aria, Cotton, what can I do for you?"

"We were looking for Velvet actually," Cotton replied.

"Oh, she decided to turn in early tonight." He glanced at Aria. "She's had rather a busy day."

"Oh dear, I really think we need to speak to her tonight."

"If it's that urgent, let me see if Beryl can call her." He turned to the wall. "Beryl?"

Beryl's face appeared. "Yes, Linen?"

"Could you call Velvet in her room? There is an urgent matter that Cotton needs to discuss with her."

"Certainly." Beryl's face faded away and seconds later Velvet appeared in the office.

"What's wrong, Cotton?"

"Velvet, it seems as though one of the trainees, a soul called Tim, has been called."

"What?" Velvet asked in shock. "A trainee? Are you sure?"

Cotton nodded and gestured to Aria. "It's a Starperson, her room-mate."

"Called?" Aria asked, confused. "What do you mean?"

"It hasn't been covered in class yet, as we assumed it would be too early, but to be called means that it is time for you to be incarnated on Earth."

"Isn't it too early yet? I mean, I know that the time has changed, but surely one week of training is not enough?" Linen asked.

Velvet shrugged. "I wouldn't have thought so. But my knowledge of the way these changes work is limited."

"So he's going to leave?" Aria asked. "What about the other trainees? They won't leave yet too, will they?" She looked at Velvet almost desperately. It was much too soon for her to lose Amethyst.

"I don't know, little one. But I think we need to visit your friend Tim and I need to call a meeting for all the trainee Earth Angels first thing in the morning. I need to explain the calling process and see if anyone else has indeed been called." She stood and moved towards the door. "Aria, would you like to come with me? Cotton, thank you for bringing this to my attention. You can return to the evening activity if you wish."

Cotton nodded and clicked her fingers.

Velvet held a hand out to Aria. Aria scrunched her eyes shut and Velvet clicked her fingers.

*   *   *

When they arrived outside room 409, they could hear someone crying. Aria rushed in, half expecting it to be Amethyst, and saw Tm sat on his bed, head in hands, sobbing.

"Tim!" she exclaimed, flying to his side. "What's wrong?"

"I don't know what they want!" Tm cried. "They just keep calling my name! What do they want?"

"Tim," Velvet said softly.

Tm looked up, surprised to see the Head of the Academy in his room.

"I'm sorry that you were not prepared for this, I thought it too soon to explain the procedure."

"Procedure?" Tm repeated, confused.

"The Angels are calling you to Earth, Tim. It's time for you to be incarnated as a human."

Tm's eyes widened. "Already? Are you sure?"

"Well the Angels seem pretty sure. Don't be afraid. When you leave here, you will meet your Guardian Angel who will explain it all to you and then you will be born as a human."

Tm bit his lip. "I wasn't expecting to go there so soon."

"I know. But if you weren't ready, they wouldn't be calling you."

Tm nodded. "Okay. What do I have to do?"

"You just close your eyes, and say in your mind; 'I'm ready.'"

"That's it?"

Velvet nodded. "Yes."

"Bye, Tim," Aria said; her voice a little sad.

"Goodbye, Aria. It was fun sharing a room with you. Tell Amethyst goodbye for me, would you?"

Aria nodded.

Tm looked at Velvet. "Thank you. I hope I see you on Earth."

"I hope so too."

Tm closed his eyes, and before Aria could blink, he was gone.

*   *   *

Aria was still sat on Tm's planet bed when Amethyst came back, in the early hours of the morning. She drifted into the room, a dreamy smile on her face. She glanced over to Aria's bed, and when she noticed it was empty, she frowned, stopped and looked over at Tm's bed.

"Aria! There you are. Why are you sitting on Tim's bed?" She looked around the room. "Where is he? I figured you'd both be in bed by now, it's late." She looked at the clock and giggled. "Well, early, oh, well, you know." She moved closer to Aria and noticed tears running down her friend's cheeks.

"Aria?" she said softly, going to sit next to her. "What's wrong, little Faerie?"

Aria wiped her face with the back of her hand and sniffled.

"Tim's gone," she whispered.

"Gone? Gone where?"

"He said to tell you goodbye. He couldn't wait any longer."

"Aria," Amethyst lifted the Faerie's head and looked at her tear-streaked face. "Where did he go?"

"Earth," Aria replied, her green eyes sad. "He heard the

call, and he left."

Amethyst frowned. "But he's a trainee! I know we're working on a different time scale now, and we won't have to be here for years before we graduate, but the trainees were still looking at being here for at the very least a few weeks. Seven days! I've never heard of an Earth Angel trainee hearing the call after seven days."

Aria's shoulders shook and more tears fell. Sobbing, she threw herself into Amethyst's arms.

"Shhh, hush now, Aria. I didn't mean that he would be unprepared or anything. He must have been ready; otherwise they wouldn't have called him. I'm sure he'll be just fine."

Aria cried harder. Amethyst just continued to stroke her friend's hair, and murmured soothing words. Eventually, Aria's sobs turned into hiccups. She looked up at Amethyst.

"I'm not crying because of Tim. I mean, I'll miss him, but I know he will be fine. I'm crying because I don't want you to go, Am! You're so ready for Earth, you're so wise and so prepared and I'm afraid that I'm going to wake up in the morning and you'll have left too!"

"Oh, little Faerie, don't be silly. I'm sure we have time yet before I hear the call. And besides, when I do hear it, there is no way, absolutely no way that I would leave without saying goodbye to you first. Do you hear me?"

Aria nodded.

"Now, it's really late, I have a full day tomorrow and I'm sure you'll be busy with Linen, so let's get some rest, okay?"

Aria managed a smile and Amethyst stood and went over to her bed. Aria looked down at Tm's star-dust covers.

"I think I'll sleep here tonight," she said, lifting the cover and snuggling underneath.

Amethyst smiled and got into her own bed. "Good night, little Faerie."

"Good night, Angel," Aria closed her eyes and whispered. "Good night, alien. I hope you're okay, wherever you are."

*   *   *

Despite Aria's fears, several days passed at the Academy, and though a dozen or so more trainees were called to Earth, along with many second years, Amethyst and Cobalt remained. By the time they had been at the Academy for just over two weeks, Aria was feeling much more optimistic. She arrived at the main office early one morning, whistling her favourite tune; which Linen had played on the piano for her the night before.

"Good morning!" she sang as she entered the office and took her usual place on the piano stool. Linen looked up from his desk and smiled. Though nothing had happened between them yet, Aria felt closer to him every day. She actually felt a little bad about ribbing Amethyst so much for being so smitten with Cobalt. But not bad enough to stop, of course.

"Good morning, Aria. Are you ready for a busy day?"

"Yes, I am! What's on the agenda for today?" Aria asked, bouncing up and down on the stool.

"I've asked all of our new recruits to be here today, we're meeting them in the main hall at twelve-thirty this afternoon. I'll need your help in sorting them into groups and then figuring out what exactly their roles at the School will be."

"Sounds good. It'll be good to see them all again. I think we found some really great Faeries and Angels to work here."

"Yes, I think we did, now we just need to get them trained and prepared. As you've probably noticed, the numbers of Earth Angels arriving at the Academy is decreasing, and the number of Earth Angels leaving is increasing slightly. We are quickly approaching the day where all of the Earth Angels will have graduated, and that's when Velvet will leave and it'll be just us then, kid."

Aria smiled. "I can't wait!"

Linen chuckled. "Yes, well, we still have a lot to do before that happens. So, how do you think we should sort the new recruits?"

"Good morning!"

Aria jumped a little when Velvet appeared behind her desk

suddenly. She still couldn't get used to the way the Old Soul just appeared like that.

"Morning!" Aria responded. She leaned across Linen's desk and looked at the different groupings Linen was suggesting.

"Busy day today?" Velvet asked.

"Uh huh," Linen responded absently, concentrating on the papers.

"Excellent, me too. In fact, I'd better be going."

This time there was no response. Rolling her eyes, Velvet clicked her fingers and disappeared.

*　　*　　*

Velvet reappeared in the empty main hall, and sat in a seat in the front row, facing the stage. She chuckled to herself. When Linen first arrived, just over two weeks ago, she couldn't get him to shut up. Peace and quiet was virtually non-existent. Now, with Aria around, she could barely get two words out of him. Not even a good morning! She shook her head. It was amazing how much had changed in a mere sixteen days. *Well,* she thought, thinking of Earth, *sixteen years for some.* Her smile dropped a little. Though she had looked in once or twice since the weather magick incident, she had tried her best not to spend too much time spying on Laguz and Magenta on Earth. They had looked quite happy the last time she had checked. But it still pained her to think about them. They would be about twelve years old by now. Because of Tm's very early departure, she had hoped that by now, more of the trainees would have left, making her own departure come just a little sooner. But there were still more than sixty trainees and a hundred and fifty second years left at the Academy. If they continued to depart at the same rate, she would be here for at least another two weeks. Or, in Earthly terms: fourteen more years. A twenty-six year age gap. Velvet sighed. Though humans were becoming more accepting and open to the unusual, she still had doubts as to whether it would work, the two of them being together. Their future, their reunion, was still uncertain.

She was jolted out of her thoughts by the sound of feet entering the hall. The seats behind her and around her began to fill. She looked up at the wall behind the stage, and when the giant clock hit nine thirty, she got to her feet and clicked her fingers, reappearing instantly on stage. Her sudden arrival caused several of the second years to jump.

She bit back a laugh and smiled. "Good morning! I trust that you are all well. First of all, has anyone heard the call since our session yesterday?"

About twenty-five hands went up. Velvet nodded. "Well, as you know, you are welcome to stay for this last session, if you can stand it, that is, otherwise, you may answer the call now."

Some of the Earth Angels closed their eyes and vanished, the rest decided to stay.

"Right then, for today, the theme of our discussions will be love. This is a pretty broad theme, which is why we will be discussing it all day. On Earth, there would seem to be many different types of love. You love your mother, you love the sunshine, you love to read, you love chocolate ice cream."

There were a few scattered laughs.

"But honestly, there is only one kind of love. We just express that love in different ways and in different amounts. Another misconception about love is that it can be exchanged between beings, given away, lost or found. Love, isn't an object. It isn't merely an emotion, either: it is pure energy. It is the feeling that we experience when we are in sync with the Universe. When we are flowing with the river of life. Therefore we do not need a partner, or a house, or the latest car or even chocolate ice cream to feel love bubble up inside and make us feel on top of the world. We can feel like this anytime we wish.

"To feel this way, we just have to surrender to the flow.

Resisting the natural course is much like trying to stop ice melting on a hot, sunny day - pointless. Yes, you could put the ice in the freezer to stop it melting, but who wants to remain frozen for the rest of their life? Let yourself melt, transform, be transfigured into another state of being. When you do, you will be in love with the world. Not to mention the fact that you will be outwardly happy, and contented. Which, in accordance with the law of attraction, will bring you more people, things and circumstances that will help you to feel the love within."

Velvet paused and looked around the room of attentive souls.

"I'd like to invite you all to split into groups of five, and between you, discuss the way in which you could surrender to the flow of life. How could you make it easier for yourself to feel love?"

The souls all shifted into groups, and a low, steady hum of conversation filled the room.

Velvet manifested her purple chair and sat down, contemplating, how she could make it easier for her human self to remember how to experience the love within her. Her hand moved to the lump underneath her velvet robes where the rune necklace lay hidden. She knew that finding Laguz would ensure that she would feel it, but now that being with Laguz was becoming a more distant prospect with every passing day, she needed to figure out how she could do so otherwise. Also, just because she might not be with her Twin Flame on Earth, she could still meet another one of her soulmates. There wasn't an abundance of them, but there was at least a better chance of meeting one of them. And it would be a good enough match, she was sure that she could feel the love that she knew was possible.

It occurred to her that perhaps the other way she could experience love, and indeed, Awaken when incarnated on Earth; would be with the help of the many, many Earth Angels who were now on Earth and were on their way to Earth shortly. She knew that many of them would Awaken this time, and would help others do the same through all different types of media. The Earth was advancing technologically, and Velvet had no doubt that communications between humans would be so superior within the next few decades, that spreading the light of the Earth Angels would become quite easy.

Every day, she felt a sense of anticipation. There were massive changes in the air, and she knew that even before she got to Earth, there would be many big changes at the Academy too. She had noticed that since regaining some of her memories from Atlantis, she had started to listen to her intuition more. She still couldn't quite See as she apparently had in those times, but often she got a sense that something was going to happen, sometimes even an idea of what it would be, and surely enough, hours or even minutes later, it would happen.

That very morning, in fact, she had awoken with the feeling that today would be a big day. That something was going to enter her existence, and possibly change the future of the world.

The Earth Angels chattered amongst themselves for an hour before she called the session to a close. She was just leaving the room and had decided to take a walk to the Atlantis Garden when Linen suddenly appeared in front of her.

"Oh!" Velvet jumped. "Linen! Don't do that to me!" She tilted her head to one side, confused. "How did you do that?"

Linen grinned. "Chiffon has been giving me lessons in the Old Soul Magick. First time I've done it by myself though."

"You've got over your travel sickness then?" Velvet asked, smiling.

"Yes, I have. I just pretend I'm on a rollercoaster."

Velvet frowned. "A what?"

Linen shook his head. "Nevermind. Look, I came to find you because I have to show you something."

"What is it?"

"Well, that's the thing, I'm not entirely sure." Linen held out his hand. "You drive, I'll steer. I'm still a learner."

Velvet chuckled. She grasped Linen's hand and he closed his eyes. She clicked her fingers, and set her intention to arrive wherever Linen was concentrating on.

*   *   *

When they reappeared, they were stood in a corridor in the Academy, outside of room 334.

Velvet looked at the door across the corridor. "Is this to do with the Children?"

Linen shrugged. "Could be. Like I said, I'm not sure what's happening. All I know is, Beryl received a notice to say that there was a new arrival in room 334, and that I should come down to greet them."

"You, specifically? Not me?"

"Yes, me. The notice said the Head of the School for the Children of the Golden Age."

"Okay, well it must have something to do with the Children then."

"See what you think." Linen reached out and tapped the door. It disappeared and they entered the brightly-lit room. Velvet looked around and let out a gasp.

"Oh, Goddess, it's so beautiful," she whispered. Linen nodded.

Before them was a sea of the most beautiful crystals Velvet had ever seen. Every different type of crystal seemed to be there, representing every possible different colour. They glittered and shined in the brightly-lit room. Velvet had not seen anything as beautiful since Atlantis, where the streets and homes had been covered with gems and crystals. She suddenly recalled another memory; one of Atlantis after the people had taken the crystals with them to the ocean. It had looked like a ghost town, a mere shadow of the breath-taking place it had formerly been.

"So what do you think?" Linen asked finally. "How do you welcome a room full of giant crystals?"

Velvet shook her head. "I have no idea. Perhaps we should ask one of the Indigo Children if they have any ideas?"

"Why didn't I think of that?" Linen muttered. He left Velvet and went across the corridor. Moments later, he returned with the Indigo Child that had spoken to them when the Golden City first arrived.

Velvet greeted the Child, who was calmly looking around the room, a smile on her young face.

"They have arrived." She looked up at Velvet. "We were unsure that this day would ever come. This means that Earth is progressing quickly, and progressing well."

Linen shook his head. "I'm afraid we don't know what you mean." He gestured to the shimmering crystals. "Can you explain?"

The Indigo Child smiled and bent down to the crystal stood at the front of the room. It was a tall, clear quartz point. She whispered something to it, and a moment later, a Child with piercing eyes, almost translucent blonde hair and a beautiful smile stood in its place.

Velvet and Linen gasped simultaneously.

"Greetings, Crystal Child," the Child of the Golden City said. She reached out and they embraced one another.

"Thank you, dear Indigo Child," the Crystal Child smiled up at Velvet. "Greetings, Old Soul." She smiled at Linen, tilted her head slightly, studying his features. "Greetings, Faerie. I apologise for interrupting your day. We were told by the Angels that the situation on Earth had reached the point where we would be needed, so we have come to the School." She looked at Linen. "Are you the Head of the School?"

Linen nodded, a little amazed that she had so quickly realised he was a Faerie. "Yes, my name is Linen, and this is Velvet, she is the current Head of what is at the moment the Earth Angel Training Academy."

The Crystal Child nodded. "When will it be formally changed into the School?"

"We are about to start training the new teachers, and are

planning to be ready to start running classes for the Children once the Earth Angels have all left and Velvet has also left."

The Crystal Child glanced at the Indigo Child. "I'm afraid that is not soon enough. We have been told that classes should commence immediately. The Indigo Children will start to hear the call very soon. You do not want to send them unprepared do you?"

Linen's eyes widened. "How soon?"

"The Angels said that the first would be called before the last of the Earth Angels leave here."

"Though we should not be surprised, considering how quickly things have progressed in the last two weeks, this is definitely news to us," Velvet told the Crystal Child. "We shall do all we can to set up the new classes for the Indigo and Crystal Children as quickly as we can." Linen nodded in agreement. "In the meantime, can we do anything for you? Is there anything you require?"

The Crystal Child smiled and shook her head. "No, we are quite happy here, thank you. We shall remain in our original states until we are called to attend the classes."

Velvet nodded. The three of them turned to leave when something occurred to her. "How do we call you?"

"The Indigos know how," the Crystal Child replied, turning back into the clear quartz point.

Velvet nodded and they left the room.

"Are there likely to be more Children coming?" Velvet asked the Indigo Child out in the corridor.

The Indigo Child nodded. "Yes. There are several different kinds of Golden Age Children, who will arrive on Earth in stages. We are the first stage, the Crystal Children are the second stage."

"And the third?"

The Child smiled. "Patience is needed here. We do not even know if the third stage will arrive. It depends on the success of the Earth Angels and the early Indigos."

"I see," Velvet said. "Will the third stage of Children come here to the School before going to Earth?"

"Perhaps. I imagine that the third stage Children will be so pure and enlightened that schooling will be entirely unnecessary, but they may pass through here on their way."

Velvet smiled. "Thank you for answering my questions."

"It is entirely my pleasure, Velvet. I shall return to my city now. When you are ready to teach us, just let us know and we in turn, will let the Crystal Children know." Before they could answer, the Indigo Child turned into the blue sphere of light and returned to the Golden City.

Velvet and Linen stood in the corridor and looked at one another.

"Wow. Could things get much weirder any faster?"

"Probably," Velvet replied wryly.

"I need to get back to the office and get going with arranging these classes. It seems we have even less time than we thought."

"So what's new?" Velvet smiled and offered her arm. "Shall we?"

Linen nodded and held onto it, closing his eyes in preparation for the click.

Chapter Twenty

"The new arrivals are crystals?" Aria asked, her green eyes wide.

"Yes, although it sounds quite odd, they were incredibly beautiful," Linen replied, looking a little harassed as he sifted through the papers on his desk. "I just don't know how we will possibly get everything ready in time. The new teachers haven't even arrived yet, let alone been trained. We haven't figured out the schedules. Basically, we're just not ready."

Aria reached across the desk and put her hand on his, bringing it to a halt.

"Linen, if the Angels believe we can do this, then so do I. We will be ready in time, and we will get those Children to Earth on time. Just relax, take a deep breath, and we'll work through everything just fine."

Linen looked at her hand on his and smiled up at her. "Thanks," he whispered.

"Perhaps a little music to relax?" Velvet suggested. She went to the piano, and Aria scooted off the stool. Velvet sat and after a moments pause, began to play.

Linen took a deep breath and closed his eyes. He listened to the notes; lost in the melody that Velvet was weaving so beautifully. After a minute, he opened his eyes and nodded at Aria. The energy in the room shifted and a more positive vibration filled the air around them. Even Aria, who was bouncing in the air in time to the music relaxed and felt more focused.

Velvet finished the song with a flourish and turned to Linen. "Ready to work now?"

Linen nodded. "Thank you, Velvet. I needed that."

"It's the least I can do considering all the times you did the same for me."

Aria's good mood lessened slightly as she witnessed the exchange between the two of them. But she dismissed her jealousy, refusing to let it spoil her time with Linen.

"So," she said, turning to Linen. "What's the first thing on the list?"

"Well," Linen said, glancing at the clock. "We have exactly three minutes to get to the main hall to welcome the new teachers. So we'd better get shifting." He grinned. "Fancy trying out a little magick?"

Aria grinned back. "Would love to!"

He held out his hand for Aria to hold, which, in Aria's mind, was the best part, and she closed her eyes tight. He closed his own and concentrating hard, clicked his fingers. He opened one eye and found himself still in the office, looking at a bemused Velvet sat on the piano stool, watching. He closed it again, and with even more concentration, and an extra loud click, they both vanished.

*   *   *

Amethyst sighed happily as she stared at the lilac flower in her hand. She entwined her other hand in Cobalt's and leant forward to kiss him.

"It's beautiful," she murmured. "Thank you."

"Anything for my Angel." He smiled and returned the kiss, but suddenly pulled back and looked behind him.

"What is it?" Amethyst asked, looking behind him but seeing nothing there.

"I thought I heard something," Cobalt said, frowning. He continued to search the gardens but saw nothing amiss. He shrugged and turned back to Amethyst.

She leant into his body and he rested his chin on her head, breathing in the scent of her hair.

"I wonder how Tim is doing," Amethyst mused. "I wonder what he's getting up to. Wow, he'll be eight years old already! Amazing."

"Mmmhmm," Cobalt replied, lost in his own thoughts.

"I wonder if-" Amethyst stopped mid-sentence and pulled away from Cobalt to look at his face. "What is it?" she asked, searching his face. His body had tensed, and the look on his face now was of a soul in pain.

"What can I do?" she asked anxiously. "What is it?"

Cobalt blinked and focused on Amethyst. "Oh, Am," he said. "I can hear them."

"Who?" Amethyst asked softly, afraid that she didn't want to know the answer.

"The Angels. They're calling me."

Amethyst shook her head, her face crumpling in pain. "No. Not yet."

Cobalt closed his eyes and nodded. "I'm afraid so." He held out his arms and Amethyst melted into them, trying desperately not to cry.

"When will you go?" she whispered.

"I should go now, before your afternoon classes-"

"I won't go to them. I won't be able to concentrate anyway. Please, please stay just a little longer."

Cobalt nodded, and held her tighter. "Okay. I'll stay."

They sat there while the other Earth Angels in the gardens went past, on their way to the afternoon classes. Every now and then, Cobalt tensed as he heard the call, getting louder and more insistent each time.

After a while, he whispered. "We will find each other. I promise you that. If it takes me all my life, I will find you."

Amethyst looked up at him, a tear finally escaping down her cheek. "I'll be there as soon as I can."

Cobalt leant forward and they kissed, their tears mingling

together upon their lips.

"I love you, Amethyst."

"I love you, Cobalt."

With all the strength he possessed, he pulled away from her and stood unsteadily. While still holding Amethyst's hand, he closed his eyes and uttered the words.

Amethyst's hand fell to her lap, now as empty as her heart.

*   *   *

Aria was exhausted when she finally returned to her room after midnight. She and Linen had worked all afternoon and most of the evening with the new teachers, bringing them up to date on all the latest developments and figuring out schedules. Everything that they were basically going to do in the next week - they did it all today. Despite the volume of information they were bombarded with, the Faeries and Angels seemed to have taken it all in their stride and were all fired up to begin classes with the Children the next day. Aria and Linen had dismissed them around nine, and then spent hours sorting out the rooms and everything needed for each class. They decided to let the Children know first thing in the morning that they were ready for them.

Aria flew slowly to her bed, and was about to crawl in under the blanket of flowers when a noise from across the room made her pause.

She heard the noise again and looked over to see what was causing it, but it was difficult to see in the dim glow of the stars on the ceiling.

"Am?" she called softly. "Is that you?"

She heard it again and realised that it was a stifled sob. Frowning, she flew over to Amethyst's bed and found the Angel under her covers, clutching a flower in her hand, her body wracked with sobs.

"Oh, Am!" Aria exclaimed. "What's wrong?"

"C-c-cobalt," Amethyst managed to get out, before

dissolving into yet more tears.

Aria understood at once, and without saying another word, put her arms around her friend and hugged her has hard as her little arms would allow.

"Shhh, it's okay, Am, everything will be okay. I promise," she whispered, having no idea if everything would be or not. She thanked the Goddess that the Angels had not called her friend yet, and exhausted, they both eventually fell asleep under the starlight.

*   *   *

It took a moment for Aria to orientate herself the next morning. She blinked sleepily as she tried to figure out where she was. She looked around her and realised she was in Amethyst's bed. There was a crumpled lilac flower next to her, some of its petals scattered across the sheets. Aria sat up then, the details of the previous night coming back to her in a flash. She looked around the empty room. "Am?" she called out.

Silence met her anxious call. Flying out of bed, she did a quick circuit of the room, and after determining that Amethyst was definitely not there, she zoomed out of the room and headed for the gardens. Blessing the Goddess that she still had her wings, she did circuits of all their favourite gardens, searching for her friend. She passed several classmates on the way, who were enjoying some peace before the morning classes started. After searching each garden once, she searched them again, this time calling out her name.

After the second round, she sat for a moment to catch her breath and thought hard. Where could her friend be? They only ever went to the gardens or their room. Surely she wouldn't have gone to class already? Aria jumped up and flew as fast as she could to the Patience 100000001 classroom. She arrived there and knocked on the door. The door vanished and she entered, but the room was empty except for Cotton, who was sat staring at a plant.

She looked up when Aria entered. "Yes?"

"I was looking for Amethyst, you haven't seen her this morning have you?"

Cotton shook her head. "No, I'm afraid I haven't."

"Thanks," Aria called over her shoulder, already heading out the door.

She paused out in the corridor, truly at a loss of where else to look. Her heart sank when she wondered if Amethyst had left for Earth already. Despite her promises to say goodbye, she might have answered the call quickly in a bid to get to Cobalt. Sighing, she decided to go to Linen, and ask if there was any way to put out a message to the whole Academy when she remembered what he had said about communicating with other souls.

"Amethyst. Amethyst. Amethyst," Aria said, crossing her fingers and praying that it would work. A second later, she thought she heard something.

"Am?" she said to the empty corridor, feeling slightly foolish.

"Aria?" Amethyst's voice replied in her ear, confused.

"Oh, Am! Where are you? I've been searching everywhere for you! I thought you'd left for Earth without saying goodbye!"

She heard a sigh. "Aria, didn't I promise you that I wouldn't do that? I haven't heard the call, I promise."

Aria heard the disappointment in her tone and bit her lip. "Where are you?" she asked quietly.

"I just needed to get away, go somewhere where no one could find me. Once I've had some time to myself, I will come back, I promise."

"But you're still in the Academy, right? You haven't left like Velvet did, have you?"

"Aria, please stop worrying. I'm in the Academy, I will be back soon."

"Okay. I'm sorry I bothered you," Aria said, and then she consciously cut the connection between them. A frown marring her impish face, she flew slowly to Linen's office; flying above the heads of the Earth Angels now heading for their morning classes.

When she reached the office, she entered as she usually did, without knocking. She sat in her usual place on the piano stool and rested her head on her hand.

"What's wrong, Aria?" Velvet asked softly from behind her desk.

Aria shook her head. "Nothing," she said quietly.

"If you need to talk..."

Aria tried to smile. "Thanks," she replied.

Linen entered then, a smile on his face. "Good morning!" he said jovially, walking over to his desk. He picked up the day's schedule and looked at Aria.

"Shall we get go-" He stopped and peered closer. "Are you okay?"

Aria shook her head and her eyes filled.

Linen set the schedule down and went to sit next to the Faerie. He put his arm around her and gave her a hug. "What is it?"

"I've got to get to class. See you later," Velvet said quietly, leaving with a soft click.

Aria's shoulders shook and a single tear dropped onto the front of her green dress. "Amethyst's Twin Flame, Cobalt, heard the call and left for Earth yesterday," she whispered. Linen leaned closer so he could hear her. "She was really upset last night, and this morning, I couldn't find her, so I said her name three times, like you told me, to contact her."

"Did you speak to her?" Linen prompted.

Aria nodded, her lip quivering. "She said she'd gone where no one could find her, and that she needed to be alone."

Linen frowned. "She's probably quite upset, Aria. I'm sure she'll be back when she's calmed herself."

"That's what she said. The thing is, I'm dreading the day she hears the call to Earth so much, but to be honest, I feel like I've lost her already. She won't let me help her, Linen. I'm her best friend, and she doesn't even want to see me." Aria buried herself in Linen's yellow robes and cried.

"Shhh," Linen soothed, holding her tight to his chest. "She's just upset, Aria. You haven't lost her. She probably just needs a little time to say goodbye to Cobalt, that's all." He glanced over at Velvet's desk. "It seems that losing a Twin Flame is quite traumatic."

Aria pulled back a little and looked up into his eyes. "Do you think I'm being silly?"

Linen smiled. "No. I think you're just being a good friend. Though I do love a good bit of silliness."

Aria smiled a little. "Me too." She frowned. "Things have been way too serious around here lately."

"You're telling me. I'm actually beginning to feel like an Old Soul. And I have to say, it's not a whole lot of fun."

"Shall we make a promise now, to do at least one silly thing every day?"

"I think that sounds like a wonderful idea." Linen held out his right hand. "Shake on it?" Aria reached out and grasped his massive hand with her tiny fingers.

"Now then. We have a ridiculously busy day ahead of us, are you ready for it?"

Aria wiped her face with the back of her hand and smiled. "Ready!"

"Excellent, first things first, we need to make a visit to the Indigos." He grabbed his schedule from the desk and held his hand out. "Shall we?"

*   *   *

Aria and Linen went with the Indigo Child to room 334, and watched while she whispered to the large clear quartz point at the front of the room. When the crystal turned into a Child, Aria gasped. The Child nodded to them both with a smile.

"You have worked very quickly, and we appreciate your great efforts, Faeries. I shall Awaken my brothers and sisters now."

She turned to the roomful of crystals and opened her mouth. She began to sing, quietly at first. Aria's heart swelled as she listened to the beautiful words.

One by one, the crystals turned into Children, all stunningly beautiful, yet all very unique. They were dressed in simple clothing that glittered as though it were woven from the very crystals they had transformed from.

Soon, the entire room was filled with Children of all sizes, staring at the two of them with benevolent smiles.

The Child finished the song and turned to Linen and Aria.

"Lead the way," she said simply.

"We're meeting with the teachers in the main hall," Linen told them. "We will take you there; the Indigo Children are already there."

He and Aria led the Crystal Children through the corridors of the Academy to the main hall.

When they arrived, the Crystal Children took their places in the rows of seats behind the Indigos. The teachers were all on the stage, all hovering, waiting nervously to meet their new students. Linen and Aria made their way up to the stage and Linen took Velvet's usual place centre stage.

He clicked his fingers so that his face appeared on the wall behind him, and then held out his arms, much like Velvet had done on the first day of the new term.

"Welcome, Indigo and Crystal Children, to the School for the Children of the Golden Age. We are so very pleased to have you here with us, and hope to learn just as much from you as you will from us in the time you are here. To start things off, I'd like introduce the Faeries and Angels who will be teaching you, guiding you, and helping you in any way they can."

He smiled and turned to Aria. "This is Aria, she is my assistant, so if you have any problems, please find either her or me. She will also be teaching classes on the importance of respecting nature on Earth." Aria grinned at the Children and waved energetically. Many of the children waved back.

Linen turned to the row of souls behind him.

"Please let me introduce to you Fraggie…"

*   *   *

During the midday break, Velvet found herself in the Atlantis Garden, sitting on the bench in front of the empty space. Although she wasn't as talented as Corduroy when it came to these things, she decided to replace the statue with another of Laguz. She closed her eyes and concentrated on what he had looked like, when they had said goodbye on the beach. Then she clicked her fingers. She opened her eyes and found herself staring at a beautiful marble statue bearing Laguz's stunning smile and green eyes. This statue had legs instead of a tail, though. She blinked back tears as she stared at the face of her beloved Twin Flame.

She pulled the rune out from under her robes and stared at it, smoothing her thumb over the engraved symbol. She wondered what he was doing right now. Whether he had Awoken to his origins at all. Whether Magenta had discovered her ability to See. Another day had passed for Velvet, another year for Laguz and Magenta. She wished she were able to See the future as she used to in Atlantis. She wished that she could See whether they would all meet up again, on Earth, as humans.

Lost in deep contemplation, a loud crackling noise made her jump and her heart constrict. She looked around wildly for the source. It was the same noise the Leprechaun used to make when they appeared and disappeared. Finally, her gaze came to rest upon a door, off to her left, that had not been there when she arrived in the garden. She stared at it, afraid of what might come through it. After a few tense moments, the wooden door creaked open, and Velvet's eyes widened as a very dishevelled Amethyst came through it. She closed the door behind her and the door disappeared with the same crackling noise. She turned and saw Velvet.

"Oh!" she said, a little surprised. Her face was tired, her eyes puffy and red.

Velvet frowned. "Dear Angel, where did you just come from?"

Amethyst smiled a little. "The Leprechaun Garden."

Velvet's eyebrows shot up. "The Leprechaun Garden? How on Earth did you manage to find your way in? I've been trying for years!"

"It wasn't me who figured it out, it was Cobalt." She stared at the ground. "My Twin Flame."

"Come sit with me a while, Angel," Velvet said softly, patting the bench.

Amethyst went over to the bench and sat beside her, and they both stared at the statue of Laguz for a while, lost in their own memories.

"When was he called?" Velvet asked.

"Yesterday afternoon."

There was a pause. "I'm so sorry, Angel."

Amethyst shook her head. "It's okay. Really. I knew it would happen. We had longer together than I thought we might. I have to admit, at first, it was difficult to accept, but I'm fine now." She smiled unconvincingly.

"You are taking it better than I did, Angel. I'm afraid I was much more human about it."

"It's a difficult thing, saying goodbye," Amethyst said softly. "Even when you know that it's only for a short time."

"Yes," Velvet agreed. "So tell me, Angel. How did you manage to get into the Leprechaun Garden? What's it like there?"

Amethyst smiled. "I'm afraid I can't tell you how, we had to swear we would keep it a secret. But before we leave, I'll take you there if you'd like."

"That would be brilliant. Despite the chaos that the Leprechaun caused in their time here, they always did know how to have fun. I should think their garden is something quite spectacular."

"It is that. It also provided an excellent getaway. Cobalt and I would go there to be alone." She paused and looked up at the statue of Laguz.

"Do you think you will find him again?" she whispered.

Velvet bit her lip and held onto the rune. "Sometimes I hope I do, other times, I hope I don't. I would rather live my whole life without him, than to meet him and realise that too much time has passed for us to be together."

"How old is he now?"

"About thirteen years old. By the time I leave for Earth, it is likely that there will be more than twenty years between us."

"Do you really think that a number could keep you apart though?"

"I don't know," Velvet said honestly. "I can only hope that the Goddess has something up her sleeve." She looked up into the green eyes she had created. "And that we will be together once again."

*   *   *

By the end of the afternoon, Aria and Linen were taking a break in the office, they were both equally tired and excited.

"The Children are amazing," Aria said, still in awe. "Despite their young and innocent appearances, they know so much! The knowledge, the wisdom, the knowing that they have; it's incredible."

"I know, I had no idea when this all began that there could be such pure beings out there. The humans on Earth are incredibly lucky to have the Children going to help them. I honestly think that with them there, the Golden Age may well become a reality."

Aria was thoughtful for a moment. "Do you wish you were there? To see it happen?"

"On Earth?" Linen pondered this. "I don't know. As interesting as I think it would be, I didn't feel right on Earth. It was too heavy, too sombre, a little like it is around the Old Souls here. Most humans have forgotten that to be human is to be happy. You see, they think that it is human nature to be miserable, but misery is a habit. It is something that they are taught, not something they are born with. Human habit is to look at the darker side of things. Human nature is to love, and to be happy and joyful. And if anyone can open the human's eyes to this fact, it is the Children." He looked at Aria. "Are you thinking of changing your mind? Going to Earth to be human after all?"

"Oh, no, not at all," Aria said quickly, noticing the relief in Linen's eyes. "I just wondered if you missed it, that's all."

"I wish I could have said goodbye to my mother in my last life. Though I knew leaving was necessary, I felt bad for not telling her I loved her, and that I was going. I hope she managed to get over losing me."

"How long ago did you leave Earth?"

"Only seventeen days ago. But in Earthly time, that's seventeen years. I would have been twenty seven by now had I stayed."

"And probably into all sorts of crazy daredevil stunts by now," Velvet joined in, suddenly appearing behind her desk.

Linen chuckled. "Yes, probably."

Aria felt a little annoyed at the intrusion on their conversation. It seemed like they barely ever got a chance to be alone outside of work.

"How has it gone today? With the Children?"

"Excellent. We were just saying how incredibly inspiring they are. The teachers are doing well, though as we suspected, we're learning more from the Children than we can teach them."

"Yes, I must say that's how I felt when it came to teaching the Earth Angel returnees. I like to think that we learn from each other. Have they mentioned the third stage of Children again yet?"

"No, I think that they only will if they do indeed turn up."

"What third stage?" Aria asked, feeling left out.

"The Indigos are the first stage, the Crystals are the second, and the Crystal Child we spoke to said that there could be a third stage of Golden Age Children to come."

"Wow, I wonder what kind of Children they-"

"Aria!" a voice shouted.

Aria broke off mid-sentence and looked around in a panic. "Did you hear that?" she asked Linen and Velvet. They both nodded, frowning, and Aria breathed a sigh of relief. There was a knock at the door then, and before they could call out to come in, Amethyst was already charging into the room.

"Am! Was that you calling me just then? You gave me a fright, I thought I was hearing the call to Earth." She peered more closely at her friend. "What's wrong?"

Amethyst's face split into a smile. "Nothing!" She rushed forward to grab the Faerie's hands. "They're calling me, Aria."

Aria's eyes widened and her heart sank. "What?"

"The Angels. They're calling me to Earth. I've heard them several times now." Her eyes were shining. "There'll be less than a couple of years between us. Cobalt and I will find each other for sure."

Aria nodded and smiled, trying to be happy for her friend.

"That's brilliant, Am," she said softly. She reached out to hug the Angel. "I'm so pleased for you, really I am."

"Congratulations, Angel. You must have learnt all that you need for Earth. You will be missed, but I wish you all the luck in finding your Twin," Velvet said, coming out from behind her desk. Amethyst smiled at her and released Aria so she could embrace the Old Soul.

"Thank you for everything, Velvet. I hope you find yours too."

They stepped back from one another and Aria threw herself into Amethyst's arms again.

"When are you leaving?" she asked.

"Now. I can't wait any longer, little one." She pulled back and looked into the Faerie's grass-green eyes. "I will never forget you my dear friend. I think the most that I have learnt here, I learnt from you. And I have thanked the Goddess every day for bringing us together on that first day of term."

Aria smiled, her eyes filling. "I'll never forget you either, Angel. You really are the best friend in the whole Universe."

Amethyst hugged her once more. "Goodbye, Aria."

"Goodbye, Amethyst."

Amethyst smiled and closed her eyes. She mouthed the words to the Angels, then disappeared, leaving behind a cloud of shimmering lilac feathers.

Aria bit her lip. She didn't want to cry in front of Velvet and Linen again, it was so completely unprofessional. But when Linen came over to her and put his arm around her, she couldn't help it. For the second time that day, she sobbed.

Chapter Twenty-one

Four days later, the Academy was becoming increasingly emptier as large groups of Earth Angels left every day. Many more trainees had now been called, meaning that some of the classes barely had two or three trainees in them. Aria moved into a different bedroom, one that was closer to the office, one that didn't remind her of her friends who had left. She had carefully pressed the lilac flower Amethyst had left and kept it next to her bed.

Classes with the Children were going well, and Aria threw herself into her work, enjoying every moment spent with Linen. She had begun to wonder though, whether they would ever be more than just friends and colleagues. Or whether she had completely misread the signs and that he didn't feel the same way at all.

She was lying in bed very early one morning, staring up at the blue sky ceiling with clouds drifting across it lazily, when she heard the most beautiful sound. It was a clear, high-pitched note that rang out and filled Aria's entire body with love. Smiling, she sat up and tried to determine its source. Deciding it was coming from outside her room; she flew to the door and peeked out into the corridor, only to find herself face to face with a bare-chested Linen, who had come out of his room which was next door. As they looked at each other, the sound drifted away.

Aria was the first to speak. "What was that?"

Linen shook his head. "I don't know." He dashed back into his room and threw his yellow robes on. He came back out to where Aria still hovered. "Let's go find out."

They made their way quickly to the office, where they found Velvet staring at a very large crystal on Linen's desk.

"Velvet, what was that noise?" Linen asked, entering the room, Aria right behind him. "And what is that?"

Velvet held up a hand to quiet him, and continued to stare at the crystal. It was clear, but cut in a way that gave it a thousand facets.

Linen and Aria moved closer to look at this unusual crystal, wondering what it could possibly have to do with the sound they just heard.

After a few moments, Velvet sighed. "I can't read it." She turned to Linen. "Can you?"

"Read what?"

"I was sat here, just doing some paperwork when I heard this beautiful high-pitched note, and when I looked up, this had appeared on your desk." She gestured to the crystal. "Because of the way it is cut, I assumed that there must be a message of some sort in it. But I can't seem to read it."

Linen walked around his desk, viewing the crystal from all angles. "It doesn't look like the Crystal Children crystals. In fact," he said, looking at it more closely. "It doesn't look like a naturally formed crystal at all. It looks like it's been manufactured."

"So what do you think it means?" Aria asked.

Linen shrugged. "That maybe Velvet is right. Maybe it contains a message of some kind. But I don't know how to read it either."

"Perhaps we should take it to the Crystal Children," Velvet suggested. "They may have some ideas."

Linen shook his head. "Why didn't I think of that? Of course they'll know. They seem to know everything before we do."

"Okay, I think if we both concentrate really hard, we

should be able to do it." She put one hand on the crystal, which was slightly warm to the touch, and her other hand on Linen's shoulder. Linen put one hand on the crystal and wrapped the other around Aria's. They all closed their eyes and within a moment, they were all stood outside room 334. Linen knocked, then entered when the door disappeared.

The Children were all back in their original crystal states and the room was very dimly lit. Velvet stopped at the doorway. "I'll go get the Indigo Child." She clicked her fingers and the crystal moved into the room and settled on the floor. Linen and Aria followed it.

They waited until Velvet returned. The Indigo Child followed her in and saw the cut crystal on the floor next to them. Her face lit up and she grinned. She danced over to where the clear quartz point stood and whispered excitedly to it. A moment later, the Crystal Child appeared. She looked at the crystal and also smiled. She clapped her hands together.

"Oh! This is such a wonderful day!" She looked up at the three of them. "Dear souls! Celebrate! Your efforts must truly be working."

Velvet, Linen and Aria all looked at one another in bemusement.

"What are you talking about, Crystal Child?" Velvet asked.

The Child knelt in front of the crystal. She reached forward to touch it lightly. "The Rainbow Children have arrived," she said joyfully.

Velvet raised an eyebrow, still perplexed. "The Rainbow Children?" she asked, looking down at the crystal.

The Crystal Child nodded. "Do you have an empty room to spare? I will show you."

Linen nodded. "There's one next door. Should we take the crystal with us?"

"Yes. Do you need help moving it?"

Linen bent down to lift the crystal, and grunting, tried to lift it, but it didn't move. The Indigo and the Crystal Child giggled. "Where are you, Faerie? On Earth, or in the Fifth Dimension?" the Indigo Child asked teasingly. She clapped her hands, and the crystal lifted off the floor and hovered. Linen rolled his eyes. He still thought like a human at times it seemed.

They all moved to the room next door, the crystal hovering in-between the two Children. Once inside, they lifted their arms and the crystal rose up and stayed hovering, halfway between the floor and the ceiling.

They grinned at each other and the Indigo Child swept her hand to one side. They all watched silently as the crystal began to revolve slowly.

The Crystal Child whispered. "Ready?" Everyone nodded, intrigued. The Crystal Child clapped her hands and the room was lit up suddenly. The ceiling had turned into a bright blue sky with a dazzling sun shining brightly onto the crystal and onto them. Linen, Velvet and Aria blinked several times, their eyes adjusting to the light. When they could see, they each gasped. Dancing around the room were thousands of rainbows.

The Crystal Child giggled happily and cried out. "Welcome, Rainbow Children! Welcome!"

Linen turned to Velvet, frowning. "They're Children?" he whispered. "Aren't they just the light being refracted through the crystal?"

"The Rainbow Children are beings of pure light," the Indigo Child said in response to his whisperings. Linen blushed a little at being caught. The Indigo Child smiled up at him. "But you do not have to take my word for it. Ask them yourself."

Linen raised an eyebrow. "And how do I do that?"

The Child reached out and a rainbow appeared on her hand. She closed her fingers around it and closed her eyes. After a moment she laughed and nodded, then she opened her hand and the rainbow drifted away.

"Try for yourself. The Rainbows wish to greet you."

Linen reached out and caught a rainbow. He closed his hand around it, and closed his eyes, as the Indigo had.

"Greetings, Linen. We are very happy to be here in your School. We hope that we will be able to assist you in your mission to Awaken the humans on Earth in readiness for the Golden Age."

Linen's eyes popped open and he stared down at the dancing coloured light on his palm.

"Unbelievable," he said, shaking his head in wonder. He looked at the Indigo and the Crystal Child. "They are the third stage?"

They both nodded. "Soon, the Indigos will begin to join the Earth Angels in their departures to Earth. We must make sure that everything is ready for the Crystals and Rainbows to join us."

Velvet gazed around the room. She too, caught a rainbow, and joy filled her face as she listened to the infinite wisdom of the incredible beings.

"Fear not, Velvet," the Rainbow Child said. "You shall be with him again, though perhaps not in the way you imagine." Velvet opened her eyes and looked down at the Rainbow in her hand.

"Thank you," she whispered.

"Will we need to arrange classes for the Rainbow Children too?" Aria asked, her wings fluttering excitedly.

"No need. The Rainbow Children know all they need to. They are here simply to provide their support to us while we prepare."

Velvet heard the sound of wind chimes. "I need to go. It appears I am late for my morning class. Thank you, Children, for helping us to welcome the Rainbows." She turned to Linen and Aria. "I will see you both later." She clicked her fingers and vanished.

"We must go too; we will be late for class." The Indigo Child took the Crystal Child's hand. They both waved to the Rainbows, then left.

Aria reached out to catch a Rainbow Child, and closed her eyes.

"It won't be long, dear Faerie. It will happen soon. Have faith."

Smiling she let the Rainbow Child go and turned to Linen. "We're going to be late too."

Linen nodded. He pulled his gaze away from the dancing Rainbow Children and took Aria's hand. With a click, they both disappeared.

*　　　*　　　*

Velvet's morning class with the second years went quickly. She told them about the arrival of the Rainbow Children, which apparently meant that things were going well on Earth. The Earth Angels were excited and encouraged by the news, and there was a renewed sense of hope that they may actually get to see the Golden Age.

"With the help of the Children, how could we possibly fail?" an Angel called Celestite remarked. "I, for one, cannot wait to join our fellow Earth Angels and help with the shift."

Many others around her nodded. There were so few of them remaining these days, that most were able to participate in the discussions.

"How long do you think it will be until the Children arrive on Earth?" an Old Soul called Terry asked.

"Apparently some Indigos will be called before all of you and the trainees have all been called. As for the Crystal and Rainbow Children, it is my assumption that they will mainly be called to be born to Earth Angel or Indigo parents. So they will be going to Earth at least fifteen to twenty years, or to us, days, after the Indigos and Earth Angels have left."

"Don't you think that they would also have some Crystal and Rainbow Children born to non-Earth Angel or Indigo parents though, in order for them to Awaken their parents? If these Children are only born to Awakened families, then how would the Awakening wisdom reach everyone in the world?"

"You could be right, Sol, it would certainly make sense to do that. And there are certainly enough Crystal and Rainbow Children to do so."

"Will we be able to meet the Rainbow Children before we leave?" a Merman called Ray asked.

"I'm not sure, I can certainly ask Linen if this would be possible," Velvet replied.

"Thank you. I just think it might be beneficial to us to see what they have to say, see if they have any advice for us," Ray continued.

"Yes, indeed." Velvet smiled, remembering what they had said to her. "They do seem to know what to say. Now then, for the rest of this morning's session, I'd like to talk a little about magick."

*   *   *

By the end of the morning session, several more of the Earth Angels had heard the call. They all decided to leave by midday, excited to reach Earth to prepare for the arrival of the Rainbow Children. One of them was Celestite.

"I guess I will just have to wait until they arrive on Earth to meet them," she said to Velvet, smiling. "I hope that we get to meet up also."

"As do I, Angel. I wish you every happiness."

Celestite smiled. "Goodbye, Velvet." She closed her eyes and disappeared. Velvet did a quick head count as the rest of the Earth Angels left the room. Only twenty-five left. And only forty-seven trainees were left. She smiled, it wouldn't be long now before they were all called and she could get to Earth.

Her fingers smoothed her robes over the bump of the rune necklace. She imagined Laguz as a sixteen year old boy, and wondered how he was. But she had promised herself that she wouldn't spy on him. If they were meant to be together when she got to Earth, they would find one another somehow. She thought again about what the Rainbow Child had told her. That they would be together, but not in the way she was thinking. Perhaps they would be related? Velvet shook her head. She didn't want to entertain that thought. The idea of Laguz being her father or uncle was an awful one. She wanted to be with him, not be related to him.

She sat and stared out over the empty seats and tried to figure out what they could have meant, but no more ideas came to mind. Finally, she gave up and decided to go for a walk in the gardens.

Upon reaching her favourite bench in front of Laguz's statue, Velvet suddenly realised that in all the excitement of Amethyst hearing the call, the Angel hadn't taken her to the Leprechaun Garden. It seemed she would be leaving the Academy with some mysteries still unsolved. She sat for some time, lost in her musings, when a young voice brought her back to the present.

"I'm very sorry to bother you, Velvet, but I wondered if I may speak with you for a moment?"

Velvet looked up and found herself eye to eye with a beautiful little boy dressed in deep blue clothing.

"My dear Indigo Child, of course you are not bothering me." She gestured to the bench. "Please, sit with me."

The Child joined her on the bench, his short legs dangling, not quite reaching the ground.

"Myself and ten other Indigos have heard the call over the course of today," he began. "They have all left already, but I was hoping to speak with you before I too, answered the call."

"What is it you wish to speak to me about?" Velvet asked.

"When I first met you, when we arrived in room 333, I sensed something that I thought you may wish to know. I was going to tell you sooner, but things have been quite busy since then. And I do not wish to leave without mentioning it."

Velvet looked at the Child quizzically. "What is it you sensed?"

"I sensed that there is a great part of you that you are

denying. There is much you are able to do, and yet you have shut it away into a box in the far corners of your self and are refusing to set it free again." The Child looked at her now, and tilted his head.

"Though I sense now that some of those things have indeed been set free. But there is still much more work to do, Old Soul, before you return to Earth. For if you cannot Awaken every part of yourself here, then your chances of Awakening at all on Earth will be that much smaller." The Child smiled innocently. "I hope I have not offended you in any way, my intuition told me that you needed to know this." He hopped off the bench.

"I will answer the call to Earth now, I hope you Awaken soon, after all, the Angels may not call you until you do." He closed his eyes, and before Velvet could even thank him, he was gone.

Velvet sat and stared at the empty space where the Child had stood, for some time after he left. She thought about what he had said. It matched what Magenta had also said, that she possessed talents and abilities that she had forgotten, or rather, had buried. She assumed that the Child had been talking of the piano playing and memories of Atlantis when he said that some things had been set free, but she wondered what it was she was still suppressing. She remembered what Magenta had said about Atlantis, about how she was able to See. That she was one of the best Seers there. Aside from the feelings of intuition, Velvet had not Seen since Atlantis. How was she supposed to learn to See again? The only Seer she knew had left already.

Suddenly, a face popped into her mind. The Faerie, Leon. He was a Seer. She knew he had not left yet, and she wondered if he could help her. Hearing the sound of wind chimes, she knew she should hurry to get to her afternoon classes on time. She checked her mental schedule and smiled. She had Leon in her very next class.

*   *   *

"Just let everything in your mind right now flow away. Don't try to hold onto any thought in particular. Just focus on your breathing, and relax."

Velvet and Leon were sat in her office, with the lights dimmed and soft music playing in the background.

"Slowly open your eyes and look into the water. Don't think, don't analyse, just tell me what you See."

Velvet opened her eyes slowly and stared into the shallow basin of water on her desk. It reminded her of the lake in the Angelic Realm, when she was watching Laguz on Earth.

"I See..." she said, letting her eyes focus softly on the surface of the water. "I See…"

"Yes?" Leon prompted.

Velvet shook her head. Her mind was still so full of Laguz that all she could see was him. But they weren't visions, they were memories.

"I'm sorry, Leon," she said, looking up at the patient Faerie sat across the desk. "I still can't seem to See anything."

Leon smiled. "Do not apologise. It takes a while to open the mind to being able to See. Especially as you have repressed the ability to do so for so long."

"Thank you, for being so patient. I will keep practising."

Leon stood. "I'm sure you will. I had better go, I'm meeting someone."

"Yes, don't let me make you late. Same time tomorrow?"

Leon nodded and left the room. Velvet looked back into the water and saw Laguz again. She sighed. Would her memories of him ever let her concentrate on being able to See again? Poor Leon had been coaching her for four days now, and she still had not Seen anything.

"Good session today?" Linen asked, appearing behind his desk.

Velvet looked up. "Same as yesterday I'm afraid."

"Still nothing?" Linen picked up his notebook. "Don't worry, Velvet, it'll come back. Just don't try to force it. If you are tense, your mind cannot relax enough to open up."

Velvet sighed in frustration. "I know. It's just difficult to relax when I know that learning to See again might be my only chance of being called and therefore my only chance to be with Laguz. But every time I close my eyes, or do the meditation exercises with Leon, all I can see is Laguz's face. Nothing else has a chance of getting in."

"Surely once all the trainees and second years have left you will be called anyway? Regardless of whether you are able to See?"

"That's what I had assumed, but the Indigo Child seemed to think that the Angels would not call me until I was fully Awake here." Velvet sat forward in her seat and stared once again into the bowl of water. "Besides, I may as well fill my time with doing something useful."

Linen frowned. "Filling time?" He glanced up at the clock. "Shouldn't you be in class right now?"

Velvet shook her head in amusement. "I don't have any evening classes anymore, Linen, or morning classes for that matter. Didn't you notice me sat here all yesterday evening staring into this damned bowl of water?"

Linen tilted his head and thought about the evening before. He'd been so wrapped up in his conversation with Aria about the Rainbow Children, that he had not even noticed Velvet's presence. "Oh, why don't you have evening classes anymore?"

"Because the last of the second year Earth Angels left yesterday morning."

"They've gone? All of them?"

"Yes, Linen, every last one."

"So how many trainees are left now?"

Velvet calculated quickly in her head. "Twenty-six."

Linen's eyes widened. "Wow, so it won't be long before you'll be leaving then?"

Velvet sighed. "Hopefully, but I like I said, if I don't remember how to See, I don't know if I'll be going at all."

"Well," Linen said, standing up. "Don't let me keep you from practising." He went to click his fingers when Velvet spoke.

"Say hi to Aria for me," she said, a smile playing on her lips.

Linen frowned. "How did you know?" Then he shook his head. "Nevermind." He clicked his fingers and left Velvet there, chuckling over the bowl of water.

*   *   *

"I'm so glad Am gave me some hints on how to get here before she left," Aria said, staring up at the luminous stars shining above them.

"Me too," Linen replied, looking at her face.

"I know the Leprechaun caused havoc when they were here, but they sure as hell know how to create a beautiful alternate dimension."

"Mmmhmm," Linen agreed.

She reached out and picked one of the four leaf clovers next to her. "I've never seen a real one of these before." She turned to Linen. "Do you think they're really lucky?"

"I think they must be."

Aria's cheeks darkened in the dim light. "I think I might just keep this one then," she said, tucking the tiny green stem into her pocket. She looked back up at the stars.

"Aria?"

"Yes?"

"What do you think we will do, after?" Linen asked.

"After what?"

"After the Children have all left."

Aria turned to look at Linen and frowned. "What's making you ask that? Surely there's plenty of time before that day comes?"

"At the rate the Indigos are leaving, I would guess that there isn't much time left before that day. A few weeks, at most."

"Oh." Aria thought for a moment. "What are you planning

to do after?"

"I don't know yet. I suppose at that point, I could either go back to the Elemental Realm, go to the next dimension to be a guide, or go to Earth."

"I thought you didn't feel right on Earth?" Aria said softly.

"I didn't. But I wonder now if that was just because it wasn't the right time for me to be there."

"Oh," Aria said again.

After a moment of silence, Linen asked quietly. "Which would you choose? Out of the three options?"

"It depends."

"On what?"

Aria tried to come up with a reply that wasn't "On where you are."

"I don't know," she said finally.

"Oh," Linen replied.

*   *   *

"Where's Shelly?" Velvet asked, looking at Leon and Amber in class the next afternoon.

"She was called last night," Amber replied. "She answered the call immediately. Her Twin Flame, Angelite, left three days ago, and she wanted to be with her."

"Okay, that's understandable. So I guess it's just us three then?"

Leon and Amber looked at one another, then looked back at Velvet and nodded.

"Though we've sped through the material, we have actually managed to cover most things you need to know, was there anything in particular you wanted to ask me about Awakening? Or indeed, anything else?"

"I was wondering, have you looked at the situation on Earth recently? If so, have things improved at all?" Amber asked.

"Actually I-"

"They have begun to improve slightly, but the real shifts in attitude will begin in the next two decades."

Velvet and Amber both looked at Leon, surprised.

"How do you know that?" Velvet asked.

Leon smiled and tapped his head. "I don't just See what will happen in this dimension. My Sight knows no boundaries."

Velvet's eyes widened. "I didn't realise that. So, tell us, have the Earth Angels and Indigos begun to Awaken yet?"

Leon nodded. "A few have. They're definitely more open-minded than the previous generations of Earth Angels. They feel…" Leon searched for the right word. "Unsettled. Like they know they are there for a purpose, but are unsure as to what their purpose is. Though most of them are still fairly young, they are wise beyond their years. The older humans are beginning to realise this, and take their views more seriously."

Velvet nodded. She hesitated, then asked. "Can you See specific people, or just a general overview?"

Leon tilted his head. "I See what I am supposed to. I See what the Universe wishes me to See. How are you getting on with the water?"

Velvet laughed. "Nothing yet I'm afraid."

"Water?" Amber inquired politely.

"Leon here is trying to teach me to See as he does. Many lifetimes ago, I was a Seer, but I seem to have buried the ability to do so."

Amber frowned. "Then surely if the ability is there, it is not so much learning how, but remembering how?"

"Well, yes, in theory. But my memories of that time are so few that I don't remember how I used to do it."

Amber nodded thoughtfully. "Have you asked the Angels for guidance with this?"

Velvet shook her head. "No, I guess I could have asked Athena, but she has already left for Earth."

Amber smiled. "No, I did not mean ask an Angel friend here in this dimension, I meant have you prayed for guidance from the Angelic Realm."

"To be honest I don't think I would have even thought to do so."

"You don't think the Angels help only humans on Earth do you?"

Velvet smiled. "I guess not. Thank you for the suggestion, Amber, I will certainly give it a try."

"You're welcome, Velvet. I hope they answer your prayer."

Chapter Twenty-two

Velvet sat on the edge of her bed that night, thinking about what Amber had said. She'd never needed any Angel intervention for anything before, and wasn't entirely sure how to go about asking for it now. After a moment, she decided that there couldn't possibly be a right or a wrong way to do it, and began to speak to the empty room.

"Angels, I need your help with something. You see, I need to get to Earth, because, I think," her voice faltered. "I think, there might just be someone waiting there for me, and I'm afraid that if I don't go soon, he might not wait any longer." She sighed. "It may already be too late for me to be with him, but I have to at least try. I hope you can understand that, and if you are able to, please help me out. I just need to be able to See again. Then I will have remembered, I will have Awakened, and I'll be ready to leave here."

She sighed again and looked up to the ceiling.

"Thank you," she whispered.

*   *   *

Late the next afternoon, Velvet found herself sat staring into a bowl of water again. After her third attempt, she sat back and looked at Leon apologetically.

"I'm sorry, Leon. Perhaps we could try a different method? I'm really not making any progress with the water."

Leon was quiet for a moment. "You mentioned that you had experienced some visions of your Twin Flame – what method of meditation did you use then?"

Velvet looked over to Linen. "It was while Linen was playing the piano."

Linen looked up at the mention of his name. "Huh?"

"Leon was just wondering how I'd had the visions of Laguz, what method of meditation. I said it was when you played the piano."

Leon turned to Linen. "Are you busy right now? Do you think you could play something, see if it works?"

Linen shrugged and put his pen down. "Sure. This can wait 'til later." He moved to the piano stool and sat, fingers hovering above the keys. He turned to Velvet. "Should I play your song?"

Velvet bit her lip and nodded. She settled back into her chair and closed her eyes as the first notes filled the room. After three deep breaths, she opened her eyes and blinked in the sunlight. She breathed in the fresh, salty air and smiled. She was about to tell Linen to play something else, because this song obviously only ever linked her to the beach and to Laguz, when she realised that she wasn't alone. She looked down at her hand to see it linked with another. She looked up into the face of the man she loved. His blond hair tangled in the ocean breeze, his green eyes and beautiful smile seemed younger than she remembered.

"I can't believe it's taken so long for us to be together," he said, reaching out to touch her cheek.

She frowned. "I'm sorry it took me so long to remember."

He put his finger to her lips. "Shhh. It wasn't your fault. Besides, it doesn't matter, we're together now."

"But all that time that we lost, all that time we could have been together."

He shook his head. "Are we or are we not together right now?"

She smiled. "We are."

"Then we have lost nothing." He leant down and kissed her. She reached up and held him close, determined not to let him go again.

"Velvet?"

Velvet opened her eyes and saw Linen and Leon both staring at her, concerned looks on their faces. Linen had stopped playing the piano.

"Did you see anything?" Leon asked.

Velvet shook her head. "It wasn't a vision, it was just a memory." She frowned. "I mean, the conversation was slightly different, but the meaning of the conversation was essentially the same."

"So nothing new? Not a vision of the future?" Leon asked, this time slightly disbelievingly.

Velvet shook her head. "No. I'm afraid not." She sighed. "I guess we'll just have to keep practising."

Leon sat back. "I'm sorry, Velvet. I really thought today would be the day."

"Why's that? Because I asked the Angels for help?"

"You did? No, that's not why."

Velvet leant forward. "Did you See something?"

Leon shook his head. "No, no. I just thought it would happen today, because I have to leave. I've been called, Velvet."

Velvet's eyes widened. "Oh, I see. Well, I appreciate all of your help Leon, I'm sorry that I wasn't a very good student, but please believe that I have learnt a lot from you."

Leon smiled. "You were an excellent student, though a little more self-belief couldn't hurt. I wish you all the best, Velvet. I think the Angels may be more on your side than you realise."

Velvet smiled. "Thank you, Leon, for everything. I hope to see you on Earth sometime."

Leon nodded. "I hope to see you, too." He stood. "Goodbye, Velvet." He turned to Linen, who was still sat on the piano stool. "Goodbye, Linen, I hope everything goes well for you." Linen nodded.

Leon took a deep breath then closed his eyes. Then he disappeared.

Velvet sighed. "What am I going to do now, Linen? There are barely any trainees left now, and even they will probably be leaving by tomorrow."

Linen shrugged. "I don't know, Velvet. I could keep playing for you?" he said, gesturing to the grand piano.

Velvet shook her head. "It's no good, Linen. Whenever I close my eyes, all I see is Laguz." She sighed again and stood up. "I think perhaps I'll go for a walk in the gardens. Are you meeting Aria again tonight?"

Linen shook his head. "No, she's with the Crystal Children and I have a ton of paperwork to do."

Velvet smiled. "Work should never get in the way of love, Linen, remember that."

Linen raised an eyebrow. "I have no idea what you're talking about."

"Course you don't," Velvet agreed, grinning. Before Linen could respond, she'd clicked her fingers.

*　　　*　　　*

"Velvet?"

Velvet turned to see who was calling her, and smiled when she saw three trainees coming up the path of the Atlantis Garden.

"Good evening, dear Earth Angels, how can I help you?"

"We're sorry to bother you, but we wanted to say good bye."

Velvet smiled. "You have been called?"

All three souls, two former Faeries and a former Angel nodded.

"I wish you all the best. I hope your lives on Earth are all that you hope for, and that you find others like yourself to help you with the shift."

The Angel smiled. "Thank you, Velvet. We hope you will be able to join us soon."

"Yes, well, when everyone has been called, I'm sure it won't be long-"

"But everyone has been called," the Faerie said.

Velvet blinked. "I'm sorry, my dear Oliva, what do you mean?"

"We are the only three left now, the others heard the call just a little earlier," Oliva explained.

"That's why we came to see you. And we wanted to wish you good luck with finding your Twin Flame," the other Faerie added.

Velvet smiled, her eyes filling up. "My dear Earth Angels. Thank you." She stood and hugged each of them. "Good luck, Oliva, Rumie, Topaz. May your lives be full and blessed with love."

She stepped back and one by one, they closed their eyes and disappeared. Velvet bit her lip and a tear fell. All of her trainees had left. This was it. The time when she herself should be called. But it wasn't going to happen, because she still couldn't See.

She sat heavily down onto the bench and pulled the rune necklace out from inside her robes. She looked up at the marble statue. "Laguz, will I ever see you again?"

Her whisper floated off on the breeze, unanswered.

*   *   *

Velvet was resting, deep in a meditative state, when she heard it. She struggled up through the layers of consciousness and sat upright in bed. She looked around the dim room and frowned. She could have sworn she'd heard someone calling her name. She sat for a few minutes, extending her awareness into the darkness, waiting to see if she heard it again. About ten minutes later, she jumped when she heard the voice again, so close she thought there was someone behind her. This time though, she heard the voice more clearly. It was an Angel's voice. She was sure of it. She clicked her fingers, lighting up the room. She wanted to be absolutely sure she was awake and fully aware before getting too excited. This time, she barely had to wait five minutes before she heard it again, and it sounded like there were two voices. Velvet gasped and bit her lip.

She was suddenly so excited she didn't quite know what to do with herself. Unable to resume her rest, she got up and dressed, then went to her office. She didn't know how long she had until the call became too unbearable to ignore, and there were things she needed to finish before she could leave.

In her office, she ran hand along the piano keys, pressing down softly. She hoped that she would continue her playing on Earth. She went to her desk and began to sort through everything. She didn't want to leave any unfinished business for Linen to deal with. She checked the time and figured that Beryl might be in her office by now.

"Beryl?"

The Angel's face appeared on the wall, looking slightly surprised. "Velvet! You're up early."

Velvet smiled. "Yes, I was awoken by the most beautiful sound."

"Oh?"

"The Angels have called me."

Beryl's eyes widened. "Oh, Velvet! That's wonderful news! Oh, congratulations! I am so pleased for you."

Velvet grinned. "Thank you, Beryl. And may I say it has been an absolute pleasure and privilege working with you all this time."

Beryl's eyes began to fill. "Oh, you! You're going to make me cry! Wait just a second."

Her face faded from the wall and a moment later she entered the office. Velvet got up and met her halfway. They hugged for a long while.

"It won't be long, and I will be joining you there," Beryl

said, wiping her cheek with a white handkerchief.

"Yes, get the new girl trained up so you can get to Earth, how will I survive without you there to organise my life?"

Beryl smiled. "I'm sure you will do just fine."

"Morning meeting?" Linen appeared behind his desk. "I don't remember seeing it on the schedule."

The Angel and the Old Soul turned to look at the Faerie.

"Well," Velvet began. She looked at Beryl who nodded. "I have been called, Linen."

The smile vanished from Linen's face and he looked from one to the other.

"Seriously?"

They both nodded.

He grinned and rushed over to Velvet. He swept her into a bear hug. "Oh, that's fantastic, Velvet! I'm so very pleased for you!"

Velvet laughed. "Why, Linen, I had no idea just how much you wanted me out of your hair!"

Linen released her and chuckled. "Oh, Velvet, stop. You know I'm going to miss you terribly. I just know how much you wanted this."

Velvet smiled. "I know, I'm just teasing. I just can't believe it's really happening. I am sorry though, that we never did have a concert as an evening activity, I'm sure the trainees would have loved to hear you play."

Linen shrugged. "Don't worry, I think I prefer to keep my audiences small, anyway."

Velvet saw him glance at the piano stool where Aria normally sat and smiled. She hoped they would admit their true feelings soon. Her smile dissolved into a wince as she heard the call again. "It's getting louder already."

"When will you be leaving?" Beryl asked.

"As soon as possible, ideally. I would like to say goodbye to the Children and to Aria before I do though."

"Aria should be here any minute now, and we're having a brief meeting with all of the Children this morning, so you could come along then?" Linen said.

"Excellent. I'll just sort out my things here, we'll go to the meeting and then, well," Velvet shrugged happily. "I guess I will be on my way!"

"My dear friend, I wish you all the best," Beryl said, pulling her in for one more hug. "We will meet again."

"I have no doubt, dear Angel."

Beryl nodded and left, tears already flowing down her cheeks.

Velvet sighed. "Why is it that even though we can be so excited to go somewhere, it is still somehow difficult to leave?"

Linen smiled. "Because though you are moving forward into new and exciting adventures, you'll still always love what you have left behind."

Velvet smiled at the Faerie. "I think I made an excellent choice you know, appointing you as Head of the School."

Linen's eyebrows rose. "Choice? As I remember it, not only did you have no choice, but you also said that given it, you would never have chosen me."

"Oh really? I don't seem to recall that particular conversation," Velvet said innocently.

Linen chuckled. "I think your memory must be going again."

Velvet laughed too. "Perhaps."

Aria arrived then, whistling to herself as she flew in. "Good morning!"

"Good morning, Aria!"

The Faerie stopped mid-flight and looked at Velvet, who was sorting through some things on her desk. She looked at Linen, as if to say: what is she so cheerful about? Linen smiled and gestured for Aria to ask Velvet herself.

"You're in early this morning, Velvet, everything alright?"

"My dear Faerie, everything is more than alright. I was called this morning, and as soon as I have said goodbye to yourself and the Children, I will be leaving for Earth."

"Oh, Velvet! That's incredible!" Aria zoomed towards the Old Soul and threw her tiny arms around her.

Velvet laughed and returned the hug. "It is indeed."

Aria pulled away. "So I guess you didn't need to See again for the Angels to call you?"

Velvet shook her head. "I guess they decided to call me anyway." She shrugged. "Maybe they felt that it didn't matter. Or perhaps the Indigo Child was wrong, who knows?"

"Oh, you must be so excited! I really do hope you find Laguz."

Velvet smiled sadly. "Yes, well, even though I've been called a little sooner than expected, I think it may still be too late for us to be together."

Aria frowned. "Why is it too late?"

"Because by the time I will be old enough to find him, he will certainly have made a life for himself, if he hasn't already. After all, he's now twenty-three years old. By the time I am that age he will be in his late forties."

Aria continued to frown. "Is that a problem?"

Velvet smiled. "If he is happily married, then yes, it is."

Aria shook her head. "I don't think he could be as happy with someone else as he would be with you. Have you actually checked in on him recently, just to see where he is, what he's doing?"

Velvet shook her head. "I have not looked in on him in a long time. I didn't want to spy on him. I have decided that if we are meant to come together on Earth, in whatever way, then it will happen. If not, then it won't. Either way, I need to go to Earth to help all the many Earth Angels to Awaken." She smiled. "I haven't given up on the idea of experiencing the Golden Age yet."

"I'm glad to hear it. Don't worry; we'll be here, working our hardest to make it happen."

"I'm sure you will, Linen. You always were a very passionate soul. I feel lucky to have you here in my place."

"Linen, we said we'd meet the Children at nine, we'd better

get going. Are you coming with us Velvet?"

"Yes I am, I just need to do one last thing." Velvet looked at her desk and chair one last time then clicked her fingers. They both vanished, and Linen's desk moved into their place. "Hmm, this room is still missing something." She smiled. "Yes, that's it." She clicked her fingers and another desk appeared in Linen's old place. "I think it's about time Aria had her own desk, don't you?"

Aria flew to her tiny bright green desk and spun around several times in the swivel chair. "Wow, this is so cool! Thanks, Velvet!"

Velvet smiled. "You're welcome, little one. Is there anything else I can do for either of you before I leave?"

There was a moment of silence, then Linen spoke up, a little shyly.

"I don't know if it's possible to reverse it, but I was wondering if I could go back to being a Faerie? I know I've mastered the clicky trick thing, but I still really do miss flying."

Aria turned to Velvet to see her response.

"Of course, Linen. I feel bad that I forced you to lose your wings and to be in an Old Soul body all this time. Do you wish to resume your old appearance?"

Linen nodded.

"Very well then." Velvet closed her eyes and pictured the fire Faerie as he had looked on the first day of term. Though less than a month had passed, it seemed like a lifetime ago. She clicked her fingers and opened her eyes to see Linen shrinking, and his wings re-growing on his back.

He flapped his wings a few times, getting used to them again. He hovered for a moment then grinned and did a few laps of the office.

"This feels so wonderful!" He turned to Aria. "Race to the main hall?"

Aria's eyes widened as she took in this more playful Linen with wings. She nodded quickly. "I must warn you though, I always win."

Linen laughed. "We'll see about that!" He zoomed out of the room and Aria followed, giggling.

Velvet shook her head. She really hoped the two of them came to their senses soon. It seemed so crazy to have Twin Flames in such close proximity to one another who wouldn't admit their true feelings. She took one last look around the office, which now didn't feel like her own, and clicked her fingers.

Chapter Twenty-three

Velvet looked around the main hall, taking in the faces of the Children, all sat quietly and patiently, waiting for the meeting to begin.

"Would you like to address them first?" Linen asked, arriving slightly out of breath.

Velvet nodded and walked to centre stage for the last time.

"Good morning, Indigo and Crystal Children," she began. "I have come to see you to say goodbye. It is time for me to go to Earth now, and help the other Earth Angels with the Awakening. I promise you that I will do my very best to ensure that the world is ready for you." She smiled at the sea of innocent faces. "Then I hope we can experience the Golden Age together. I hope to see you all there in the next few years; if you recognise me there, please don't hesitate to say something. Especially if I have not yet Awoken. Before I leave you in Linen and Aria's very capable hands, is there anything you wish to ask me?"

After a moment, a hand was raised in the middle of the room. Velvet nodded towards the Indigo Child and she stood up to speak.

"I have received a message from my brother, who I believe spoke to you before he left for Earth. He says to tell you how pleased he is that you finally asked for help and was able to Awaken. He wishes you well on your journey to Earth and to Awakening both yourself, and the world."

Velvet frowned. "How did you receive a message from him? Has he left Earth already?"

"No, he is still there."

"You can communicate with other Children on Earth?" Velvet asked, surprised.

The Child smiled. "Of course. We are all one. If we wish to speak with someone, all we need to do is tune into their frequency. We keep in touch with our brothers and sisters on Earth so that we know what we need to do before we get there."

"I see. Please thank your brother for the information for me. I hope he is doing well."

"He is. I will pass along your greetings." The Child nodded and sat down.

"Anyone else?" Velvet asked. No one raised their hand. "Goodbye then, my dear Children. May the Goddess and God bless you all." She turned to Linen and Aria. "This is it. I hope everything goes well for you both."

Linen flew forward to hug her. "Goodbye, Velvet. Thank you for everything."

They pulled back and smiled at one another. Aria flew forward for another hug, her big green eyes sad.

"I'll miss you," she said.

"No, you won't," Velvet whispered in her ear. "Now you'll have the office to yourselves."

Aria pulled back from Velvet, blushing. "Good luck," she said, slightly flustered.

Velvet nodded. "Goodbye." She clicked her fingers and then was gone.

Aria turned to Linen, frowning. "Did she just go to Earth? Or has she gone somewhere else in the Academy first?"

Linen smiled, his wings fluttering. "I think she's gone to the Atlantis Garden, to say her final goodbye."

*   *   *

Empty of life, the garden was still when Velvet reappeared in front of the statue. Wincing, she knew she could not put off leaving for Earth much longer. She stepped forward and looked up at Laguz. She pulled out the rune necklace and traced the symbol with her finger. Fighting tears, she untied the worn cord from around her neck, and refastened it around Laguz's cold marble neck.

"I hope that wherever you are, whomever you are with; you are happy. I had hoped to see you again, but I don't think it will be possible." She reached up and touched his cold cheek.

"I love you." A single tear fell and she heard the Angels call once more. It was like having a whole choir sing her name in her ear. She took one last look at the man she loved more dearly than anything else in the whole Universe, and then closed her eyes.

"I'm ready."

*   *   *

"Aria, are you okay?" Linen asked, concerned. Aria looked up from her desk and nodded.

"I was just thinking about Velvet. About how she won't get to be with her Twin Flame." A tear trickled down the Faerie's cheek and she sniffled.

Linen flew over to her, hovering by her side, unsure of what to do.

Aria looked into his orange eyes. "Let's not head for the same fate," she whispered. She reached out to touch Linen's face. "I love you, Linen."

Linen smiled and breathed a small sigh of relief. He reached out and pulled Aria close. "I love you, too," he breathed.

Aria's eyes widened happily and she leant forward to kiss him. Lost in their passionate embrace, their wings fluttered crazily, taking them all over the room. Finally, they ended up on top of the piano, kissing as if there would be no tomorrow.

A cool breeze swept over them suddenly and someone cleared their throat. The two Faeries flew apart and turned to the door. Their eyes widened and Aria let out a shocked squeak.

Linen found his voice first.

"Laguz! What are you doing here?"

Laguz smiled, his green eyes sparkling. "Well, I certainly don't need to ask what you two were doing in here." Aria blushed for the second time that morning. Laguz peered at them more closely and frowned. "Linen? Is that you? You've changed a bit; I thought you were an Old Soul?"

Linen shook his head. "Uh, no, I'm a Faerie, Velvet changed me back, uh, when uh…" his voice trailed off.

Laguz looked around the room, taking in the new arrangement. He frowned. "Isn't this Velvet's office anymore? Where is she?"

Linen and Aria looked at one another, dismayed.

Laguz noticed their look. "What's going on?"

Finally, Aria turned to Laguz and practically whispered. "She left, Laguz. She heard the call, so she left."

Laguz shook his head in disbelief. "She can't have. She wouldn't have. She knew I was coming, she would have waited."

Linen frowned and shook his head. "She didn't know you were coming, Laguz. In fact," he looked down at his tiny red felt-clad feet. "She had given up on the idea of being with you. She said you would be too old by now."

Laguz was horrified. "But the Guardian Angel I spoke to when I left, told me that by the time I exited Earth, though all of the Earth Angels would have been called, Velvet would have a vision of us together on Earth, and would know that I was coming back for her. Because in the vision, we are the same age. The Angel said she would still be here, and that we could go to Earth together."

Aria and Linen shook their heads. "She tried," Aria said

softly. "She did everything she could to allow the visions in after blocking them for so long. But she told me that all she could See were memories of the two of you."

Laguz took this in and slumped against the wall. "So she left thinking that I was on Earth, but that it was too late for us to be together?"

"Yes," Linen said, his eyes still downcast. "I'm sorry, Laguz."

"Me, too," Aria added.

Laguz stared at the floor, his lip trembling. Suddenly, something occurred to him. "Wait, when I arrived on the Other Side, the Angels told me she was still here." He looked up at the two of them. "When did she leave?"

Aria glanced at the clock. "She came to the meeting at nine, and spoke with the Children for a few minutes, then she left. So about twenty minutes ago?"

Laguz stood up quickly. "When she left – did she go straight to Earth or did she go anywhere else first, to say goodbye to anyone?"

"She didn't leave immediately; I assumed she was going to the Atlantis Garden."

Laguz's eyes widened. "So no one actually saw her answer the call? She could still be in the Academy somewhere?"

Linen shrugged. "I suppose she cou-" Before he could finish his sentence, Laguz had clicked his fingers and disappeared. Linen and Aria looked at one another.

"Wow. I can't believe he came back," Aria said, awed. "Only to miss Velvet by minutes."

Linen shook his head. "It's unbelievable. He must be feeling so awful right now."

Aria flew closer to Linen. He pulled her to him and she rested her head on his chest. "Let's not ever lose each other."

"Okay," Linen whispered.

*   *   *

"Velvet!"

Laguz started shouting as he reappeared in the Atlantis Garden. He ran to the bench where he'd found her the day he'd transformed. The garden was empty. He looked around wildly and his gaze caught on a marble statue that stood out from the other gold statues. He looked it up and down, noting that it no longer had a tail. Something else about the statue was unusual. He stepped towards it, and focused on the neck. Or, rather, the leather cord around the neck from which hung a simple wooden rune pendant. His lip began to tremble again as he reached out to touch the wooden rune. He let out a sob and fell to his knees.

How could she have left without him? How could she have given up on him like that? Why didn't she know he would be returning for her? Hadn't she had the vision? Didn't she believe in their love at all? They were Twin Flames! They were meant to be together. It couldn't all be lost.

Laguz looked up, the last thought stuck in his mind. Nothing was ever lost. Everything was connected. Anything was possible. He wiped his face with the back of his hand and stood, a little unsteadily. He reached out and removed the rune from the statue. He tied it around his own neck, and smoothed his thumb over the engraved symbol.

"Nothing is ever lost," he muttered. He took a deep breath and was about to click his fingers to leave, when something occurred to him. With a smile, he closed his eyes and concentrated on how Velvet had looked, the last time he saw her laughing, and clicked his fingers.

When he opened his eyes, next to his own statue stood a gleaming marble replica of his Twin Flame. He reached out to touch her cold cheek. "I'll find you. I promise." He smiled. "I love you."

Then he clicked his fingers.

This time, the breeze and a throat clearing wasn't enough to disentangle the two Faeries, so Laguz clapped his hands twice instead. Once again, the Faeries flew apart, their faces shocked and slightly guilty.

"Laguz!" Linen exclaimed. He smoothed his hair back in an attempt to straighten himself up. "Did you find her?"

Laguz raised an eyebrow. "Do you think I'd be standing here watching you two going at it if I had? I need to speak to someone about getting to Earth. I need to get there as soon as I can. Then I'll only be a few months younger than Velvet."

Linen's eyes widened. "Oh, um, I don't know who could arrange that, I mean, Athena was the Head of the Guardian Angels, but she left ages ago, we could ask Beryl?"

"Please do," Laguz said, his voice strained.

"Okay, um, Beryl?" Linen called. The Angel appeared on the wall.

"Yes, Linen?"

"Would you happen to know how to get a soul called to Earth?"

Beryl frowned. "I thought everyone had left now?" Laguz moved into her line of sight and she clapped a hand over her mouth in shock. "Laguz! What are you doing here?"

"I came back for Velvet. But I was too late. Now I need to get back to Earth as soon as possible. Please, Beryl, do you know who I need to speak to?"

Beryl blinked. "Um, well, I haven't ever heard of a soul returning to Earth so quickly and without being called. I suppose the only soul I know who might be able to help is Elder Damask. I'll call him now."

"Thank you, Beryl."

Beryl smiled and faded. A moment later, Gold's face appeared.

"Laguz! You're back!"

"Gold," Linen cut in. "You know why we have called you, is it possible? Can we get the Angels to call Laguz back?" He glanced at the blond soul, who seemed to have lost his spirit.

"Um, well, I'm not sure," Gold dithered, his right eye beginning to twitch.

"Gold," Laguz said quietly. "I have to go back. I cannot

stay here knowing that she is there without me. We have to be together. Surely you can understand that? Please, if there is anything at all you can do, please do it." He closed his eyes and whispered again. "Please."

Gold sighed. "Well, there is an Angel I could speak with, I cannot promise anything though; there is a process after all."

Laguz opened his eyes and nodded. "I would appreciate anything you are able to do, Gold."

Gold nodded hurriedly. "Yes, well, leave it with me." His face softened. "Velvet was an incredible soul, and did a wonderful job here in the Academy. She deserves to be happy. That should sway the Angels if there are any problems."

Laguz sighed in relief. "I hope so."

Gold nodded again and faded away. Laguz's shoulders slumped. "I guess all I can do now is wait."

Aria bit her lip thoughtfully. "I know where you can wait if you don't want to be alone."

"Where?"

"Would you like to meet the Rainbow Children?"

*   *   *

The room shifted and swayed as Laguz looked around in wonder at the thousand beams of pure light. He smiled as he took in the beauty of the tiny souls. The tension left his body and he relaxed.

"If you reach out and hold one," Aria said, demonstrating, "They can speak to you." She held the Rainbow for a few seconds then giggled. "Try it." She flew towards the door. "If you need anything else, just come find us." She flew out the door, then flew back in. "Oh, but do you think you could knock next time?"

Laguz laughed, his deep chuckle filling the sunny room. "Sure. Thank you, Aria."

Aria grinned and left.

Laguz stood amongst the Rainbow Children for several

minutes, breathing deeply. He was instantly filled with a sense of peace and calm. Still smiling, he reached out and caught one of the tiny Rainbow Children. He gently closed his fingers around it.

"Greetings, Laguz. We are very pleased that you have come to join us today. We sense your sorrow, and wish to tell you not to fear. Though Velvet may seem to have given up on you, deep in her soul, she has not. She knows she will be with you again."

Laguz opened his fingers looked in amazement at the dancing light in his hand. Unsure as to how to communicate back, he just whispered. "Thank you. I appreciate your certainty. I only hope that you are right."

"We are always right," the Rainbow Child replied. "Because there is no such thing as wrong. Everything just is."

Laguz nodded. "Can you see us together? On Earth?"

"We can see your love surviving. We can see you both being very important to the humans during the shift in consciousness. But when or how you will be together is not something we wish to predict. What fun is it, being human, if you know your life's path before you have lived it?"

"It may not be fun, but it is definitely easier," Laguz replied.

"Life does not need to be easy, Laguz. It does not need to be hard, either. As a human, you get to choose which it is. Your perception of events is your experience of events. It is entirely in your hands. But as we said, fear not. Your love will survive. Of that we have no doubt."

Laguz nodded. "Thank you for your counsel, Rainbow Children. I hope to see you on Earth soon."

"As do we. Goodbye, Laguz."

*   *   *

An hour later, after Laguz had walked around the entire Academy, taking in all the different gardens, he found himself once again in the Atlantis Garden. He sat on the bench and stared at the two marble statues. He wrapped his fingers around the wooden rune on his chest.

"Come on, Gold," he whispered. "Please, Angels. Please call me to Earth. We need to be together. We deserve to be together."

He closed his eyes and leant back, trying to regain the sense of peace and calm he had felt in the presence of the Rainbow Children. Suddenly, he sat up and looked around him. "Was that?" he muttered, listening carefully. It was a few minutes later when he heard the heavenly sound again. Almost crying in relief, he jumped up.

"Gold! You are amazing! Thank you!" he shouted. He looked up at the statue of Velvet and smiled. He stepped towards it and removed the rune from his neck for the last time. He fastened it around her neck and stepped back.

"I'm coming, Velvet. Please wait for me," he said. Then with one last look at the intertwined marble hands, he took a deep breath and answered the call.

Chapter Twenty-four

Earth. Twenty-five years later.

The sun was rising over the silent waves as the couple walked hand in hand along the sand. Her long dark hair glittered in the morning sunlight as it danced in the salty breeze. His tangled blond hair framed his head like a halo.

Suddenly, she stopped on the sand and breathed in deeply. She looked down at their intertwined hands and smiling, looked up into the face of the man she loved. He smiled back.

"I can't believe it's taken so long for us to be together," he said, reaching out to touch her cheek.

She frowned. "I'm sorry it took me so long to remember."

He put his finger to her lips. "Shhh. It wasn't your fault. Besides, it doesn't matter, we're together now."

"But all that time that we lost, all that time we could have been together."

He shook his head. "Are we or are we not together right now?"

She smiled. "We are."

"Then we have lost nothing." He leant down and kissed her. She reached up and held him close, determined not to let him go again. He pulled back slightly and gazed into her deep brown eyes.

"I'll love you for eternity," he said, his voice filled with unwavering certainty.

She blinked, and a distant memory resurfaced in her mind. She smiled up at him and whispered back:

"Our love will outlast eternity itself."

Earth Angel Series:

The Earth Angel Awakening *(book 2)*

'No matter how overcast the sky, the stars continue to shine. We just have to be patient enough to wait for clouds to lift.'

Twenty-five years after leaving the Earth Angel Training Academy to be born on Earth as a human, Velvet (now known on Earth as Violet) is beginning to Awaken. But when she repeatedly ignores her dreams and intuition, she misses the opportunity to be with her Twin Flame, Laguz. Without the long-awaited reunion with her Twin Flame, can Violet possibly Awaken fully, and help to bring the world into the elusive Golden Age?

The Other Side (of The Earth Angel Training Academy) *(book 3)*

Mikey is an ordinary boy who just happens to talk to the Faeries at the bottom of his garden. So when an Angel visits him in his dream and tells him he must return to the Earth Angel Training Academy in order to save the world, despite his fears, he understands and accepts the task.

Starlight is the Angel of Destiny. By carefully orchestrating events at the Academy and on Earth, she can make sure that everything works out the way that it should, even though it may not make sense to those around her.

Leon is a Faerie Seer. He arrives at the Academy as a trainee, but through his visions he realises that his role in the Awakening is far more important than he ever imagined.

The Twin Flame Reunion *(book 4)*

Greg and Violet are among many other Earth Angels who are reuniting with their Twin Flames. They must work through their own fears in order to be together, but at times, it's just too overwhelming.

Aria and Linen left the Other Side hand in hand, to become humans on Earth. Despite being afraid of forgetting everything, Aria's memory remains intact. But when she finds Linen, he has no memory of her at all.

Charlie experiences an Awakening, and meets his Twin Flame. But when he is unable to control his anger, he changes his future forever.

Starlight leaves her Twin Flame on the Other Side, and goes to Earth, so she can assist Violet and the other Earth Angels with the Awakening. But she is not prepared for everything that comes with being human.

Leona has a vision of her Twin Flame, and decides to search for her. But when they find each other, Leona can See that it may not last.

The Twin Flame Retreat *(book 5)*

A lost Starperson, an out-of-control Faerie, a lonely Angel and an Indigo searching for love all attend the Twin Flame Retreat, which is now owned by Violet and Greg.
The three days they spend in the woods will change their lives forever.

The Twin Flame Resurrection *(book 6)*

Meeting, loving and losing a Twin Flame are all very intense experiences, and can be completely unexpected, painful, joyful and destroying.

But when two souls are meant to come together, there is nothing on Earth or in any other dimension that can stop it from happening.

Equally, if they're not meant to come together, there is nothing on this Earth that can make it happen.

Join five Earth Angels on their journeys to find their Twin Flames, and themselves.

Visionary Collection:

Heaven dot com

When Christina goes into hospital for the final time, and knows that she is about to lose her battle with cancer, she asks her boyfriend, James, to help her deliver messages to her family and friends after she has gone.

She also asks him to do something for her, but she dies before he can make it happen, and he finds it difficult to forgive himself.

After her death, her messages are received by her loved ones, and the impact her words have will change their lives forever.

The Doorway to PAM

Natalie is an ordinary girl who has lost her way. There is nothing particularly special about her or her life. She has no exceptional abilities. She hasn't achieved anything miraculous. Her life has very little meaning to it.

Evelyn is the caretaker at Pam's. The alternate dimension where souls at their lowest point find the answers they need to turn their lives around. The dimension dreamers visit, to help people while they sleep.

One ordinary girl, one extraordinary woman.
One fated meeting that will change lives.

The Elphite

Ellie's life is just one long, bad case of déjà vu. She has lived her life before - a hundred times before - and she remembers each and every lifetime.

Each time, she has changed things, but has never managed to change the ending.

This time, in this life, she hopes that it will be different. So she makes the biggest change of all - she tries to avoid meeting him.

Her soulmate. The love of her life.

Because maybe if they don't meet, she can finally change her destiny.

But fate has other ideas...

I'm Here

When Marielle finds out that a guy she had a crush on in school has passed away, the strange occurrences of the previous week begin to make sense. She suspects that he is trying to give her a message from the other side, and so opens up to communicate with him, She has no idea that by doing so, she will be forming a bond so strong, that life as she knows it will forever be changed.

Nathan assumed that when he died, he would move on, and continue his spiritual journey. But instead he finds himself drawn to a girl that he once knew. The more he watches her, and gets to know her, he realises that he was drawn to her for a reason, and that once he knows what that is, he will be able to change his destiny.

About the Author

Michelle lives in England, in the middle of the woods. When not writing and publishing her own books, she helps other Indie Authors with their own publishing adventures. She has known all her life that she is a writer. It is more of a calling than simply a passion, and despite her attempts to live in the normal world, she has finally realised that she would much rather live in a world of Angels, Faeries, Mermaids and Leprechaun.

Please feel free to write a review of this book on Amazon. Michelle loves to get direct feedback, so if you would like to contact her, please e-mail theamethystangel@hotmail.co.uk or keep up to date by following her blog – **TwinFlameBlog.com.** You can also follow her on Twitter **@themiraclemuse** or 'like' her page on Facebook.

To sign up to her mailing list, visit:
www.michellegordon.co.uk

designs from a
different planet

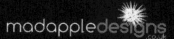

Earth Angel Sanctuary

A safe space to Learn, Grow, Heal and Evolve.

The Earth Angel Sanctuary is an online space where Earth Angels can watch videos on the 'basics' to shifting emotions with advanced energy clearings, rituals, interviews plus so much more, all to help Earth Angels help themselves.

Founded by Sarah Rebecca Vine in 2014, the Earth Angel Sanctuary has several contributors and has new videos and information added to it every month.

To join simply visit:

earthangelsanctuary.com

You can sign up for a monthly or yearly membership.

Emp⊿wered
by John

Providing Publicity, Networking & Social Media Services for Spiritual Authors, Inspirational Musicians, Lightworkers & Healers.

EmpoweredByJohn.com

This book was published by The Amethyst Angel.

A selection of books bought to publication by The Amethyst Angel. To view more of our published books visit **theamethystangel.com**

We have a selection of publishing packages available or we can tailor a package to suit each author's individual needs and budget. We also run workshops for groups and individuals on 'How to publish' your own books.

For more information on Independent publishing packages and workshops offered by The Amethyst Angel, please visit **theamethystangel.com**

Made in the USA
Charleston, SC
29 May 2016